GLITCH

SARAH GRALEY

PLAYBOX
DUNGEON CITY
DUNGEON CITY

graphix
An Imprint of
SCHOLASTIC

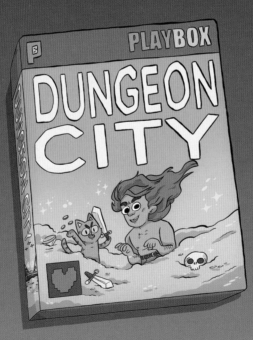

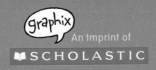

All rights reserved. Published by Graphix, an imprint of Scholastic Inc.,
Publishers since 1920. SCHOLASTIC, GRAPHIX, and associated logos are
trademarks and/or registered trademarks of Scholastic Inc.

Library of Congress Control Number: 2018948934

ISBN 978-1-338-17452-6 (hardcover)
ISBN 978-1-338-17451-9 (paperback)

10 9 8 7 6 5 4 3 2 1   19 20 21 22 23

Printed in China   62
First edition, May 2019
Edited by Cassandra Pelham Fulton
Book design by Shivana Sookdeo
Lettering and color flatting by Stef Purenins
Creative Director: Phil Falco
Publisher: David Saylor

For my parents.
Thank you for believing in me
and for getting me into
video games at an early age.

♥ ♥ ♥ ♥

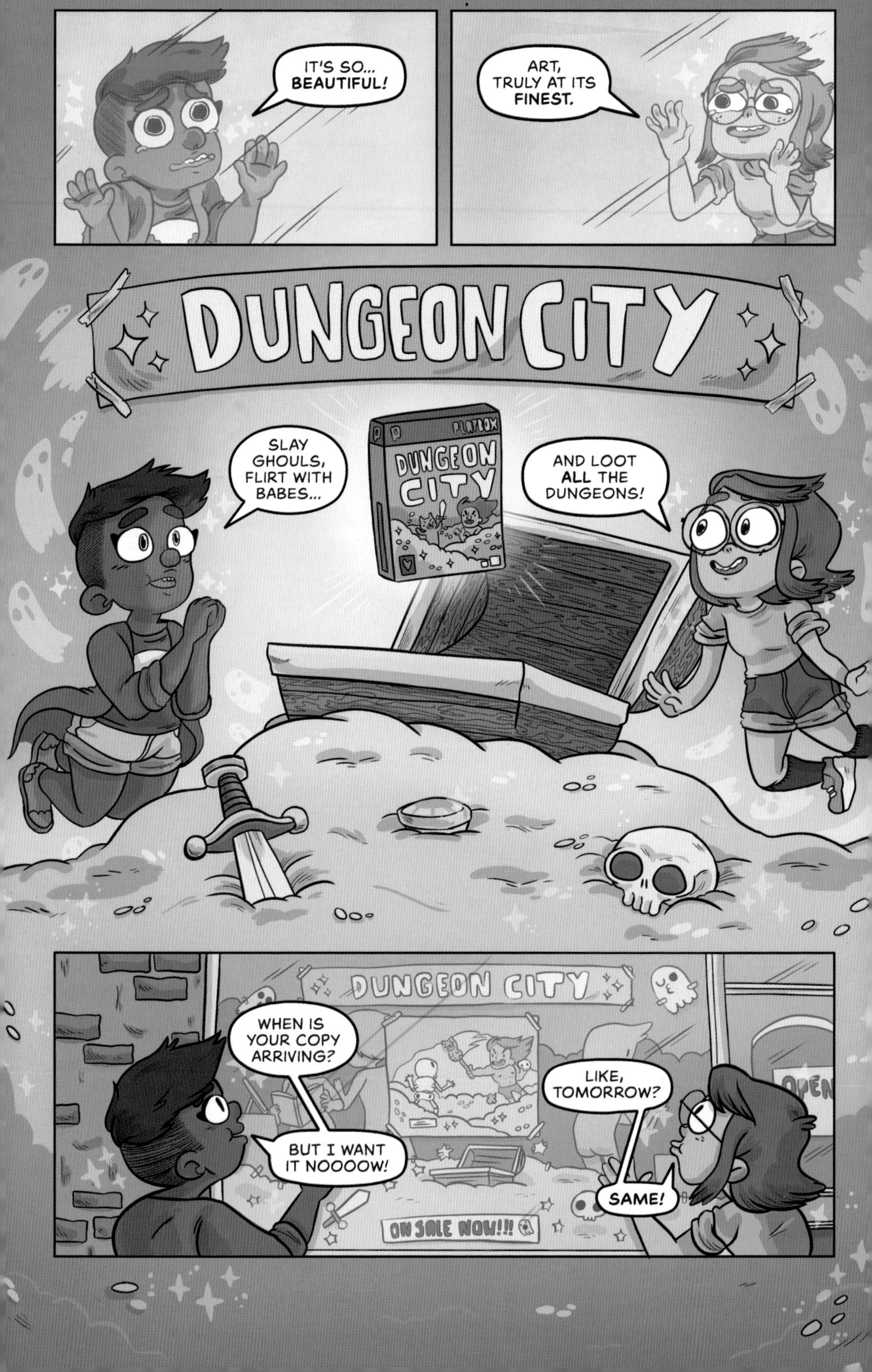
IT'S SO... BEAUTIFUL!
ART, TRULY AT ITS FINEST.
DUNGEON CITY
SLAY GHOULS, FLIRT WITH BABES...
PLAYBOX
DUNGEON CITY
AND LOOT ALL THE DUNGEONS!
DUNGEON CITY
WHEN IS YOUR COPY ARRIVING?
BUT I WANT IT NOOOOW!
LIKE, TOMORROW?
SAME!
ON SALE NOW!!!

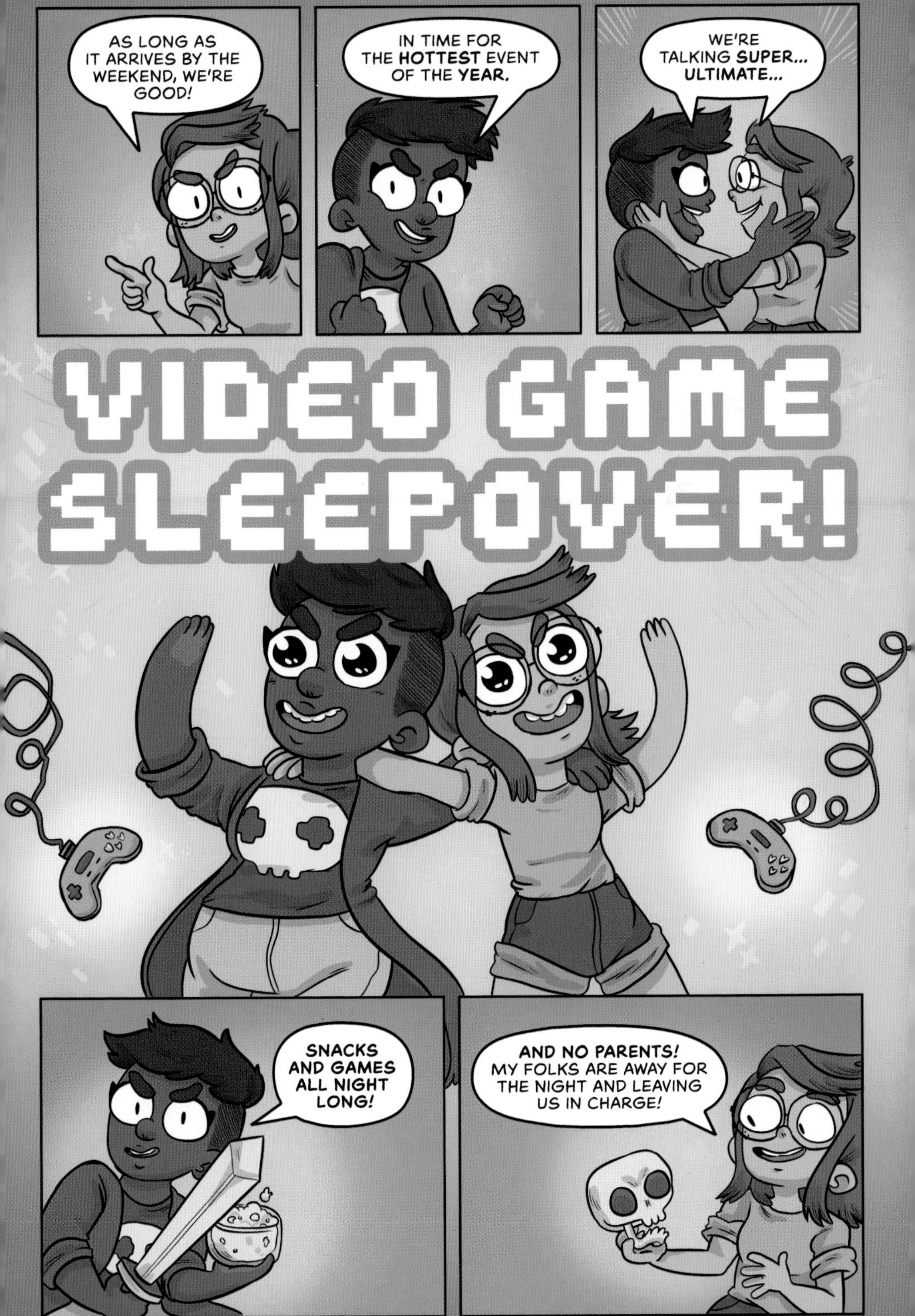
AS LONG AS IT ARRIVES BY THE WEEKEND, WE'RE GOOD!
IN TIME FOR THE **HOTTEST** EVENT OF THE **YEAR.**
WE'RE TALKING **SUPER... ULTIMATE...**
VIDEO GAME SLEEPOVER!
SNACKS AND GAMES ALL NIGHT LONG!
AND NO PARENTS! MY FOLKS ARE AWAY FOR THE NIGHT AND LEAVING US IN CHARGE!

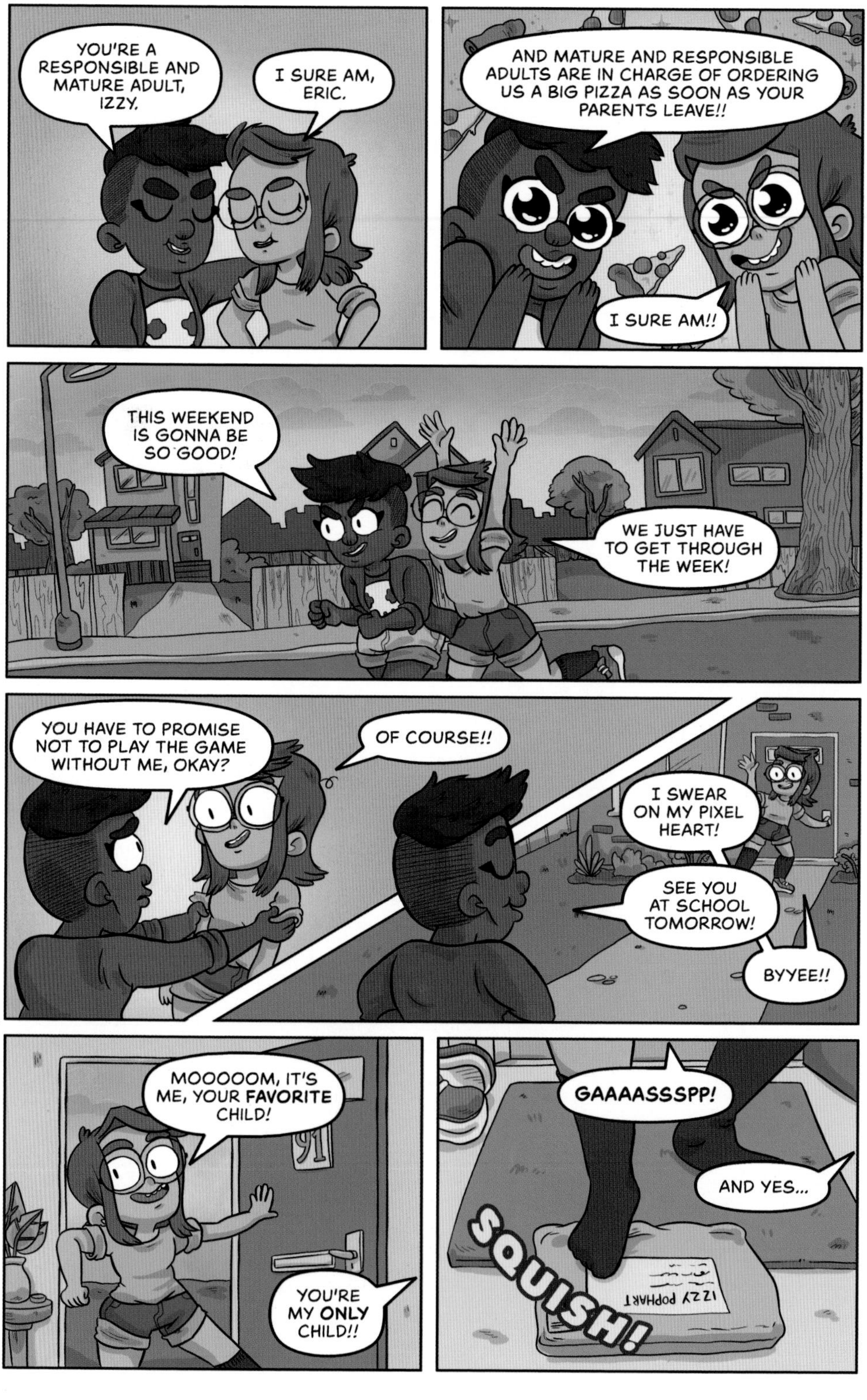
YOU'RE A RESPONSIBLE AND MATURE ADULT, IZZY.
I SURE AM, ERIC.
AND MATURE AND RESPONSIBLE ADULTS ARE IN CHARGE OF ORDERING US A BIG PIZZA AS SOON AS YOUR PARENTS LEAVE!!
I SURE AM!!
THIS WEEKEND IS GONNA BE SO GOOD!
WE JUST HAVE TO GET THROUGH THE WEEK!
YOU HAVE TO PROMISE NOT TO PLAY THE GAME WITHOUT ME, OKAY?
OF COURSE!!
I SWEAR ON MY PIXEL HEART!
SEE YOU AT SCHOOL TOMORROW!
BYYEE!!
MOOOOOM, IT'S ME, YOUR **FAVORITE** CHILD!
91
YOU'RE MY **ONLY** CHILD!!
GAAAASSSPP!
AND YES...
SQUISH!
IZZY POPHART

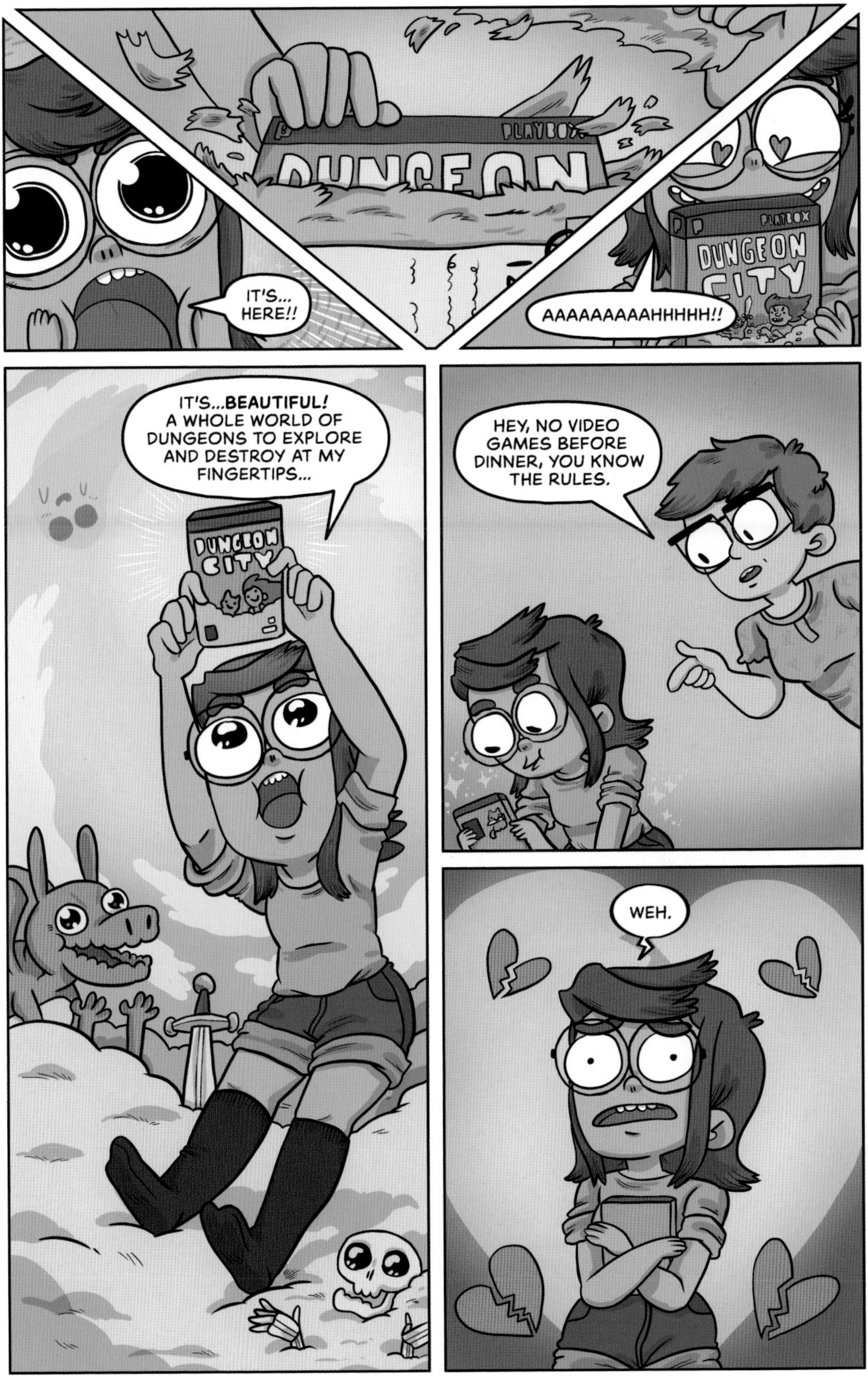
IT'S... HERE!!
PLAYBOX
DUNGEON
PLAYBOX
DUNGEON CITY
AAAAAAAAAHHHHH!!
IT'S...**BEAUTIFUL!** A WHOLE WORLD OF DUNGEONS TO EXPLORE AND DESTROY AT MY FINGERTIPS...
DUNGEON CITY
HEY, NO VIDEO GAMES BEFORE DINNER, YOU KNOW THE RULES.
WEH.

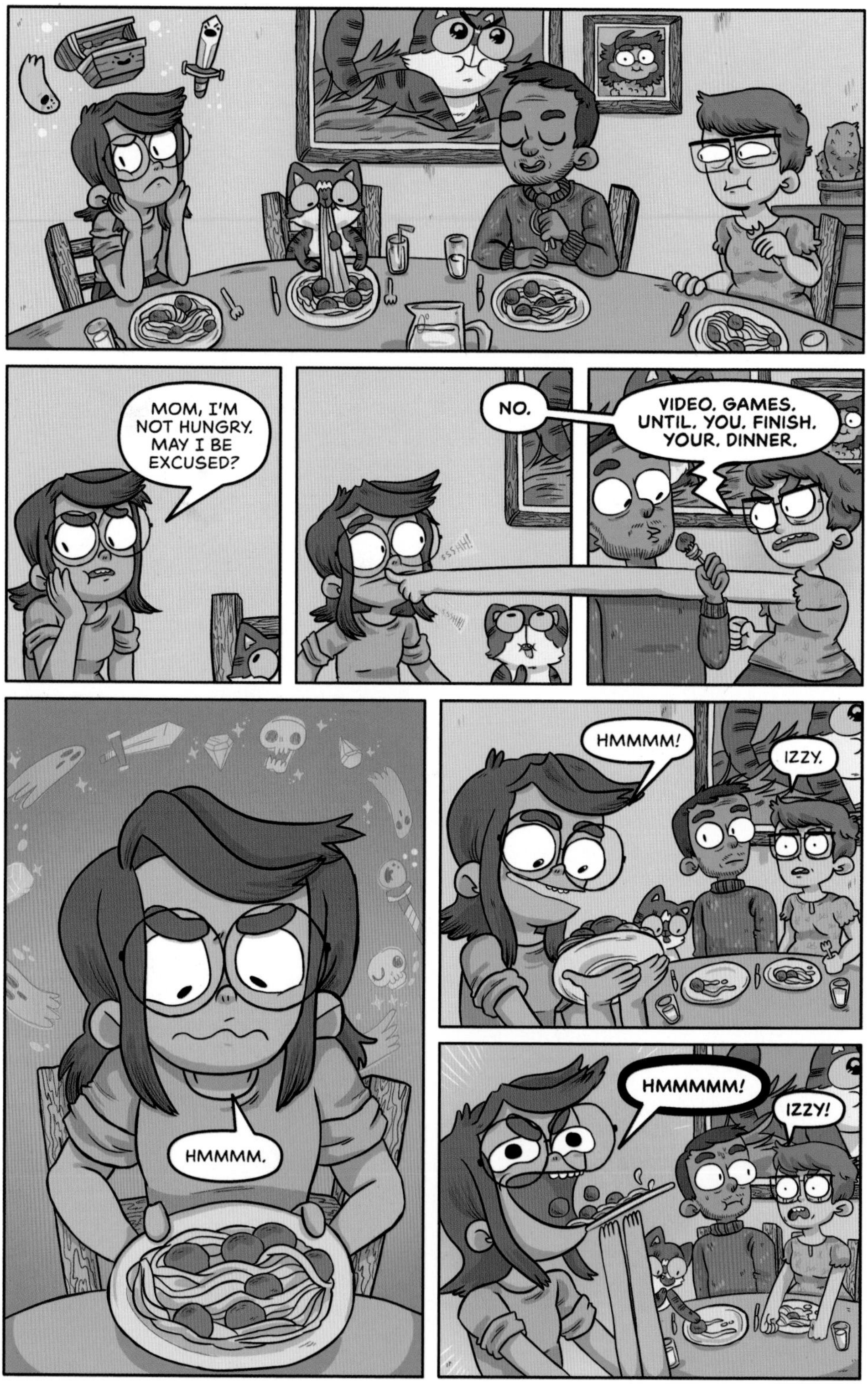
MOM, I'M NOT HUNGRY. MAY I BE EXCUSED?
NO.
VIDEO. GAMES. UNTIL. YOU. FINISH. YOUR. DINNER.
HMMMM.
HMMMM!
IZZY.
HMMMMM!
IZZY!

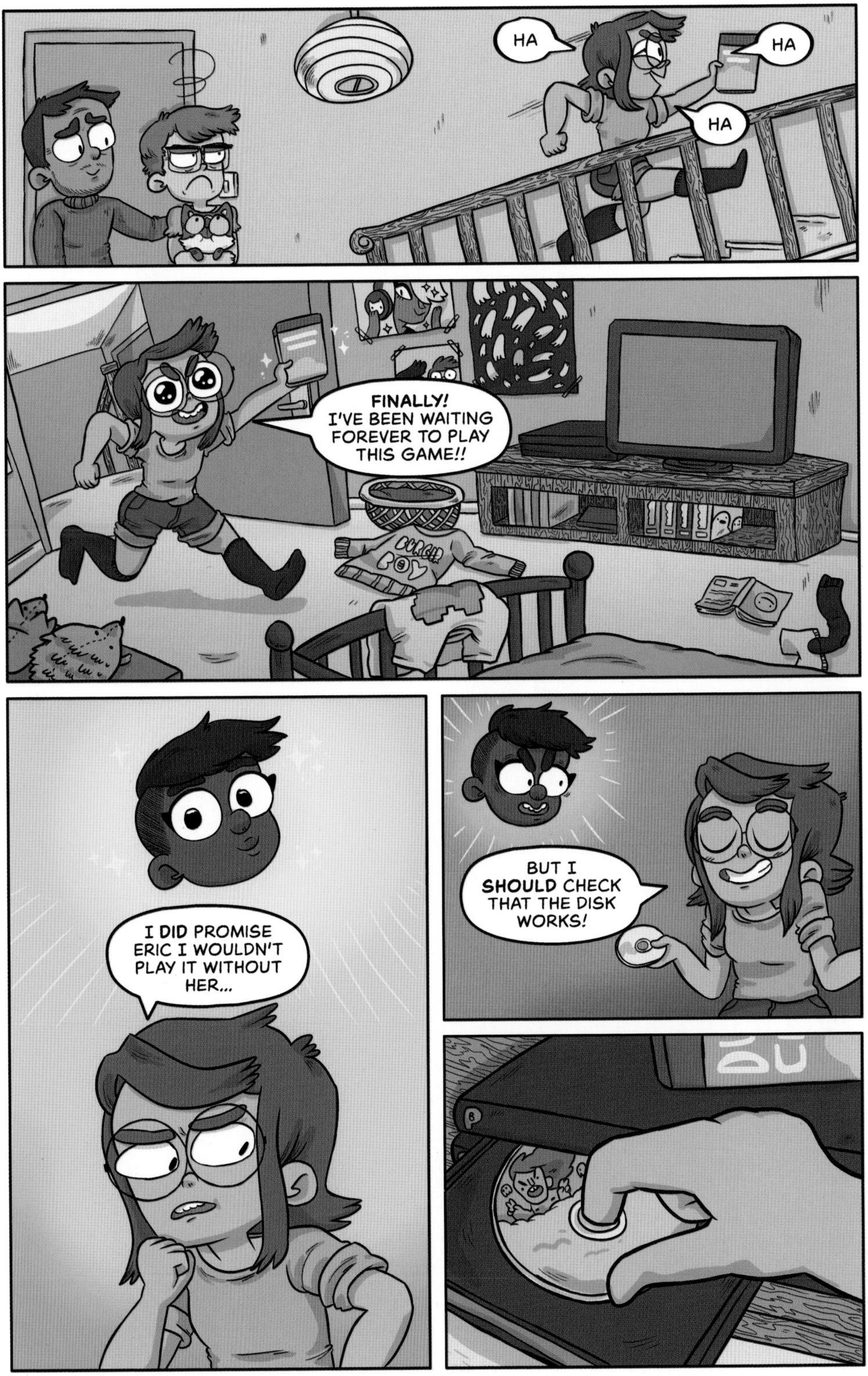
HA
HA
HA
FINALLY! I'VE BEEN WAITING FOREVER TO PLAY THIS GAME!!
BURGER BOY
I DID PROMISE ERIC I WOULDN'T PLAY IT WITHOUT HER...
BUT I SHOULD CHECK THAT THE DISK WORKS!

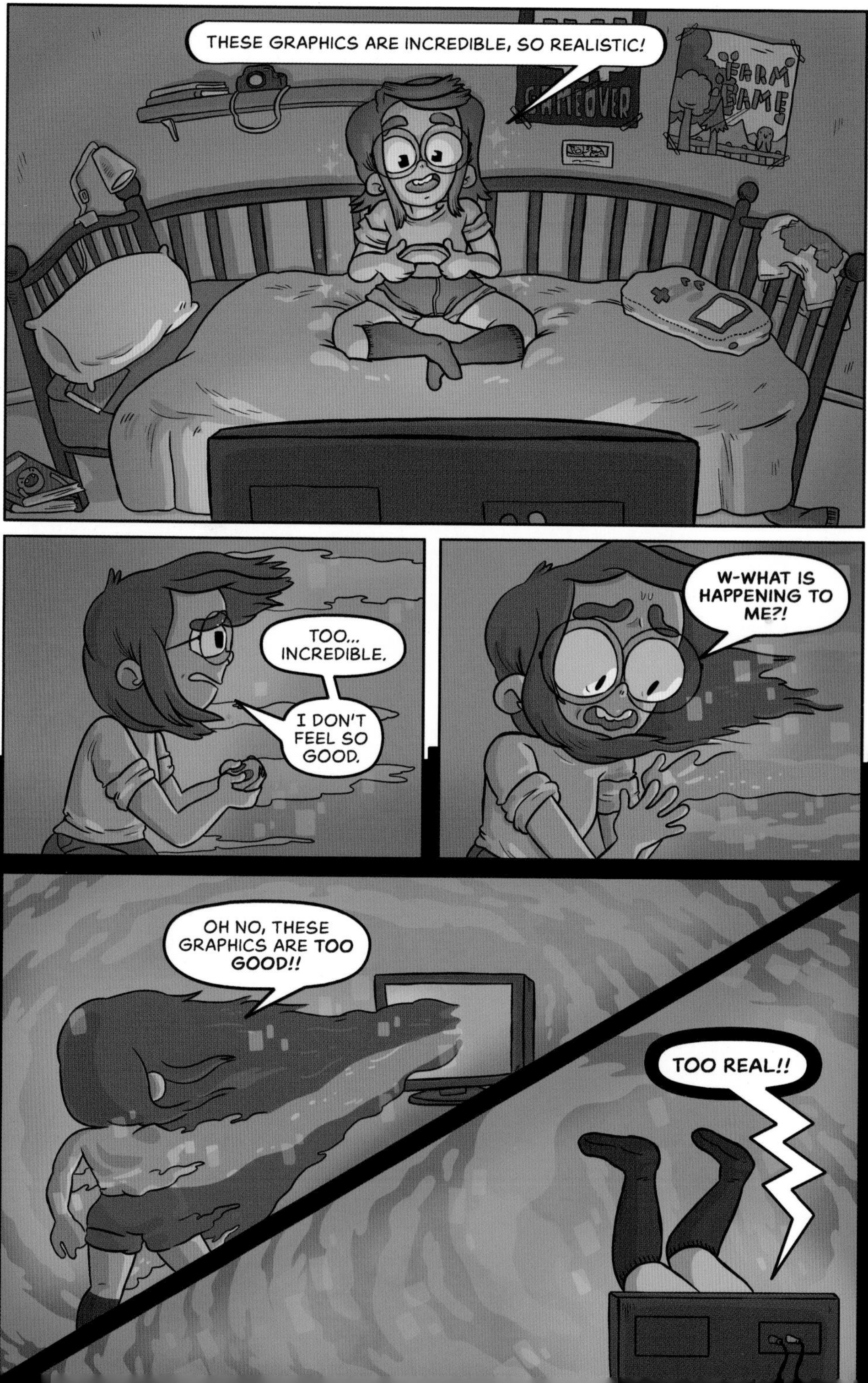
THESE GRAPHICS ARE INCREDIBLE, SO REALISTIC!
GAME OVER
FARM GAME
TOO... INCREDIBLE.
I DON'T FEEL SO GOOD.
W-WHAT IS HAPPENING TO ME?!
OH NO, THESE GRAPHICS ARE TOO GOOD!!
TOO REAL!!

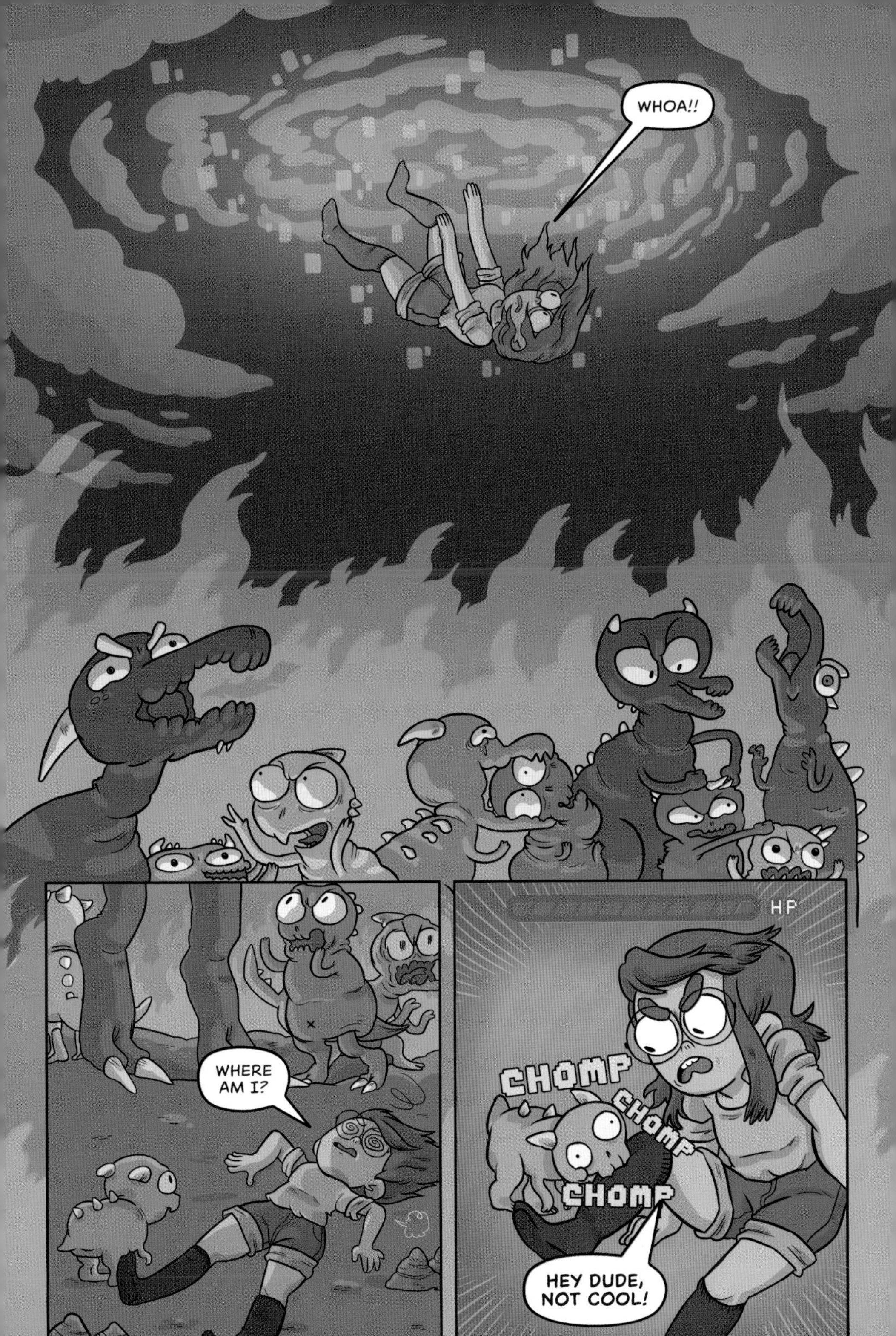
WHOA!!
WHERE AM I?
HP
CHOMP
CHOMP
CHOMP
HEY DUDE, NOT COOL!

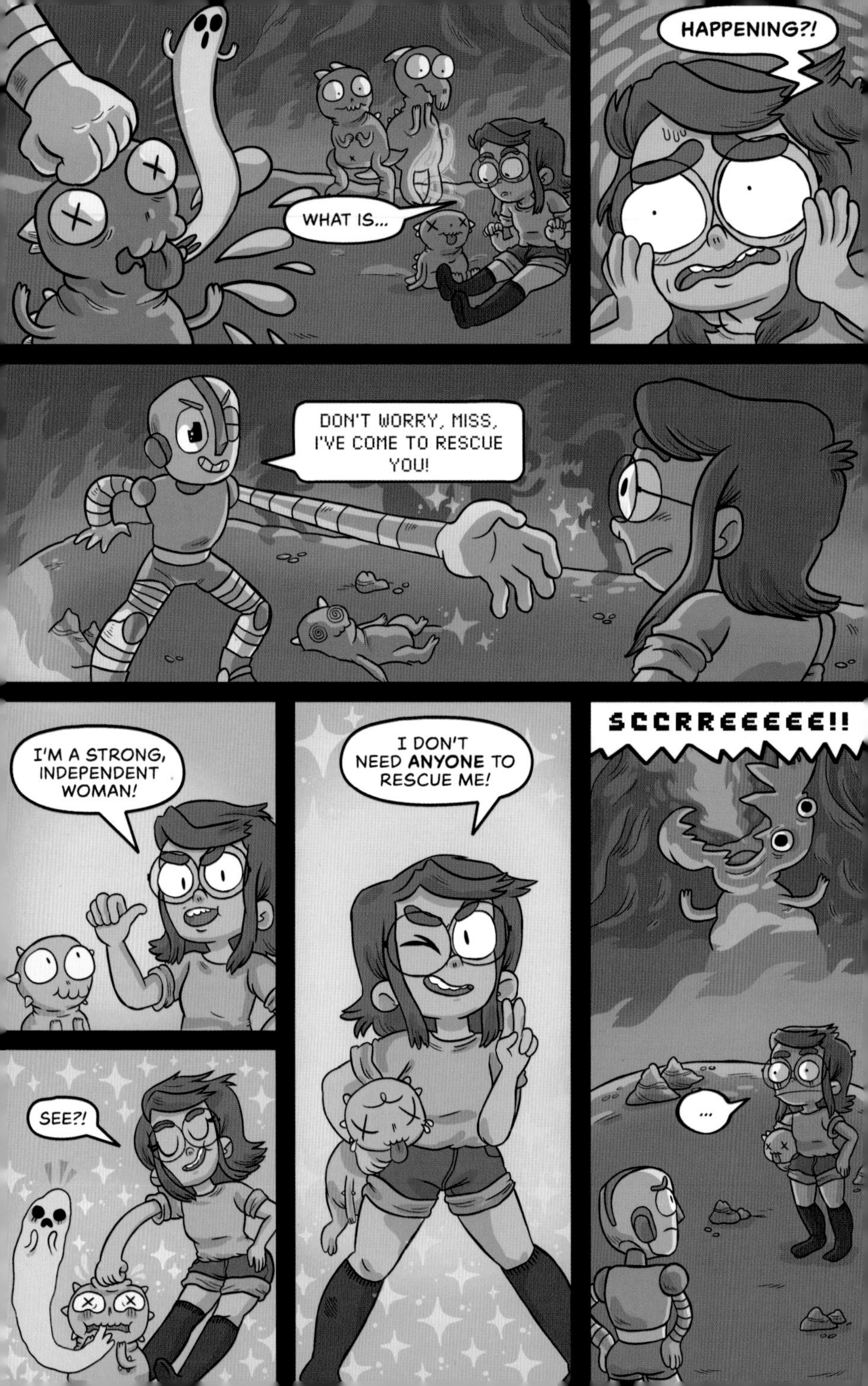
WHAT IS...
HAPPENING?!
DON'T WORRY, MISS, I'VE COME TO RESCUE YOU!
I'M A STRONG, INDEPENDENT WOMAN!
SEE?!
I DON'T NEED **ANYONE** TO RESCUE ME!
SCCRREEEEEE!!
...

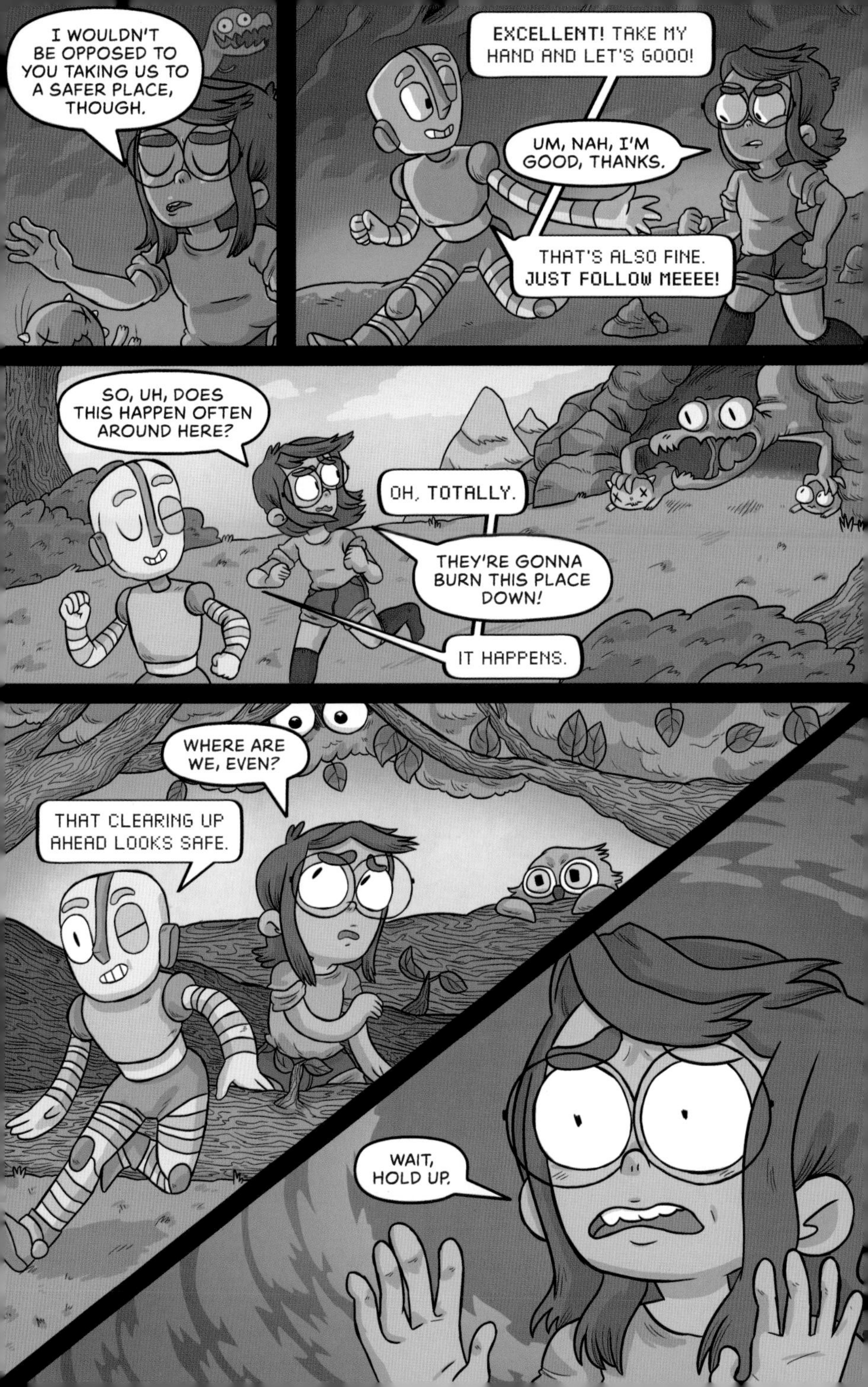
I WOULDN'T BE OPPOSED TO YOU TAKING US TO A SAFER PLACE, THOUGH.
EXCELLENT! TAKE MY HAND AND LET'S GOOO!
UM, NAH, I'M GOOD, THANKS.
THAT'S ALSO FINE. JUST FOLLOW MEEEE!
SO, UH, DOES THIS HAPPEN OFTEN AROUND HERE?
OH, TOTALLY.
THEY'RE GONNA BURN THIS PLACE DOWN!
IT HAPPENS.
WHERE ARE WE, EVEN?
THAT CLEARING UP AHEAD LOOKS SAFE.
WAIT, HOLD UP.

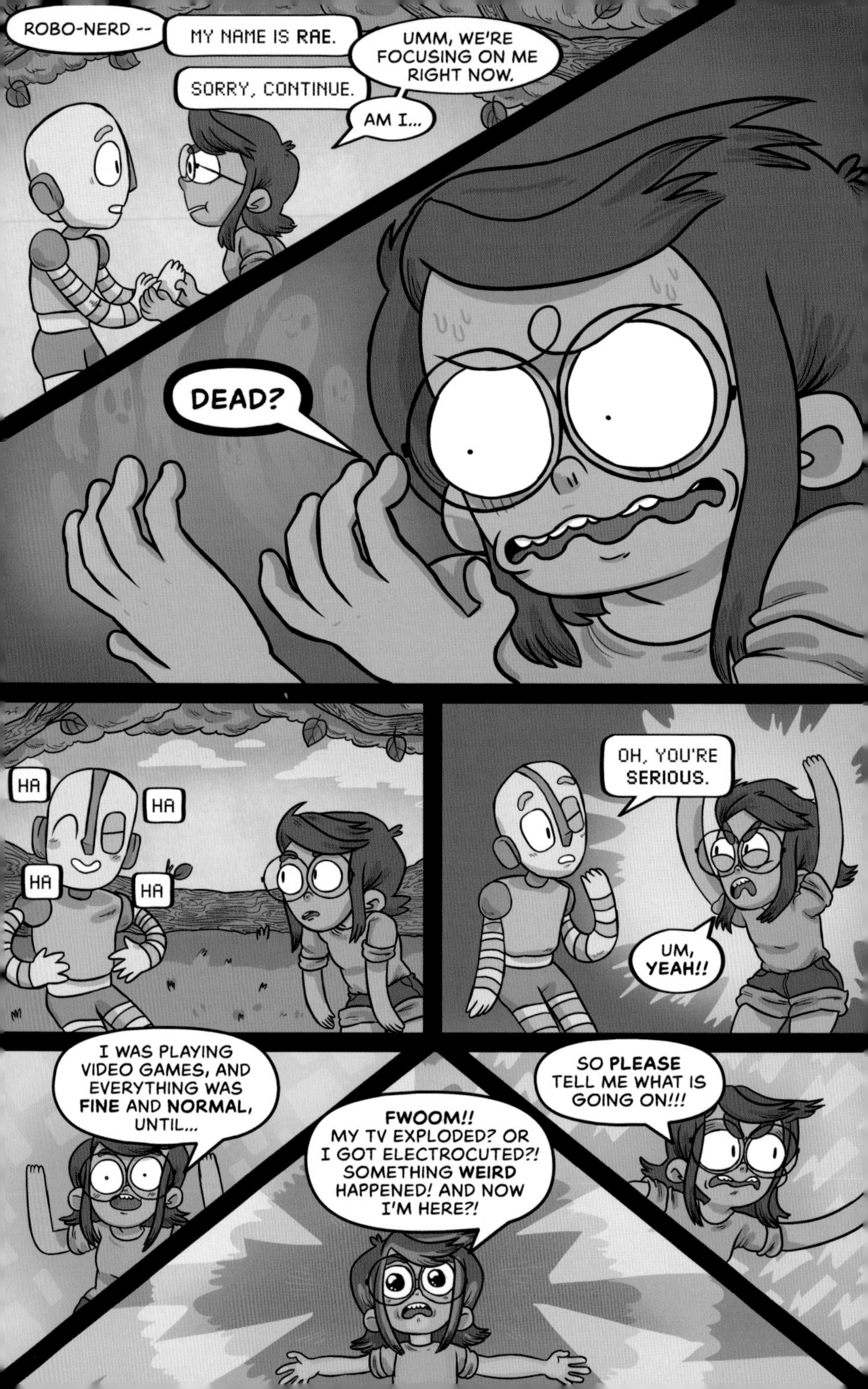
ROBO-NERD --
MY NAME IS RAE.
UMM, WE'RE FOCUSING ON ME RIGHT NOW.
SORRY, CONTINUE.
AM I...
DEAD?
HA
HA
HA
HA
OH, YOU'RE SERIOUS.
UM, YEAH!!
I WAS PLAYING VIDEO GAMES, AND EVERYTHING WAS FINE AND NORMAL, UNTIL...
FWOOM!! MY TV EXPLODED? OR I GOT ELECTROCUTED?! SOMETHING WEIRD HAPPENED! AND NOW I'M HERE?!
SO PLEASE TELL ME WHAT IS GOING ON!!!

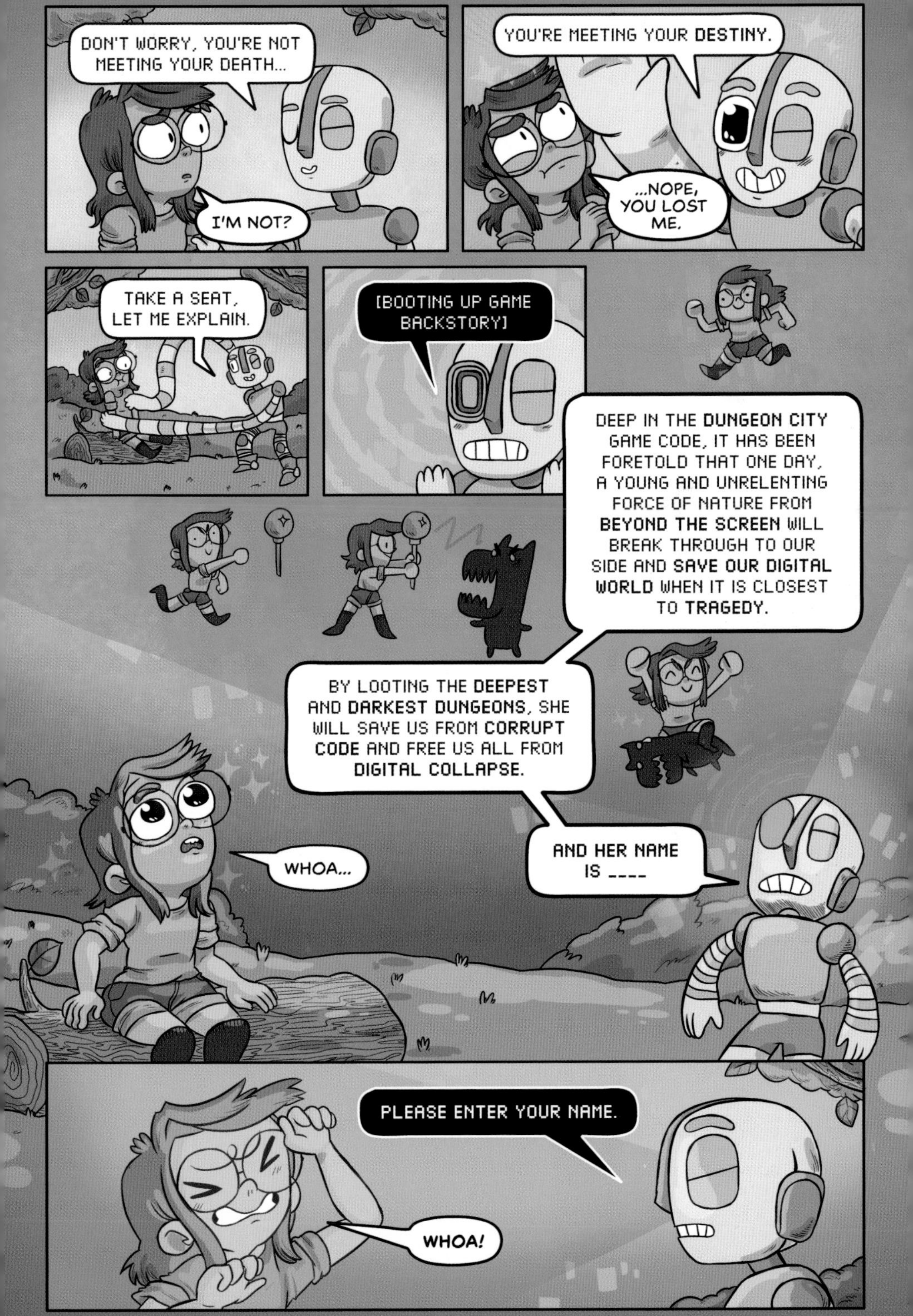
DON'T WORRY, YOU'RE NOT MEETING YOUR DEATH...
I'M NOT?
YOU'RE MEETING YOUR DESTINY.
...NOPE, YOU LOST ME.
TAKE A SEAT, LET ME EXPLAIN.
[BOOTING UP GAME BACKSTORY]
DEEP IN THE DUNGEON CITY GAME CODE, IT HAS BEEN FORETOLD THAT ONE DAY, A YOUNG AND UNRELENTING FORCE OF NATURE FROM BEYOND THE SCREEN WILL BREAK THROUGH TO OUR SIDE AND SAVE OUR DIGITAL WORLD WHEN IT IS CLOSEST TO TRAGEDY.
BY LOOTING THE DEEPEST AND DARKEST DUNGEONS, SHE WILL SAVE US FROM CORRUPT CODE AND FREE US ALL FROM DIGITAL COLLAPSE.
WHOA...
AND HER NAME IS ____
PLEASE ENTER YOUR NAME.
WHOA!

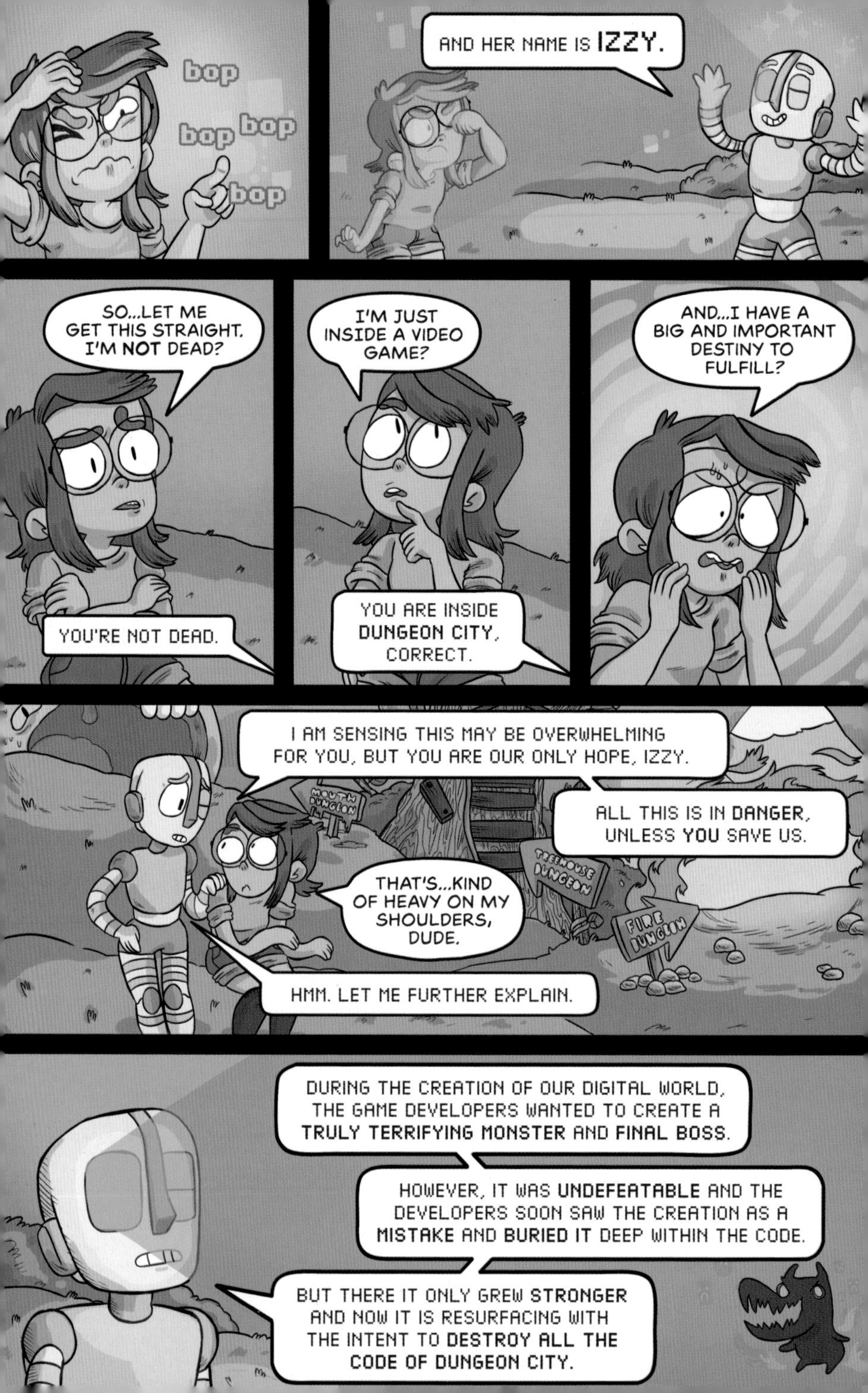
bop
bop bop
bop
AND HER NAME IS IZZY.
SO...LET ME GET THIS STRAIGHT. I'M NOT DEAD?
YOU'RE NOT DEAD.
I'M JUST INSIDE A VIDEO GAME?
YOU ARE INSIDE DUNGEON CITY, CORRECT.
AND...I HAVE A BIG AND IMPORTANT DESTINY TO FULFILL?
I AM SENSING THIS MAY BE OVERWHELMING FOR YOU, BUT YOU ARE OUR ONLY HOPE, IZZY.
ALL THIS IS IN DANGER, UNLESS YOU SAVE US.
MOUTH DUNGEON
TREEHOUSE DUNGEON
FIRE DUNGEON
THAT'S...KIND OF HEAVY ON MY SHOULDERS, DUDE.
HMM. LET ME FURTHER EXPLAIN.
DURING THE CREATION OF OUR DIGITAL WORLD, THE GAME DEVELOPERS WANTED TO CREATE A TRULY TERRIFYING MONSTER AND FINAL BOSS.
HOWEVER, IT WAS UNDEFEATABLE AND THE DEVELOPERS SOON SAW THE CREATION AS A MISTAKE AND BURIED IT DEEP WITHIN THE CODE.
BUT THERE IT ONLY GREW STRONGER AND NOW IT IS RESURFACING WITH THE INTENT TO DESTROY ALL THE CODE OF DUNGEON CITY.

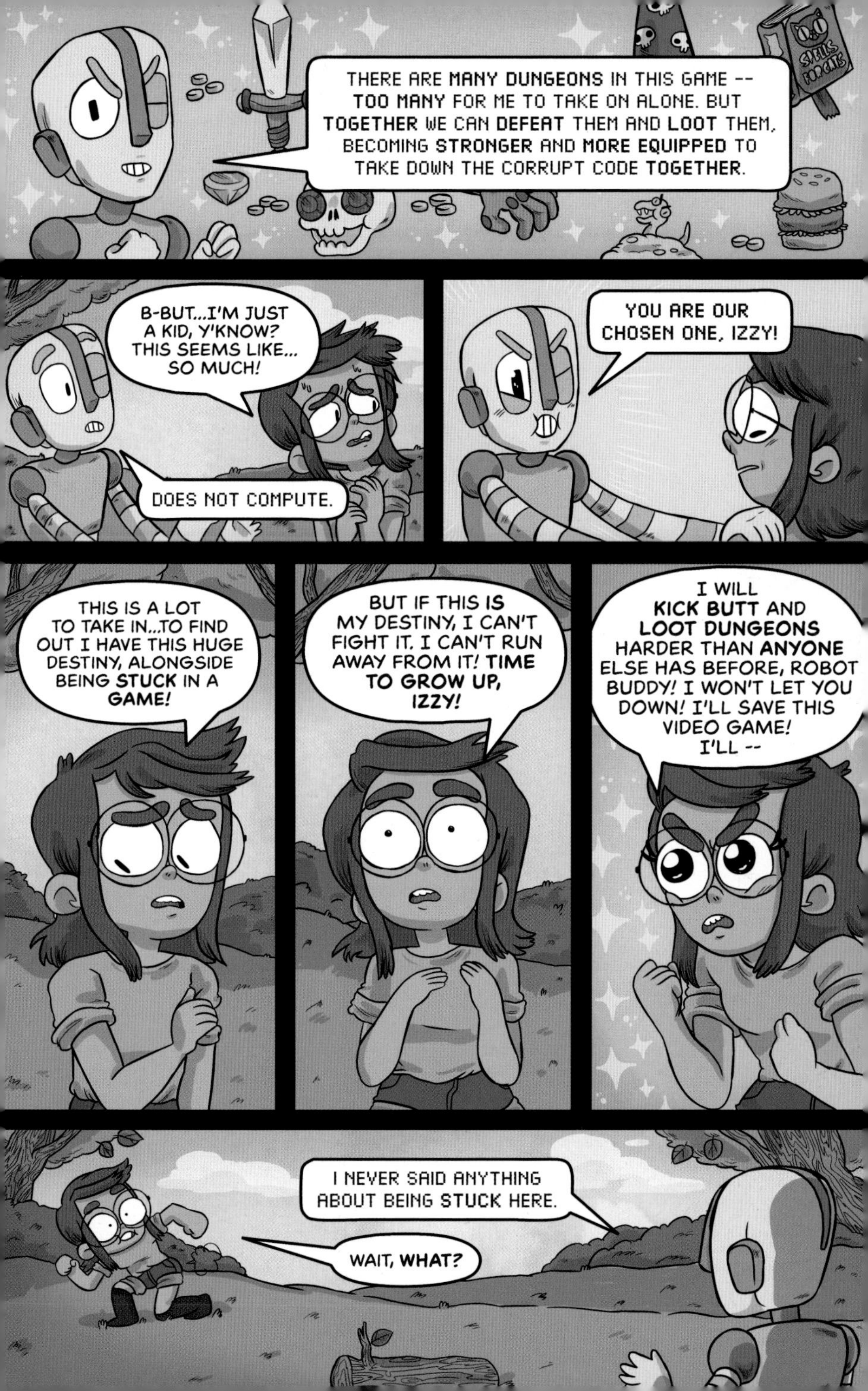
THERE ARE MANY DUNGEONS IN THIS GAME -- TOO MANY FOR ME TO TAKE ON ALONE. BUT TOGETHER WE CAN DEFEAT THEM AND LOOT THEM, BECOMING STRONGER AND MORE EQUIPPED TO TAKE DOWN THE CORRUPT CODE TOGETHER.
SPELLS FOR CATS
B-BUT...I'M JUST A KID, Y'KNOW? THIS SEEMS LIKE... SO MUCH!
DOES NOT COMPUTE.
YOU ARE OUR CHOSEN ONE, IZZY!
THIS IS A LOT TO TAKE IN...TO FIND OUT I HAVE THIS HUGE DESTINY, ALONGSIDE BEING STUCK IN A GAME!
BUT IF THIS IS MY DESTINY, I CAN'T FIGHT IT. I CAN'T RUN AWAY FROM IT! TIME TO GROW UP, IZZY!
I WILL KICK BUTT AND LOOT DUNGEONS HARDER THAN ANYONE ELSE HAS BEFORE, ROBOT BUDDY! I WON'T LET YOU DOWN! I'LL SAVE THIS VIDEO GAME! I'LL --
I NEVER SAID ANYTHING ABOUT BEING STUCK HERE.
WAIT, WHAT?

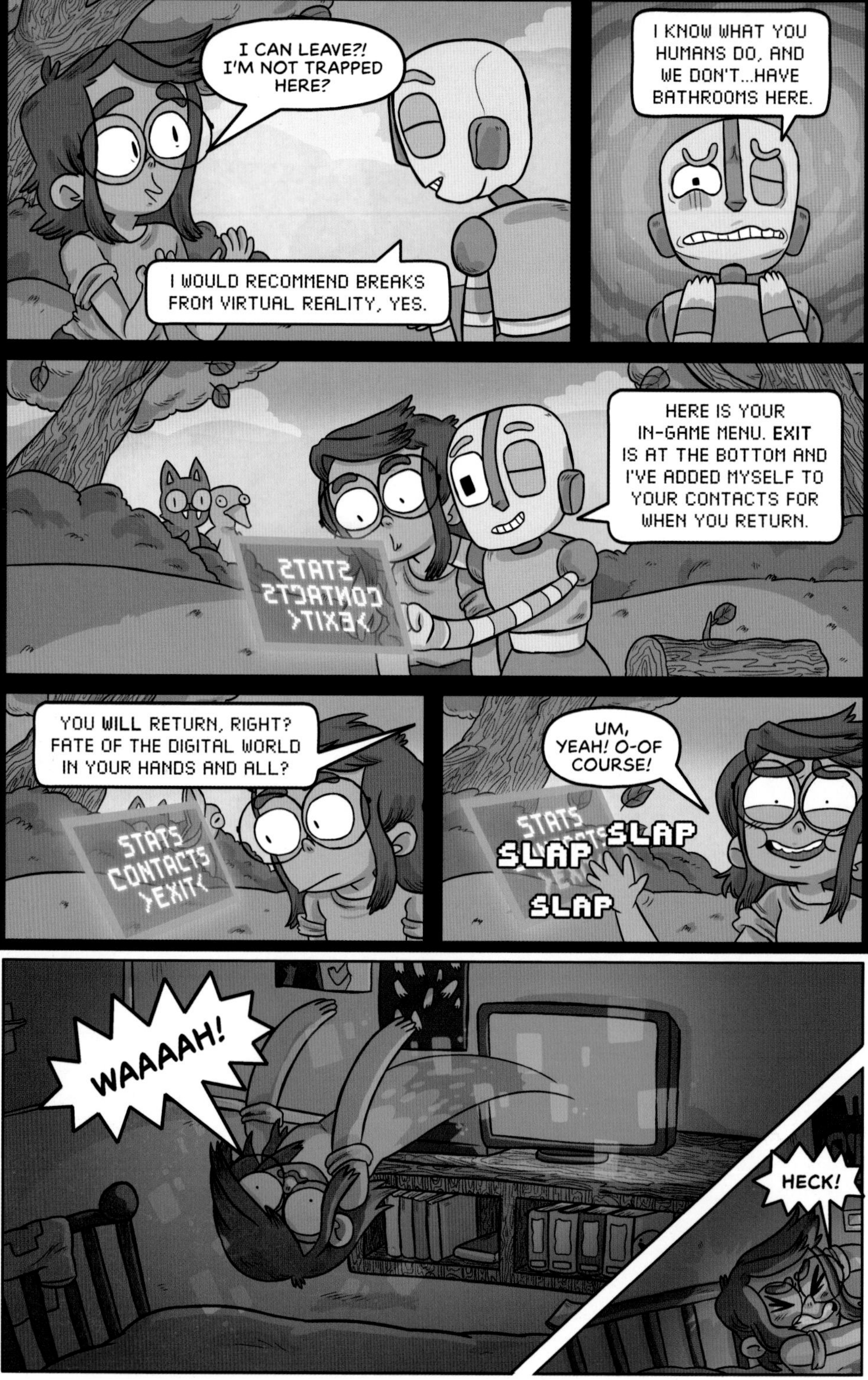
I CAN LEAVE?! I'M NOT TRAPPED HERE?
I WOULD RECOMMEND BREAKS FROM VIRTUAL REALITY, YES.
I KNOW WHAT YOU HUMANS DO, AND WE DON'T...HAVE BATHROOMS HERE.
HERE IS YOUR IN-GAME MENU. EXIT IS AT THE BOTTOM AND I'VE ADDED MYSELF TO YOUR CONTACTS FOR WHEN YOU RETURN.
YOU WILL RETURN, RIGHT? FATE OF THE DIGITAL WORLD IN YOUR HANDS AND ALL?
STATS
CONTACTS
>EXIT<
UM, YEAH! O-OF COURSE!
SLAP
SLAP
SLAP
WAAAAH!
HECK!

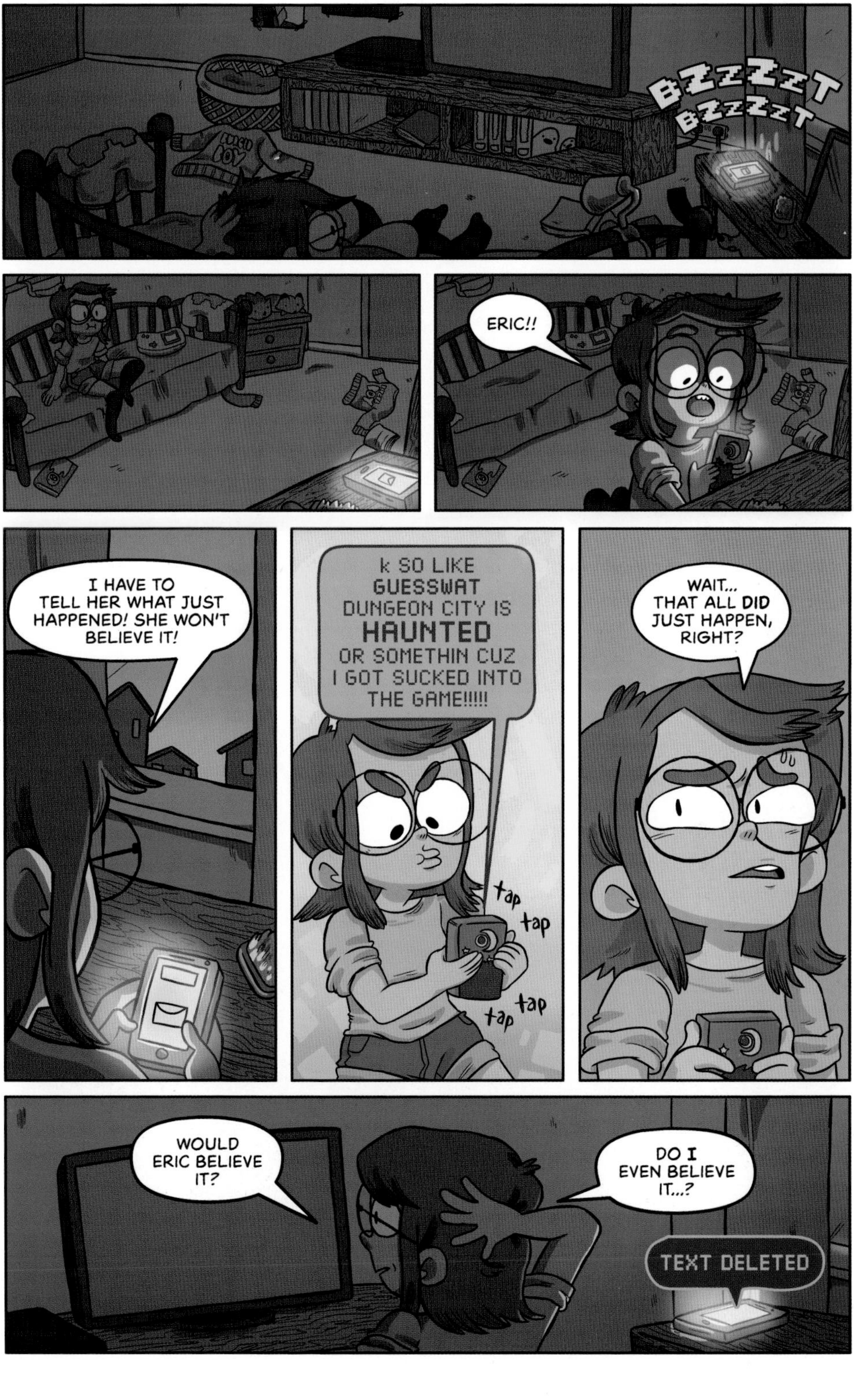
BZZZZZT
BZZZZZT
ERIC!!
I HAVE TO TELL HER WHAT JUST HAPPENED! SHE WON'T BELIEVE IT!
k SO LIKE GUESSWAT DUNGEON CITY IS HAUNTED OR SOMETHIN CUZ I GOT SUCKED INTO THE GAME!!!!!
tap tap
tap tap
WAIT... THAT ALL DID JUST HAPPEN, RIGHT?
WOULD ERIC BELIEVE IT?
DO I EVEN BELIEVE IT...?
TEXT DELETED

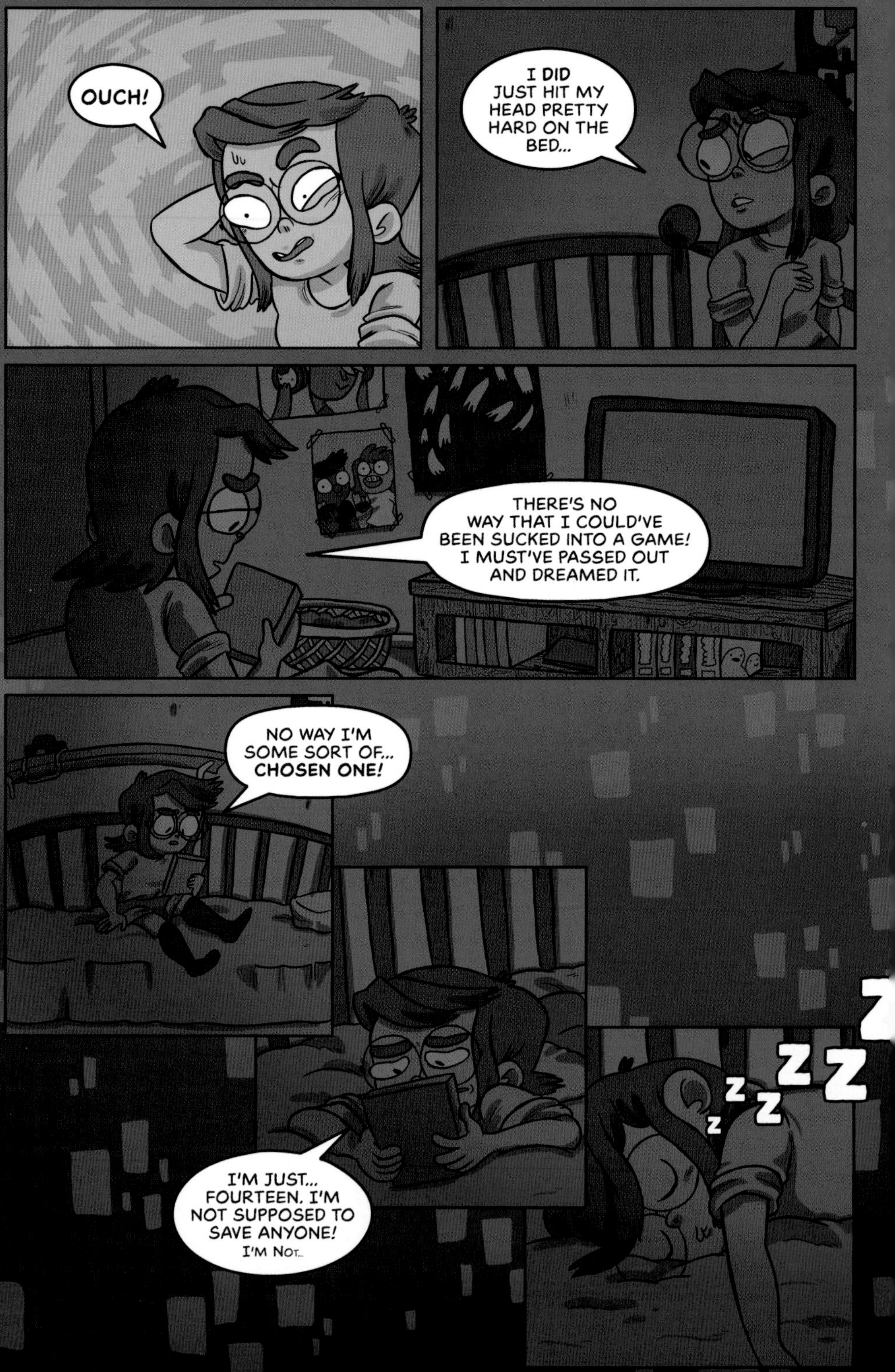
OUCH!
I DID JUST HIT MY HEAD PRETTY HARD ON THE BED...
THERE'S NO WAY THAT I COULD'VE BEEN SUCKED INTO A GAME! I MUST'VE PASSED OUT AND DREAMED IT.
NO WAY I'M SOME SORT OF... CHOSEN ONE!
I'M JUST... FOURTEEN. I'M NOT SUPPOSED TO SAVE ANYONE! I'M NOT...
z Z Z Z Z Z

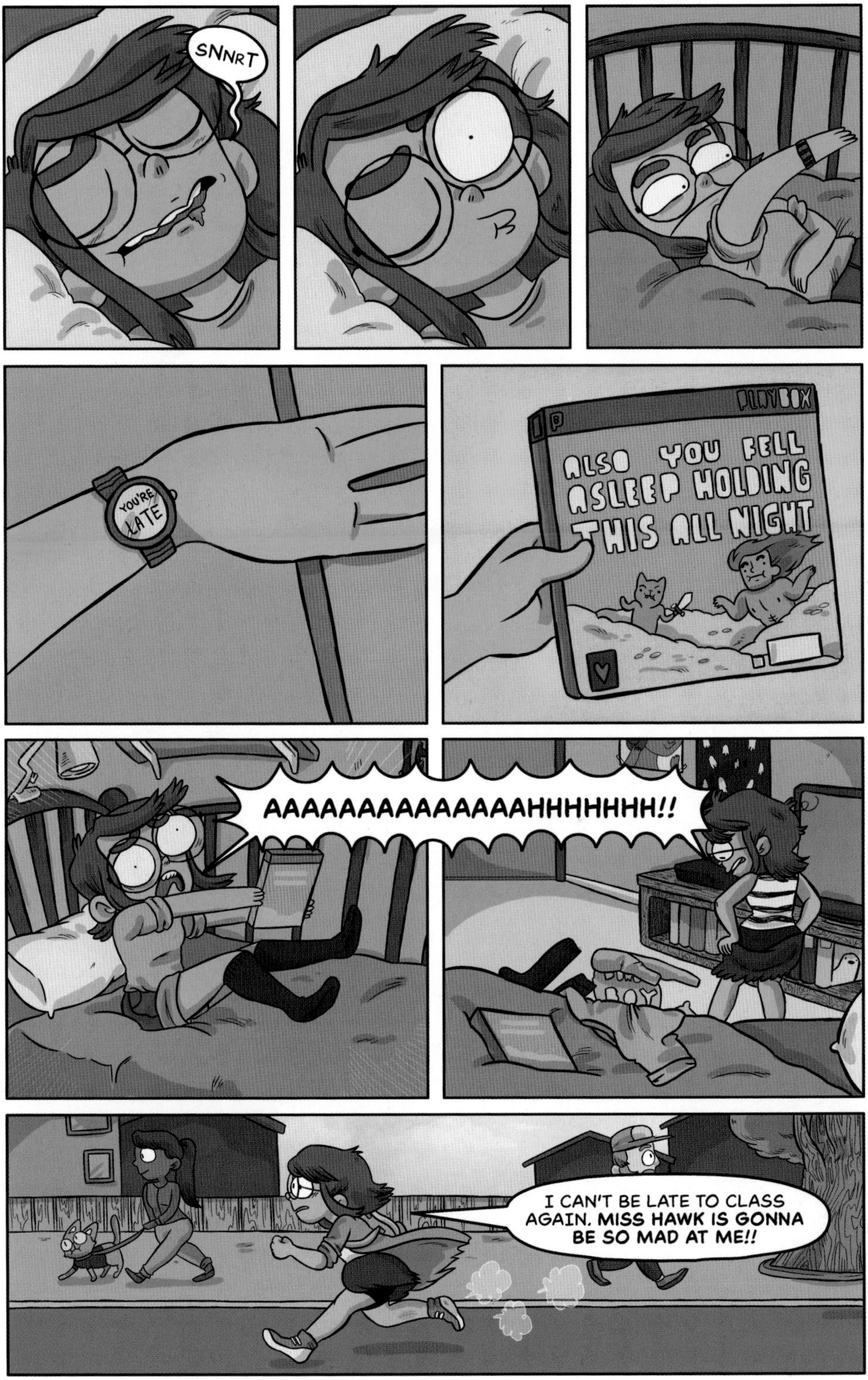
SNNRT
YOU'RE LATE
PLAYBOX
ALSO YOU FELL ASLEEP HOLDING THIS ALL NIGHT
AAAAAAAAAAAAAAHHHHHHH!!
I CAN'T BE LATE TO CLASS AGAIN. MISS HAWK IS GONNA BE SO MAD AT ME!!

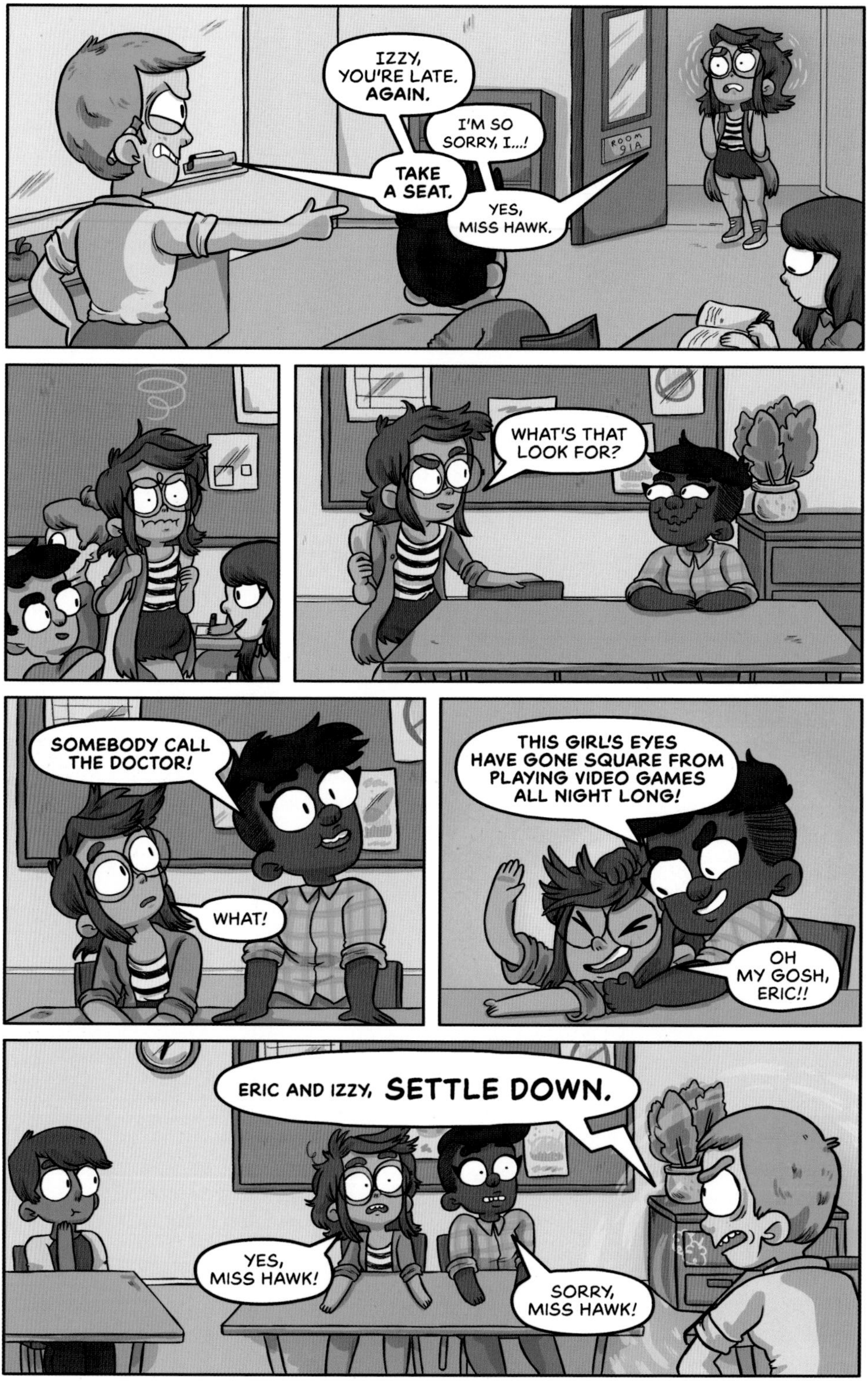
IZZY, YOU'RE LATE. AGAIN.
I'M SO SORRY, I...!
TAKE A SEAT.
YES, MISS HAWK.
ROOM 91A
WHAT'S THAT LOOK FOR?
SOMEBODY CALL THE DOCTOR!
WHAT!
THIS GIRL'S EYES HAVE GONE SQUARE FROM PLAYING VIDEO GAMES ALL NIGHT LONG!
OH MY GOSH, ERIC!!
ERIC AND IZZY, SETTLE DOWN.
YES, MISS HAWK!
SORRY, MISS HAWK!

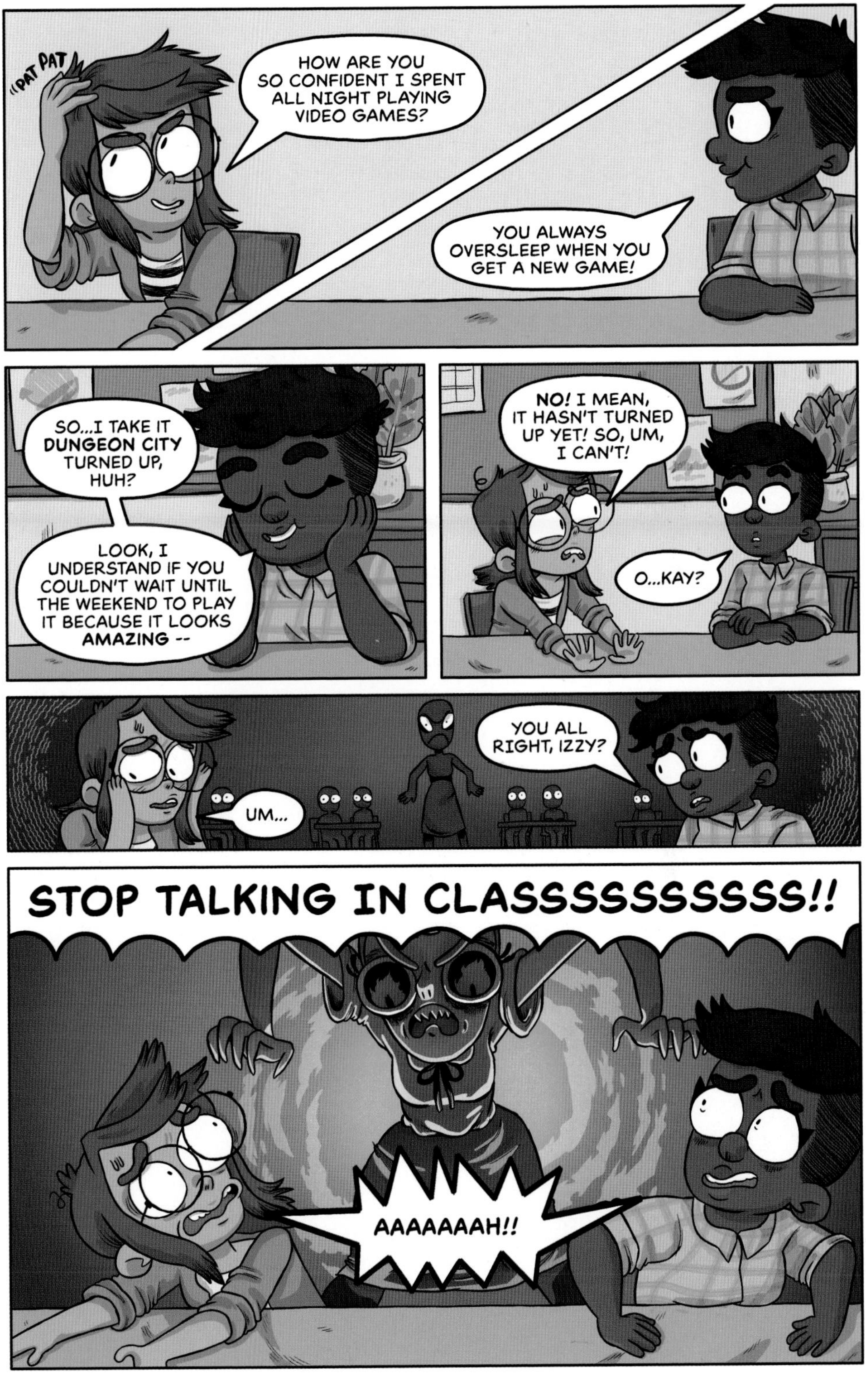
PAT PAT
HOW ARE YOU SO CONFIDENT I SPENT ALL NIGHT PLAYING VIDEO GAMES?
YOU ALWAYS OVERSLEEP WHEN YOU GET A NEW GAME!
SO...I TAKE IT DUNGEON CITY TURNED UP, HUH?
LOOK, I UNDERSTAND IF YOU COULDN'T WAIT UNTIL THE WEEKEND TO PLAY IT BECAUSE IT LOOKS AMAZING --
NO! I MEAN, IT HASN'T TURNED UP YET! SO, UM, I CAN'T!
O...KAY?
YOU ALL RIGHT, IZZY?
UM...
STOP TALKING IN CLASSSSSSSSSS!!
AAAAAAAH!!

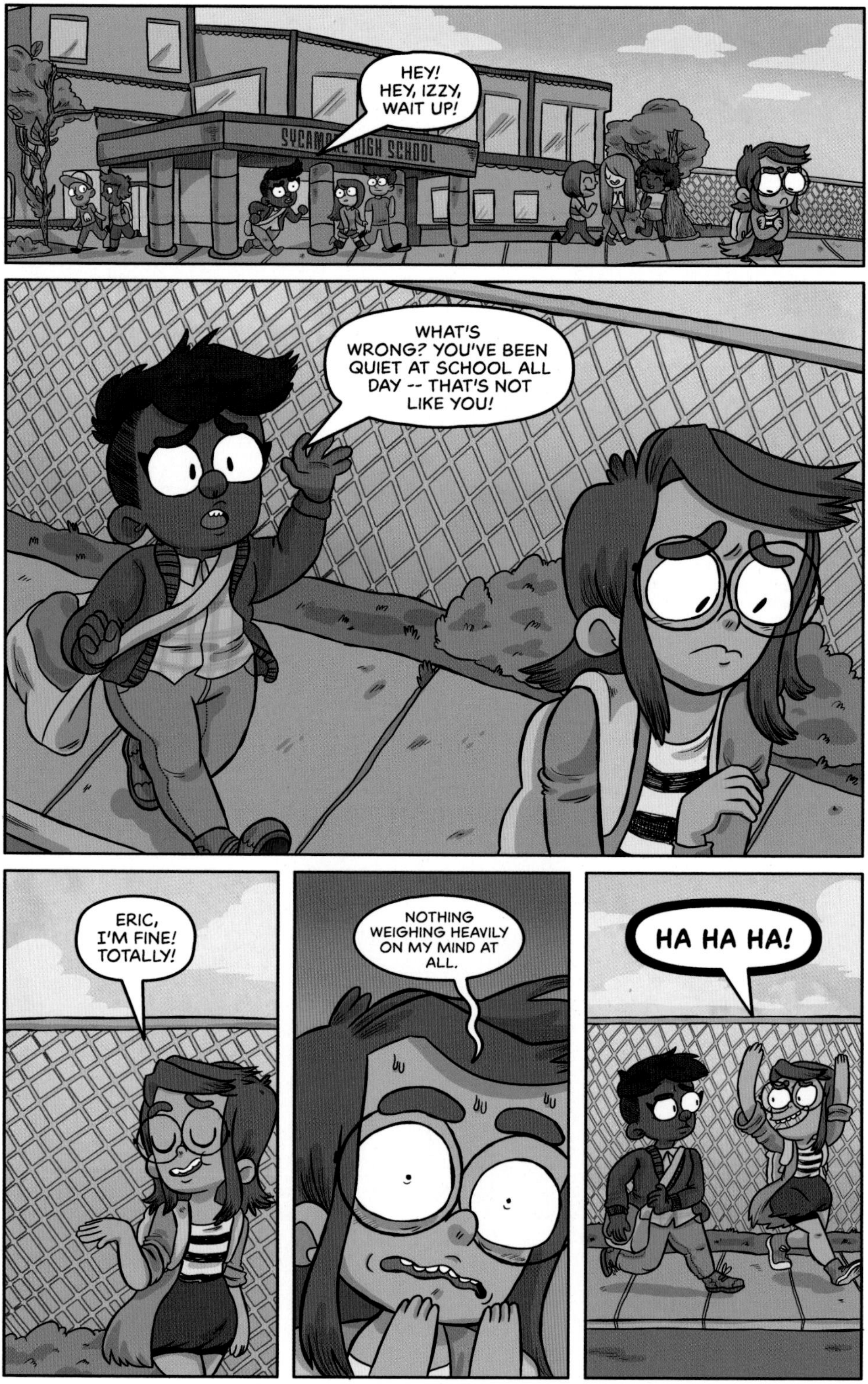
SYCAMORE HIGH SCHOOL
HEY! HEY, IZZY, WAIT UP!
WHAT'S WRONG? YOU'VE BEEN QUIET AT SCHOOL ALL DAY -- THAT'S NOT LIKE YOU!
ERIC, I'M FINE! TOTALLY!
NOTHING WEIGHING HEAVILY ON MY MIND AT ALL.
HA HA HA!

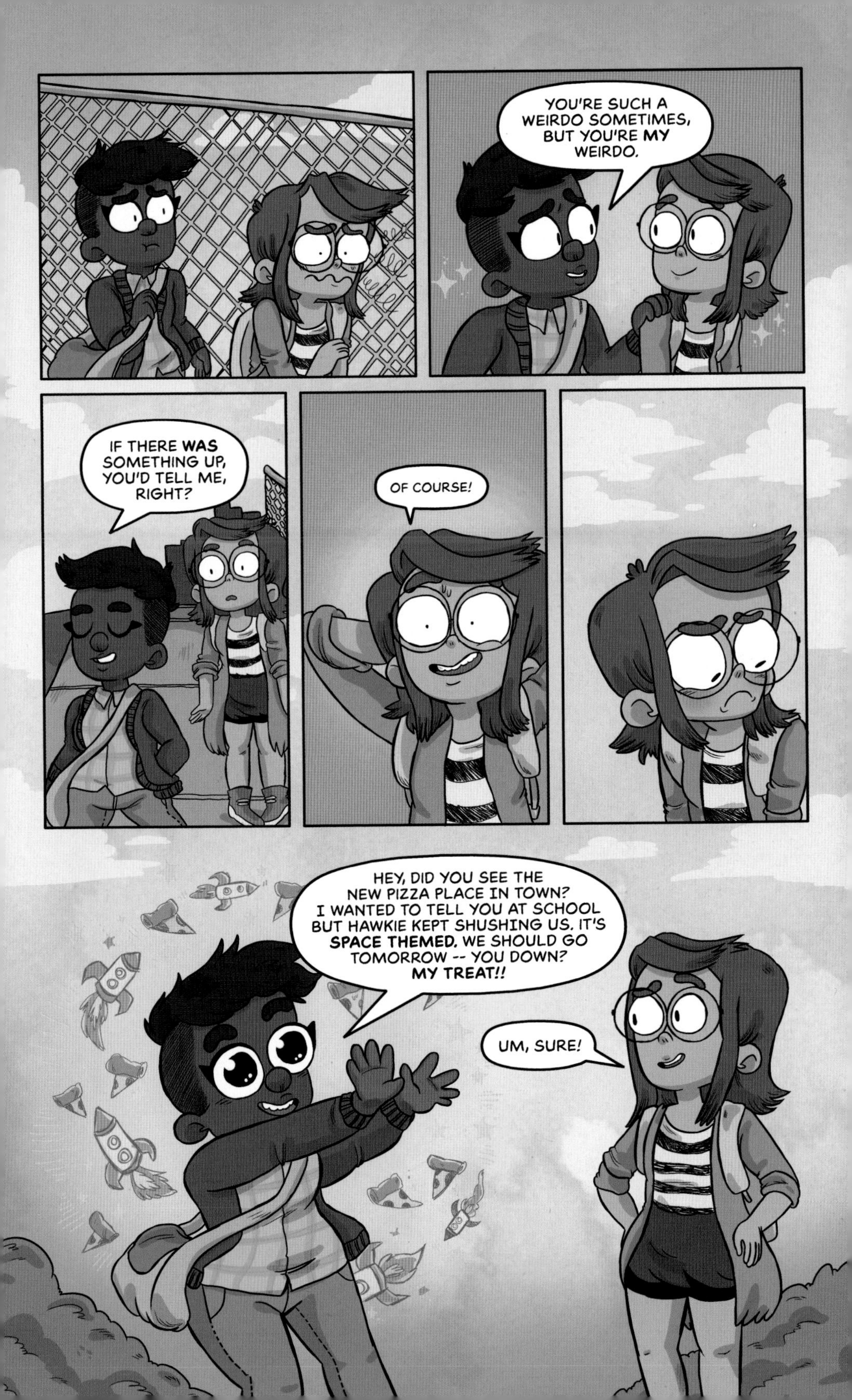
YOU'RE SUCH A WEIRDO SOMETIMES, BUT YOU'RE MY WEIRDO.
IF THERE WAS SOMETHING UP, YOU'D TELL ME, RIGHT?
OF COURSE!
HEY, DID YOU SEE THE NEW PIZZA PLACE IN TOWN? I WANTED TO TELL YOU AT SCHOOL BUT HAWKIE KEPT SHUSHING US. IT'S SPACE THEMED. WE SHOULD GO TOMORROW -- YOU DOWN? MY TREAT!!
UM, SURE!

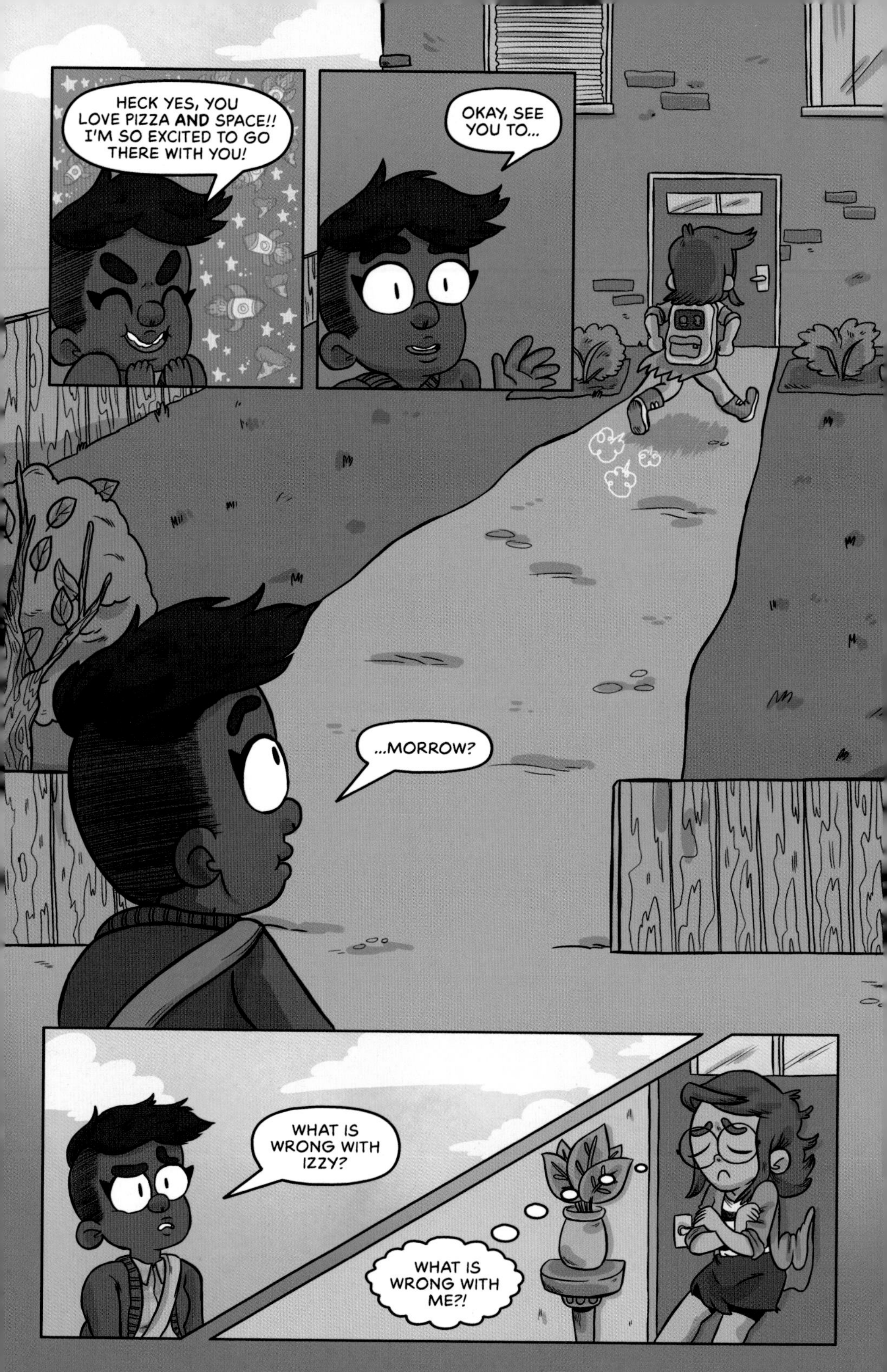
HECK YES, YOU LOVE PIZZA AND SPACE!! I'M SO EXCITED TO GO THERE WITH YOU!
OKAY, SEE YOU TO...
...MORROW?
WHAT IS WRONG WITH IZZY?
WHAT IS WRONG WITH ME?!

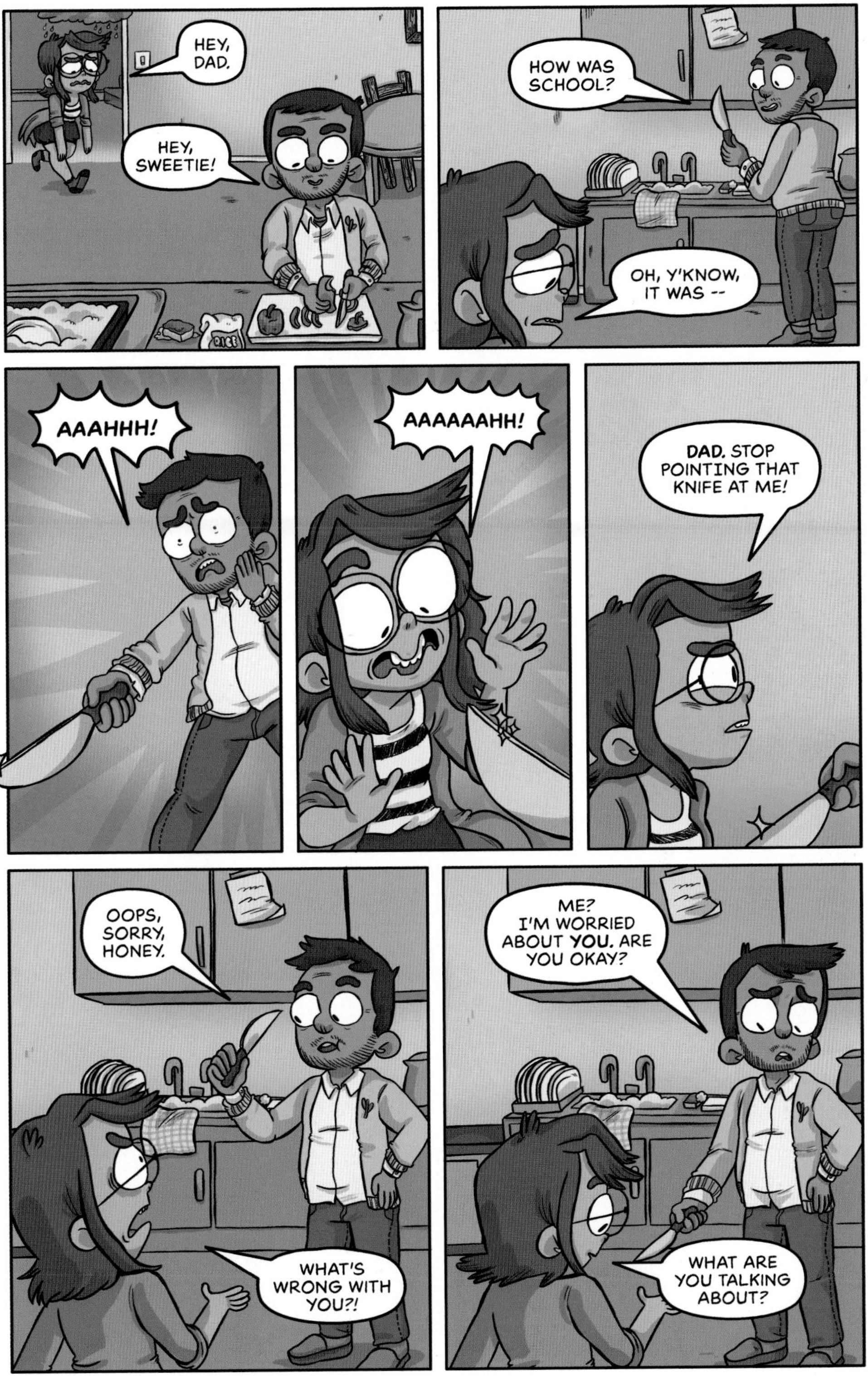
HEY, DAD.
HEY, SWEETIE!
HOW WAS SCHOOL?
OH, Y'KNOW, IT WAS --
AAAHHH!
AAAAAAHH!
DAD. STOP POINTING THAT KNIFE AT ME!
OOPS, SORRY, HONEY.
WHAT'S WRONG WITH YOU?!
ME? I'M WORRIED ABOUT YOU. ARE YOU OKAY?
WHAT ARE YOU TALKING ABOUT?

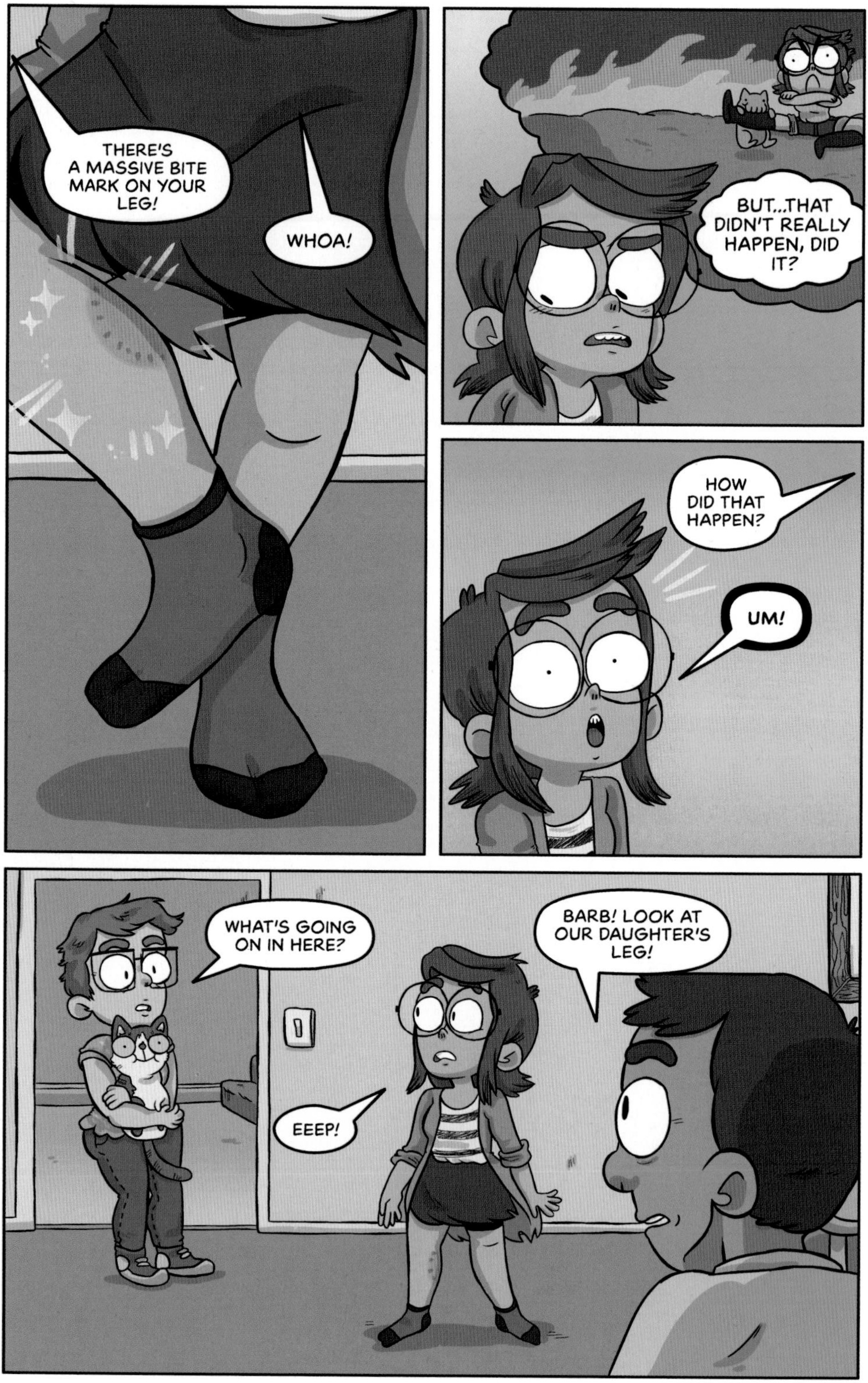
THERE'S A MASSIVE BITE MARK ON YOUR LEG!
WHOA!
BUT...THAT DIDN'T REALLY HAPPEN, DID IT?
HOW DID THAT HAPPEN?
UM!
WHAT'S GOING ON IN HERE?
BARB! LOOK AT OUR DAUGHTER'S LEG!
EEEP!

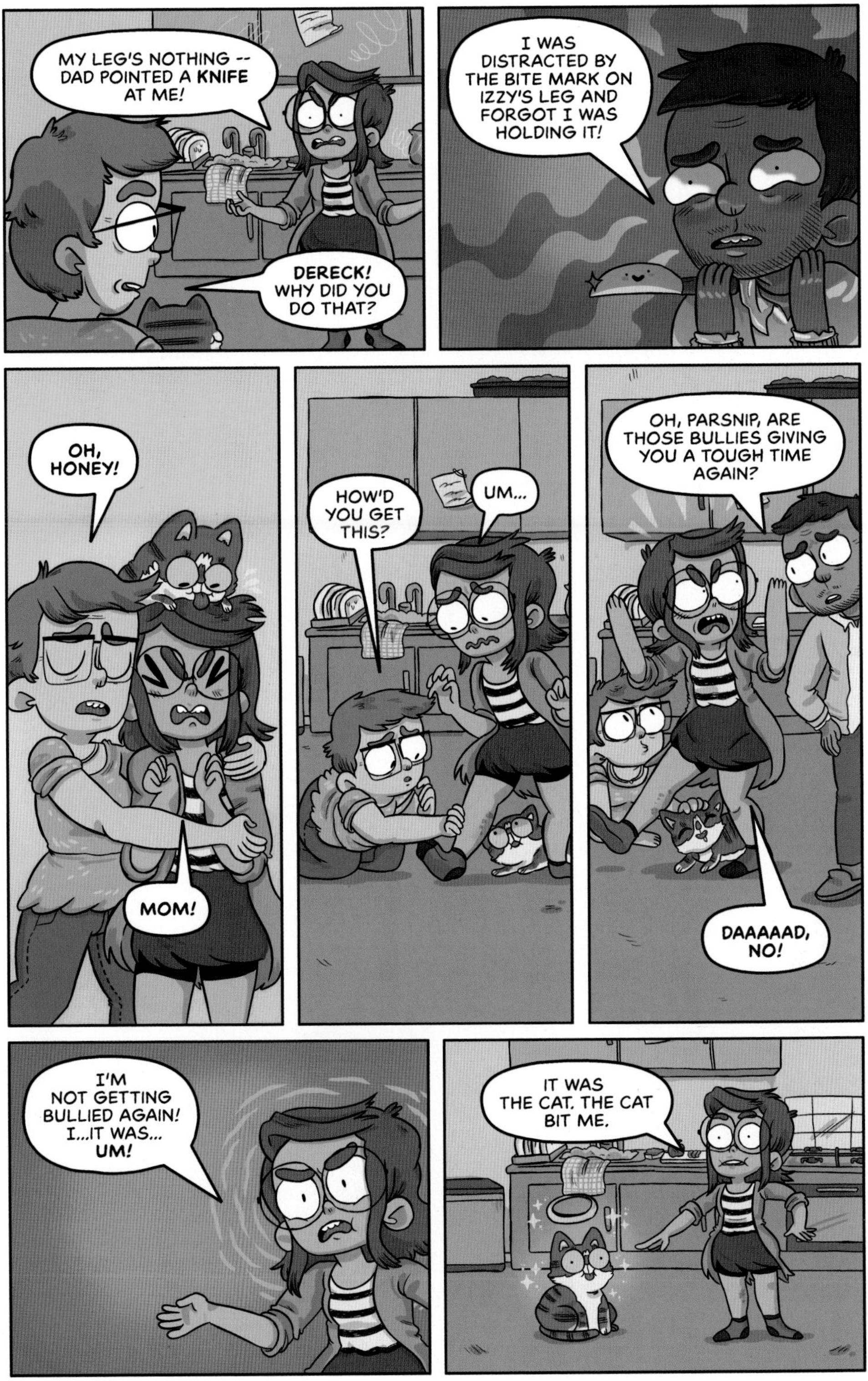

MY LEG'S NOTHING -- DAD POINTED A KNIFE AT ME!
DERECK! WHY DID YOU DO THAT?
I WAS DISTRACTED BY THE BITE MARK ON IZZY'S LEG AND FORGOT I WAS HOLDING IT!
OH, HONEY!
MOM!
HOW'D YOU GET THIS?
UM...
OH, PARSNIP, ARE THOSE BULLIES GIVING YOU A TOUGH TIME AGAIN?
DAAAAAD, NO!
I'M NOT GETTING BULLIED AGAIN! I...IT WAS... UM!
IT WAS THE CAT. THE CAT BIT ME.

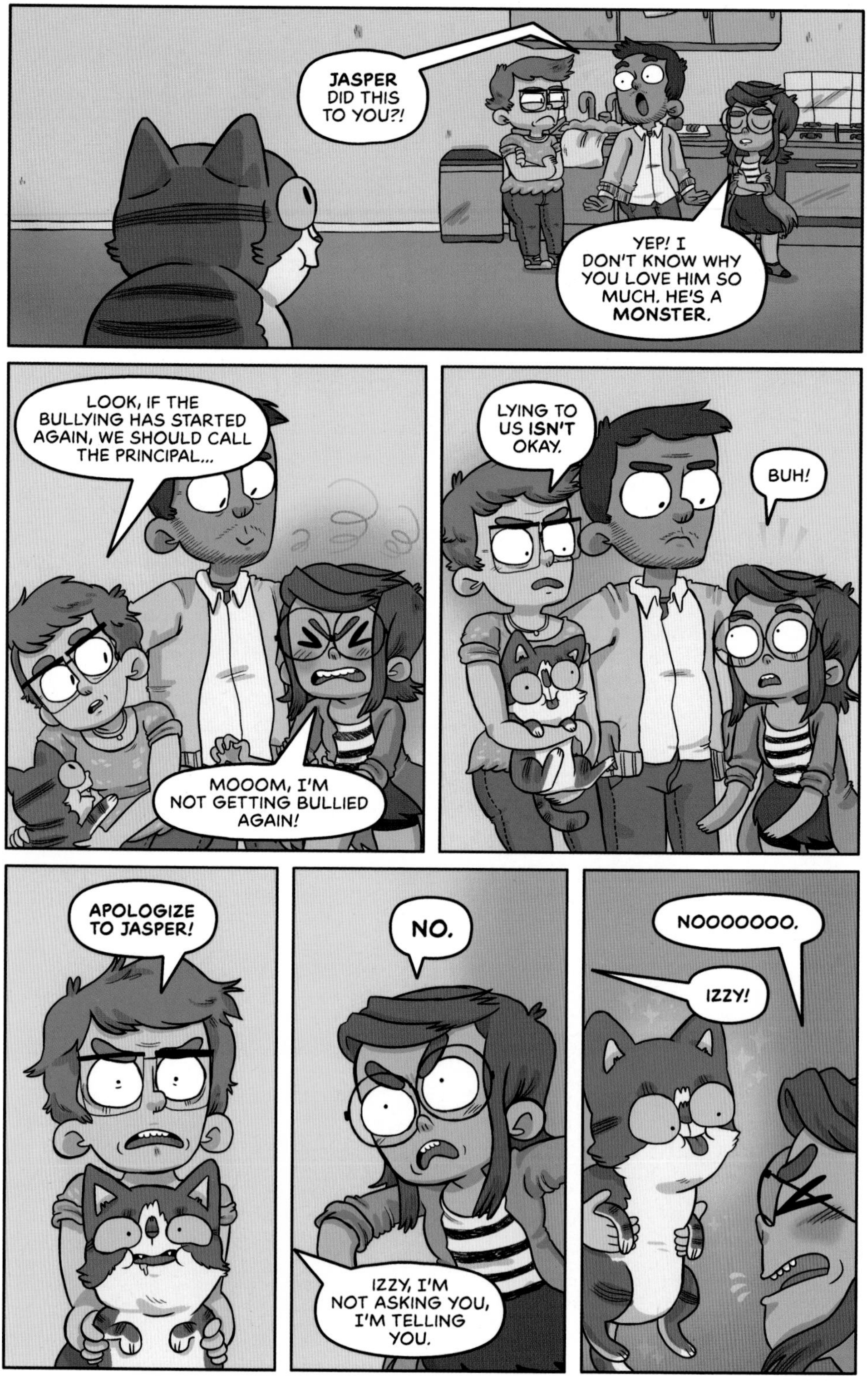
JASPER DID THIS TO YOU?!
YEP! I DON'T KNOW WHY YOU LOVE HIM SO MUCH. HE'S A **MONSTER**.
LOOK, IF THE BULLYING HAS STARTED AGAIN, WE SHOULD CALL THE PRINCIPAL...
MOOOM, I'M NOT GETTING BULLIED AGAIN!
LYING TO US **ISN'T** OKAY.
BUH!
APOLOGIZE TO JASPER!
NO.
IZZY, I'M NOT ASKING YOU, I'M TELLING YOU.
NOOOOOOO.
IZZY!

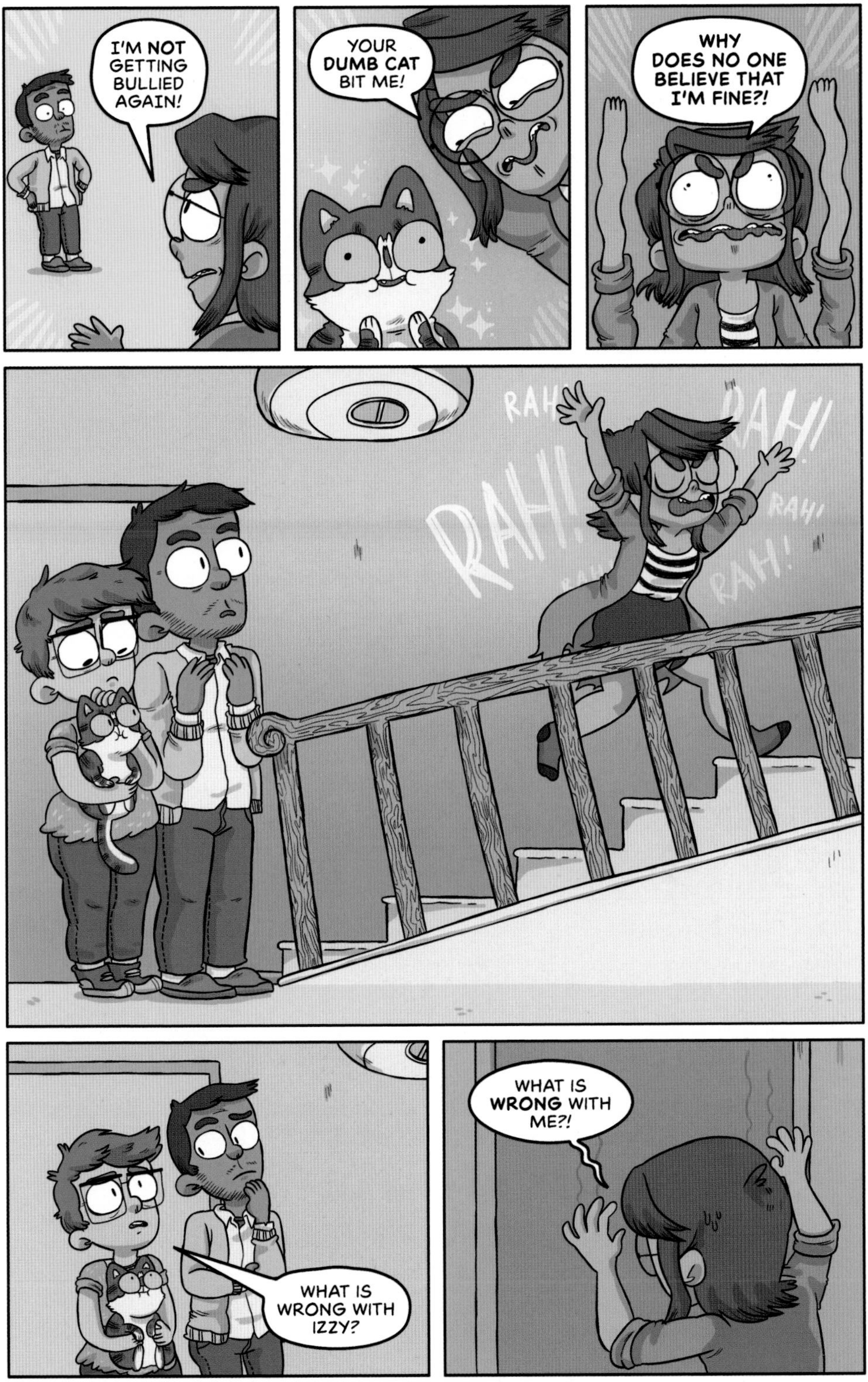
I'M NOT GETTING BULLIED AGAIN!
YOUR DUMB CAT BIT ME!
WHY DOES NO ONE BELIEVE THAT I'M FINE?!
RAH RAH! RAH! RAH RAH!
WHAT IS WRONG WITH IZZY?
WHAT IS WRONG WITH ME?!

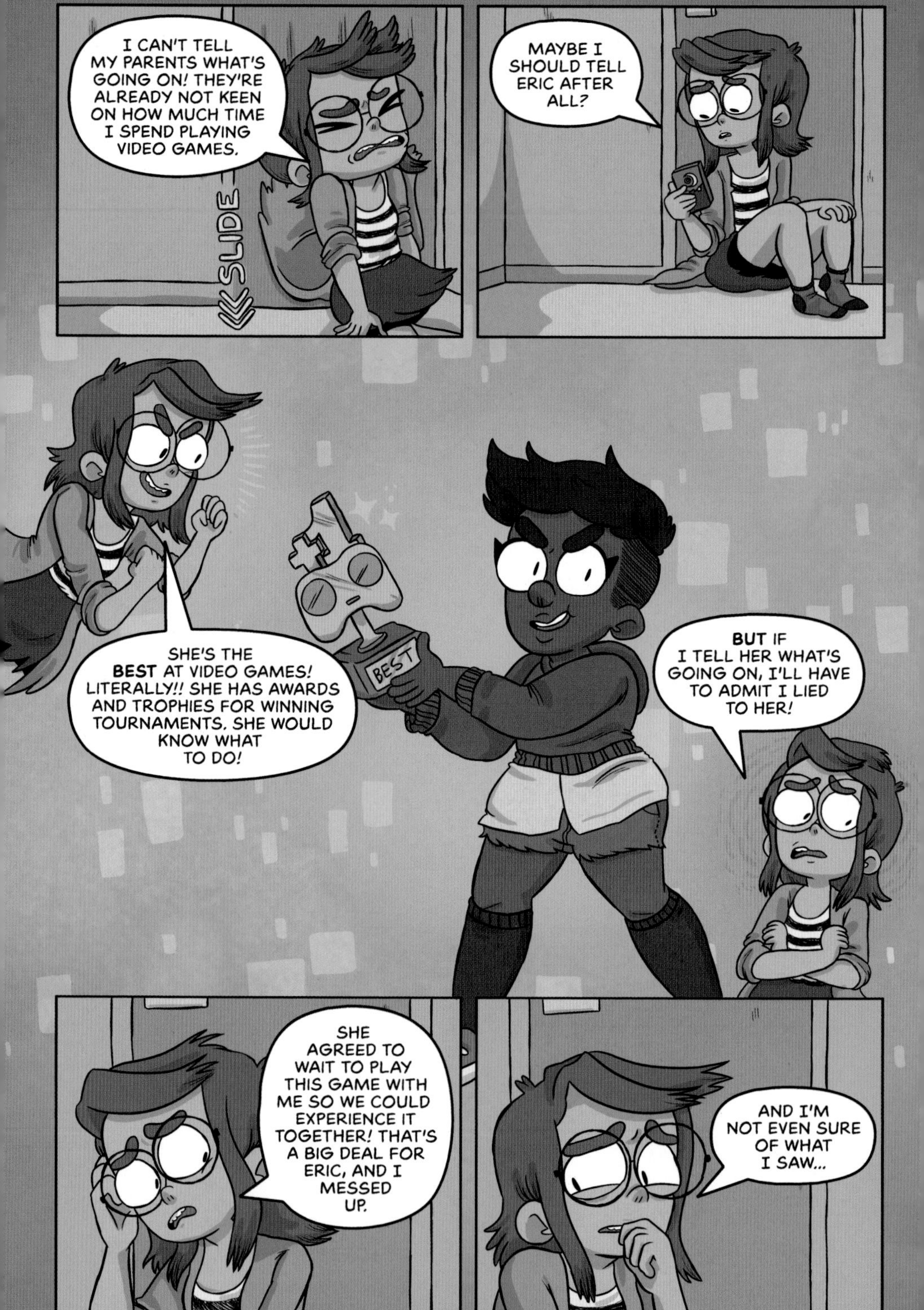
I CAN'T TELL MY PARENTS WHAT'S GOING ON! THEY'RE ALREADY NOT KEEN ON HOW MUCH TIME I SPEND PLAYING VIDEO GAMES.
SLIDE
MAYBE I SHOULD TELL ERIC AFTER ALL?
SHE'S THE **BEST** AT VIDEO GAMES! LITERALLY!! SHE HAS AWARDS AND TROPHIES FOR WINNING TOURNAMENTS. SHE WOULD KNOW WHAT TO DO!
BEST
BUT IF I TELL HER WHAT'S GOING ON, I'LL HAVE TO ADMIT I LIED TO HER!
SHE AGREED TO WAIT TO PLAY THIS GAME WITH ME SO WE COULD EXPERIENCE IT TOGETHER! THAT'S A BIG DEAL FOR ERIC, AND I MESSED UP.
AND I'M NOT EVEN SURE OF WHAT I SAW...

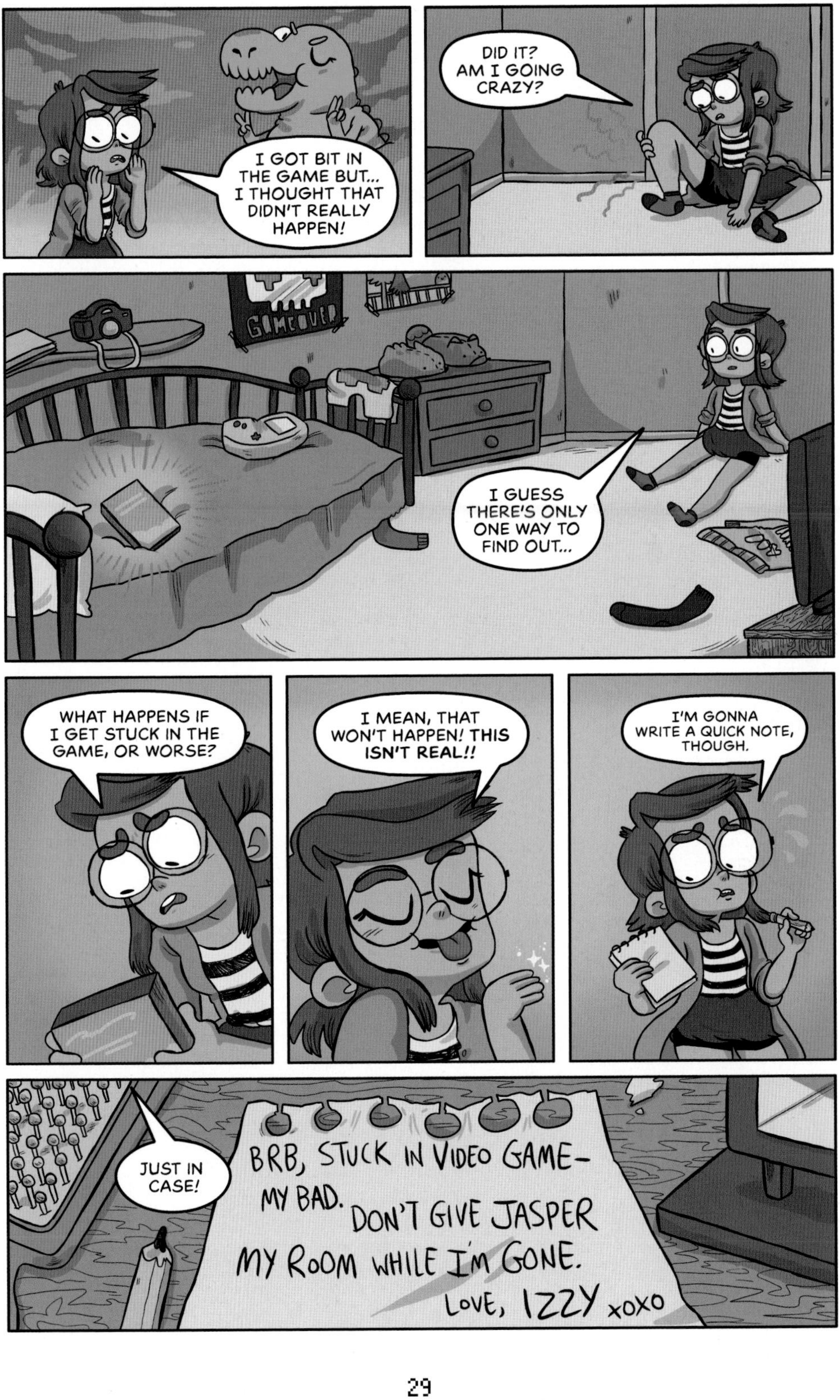
I GOT BIT IN THE GAME BUT... I THOUGHT THAT DIDN'T REALLY HAPPEN!
DID IT? AM I GOING CRAZY?
GAMEOVER
I GUESS THERE'S ONLY ONE WAY TO FIND OUT...
WHAT HAPPENS IF I GET STUCK IN THE GAME, OR WORSE?
I MEAN, THAT WON'T HAPPEN! THIS ISN'T REAL!!
I'M GONNA WRITE A QUICK NOTE, THOUGH.
JUST IN CASE!
BRB, STUCK IN VIDEO GAME- MY BAD. DON'T GIVE JASPER MY ROOM WHILE I'M GONE.
LOVE, IZZY xoxo

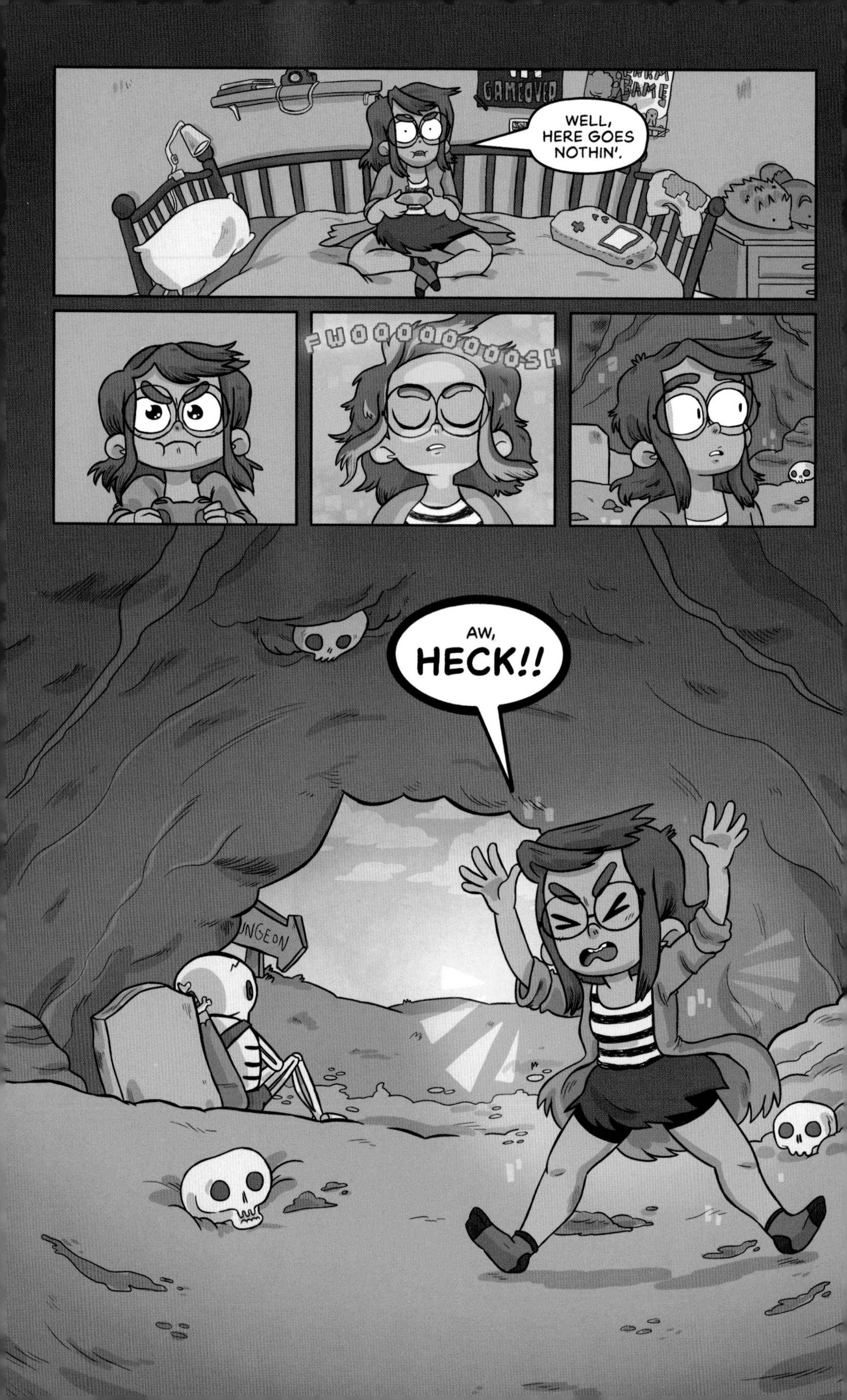
GAMEOVER
FARM GAME
WELL, HERE GOES NOTHIN'.
FWOOOOOOOOOOSH
AW, HECK!!
UNGEON

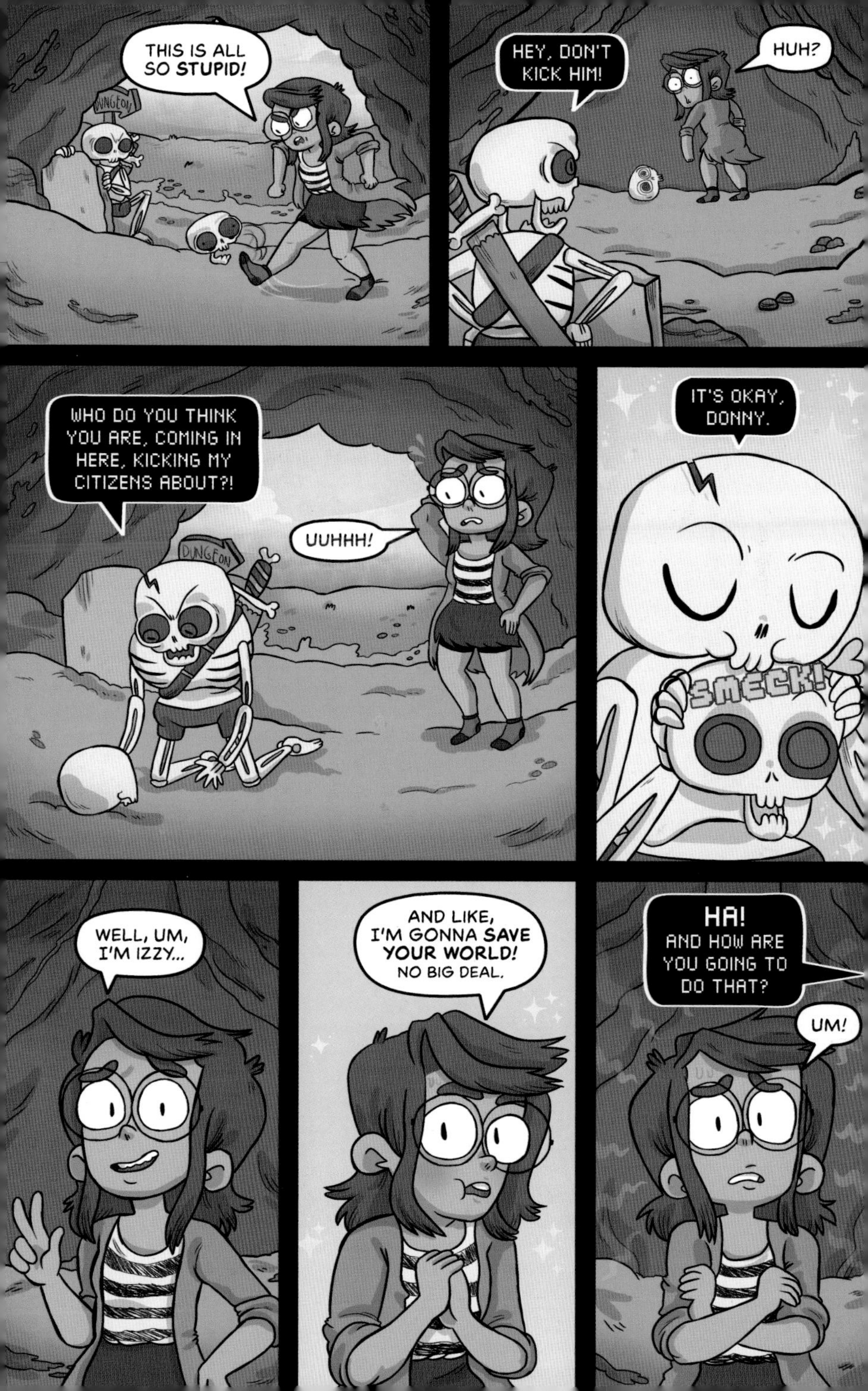
THIS IS ALL SO **STUPID!**
DUNGEON
HEY, DON'T KICK HIM!
HUH?
WHO DO YOU THINK YOU ARE, COMING IN HERE, KICKING MY CITIZENS ABOUT?!
UUHHH!
DUNGEON
IT'S OKAY, DONNY.
SMECK!
WELL, UM, I'M IZZY...
AND LIKE, I'M GONNA **SAVE YOUR WORLD!** NO BIG DEAL.
HA! AND HOW ARE YOU GOING TO DO THAT?
UM!

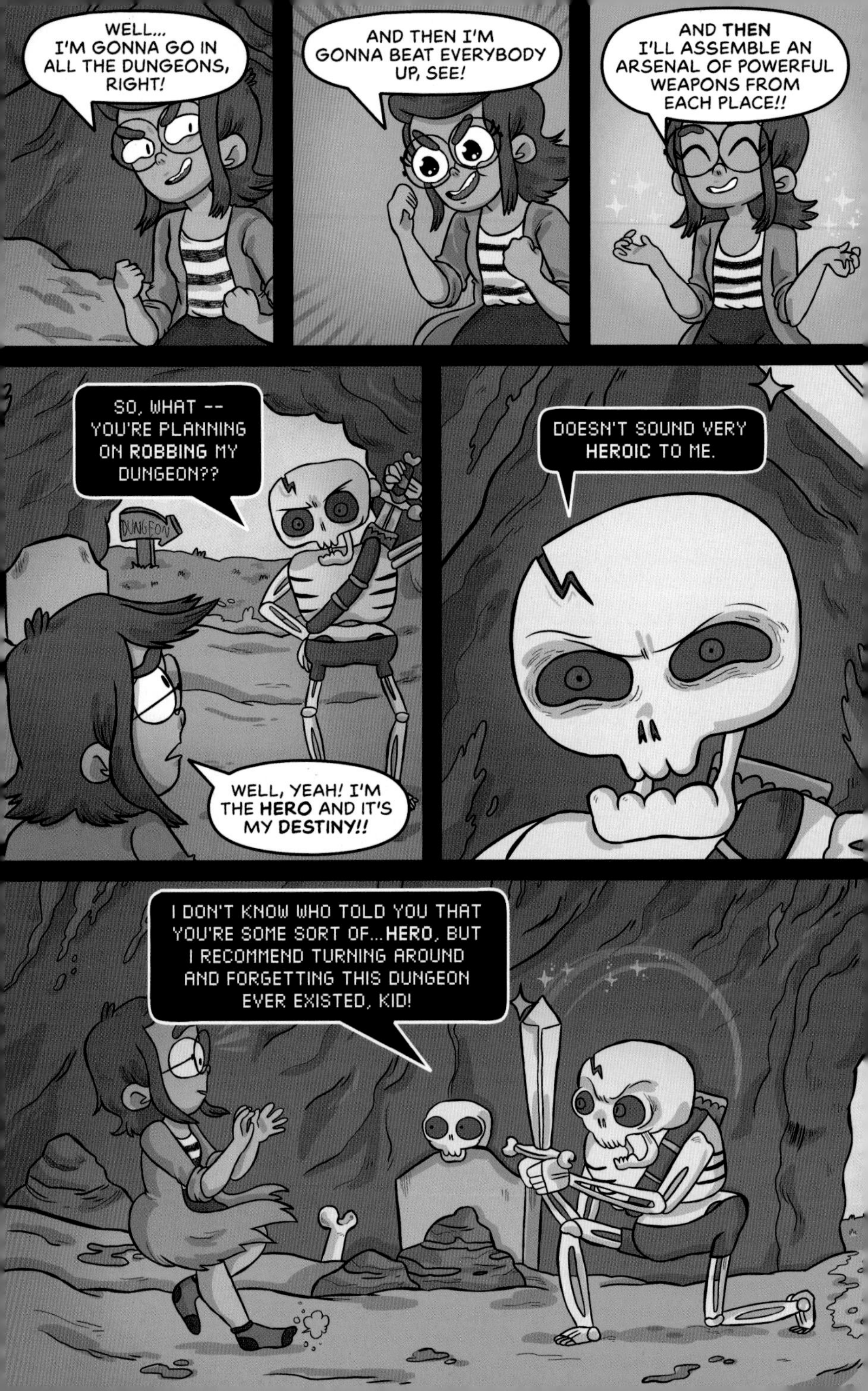
WELL... I'M GONNA GO IN ALL THE DUNGEONS, RIGHT!
AND THEN I'M GONNA BEAT EVERYBODY UP, SEE!
AND **THEN** I'LL ASSEMBLE AN ARSENAL OF POWERFUL WEAPONS FROM EACH PLACE!!
SO, WHAT -- YOU'RE PLANNING ON **ROBBING** MY DUNGEON??
DUNGEON
WELL, YEAH! I'M THE **HERO** AND IT'S MY **DESTINY!!**
DOESN'T SOUND VERY **HEROIC** TO ME.
I DON'T KNOW WHO TOLD YOU THAT YOU'RE SOME SORT OF... **HERO**, BUT I RECOMMEND TURNING AROUND AND FORGETTING THIS DUNGEON EVER EXISTED, KID!

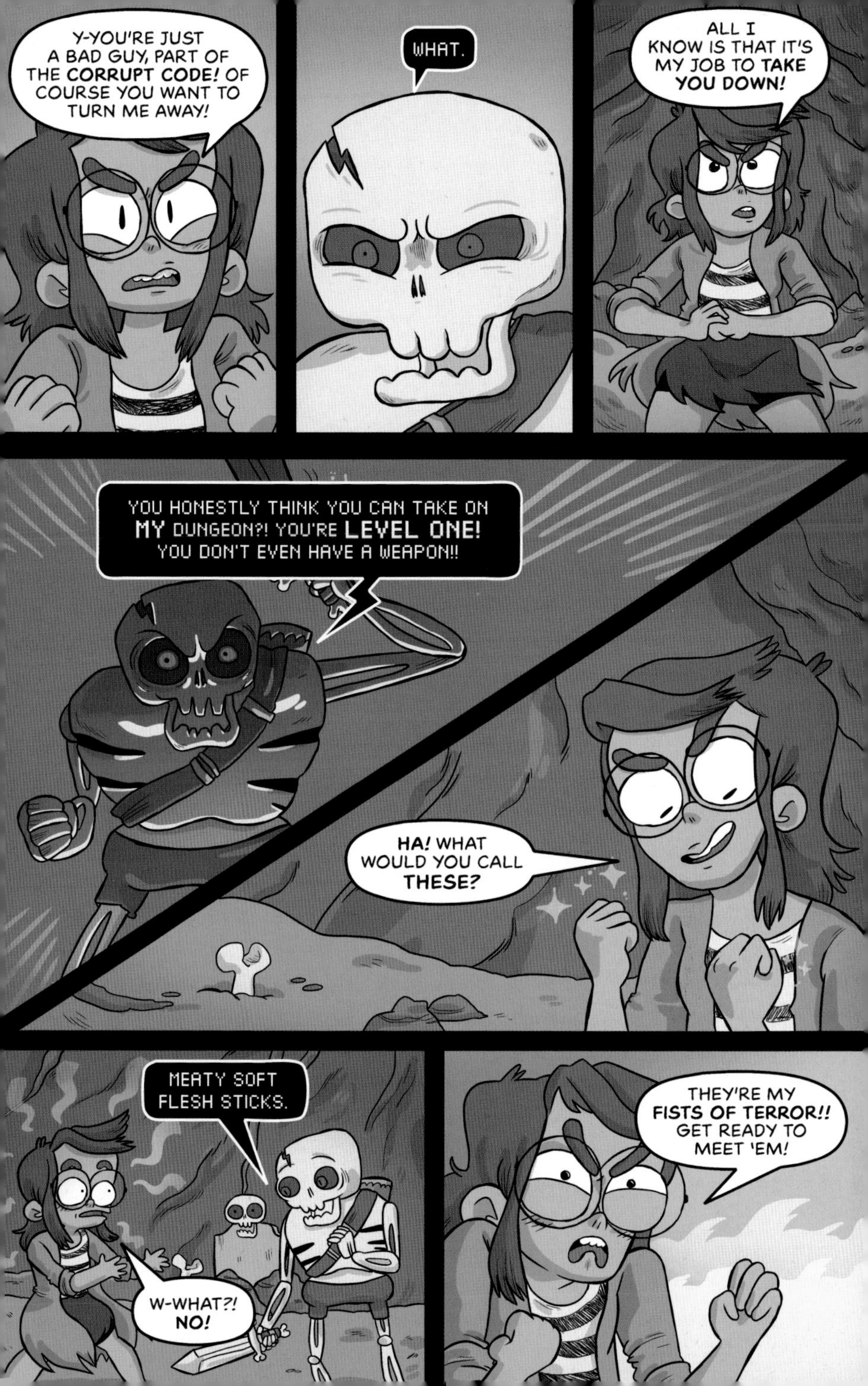
Y-YOU'RE JUST A BAD GUY, PART OF THE **CORRUPT CODE!** OF COURSE YOU WANT TO TURN ME AWAY!
WHAT.
ALL I KNOW IS THAT IT'S MY JOB TO **TAKE YOU DOWN!**
YOU HONESTLY THINK YOU CAN TAKE ON **MY** DUNGEON?! YOU'RE **LEVEL ONE!** YOU DON'T EVEN HAVE A WEAPON!!
HA! WHAT WOULD YOU CALL **THESE?**
MEATY SOFT FLESH STICKS.
W-WHAT?! **NO!**
THEY'RE MY **FISTS OF TERROR!!** GET READY TO MEET 'EM!

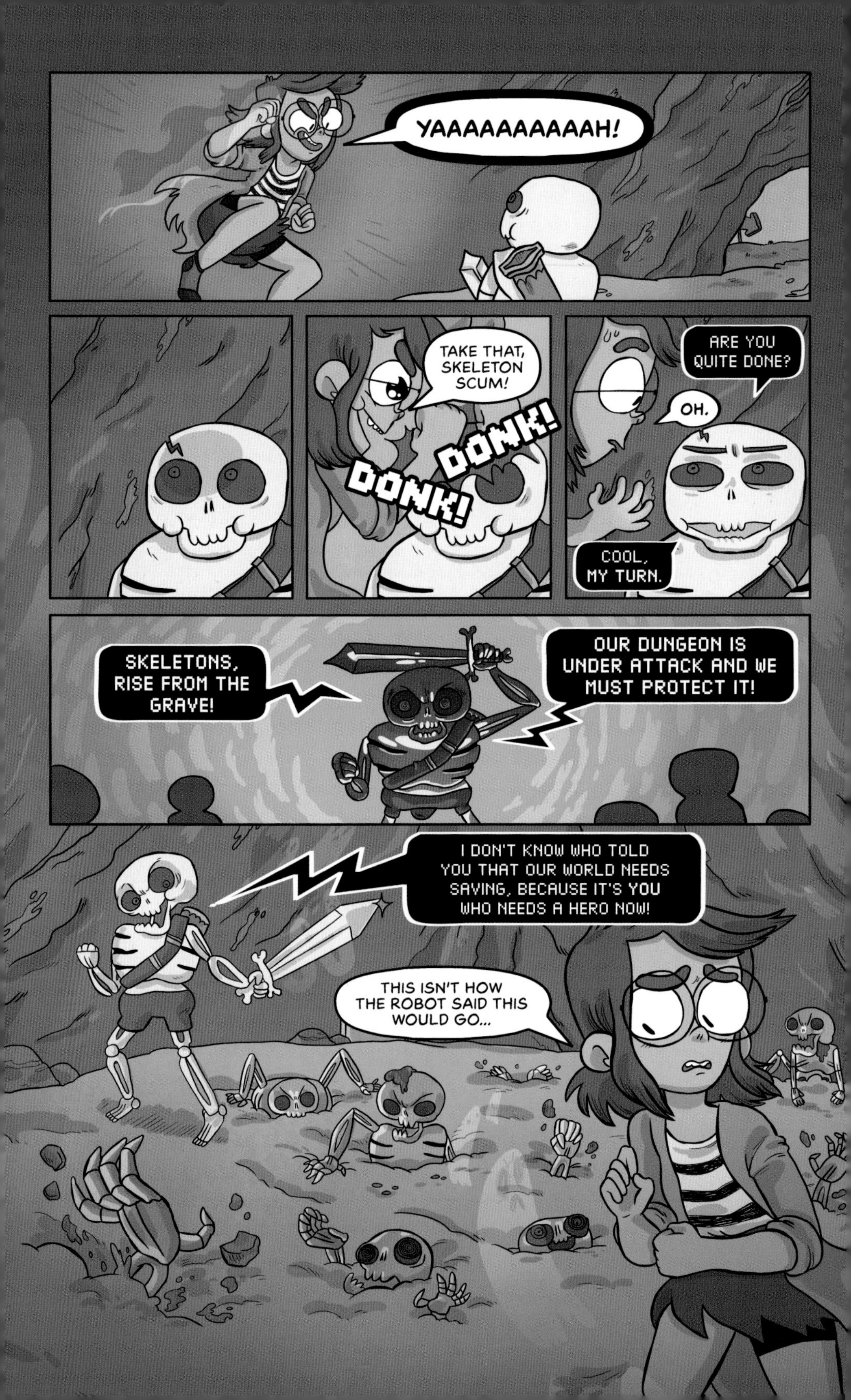
YAAAAAAAAAAH!
TAKE THAT, SKELETON SCUM!
DONK!
DONK!
ARE YOU QUITE DONE?
OH.
COOL, MY TURN.
SKELETONS, RISE FROM THE GRAVE!
OUR DUNGEON IS UNDER ATTACK AND WE MUST PROTECT IT!
I DON'T KNOW WHO TOLD YOU THAT OUR WORLD NEEDS SAVING, BECAUSE IT'S YOU WHO NEEDS A HERO NOW!
THIS ISN'T HOW THE ROBOT SAID THIS WOULD GO...

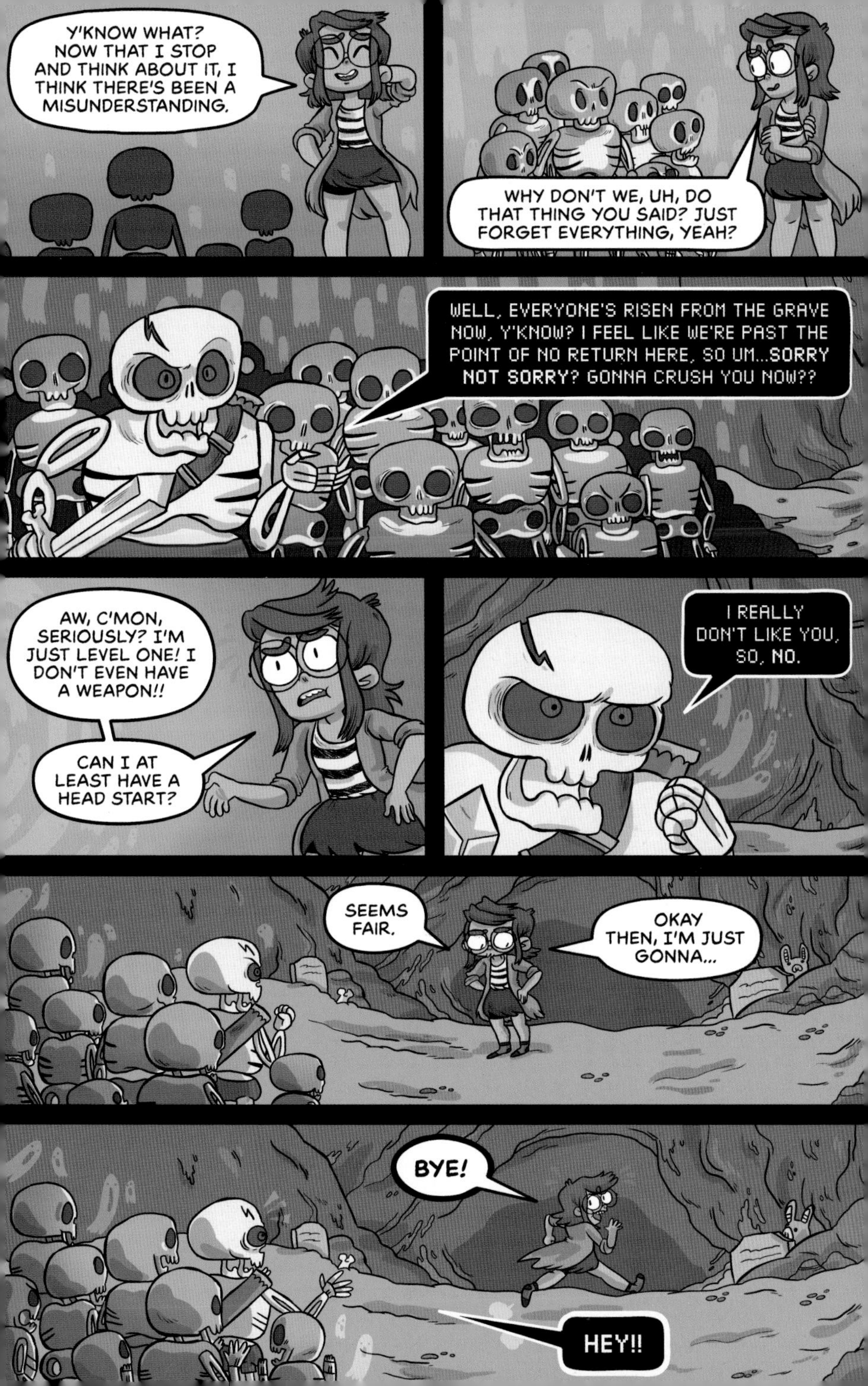
Y'KNOW WHAT? NOW THAT I STOP AND THINK ABOUT IT, I THINK THERE'S BEEN A MISUNDERSTANDING.
WHY DON'T WE, UH, DO THAT THING YOU SAID? JUST FORGET EVERYTHING, YEAH?
WELL, EVERYONE'S RISEN FROM THE GRAVE NOW, Y'KNOW? I FEEL LIKE WE'RE PAST THE POINT OF NO RETURN HERE, SO UM...SORRY NOT SORRY? GONNA CRUSH YOU NOW??
AW, C'MON, SERIOUSLY? I'M JUST LEVEL ONE! I DON'T EVEN HAVE A WEAPON!!
CAN I AT LEAST HAVE A HEAD START?
I REALLY DON'T LIKE YOU, SO, NO.
SEEMS FAIR.
OKAY THEN, I'M JUST GONNA...
BYE!
HEY!!

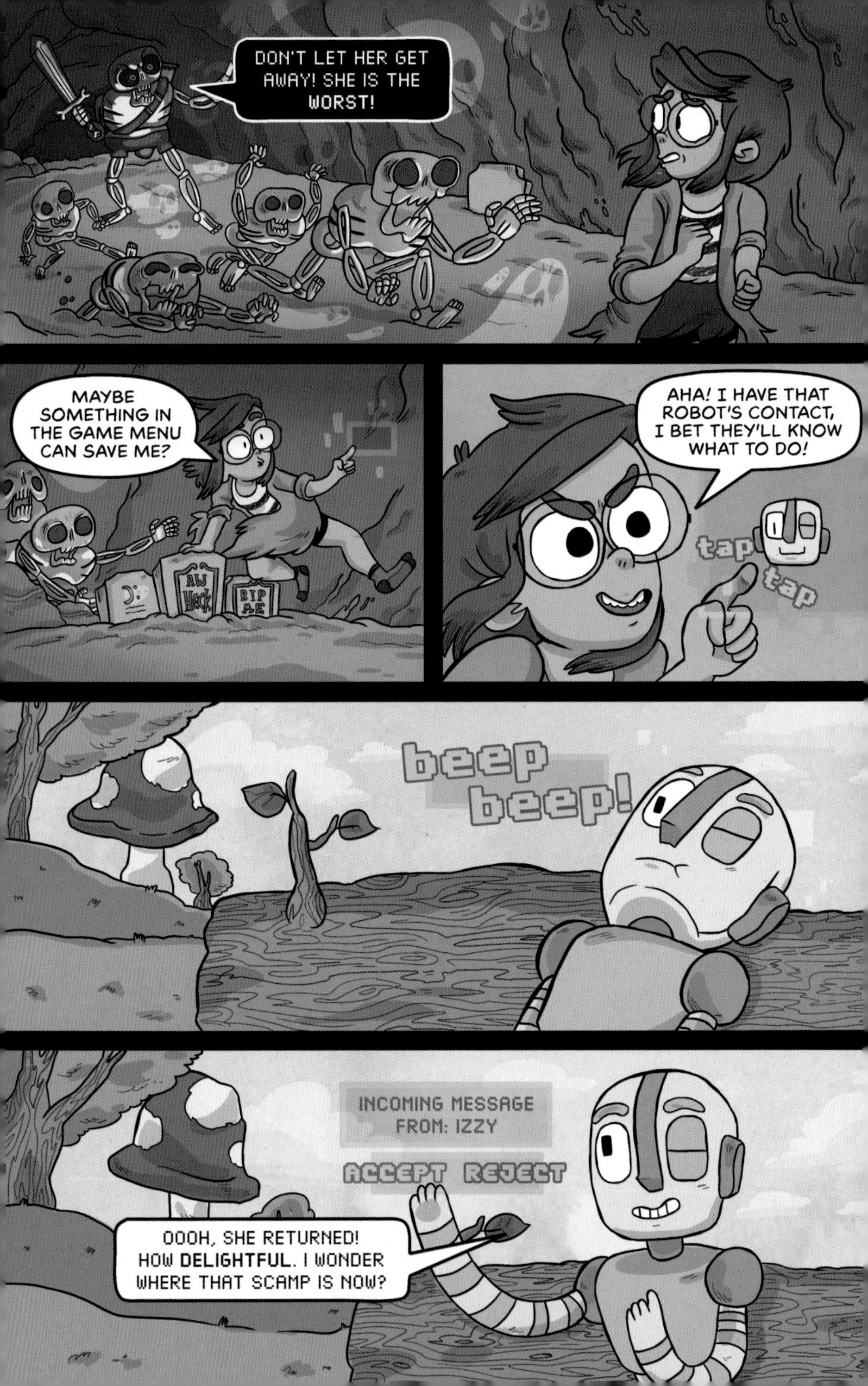
DON'T LET HER GET AWAY! SHE IS THE WORST!
MAYBE SOMETHING IN THE GAME MENU CAN SAVE ME?
AW HECK
RIP ME
AHA! I HAVE THAT ROBOT'S CONTACT, I BET THEY'LL KNOW WHAT TO DO!
tap tap
beep beep!
INCOMING MESSAGE FROM: IZZY
ACCEPT REJECT
OOOH, SHE RETURNED! HOW **DELIGHTFUL**. I WONDER WHERE THAT SCAMP IS NOW?

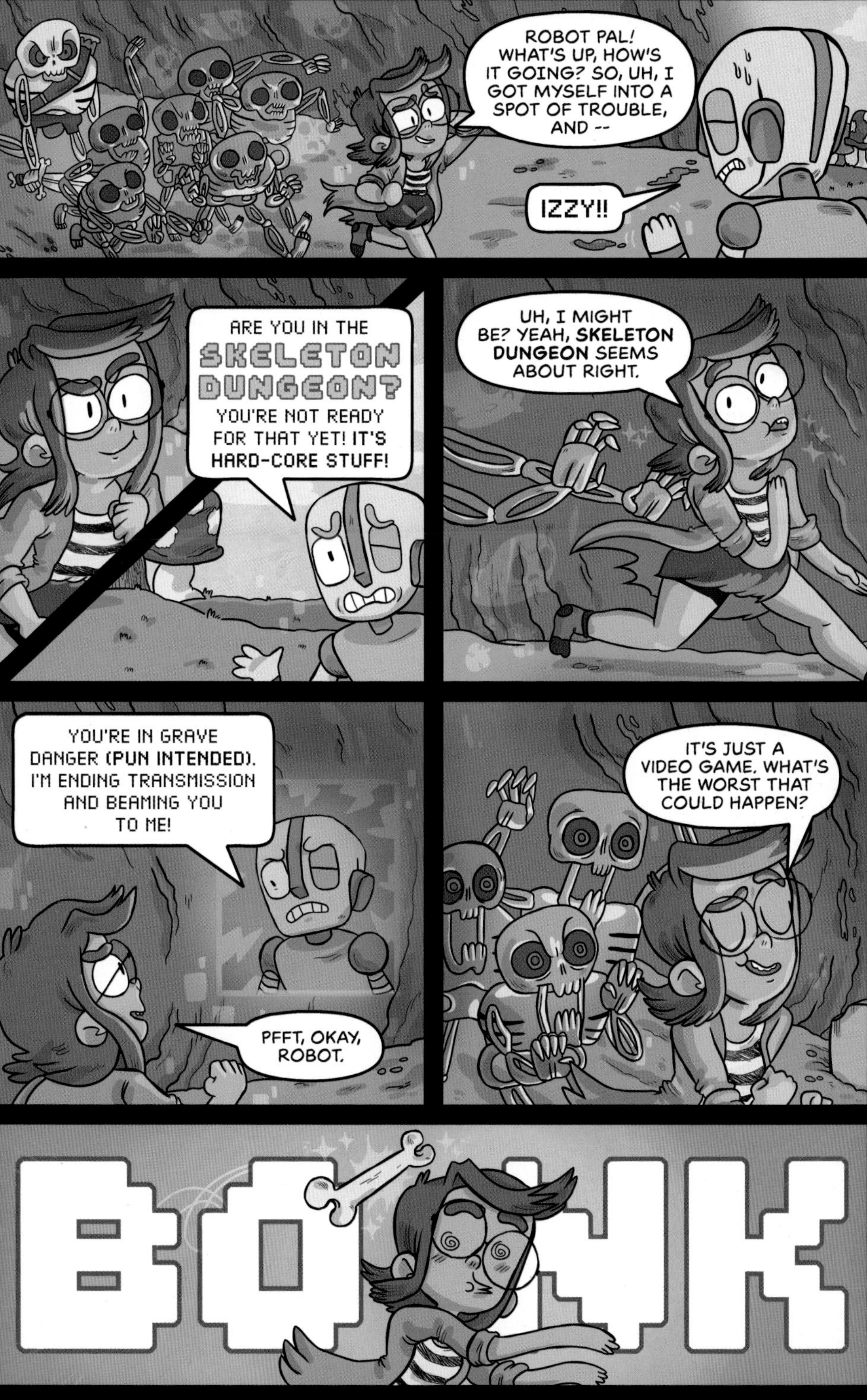
ROBOT PAL! WHAT'S UP, HOW'S IT GOING? SO, UH, I GOT MYSELF INTO A SPOT OF TROUBLE, AND --
IZZY!!
ARE YOU IN THE SKELETON DUNGEON? YOU'RE NOT READY FOR THAT YET! IT'S HARD-CORE STUFF!
UH, I MIGHT BE? YEAH, SKELETON DUNGEON SEEMS ABOUT RIGHT.
YOU'RE IN GRAVE DANGER (PUN INTENDED). I'M ENDING TRANSMISSION AND BEAMING YOU TO ME!
PFFT, OKAY, ROBOT.
IT'S JUST A VIDEO GAME. WHAT'S THE WORST THAT COULD HAPPEN?
BONK

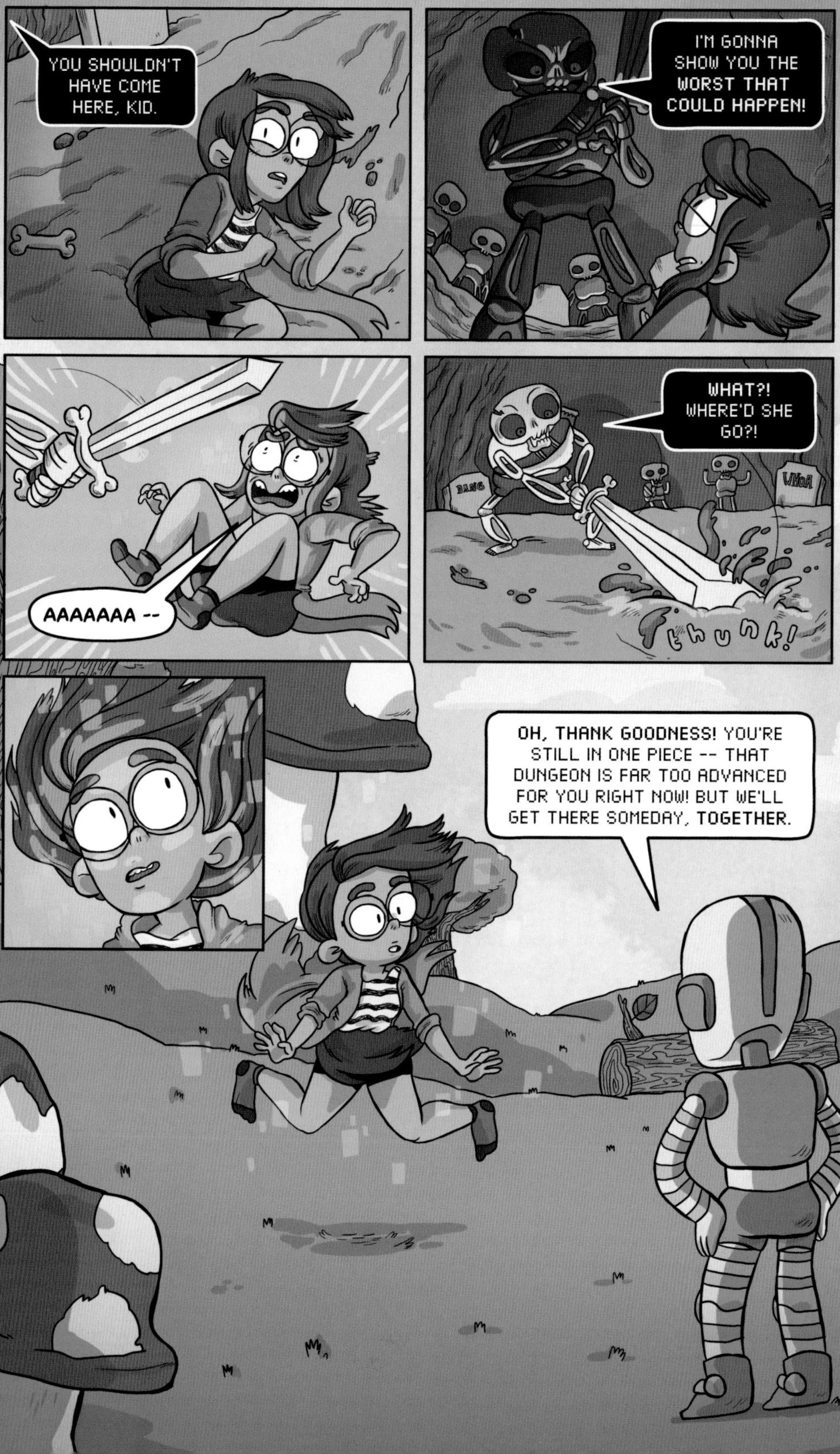

YOU SHOULDN'T HAVE COME HERE, KID.
I'M GONNA SHOW YOU THE WORST THAT COULD HAPPEN!
AAAAAAA --
WHAT?! WHERE'D SHE GO?!
DANG
WHOA
thunk!
OH, THANK GOODNESS! YOU'RE STILL IN ONE PIECE -- THAT DUNGEON IS FAR TOO ADVANCED FOR YOU RIGHT NOW! BUT WE'LL GET THERE SOMEDAY, TOGETHER.

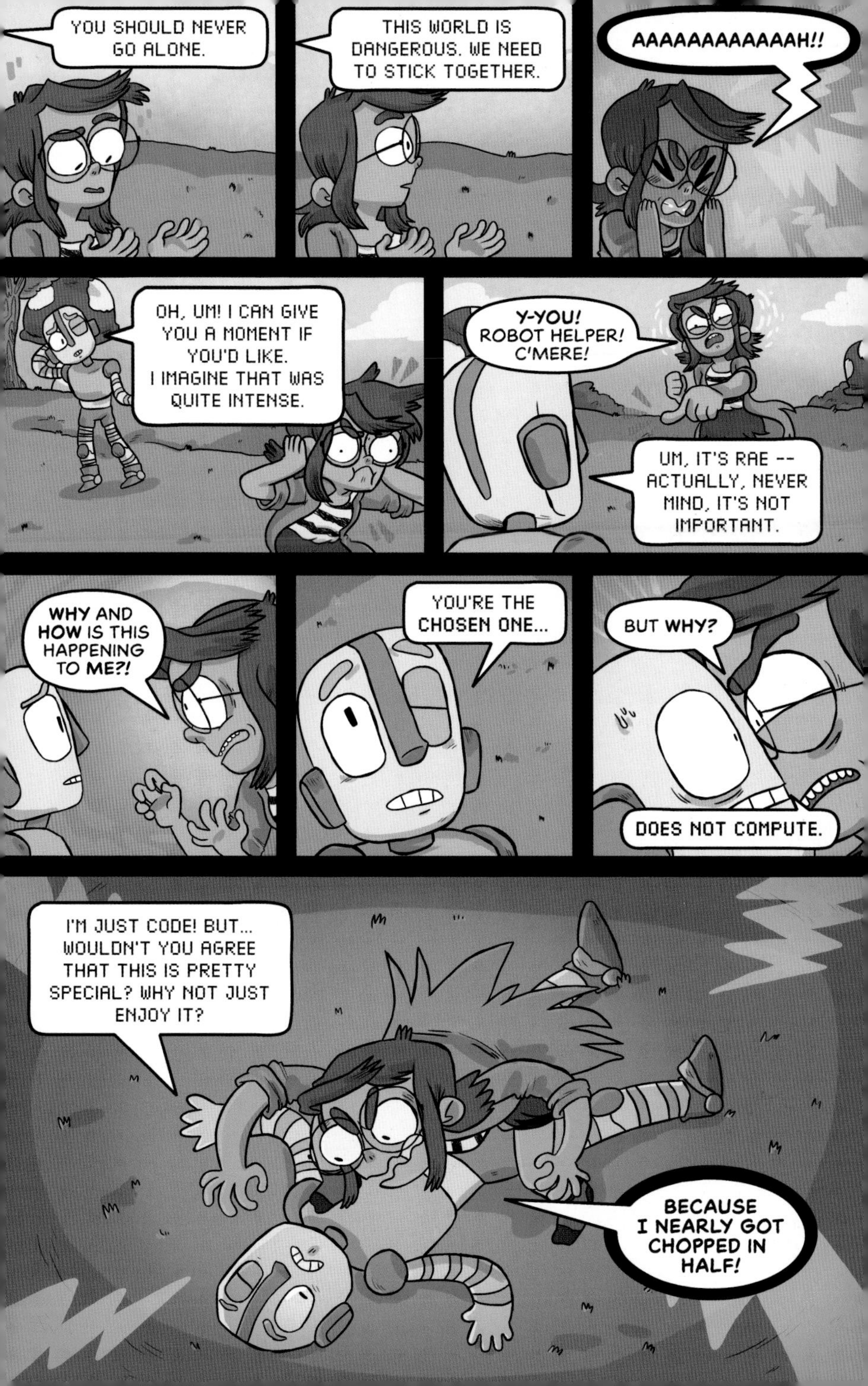
YOU SHOULD NEVER GO ALONE.
THIS WORLD IS DANGEROUS. WE NEED TO STICK TOGETHER.
AAAAAAAAAAAAH!!
OH, UM! I CAN GIVE YOU A MOMENT IF YOU'D LIKE. I IMAGINE THAT WAS QUITE INTENSE.
Y-YOU! ROBOT HELPER! C'MERE!
UM, IT'S RAE -- ACTUALLY, NEVER MIND, IT'S NOT IMPORTANT.
WHY AND HOW IS THIS HAPPENING TO ME?!
YOU'RE THE CHOSEN ONE...
BUT WHY?
DOES NOT COMPUTE.
I'M JUST CODE! BUT... WOULDN'T YOU AGREE THAT THIS IS PRETTY SPECIAL? WHY NOT JUST ENJOY IT?
BECAUSE I NEARLY GOT CHOPPED IN HALF!

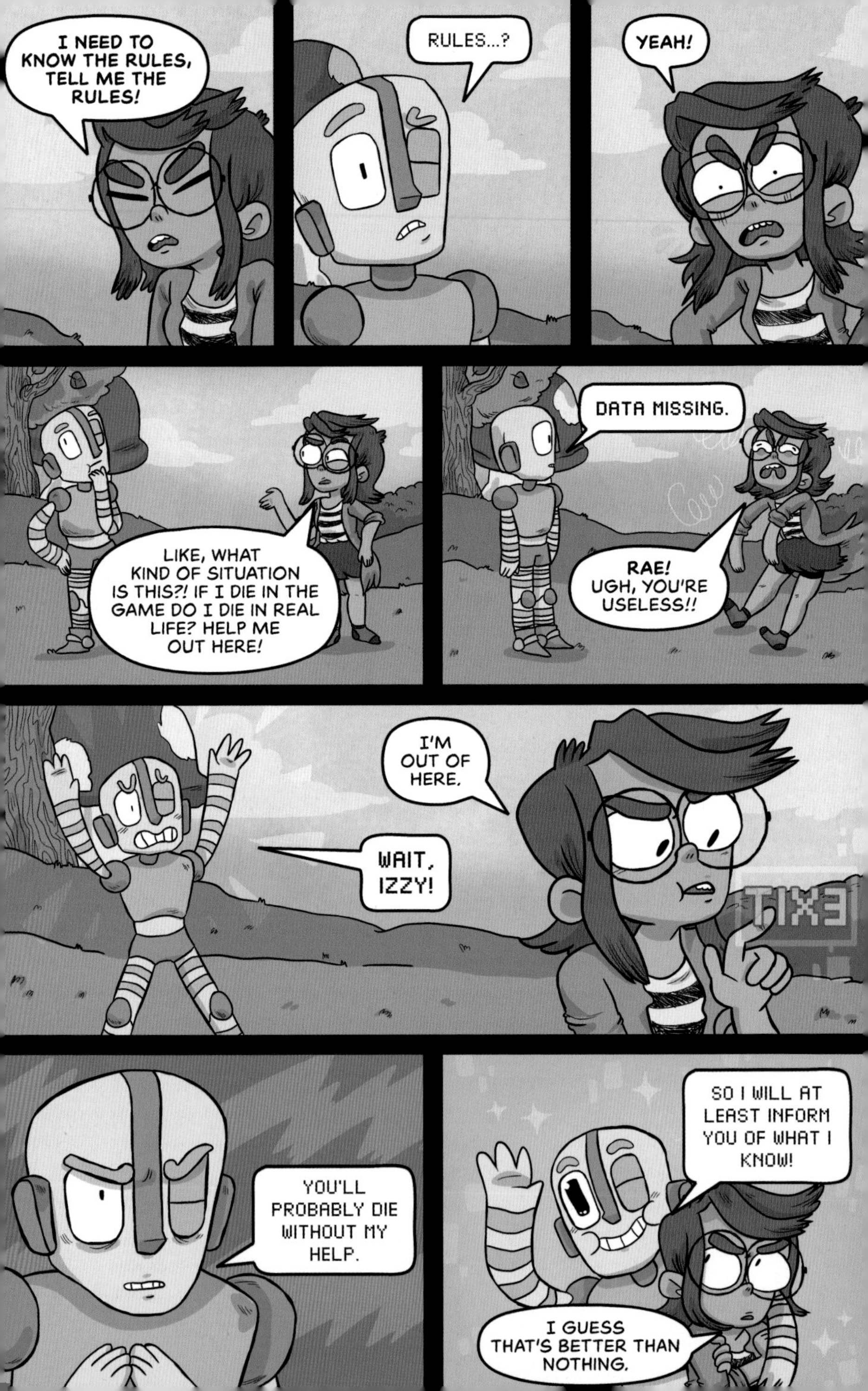

I NEED TO KNOW THE RULES, TELL ME THE RULES!
RULES...?
YEAH!
LIKE, WHAT KIND OF SITUATION IS THIS?! IF I DIE IN THE GAME DO I DIE IN REAL LIFE? HELP ME OUT HERE!
DATA MISSING.
RAE! UGH, YOU'RE USELESS!!
I'M OUT OF HERE.
EXIT
WAIT, IZZY!
YOU'LL PROBABLY DIE WITHOUT MY HELP.
SO I WILL AT LEAST INFORM YOU OF WHAT I KNOW!
I GUESS THAT'S BETTER THAN NOTHING.

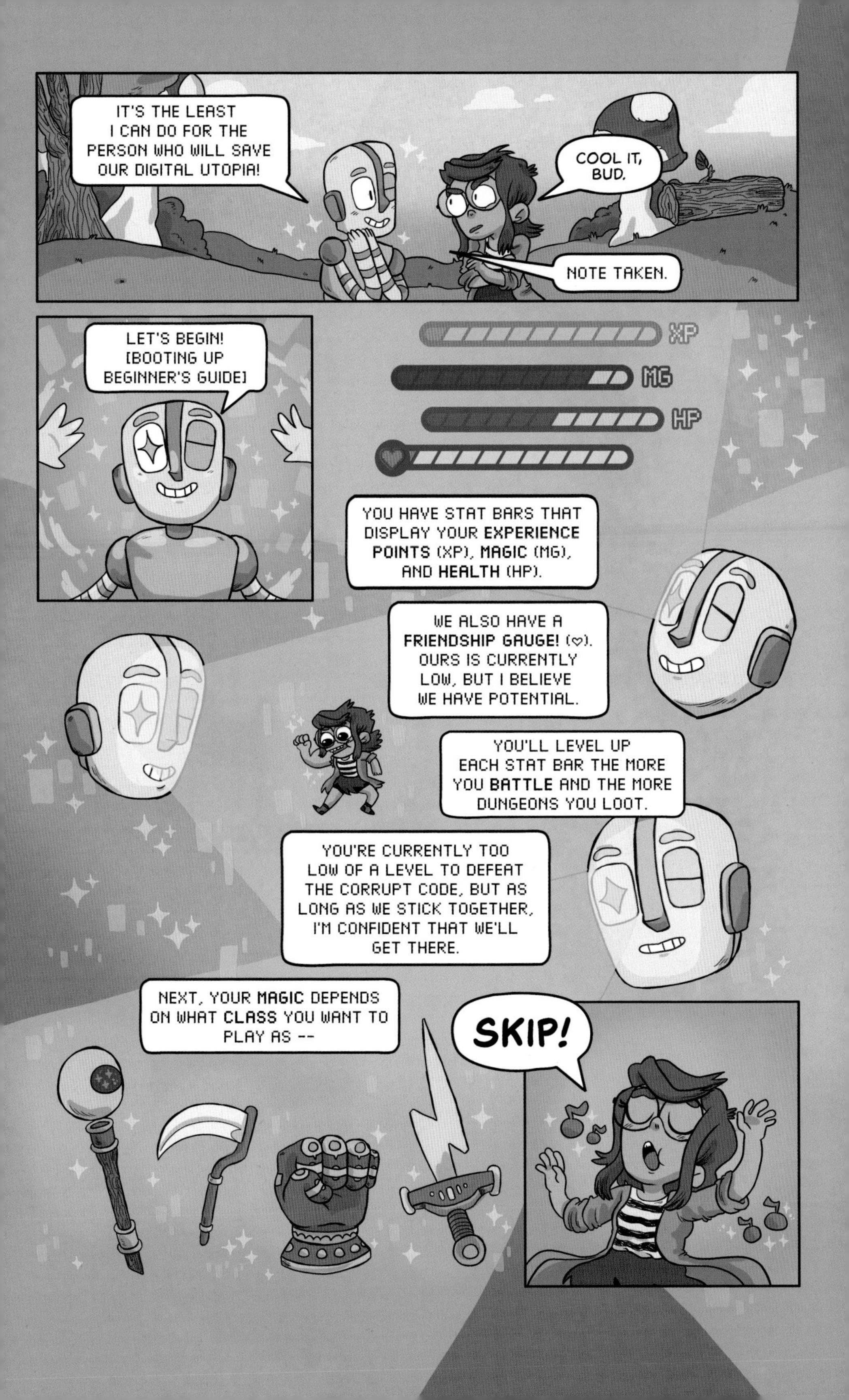
IT'S THE LEAST I CAN DO FOR THE PERSON WHO WILL SAVE OUR DIGITAL UTOPIA!
COOL IT, BUD.
NOTE TAKEN.
LET'S BEGIN! [BOOTING UP BEGINNER'S GUIDE]
XP
MG
HP
YOU HAVE STAT BARS THAT DISPLAY YOUR EXPERIENCE POINTS (XP), MAGIC (MG), AND HEALTH (HP).
WE ALSO HAVE A FRIENDSHIP GAUGE! (♡). OURS IS CURRENTLY LOW, BUT I BELIEVE WE HAVE POTENTIAL.
YOU'LL LEVEL UP EACH STAT BAR THE MORE YOU BATTLE AND THE MORE DUNGEONS YOU LOOT.
YOU'RE CURRENTLY TOO LOW OF A LEVEL TO DEFEAT THE CORRUPT CODE, BUT AS LONG AS WE STICK TOGETHER, I'M CONFIDENT THAT WE'LL GET THERE.
NEXT, YOUR MAGIC DEPENDS ON WHAT CLASS YOU WANT TO PLAY AS --
SKIP!

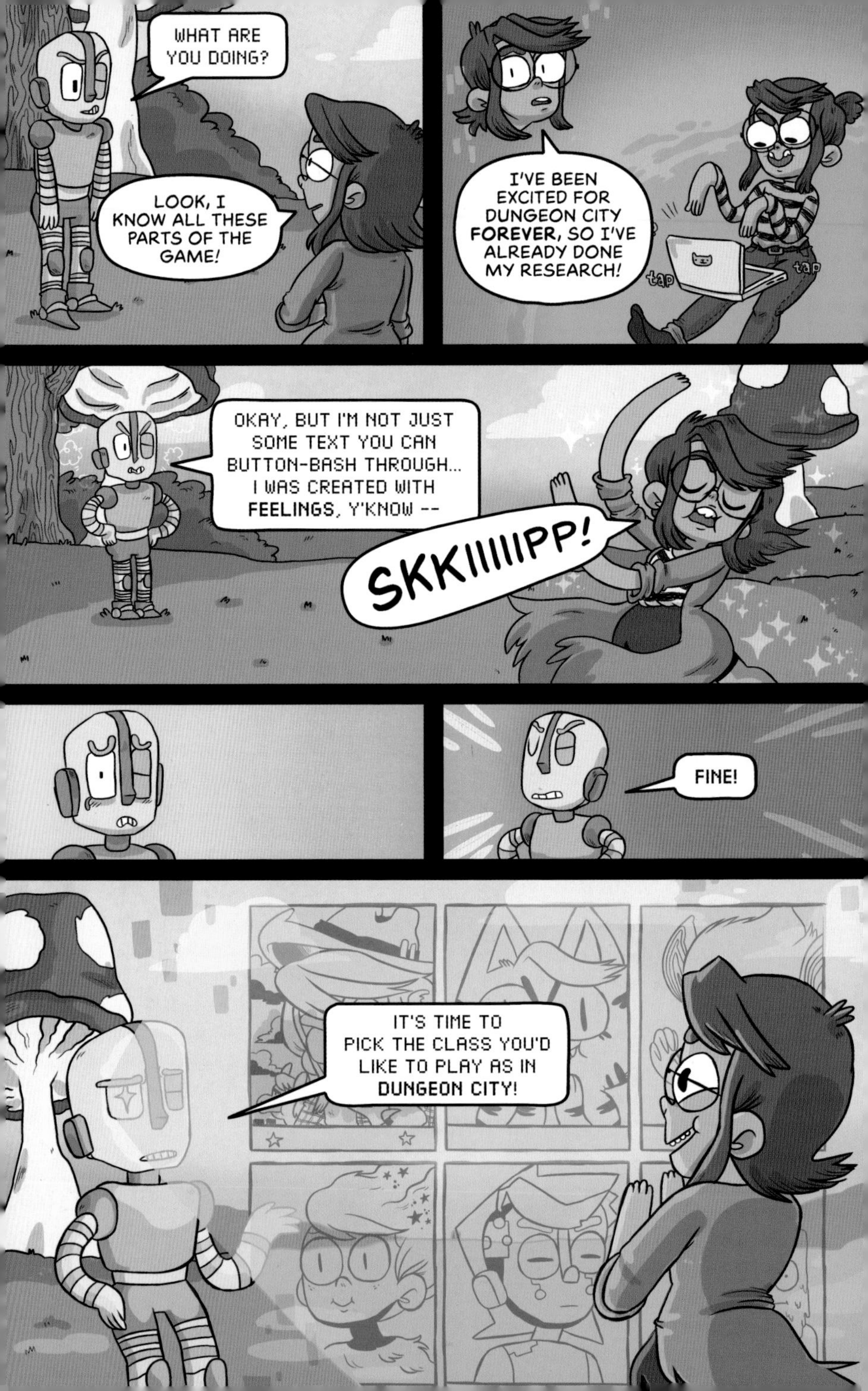
WHAT ARE YOU DOING?
LOOK, I KNOW ALL THESE PARTS OF THE GAME!
I'VE BEEN EXCITED FOR DUNGEON CITY FOREVER, SO I'VE ALREADY DONE MY RESEARCH!
tap
tap
OKAY, BUT I'M NOT JUST SOME TEXT YOU CAN BUTTON-BASH THROUGH... I WAS CREATED WITH FEELINGS, Y'KNOW --
SKKIIIIIPP!
FINE!
IT'S TIME TO PICK THE CLASS YOU'D LIKE TO PLAY AS IN DUNGEON CITY!

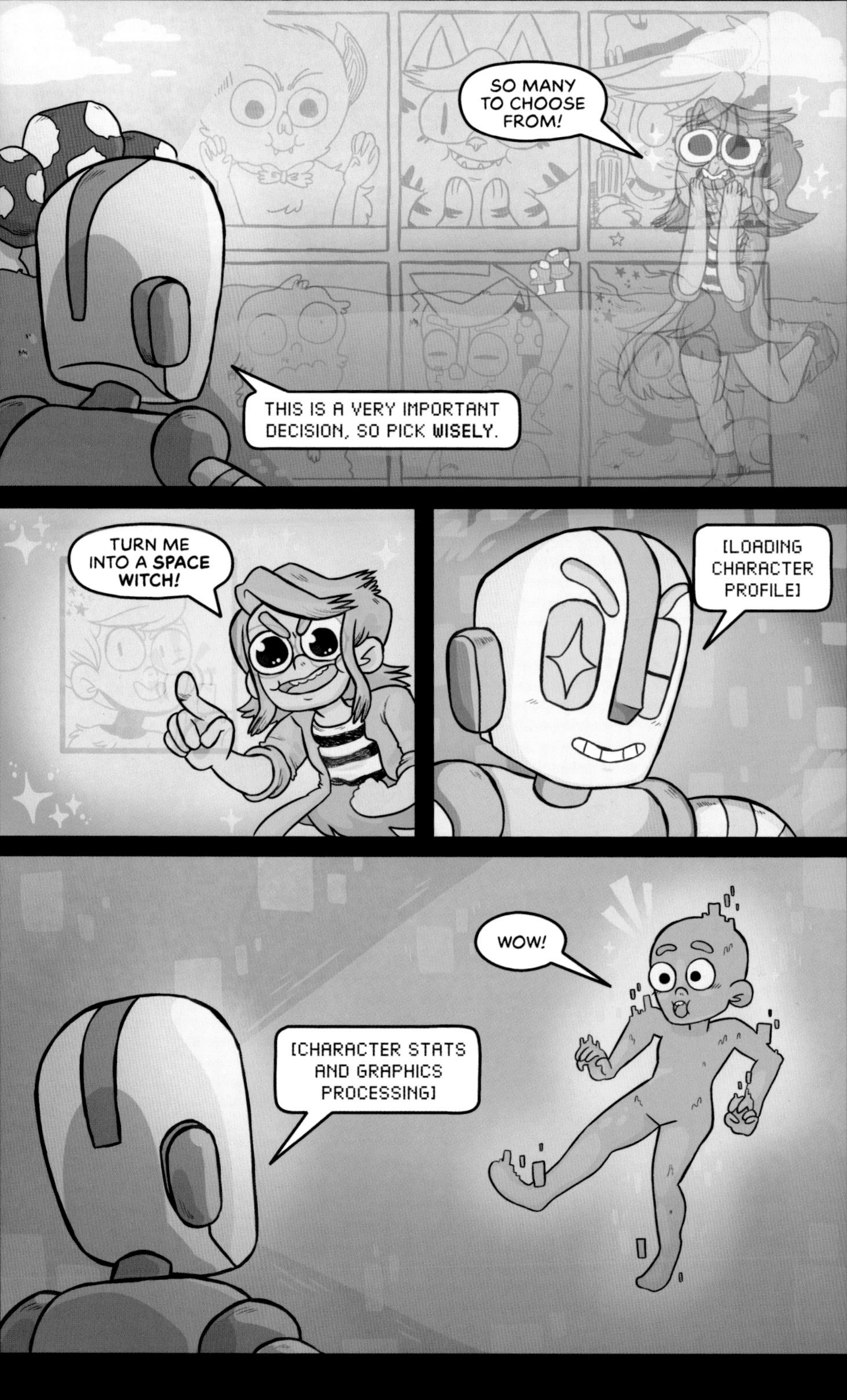
SO MANY TO CHOOSE FROM!
THIS IS A VERY IMPORTANT DECISION, SO PICK WISELY.
TURN ME INTO A SPACE WITCH!
[LOADING CHARACTER PROFILE]
WOW!
[CHARACTER STATS AND GRAPHICS PROCESSING]

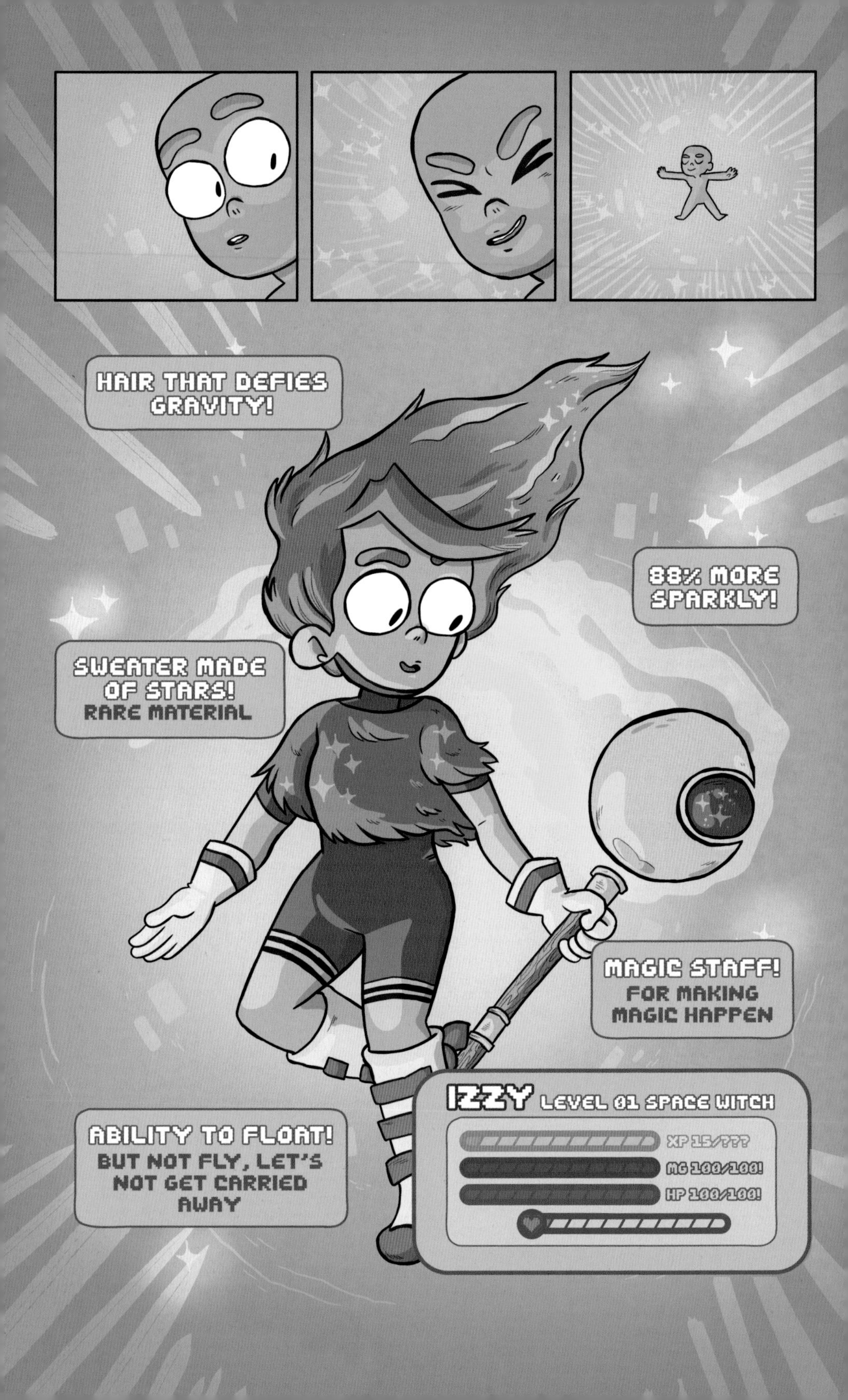
HAIR THAT DEFIES GRAVITY!
88% MORE SPARKLY!
SWEATER MADE OF STARS! RARE MATERIAL
MAGIC STAFF! FOR MAKING MAGIC HAPPEN
ABILITY TO FLOAT! BUT NOT FLY, LET'S NOT GET CARRIED AWAY
IZZY LEVEL 01 SPACE WITCH
XP 15/???
MG 100/100!
HP 100/100!

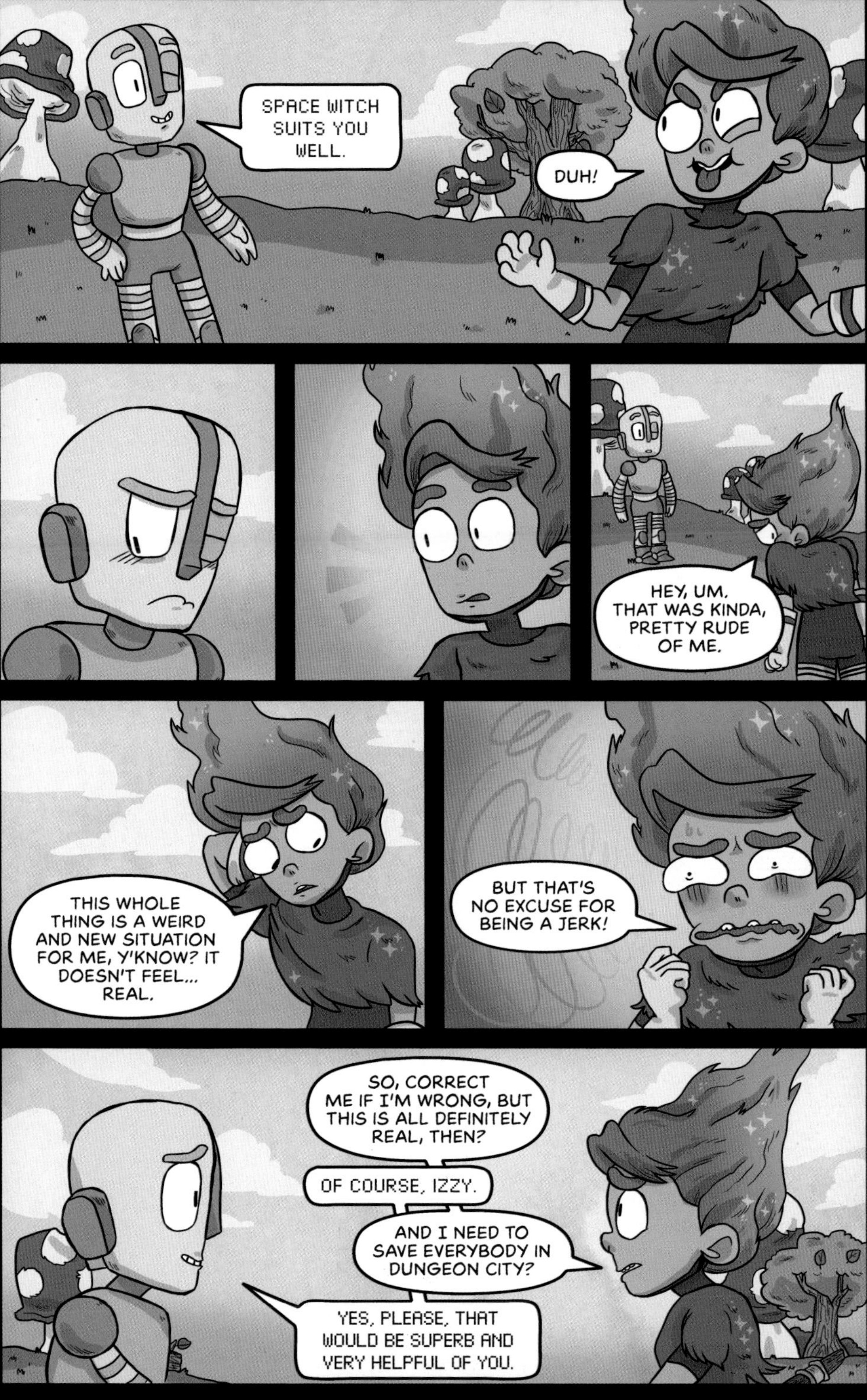
SPACE WITCH SUITS YOU WELL.
DUH!
HEY, UM. THAT WAS KINDA, PRETTY RUDE OF ME.
THIS WHOLE THING IS A WEIRD AND NEW SITUATION FOR ME, Y'KNOW? IT DOESN'T FEEL... REAL.
BUT THAT'S NO EXCUSE FOR BEING A JERK!
SO, CORRECT ME IF I'M WRONG, BUT THIS IS ALL DEFINITELY REAL, THEN?
OF COURSE, IZZY.
AND I NEED TO SAVE EVERYBODY IN DUNGEON CITY?
YES, PLEASE, THAT WOULD BE SUPERB AND VERY HELPFUL OF YOU.

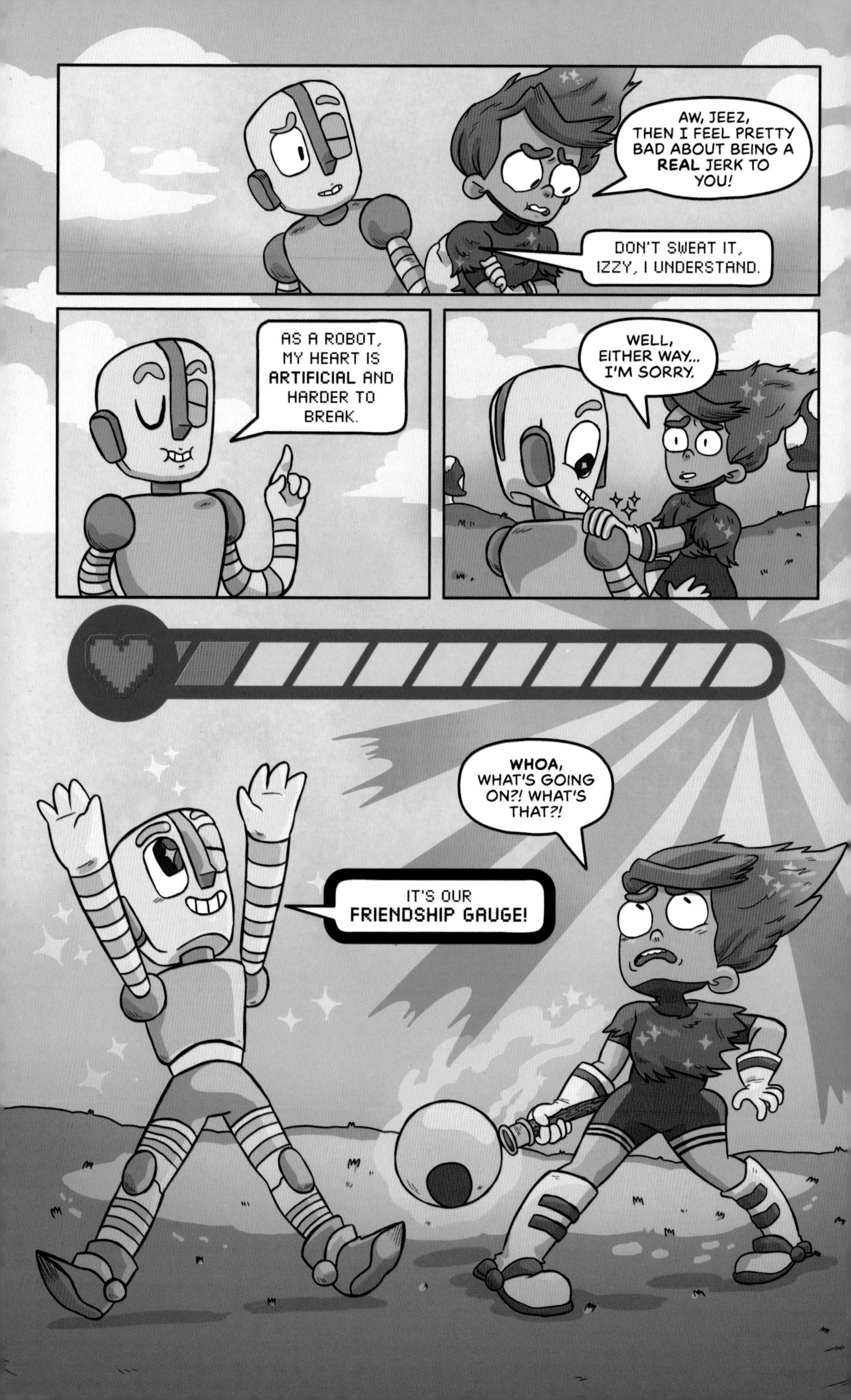
AW, JEEZ, THEN I FEEL PRETTY BAD ABOUT BEING A **REAL** JERK TO YOU!
DON'T SWEAT IT, IZZY, I UNDERSTAND.
AS A ROBOT, MY HEART IS **ARTIFICIAL** AND HARDER TO BREAK.
WELL, EITHER WAY... I'M SORRY.
WHOA, WHAT'S GOING ON?! WHAT'S THAT?!
IT'S OUR **FRIENDSHIP GAUGE!**

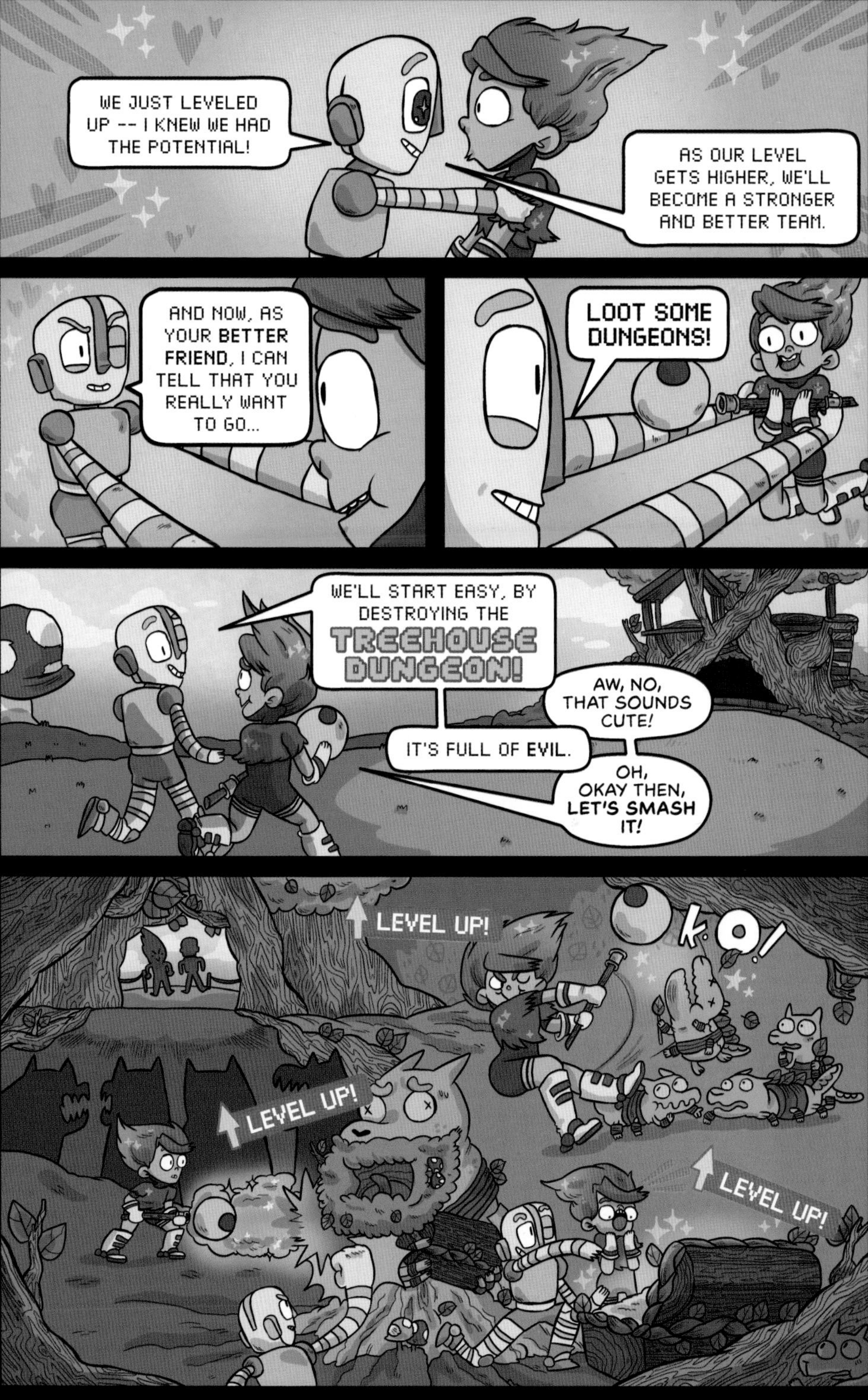

WE JUST LEVELED UP -- I KNEW WE HAD THE POTENTIAL!
AS OUR LEVEL GETS HIGHER, WE'LL BECOME A STRONGER AND BETTER TEAM.
AND NOW, AS YOUR BETTER FRIEND, I CAN TELL THAT YOU REALLY WANT TO GO...
LOOT SOME DUNGEONS!
WE'LL START EASY, BY DESTROYING THE TREEHOUSE DUNGEON!
AW, NO, THAT SOUNDS CUTE!
IT'S FULL OF EVIL.
OH, OKAY THEN, LET'S SMASH IT!
LEVEL UP!
K.O!
LEVEL UP!
LEVEL UP!

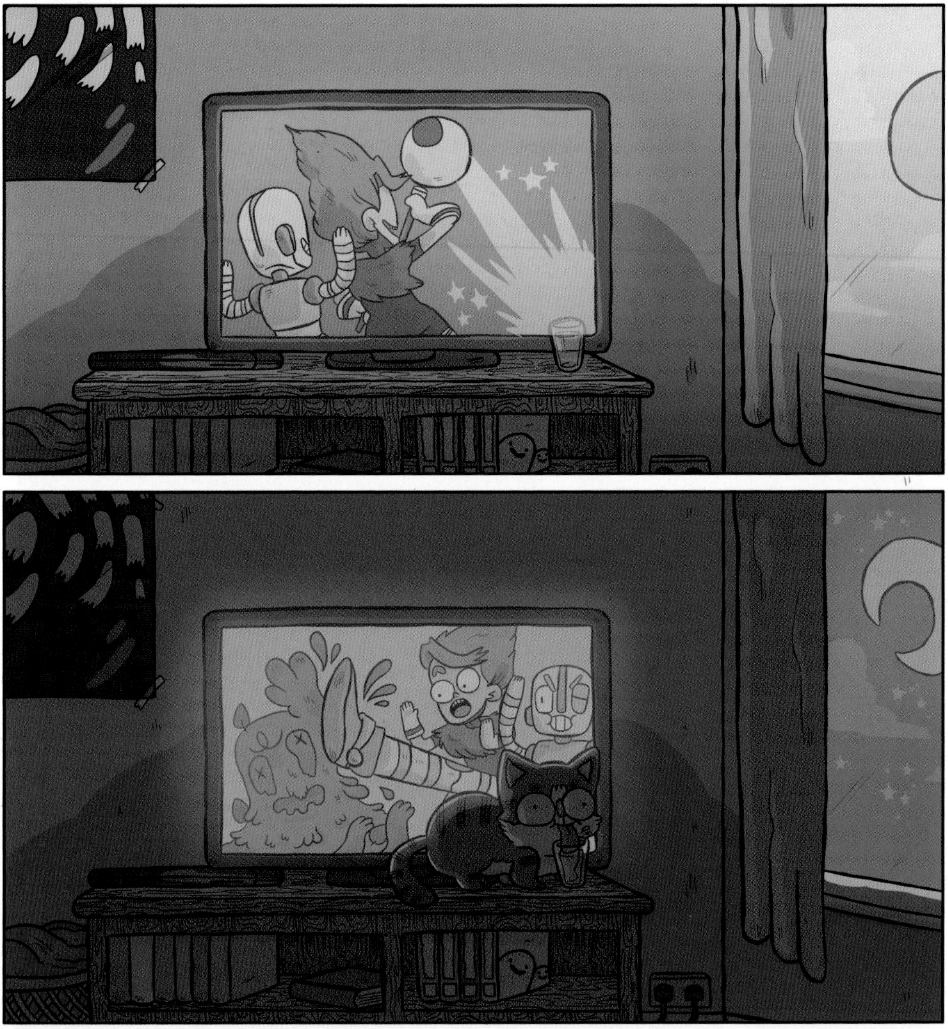

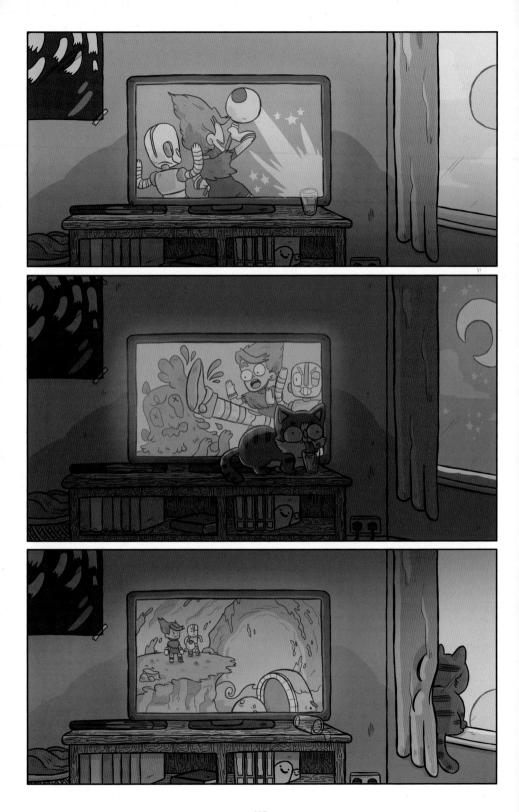

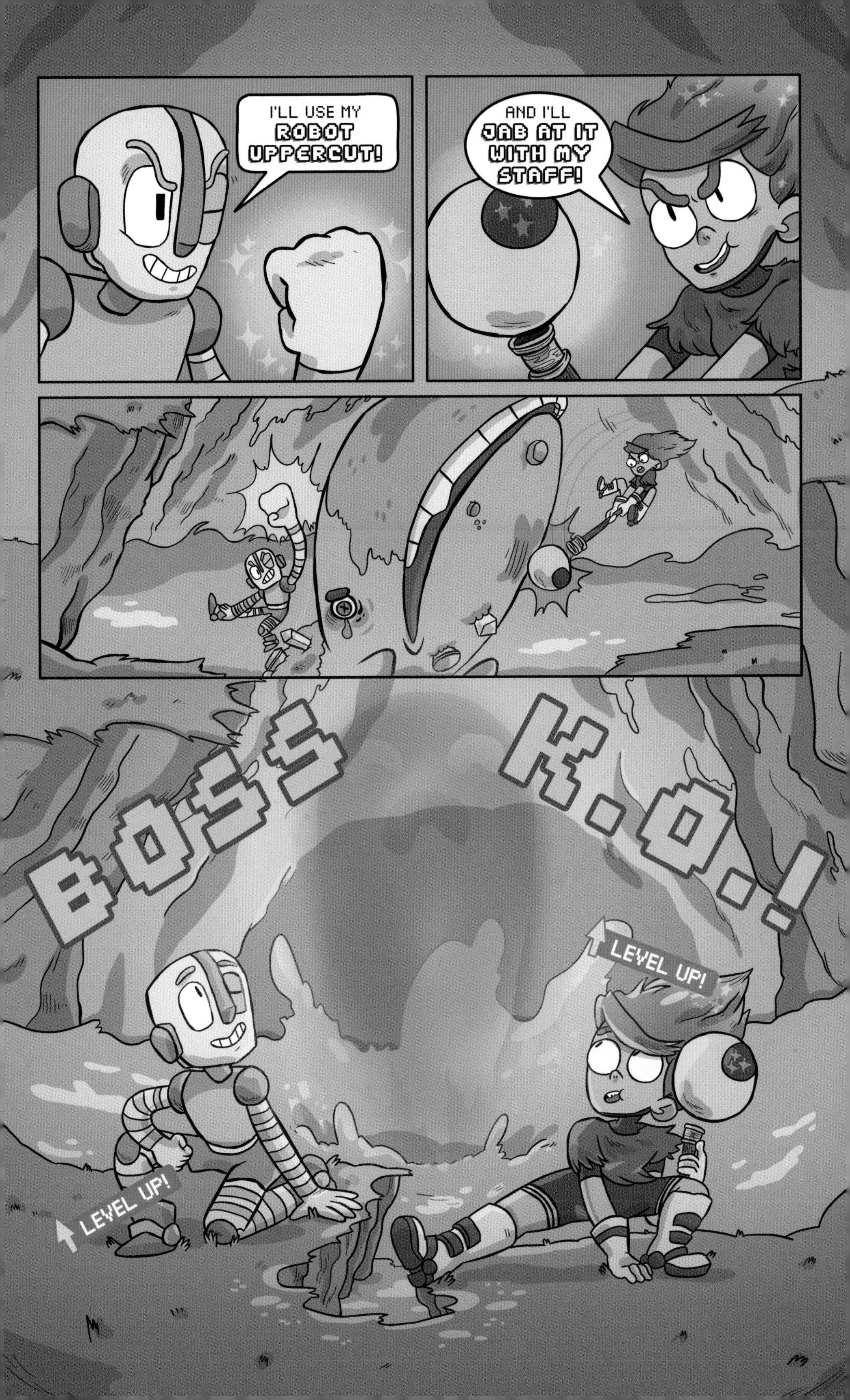

I'LL USE MY ROBOT UPPERCUT!
AND I'LL JAB AT IT WITH MY STAFF!
BOSS K.O.!
LEVEL UP!
LEVEL UP!

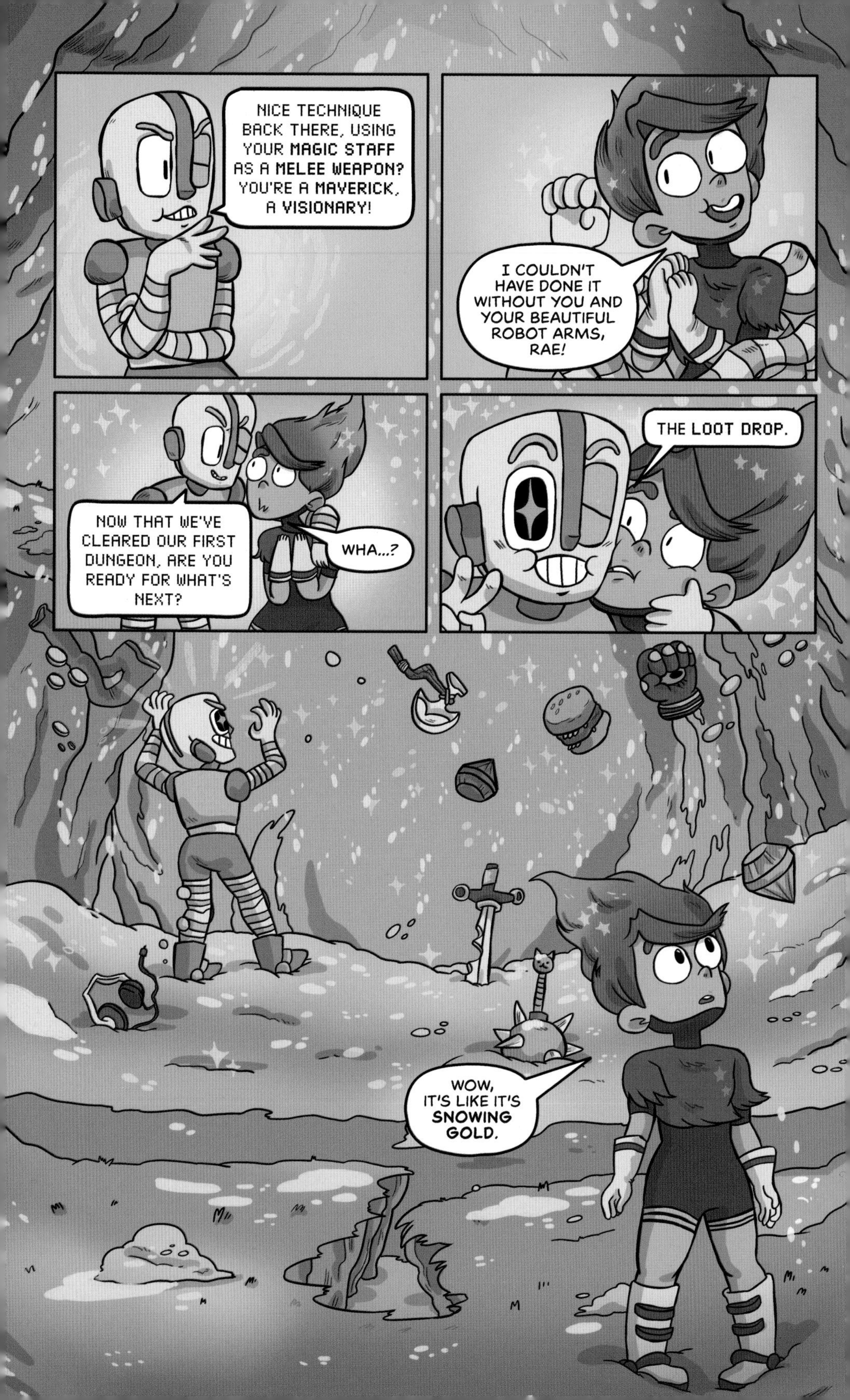
NICE TECHNIQUE BACK THERE, USING YOUR MAGIC STAFF AS A MELEE WEAPON? YOU'RE A MAVERICK, A VISIONARY!
I COULDN'T HAVE DONE IT WITHOUT YOU AND YOUR BEAUTIFUL ROBOT ARMS, RAE!
NOW THAT WE'VE CLEARED OUR FIRST DUNGEON, ARE YOU READY FOR WHAT'S NEXT?
WHA...?
THE LOOT DROP.
WOW, IT'S LIKE IT'S SNOWING GOLD.

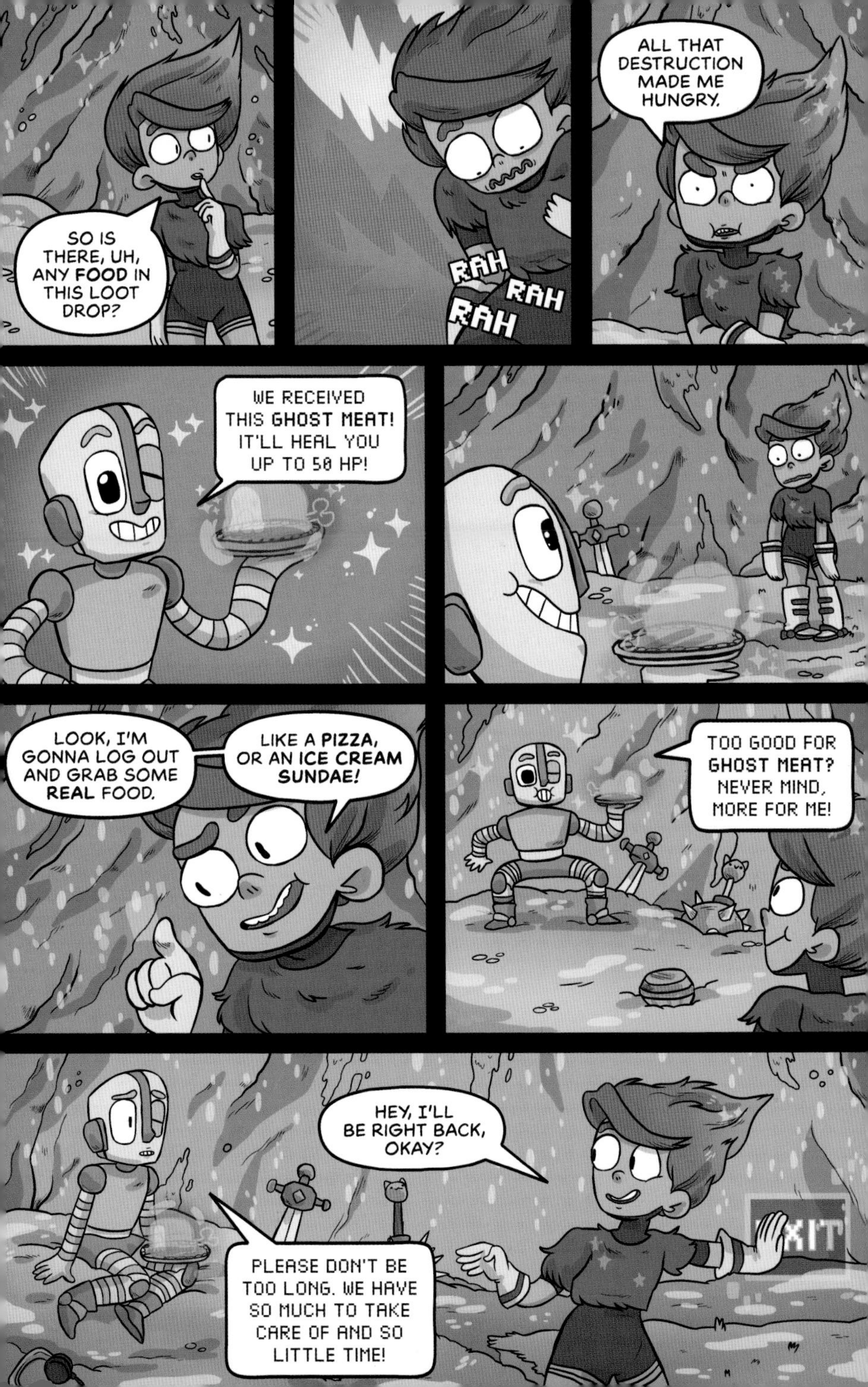

SO IS THERE, UH, ANY FOOD IN THIS LOOT DROP?
RAH RAH RAH
ALL THAT DESTRUCTION MADE ME HUNGRY.
WE RECEIVED THIS GHOST MEAT! IT'LL HEAL YOU UP TO 50 HP!
LOOK, I'M GONNA LOG OUT AND GRAB SOME REAL FOOD.
LIKE A PIZZA, OR AN ICE CREAM SUNDAE!
TOO GOOD FOR GHOST MEAT? NEVER MIND, MORE FOR ME!
HEY, I'LL BE RIGHT BACK, OKAY?
PLEASE DON'T BE TOO LONG. WE HAVE SO MUCH TO TAKE CARE OF AND SO LITTLE TIME!

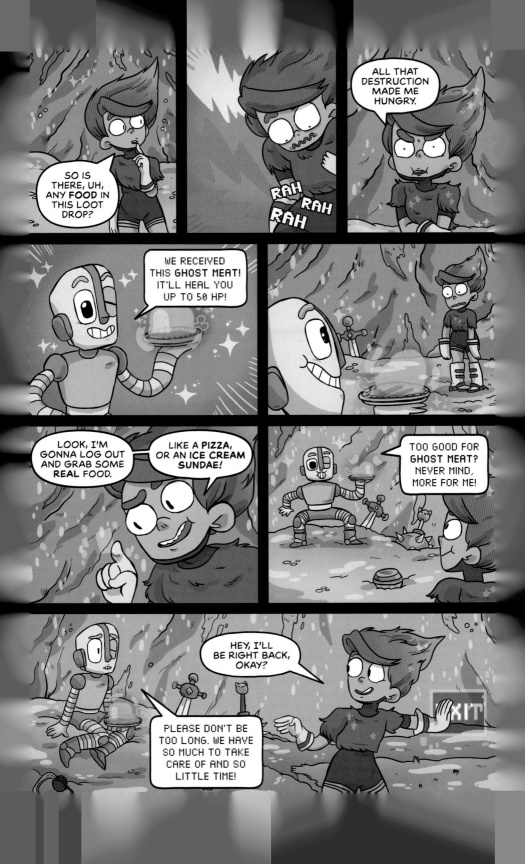

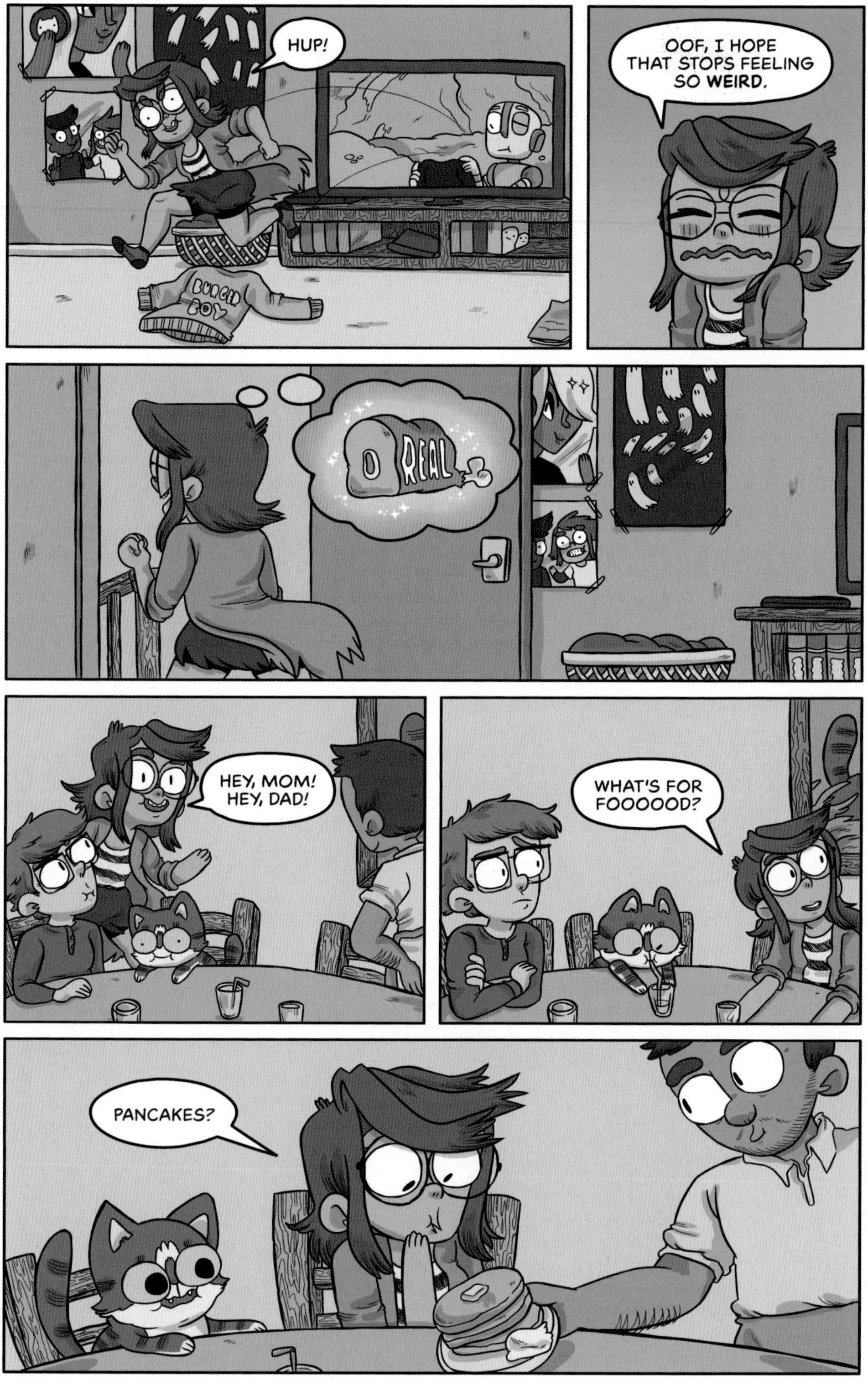
HUP!
OOF, I HOPE THAT STOPS FEELING SO WEIRD.
REAL
HEY, MOM! HEY, DAD!
WHAT'S FOR FOOOOOD?
PANCAKES?

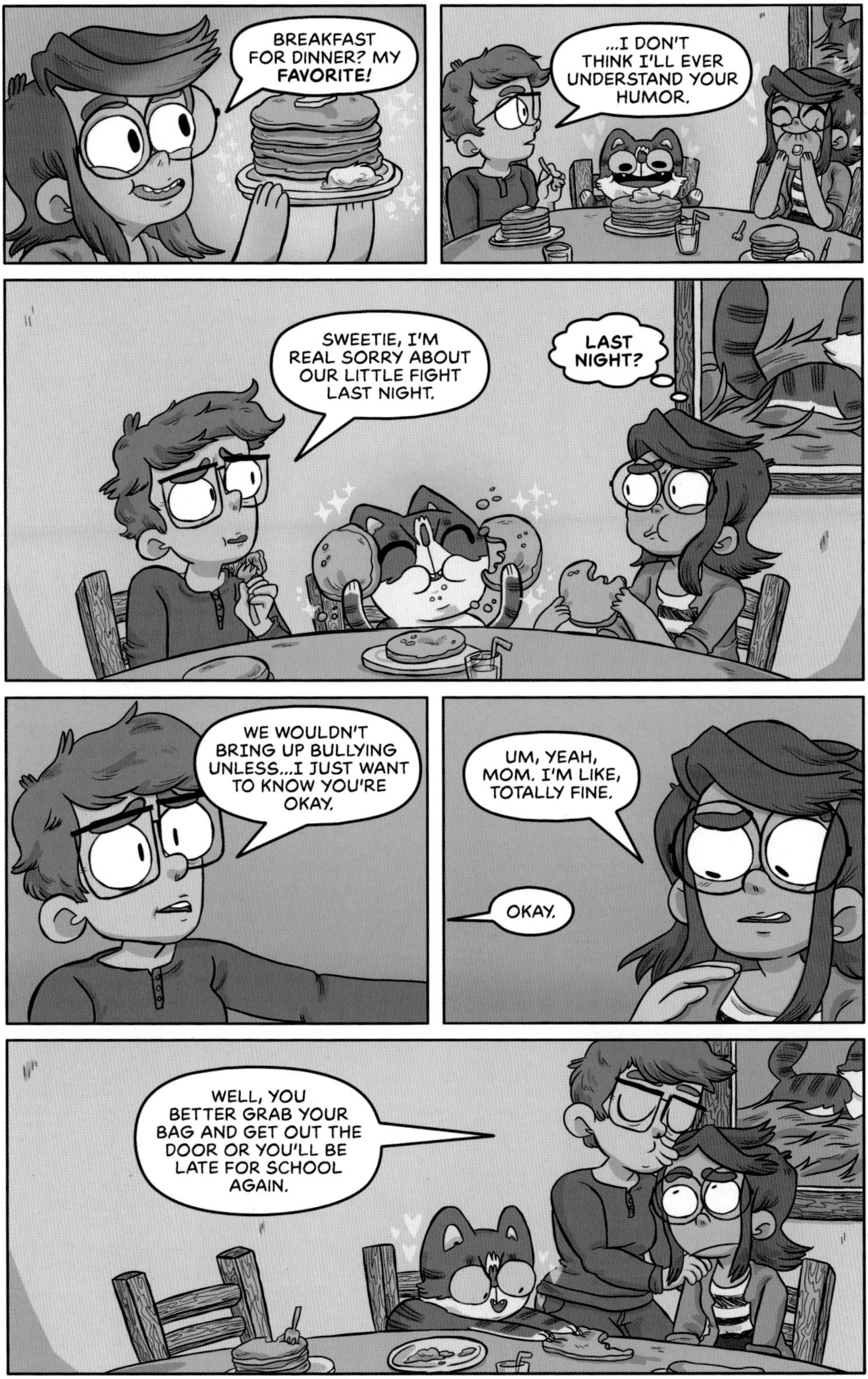
BREAKFAST FOR DINNER? MY **FAVORITE!**
...I DON'T THINK I'LL EVER UNDERSTAND YOUR HUMOR.
SWEETIE, I'M REAL SORRY ABOUT OUR LITTLE FIGHT LAST NIGHT.
LAST NIGHT?
WE WOULDN'T BRING UP BULLYING UNLESS...I JUST WANT TO KNOW YOU'RE OKAY.
UM, YEAH, MOM. I'M LIKE, TOTALLY FINE.
OKAY.
WELL, YOU BETTER GRAB YOUR BAG AND GET OUT THE DOOR OR YOU'LL BE LATE FOR SCHOOL AGAIN.

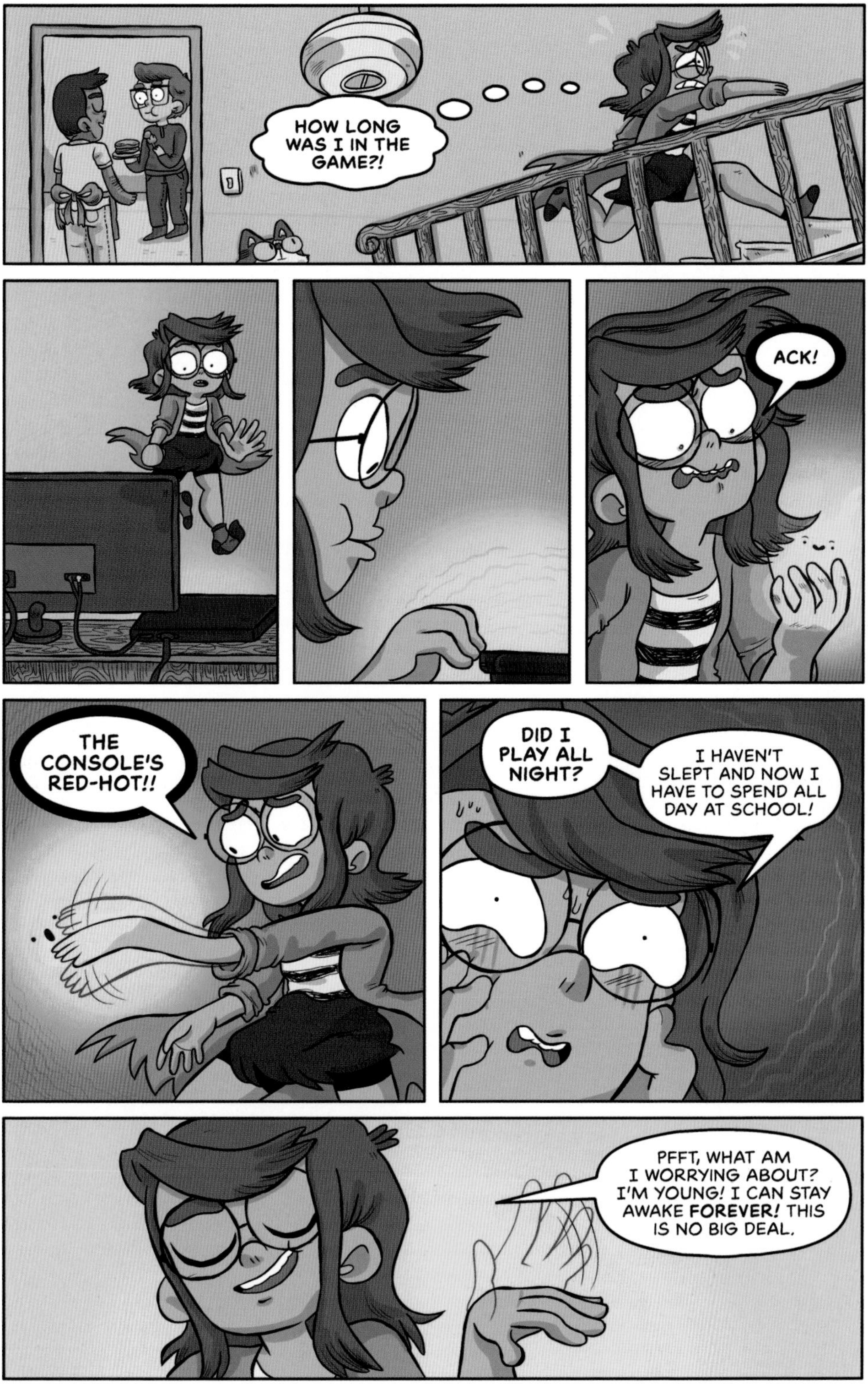
HOW LONG WAS I IN THE GAME?!
ACK!
THE CONSOLE'S RED-HOT!!
DID I PLAY ALL NIGHT?
I HAVEN'T SLEPT AND NOW I HAVE TO SPEND ALL DAY AT SCHOOL!
PFFT, WHAT AM I WORRYING ABOUT? I'M YOUNG! I CAN STAY AWAKE **FOREVER!** THIS IS NO BIG DEAL.

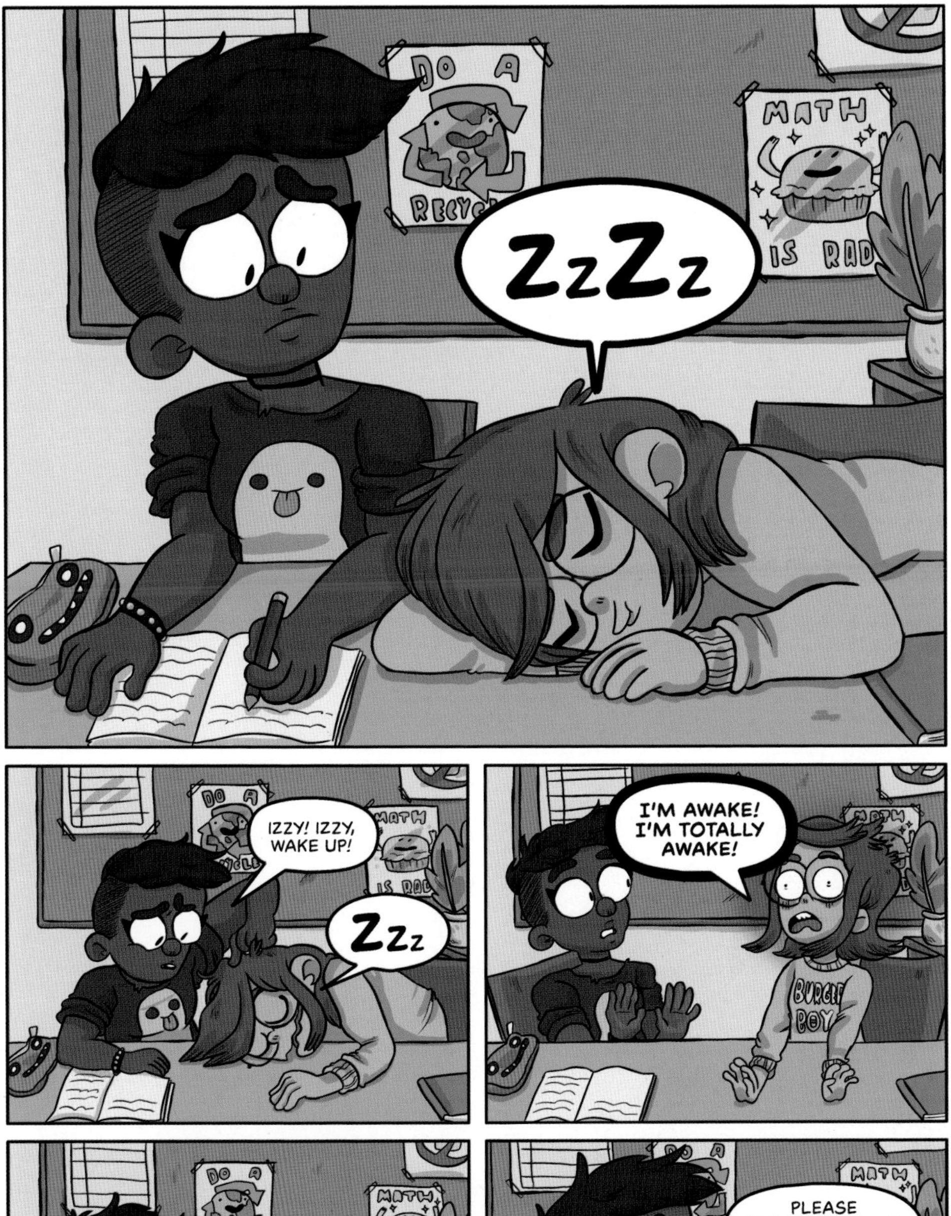
DO A RECYCLE
MATH IS RAD
ZzZz
IZZY! IZZY, WAKE UP!
Zzz
I'M AWAKE! I'M TOTALLY AWAKE!
!!!
DONK
PLEASE WAKE UP! SCHOOL IS SOOO BORING WITHOUT YOU!!

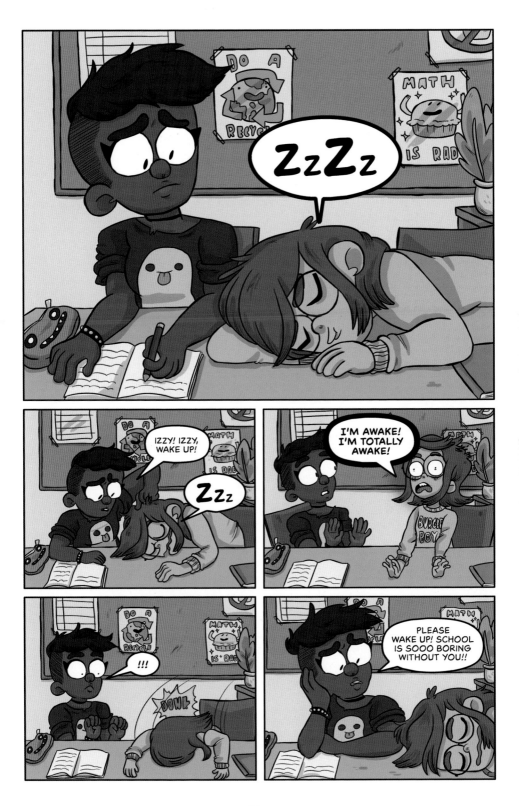

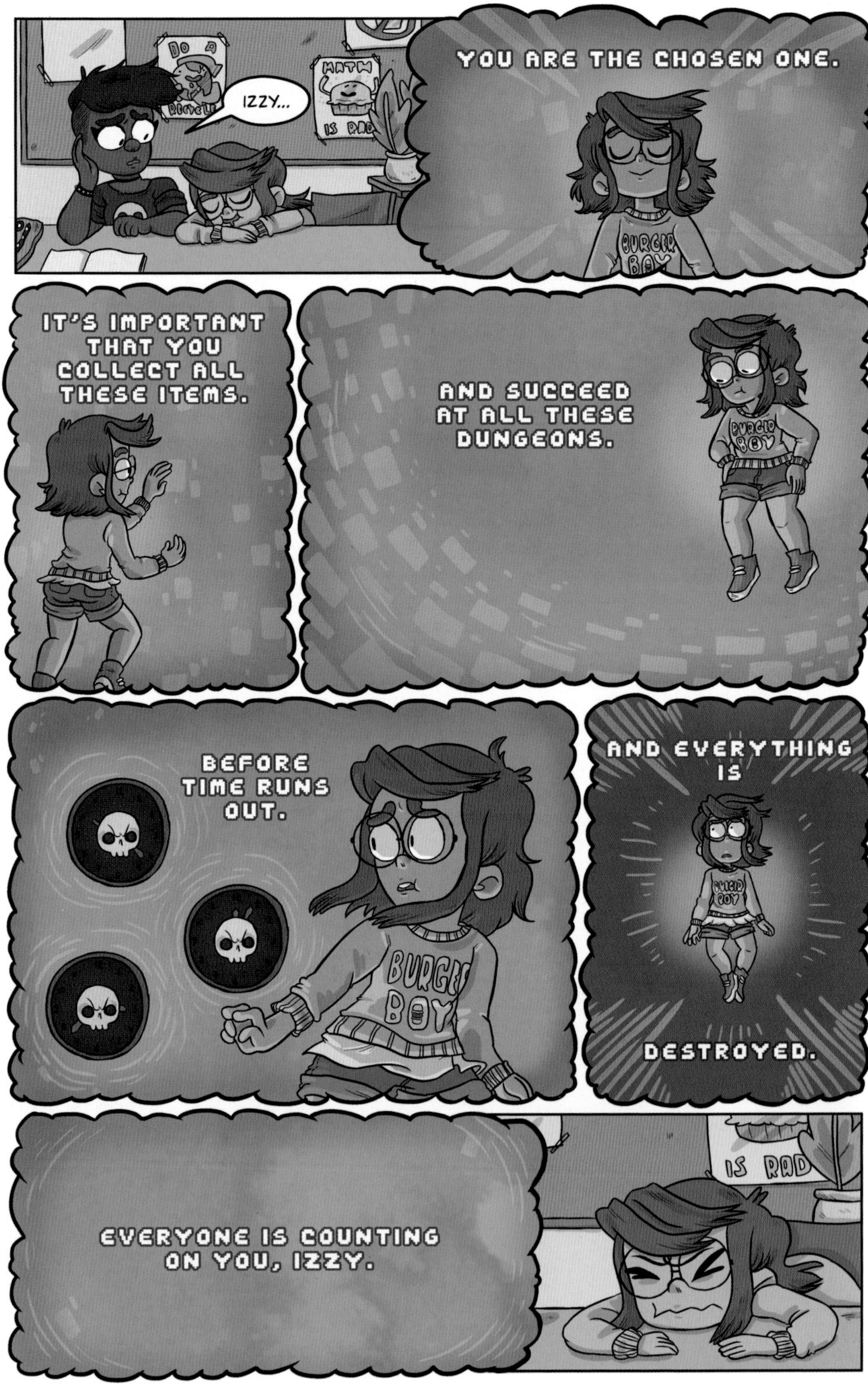
DO A
RECYCLE
MATH
IS RAD
IZZY...
YOU ARE THE CHOSEN ONE.
BURGER BOY
IT'S IMPORTANT THAT YOU COLLECT ALL THESE ITEMS.
AND SUCCEED AT ALL THESE DUNGEONS.
BEFORE TIME RUNS OUT.
BURGER BOY
AND EVERYTHING IS
DESTROYED.
EVERYONE IS COUNTING ON YOU, IZZY.
IS RAD

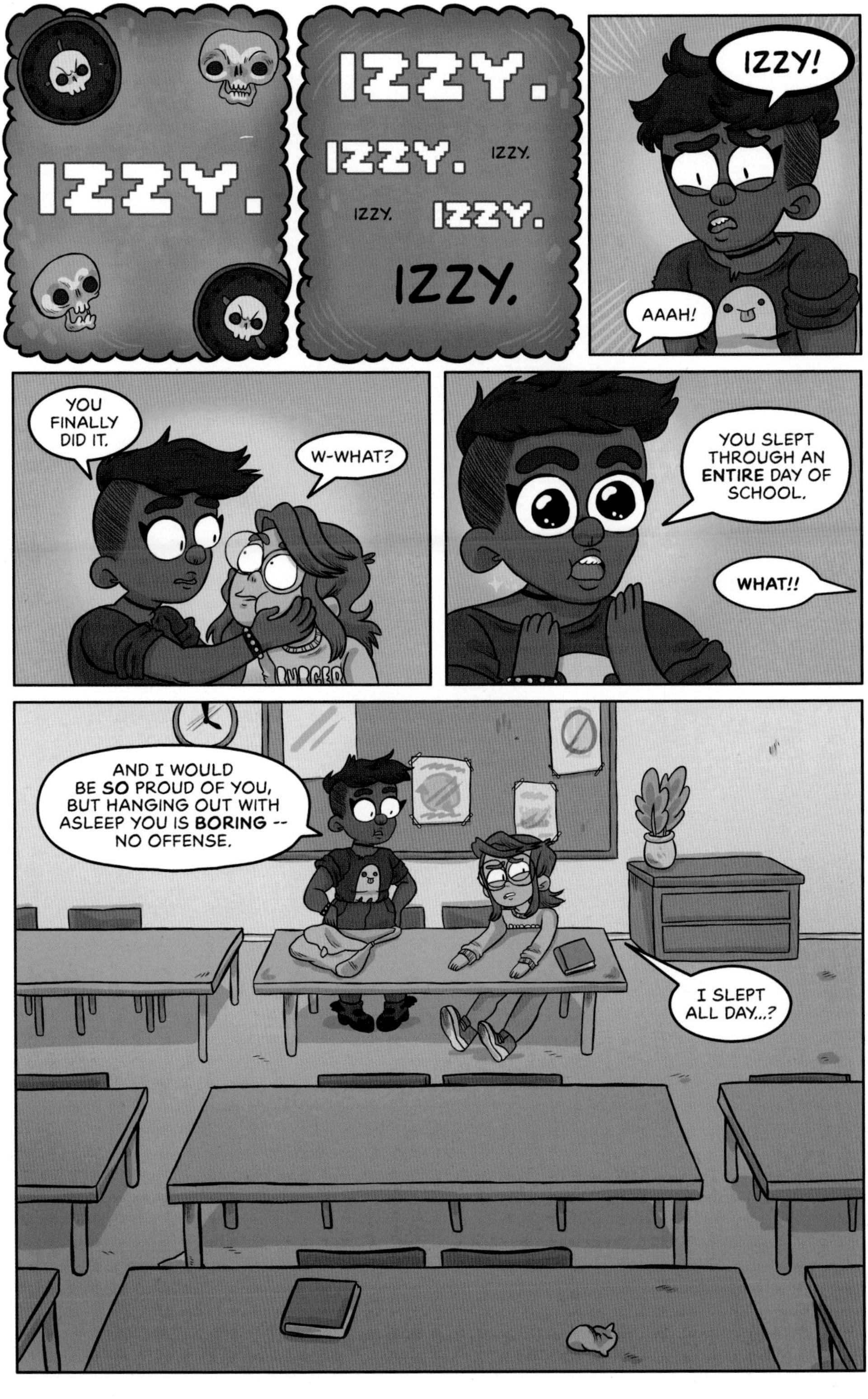
IZZY.
IZZY.
IZZY.
IZZY.
IZZY.
IZZY.
IZZY.
IZZY!
AAAH!
YOU FINALLY DID IT.
W-WHAT?
YOU SLEPT THROUGH AN ENTIRE DAY OF SCHOOL.
WHAT!!
AND I WOULD BE SO PROUD OF YOU, BUT HANGING OUT WITH ASLEEP YOU IS BORING -- NO OFFENSE.
I SLEPT ALL DAY...?

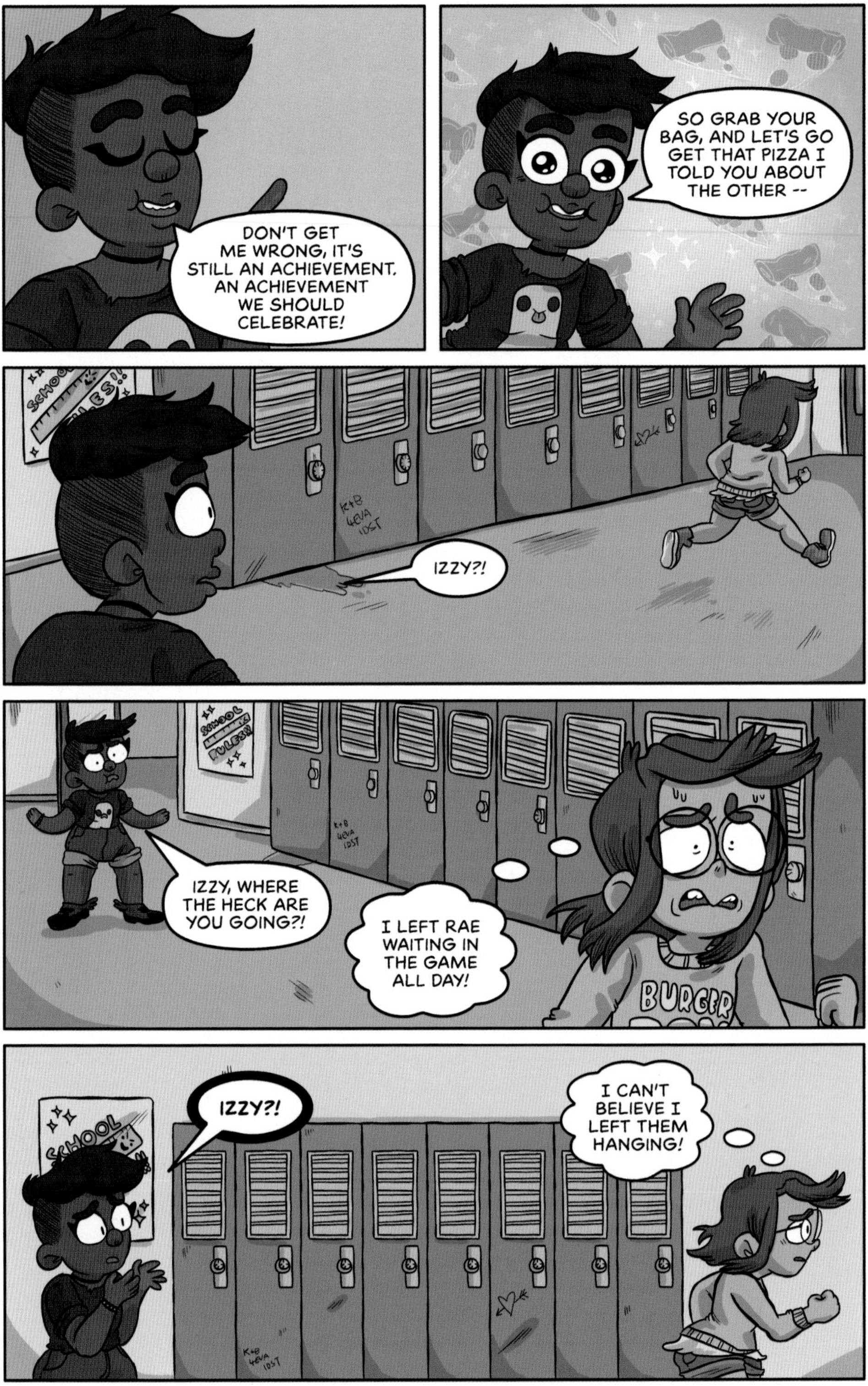
DON'T GET ME WRONG, IT'S STILL AN ACHIEVEMENT. AN ACHIEVEMENT WE SHOULD CELEBRATE!
SO GRAB YOUR BAG, AND LET'S GO GET THAT PIZZA I TOLD YOU ABOUT THE OTHER --
IZZY?!
IZZY, WHERE THE HECK ARE YOU GOING?!
I LEFT RAE WAITING IN THE GAME ALL DAY!
IZZY?!
I CAN'T BELIEVE I LEFT THEM HANGING!

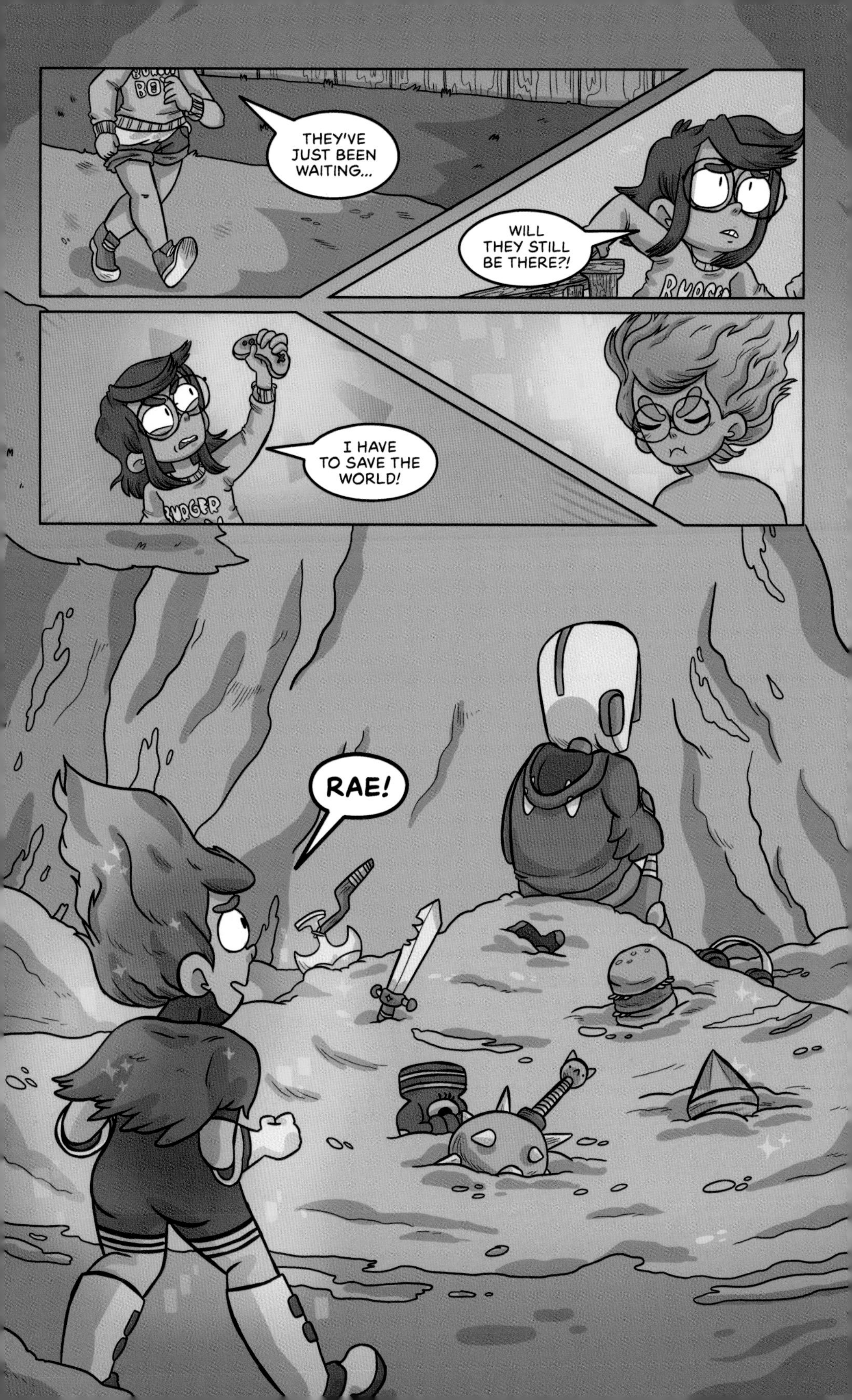
THEY'VE JUST BEEN WAITING...
WILL THEY STILL BE THERE?!
I HAVE TO SAVE THE WORLD!
RAE!

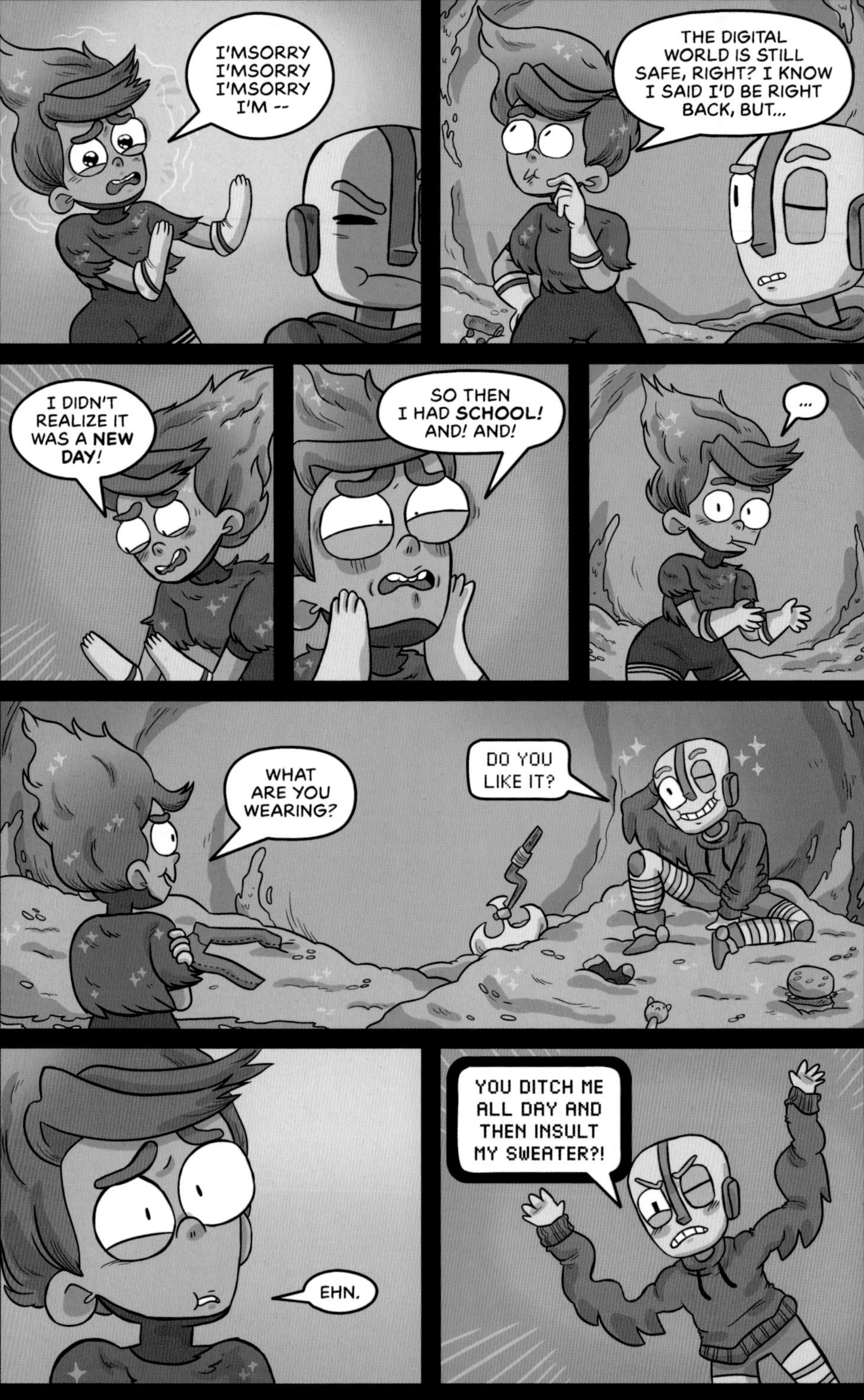
I'MSORRY I'MSORRY I'MSORRY I'M --
THE DIGITAL WORLD IS STILL SAFE, RIGHT? I KNOW I SAID I'D BE RIGHT BACK, BUT...
I DIDN'T REALIZE IT WAS A NEW DAY!
SO THEN I HAD SCHOOL! AND! AND!
...
WHAT ARE YOU WEARING?
DO YOU LIKE IT?
EHN.
YOU DITCH ME ALL DAY AND THEN INSULT MY SWEATER?!

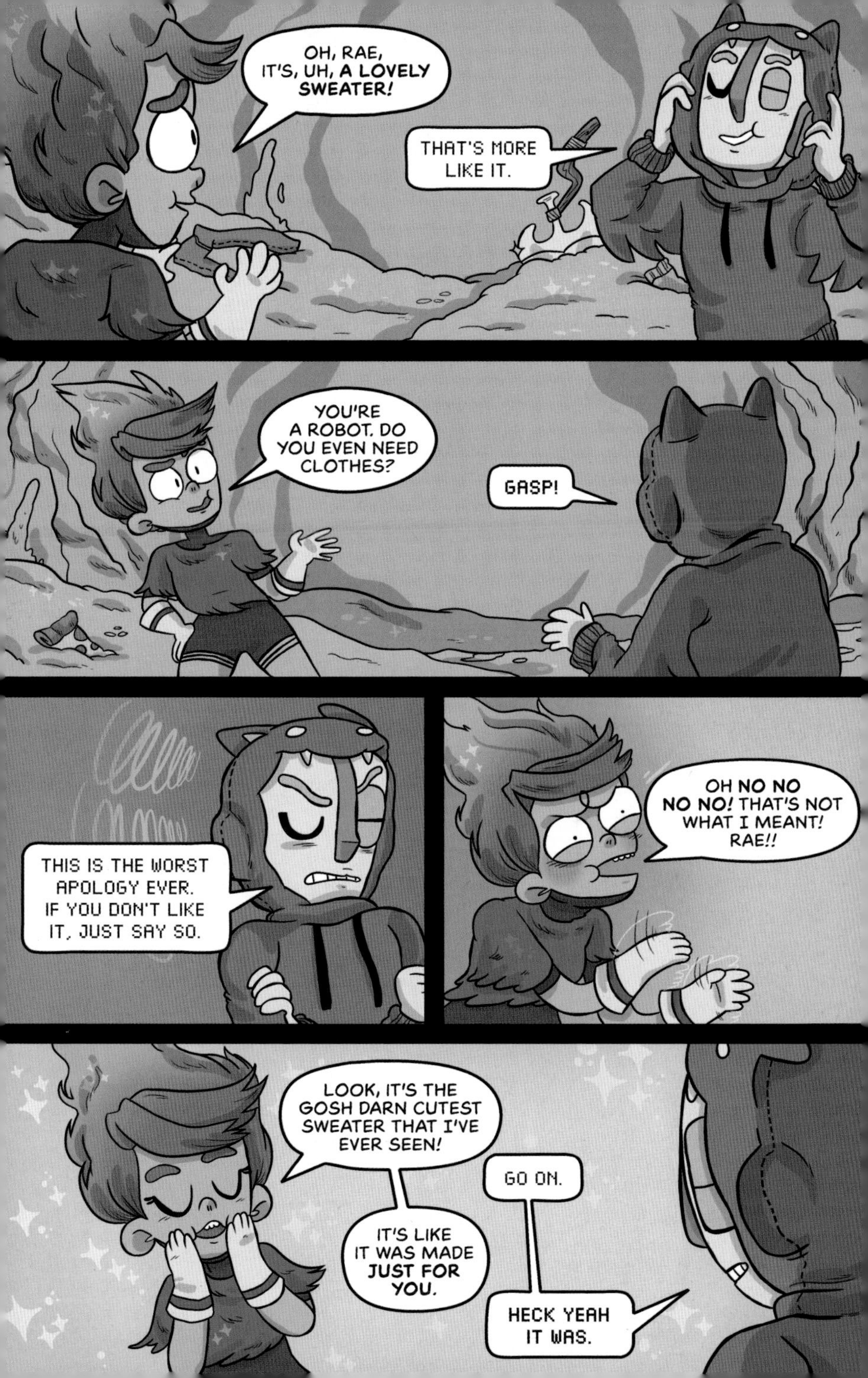
OH, RAE, IT'S, UH, **A LOVELY SWEATER!**
THAT'S MORE LIKE IT.
YOU'RE A ROBOT. DO YOU EVEN NEED CLOTHES?
GASP!
THIS IS THE WORST APOLOGY EVER. IF YOU DON'T LIKE IT, JUST SAY SO.
OH **NO NO NO NO!** THAT'S NOT WHAT I MEANT! RAE!!
LOOK, IT'S THE GOSH DARN CUTEST SWEATER THAT I'VE EVER SEEN!
GO ON.
IT'S LIKE IT WAS MADE **JUST FOR YOU.**
HECK YEAH IT WAS.

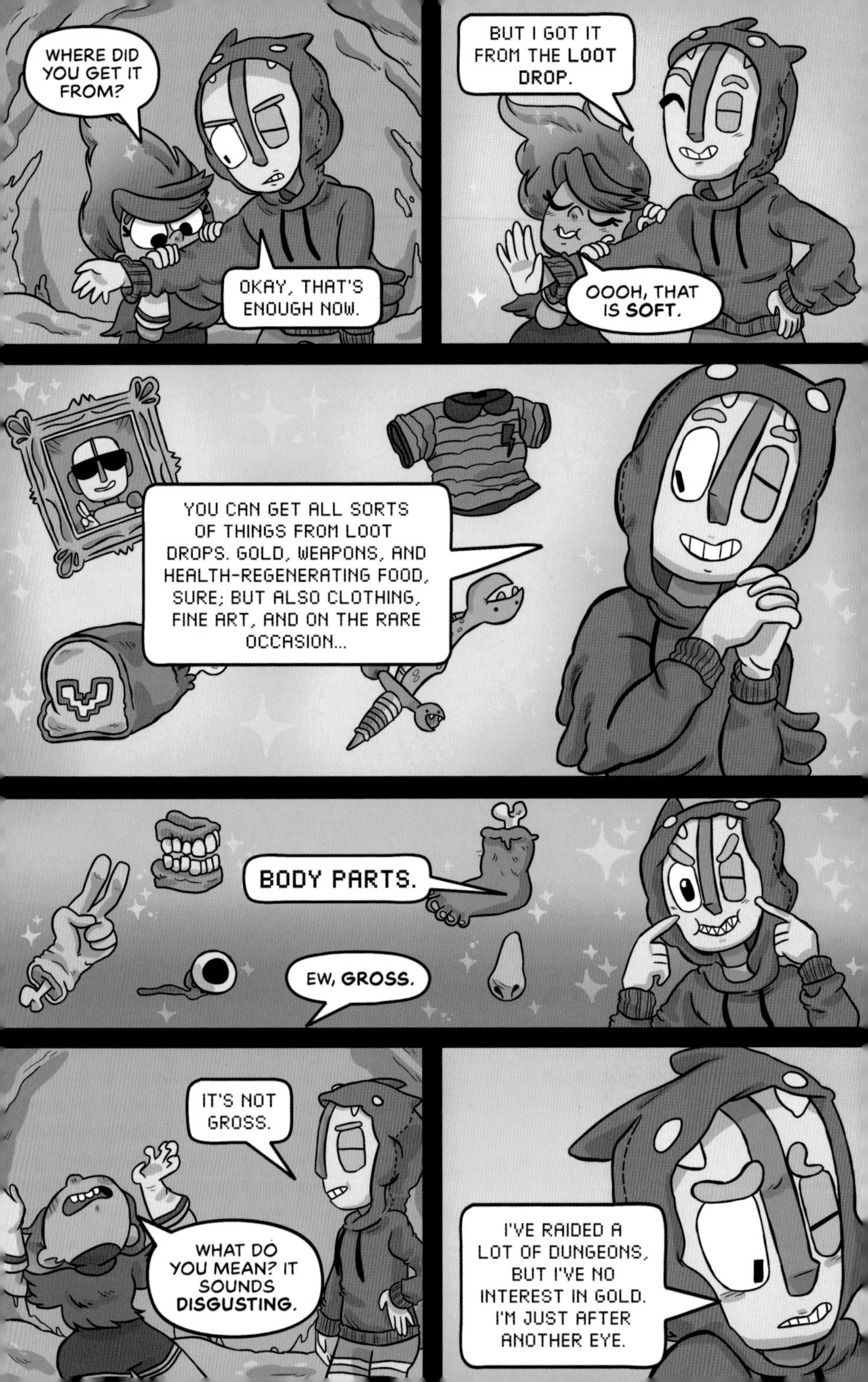
WHERE DID YOU GET IT FROM?
OKAY, THAT'S ENOUGH NOW.
BUT I GOT IT FROM THE LOOT DROP.
OOOH, THAT IS SOFT.
YOU CAN GET ALL SORTS OF THINGS FROM LOOT DROPS. GOLD, WEAPONS, AND HEALTH-REGENERATING FOOD, SURE; BUT ALSO CLOTHING, FINE ART, AND ON THE RARE OCCASION...
BODY PARTS.
EW, GROSS.
IT'S NOT GROSS.
WHAT DO YOU MEAN? IT SOUNDS DISGUSTING.
I'VE RAIDED A LOT OF DUNGEONS, BUT I'VE NO INTEREST IN GOLD. I'M JUST AFTER ANOTHER EYE.

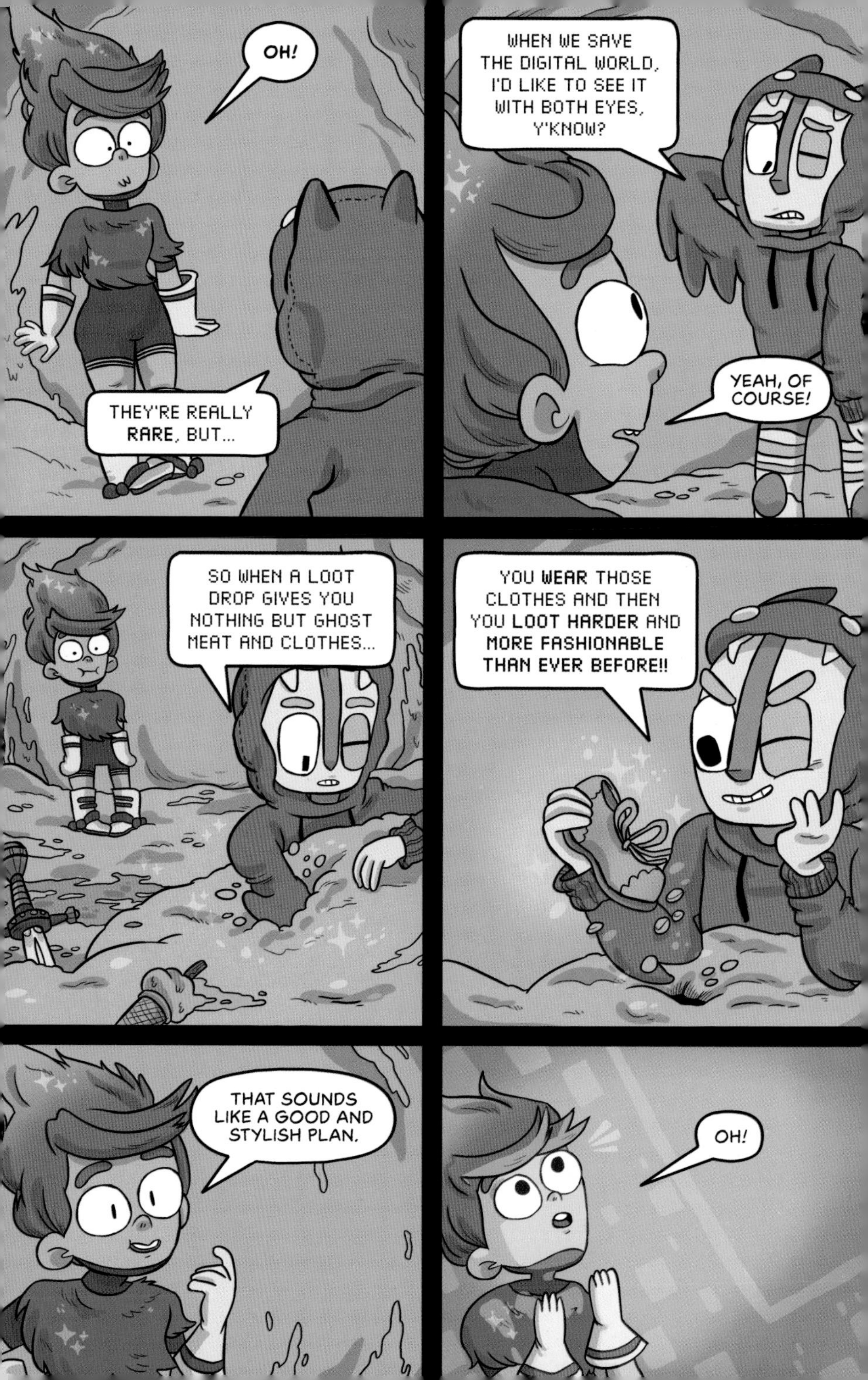
OH!
THEY'RE REALLY RARE, BUT...
WHEN WE SAVE THE DIGITAL WORLD, I'D LIKE TO SEE IT WITH BOTH EYES, Y'KNOW?
YEAH, OF COURSE!
SO WHEN A LOOT DROP GIVES YOU NOTHING BUT GHOST MEAT AND CLOTHES...
YOU WEAR THOSE CLOTHES AND THEN YOU LOOT HARDER AND MORE FASHIONABLE THAN EVER BEFORE!!
THAT SOUNDS LIKE A GOOD AND STYLISH PLAN.
OH!

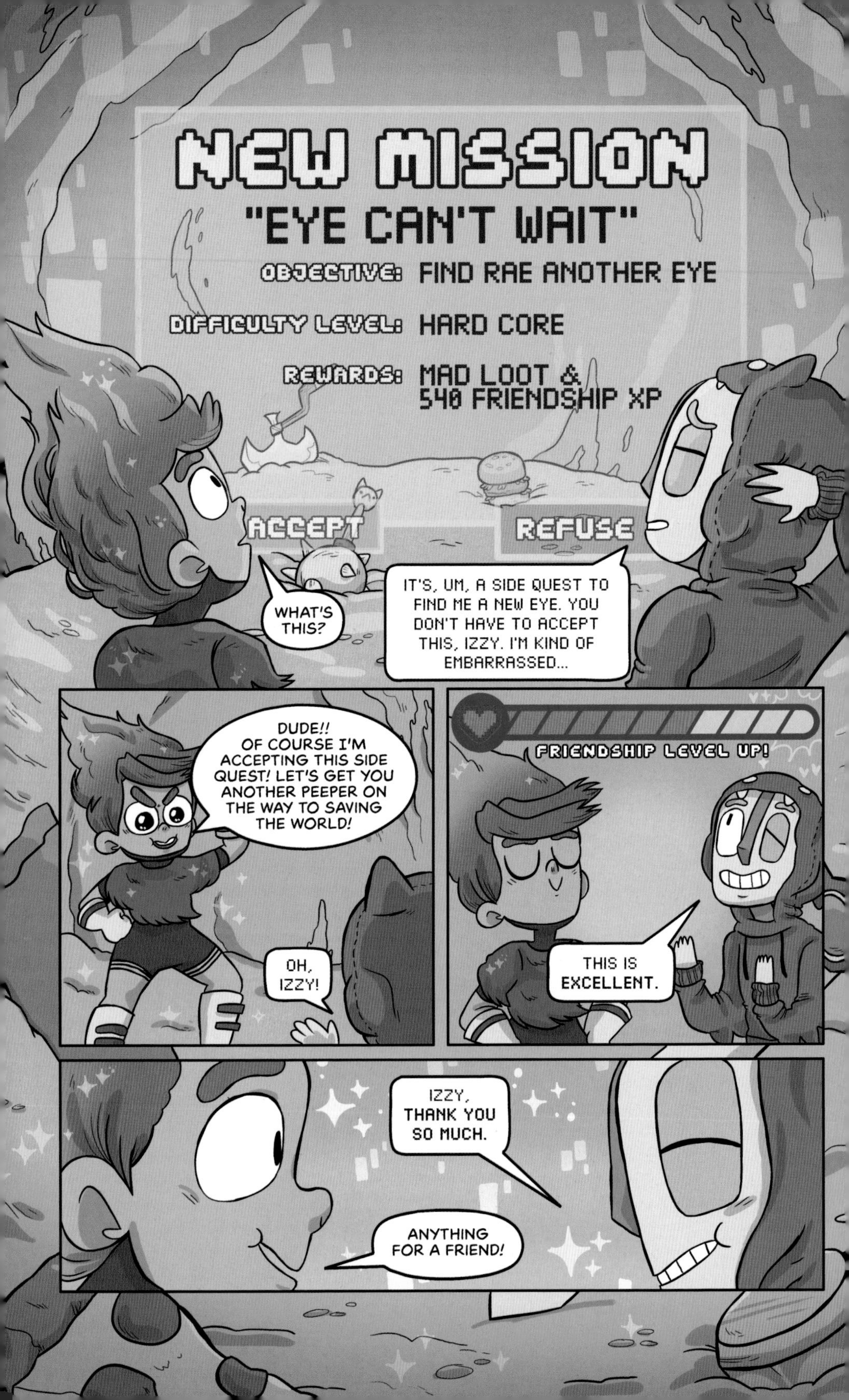

NEW MISSION
"EYE CAN'T WAIT"
OBJECTIVE: FIND RAE ANOTHER EYE
DIFFICULTY LEVEL: HARD CORE
REWARDS: MAD LOOT & 540 FRIENDSHIP XP
ACCEPT
REFUSE
WHAT'S THIS?
IT'S, UM, A SIDE QUEST TO FIND ME A NEW EYE. YOU DON'T HAVE TO ACCEPT THIS, IZZY. I'M KIND OF EMBARRASSED...
DUDE!! OF COURSE I'M ACCEPTING THIS SIDE QUEST! LET'S GET YOU ANOTHER PEEPER ON THE WAY TO SAVING THE WORLD!
OH, IZZY!
FRIENDSHIP LEVEL UP!
THIS IS EXCELLENT.
IZZY, THANK YOU SO MUCH.
ANYTHING FOR A FRIEND!

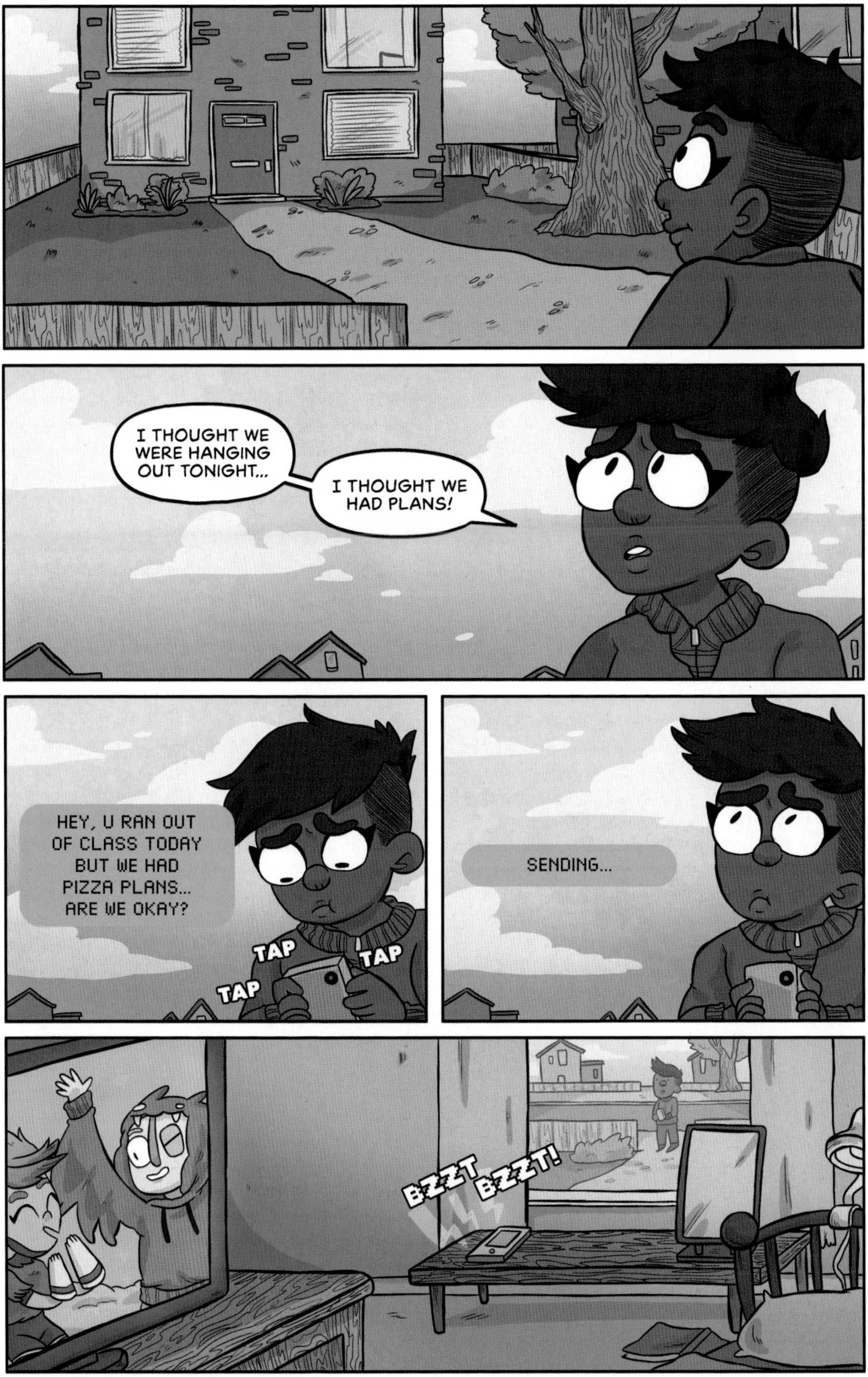
I THOUGHT WE WERE HANGING OUT TONIGHT...
I THOUGHT WE HAD PLANS!
HEY, U RAN OUT OF CLASS TODAY BUT WE HAD PIZZA PLANS... ARE WE OKAY?
TAP
TAP
TAP
SENDING...
BZZT BZZT!

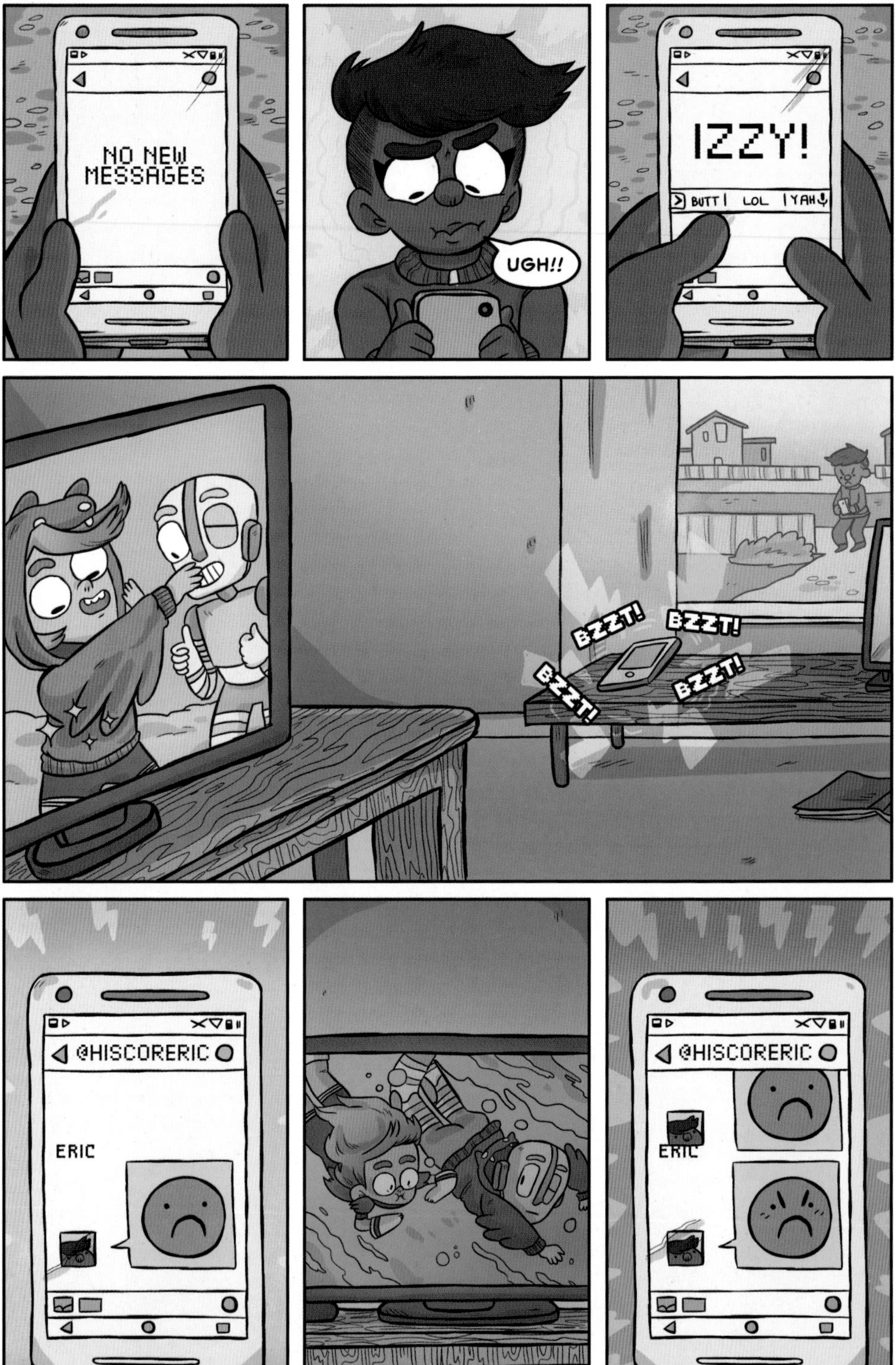
NO NEW MESSAGES
UGH!!
IZZY!
BUTT | LOL | YAH
BZZT!
BZZT!
BZZT!
BZZT!
@HISCORERIC
ERIC
@HISCORERIC
ERIC

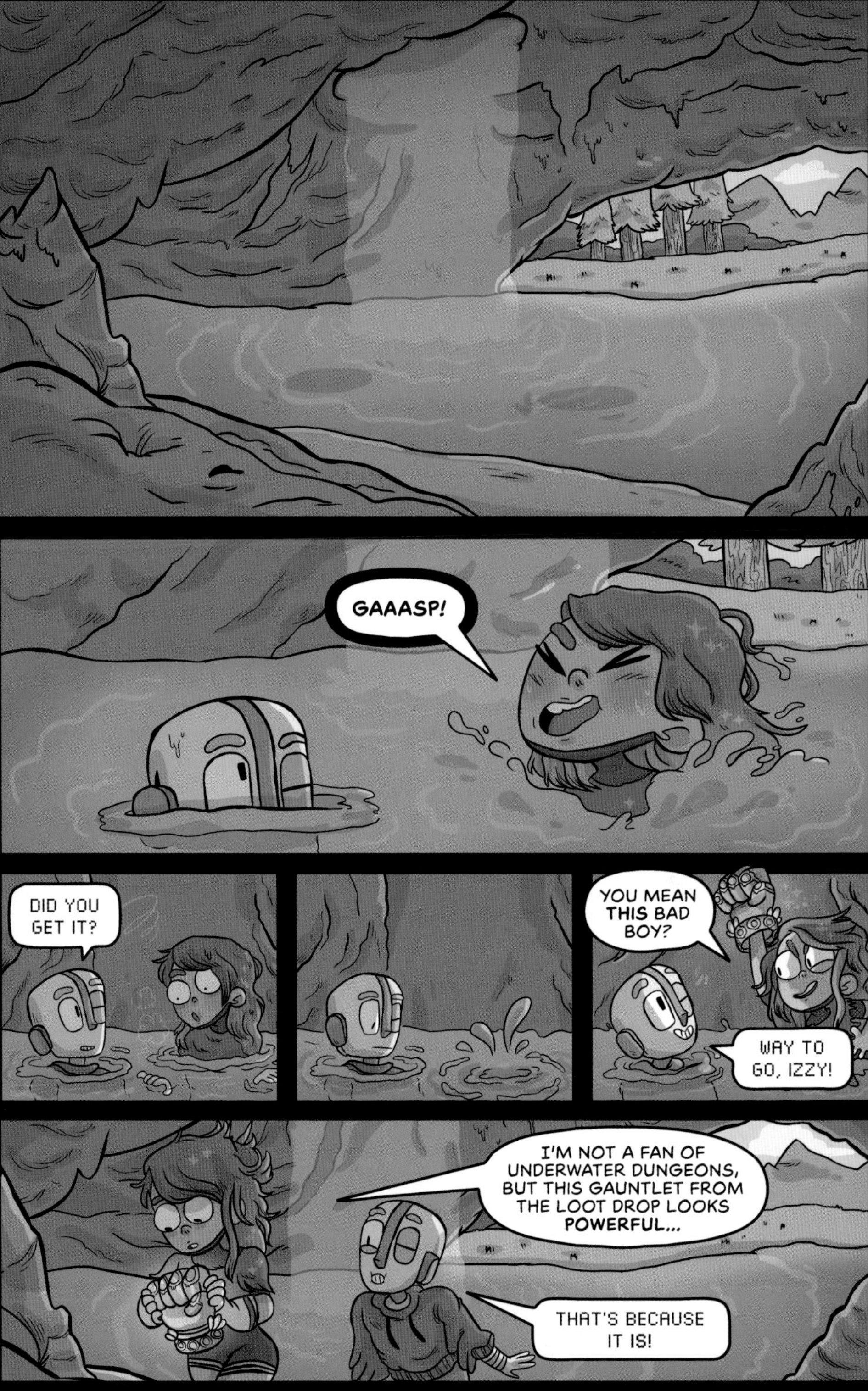
GAAASP!
DID YOU GET IT?
YOU MEAN THIS BAD BOY?
WAY TO GO, IZZY!
I'M NOT A FAN OF UNDERWATER DUNGEONS, BUT THIS GAUNTLET FROM THE LOOT DROP LOOKS POWERFUL...
THAT'S BECAUSE IT IS!

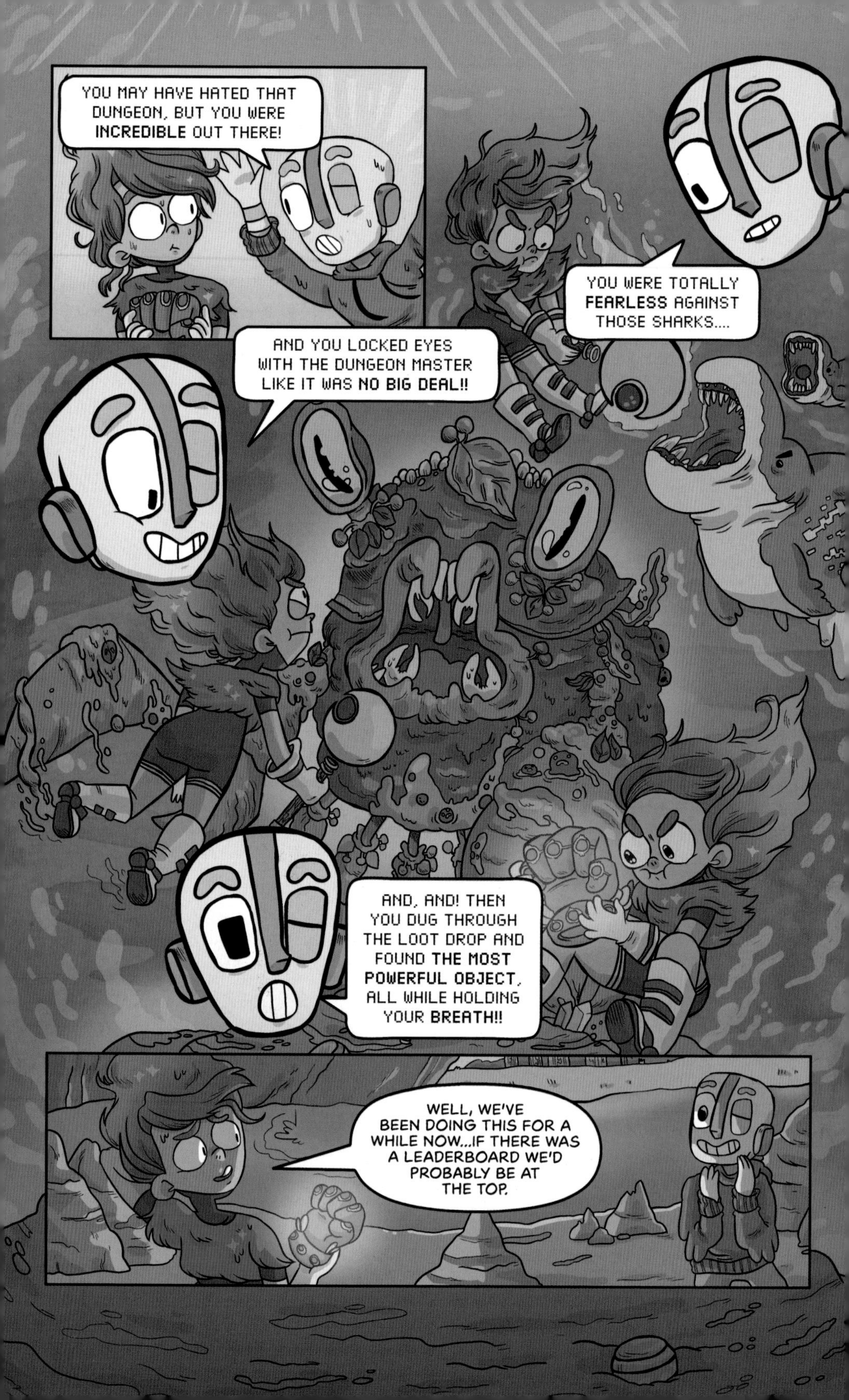
YOU MAY HAVE HATED THAT DUNGEON, BUT YOU WERE **INCREDIBLE** OUT THERE!
YOU WERE TOTALLY **FEARLESS** AGAINST THOSE SHARKS....
AND YOU LOCKED EYES WITH THE DUNGEON MASTER LIKE IT WAS **NO BIG DEAL!!**
AND, AND! THEN YOU DUG THROUGH THE LOOT DROP AND FOUND **THE MOST POWERFUL OBJECT**, ALL WHILE HOLDING YOUR **BREATH!!**
WELL, WE'VE BEEN DOING THIS FOR A WHILE NOW...IF THERE WAS A LEADERBOARD WE'D PROBABLY BE AT THE TOP.

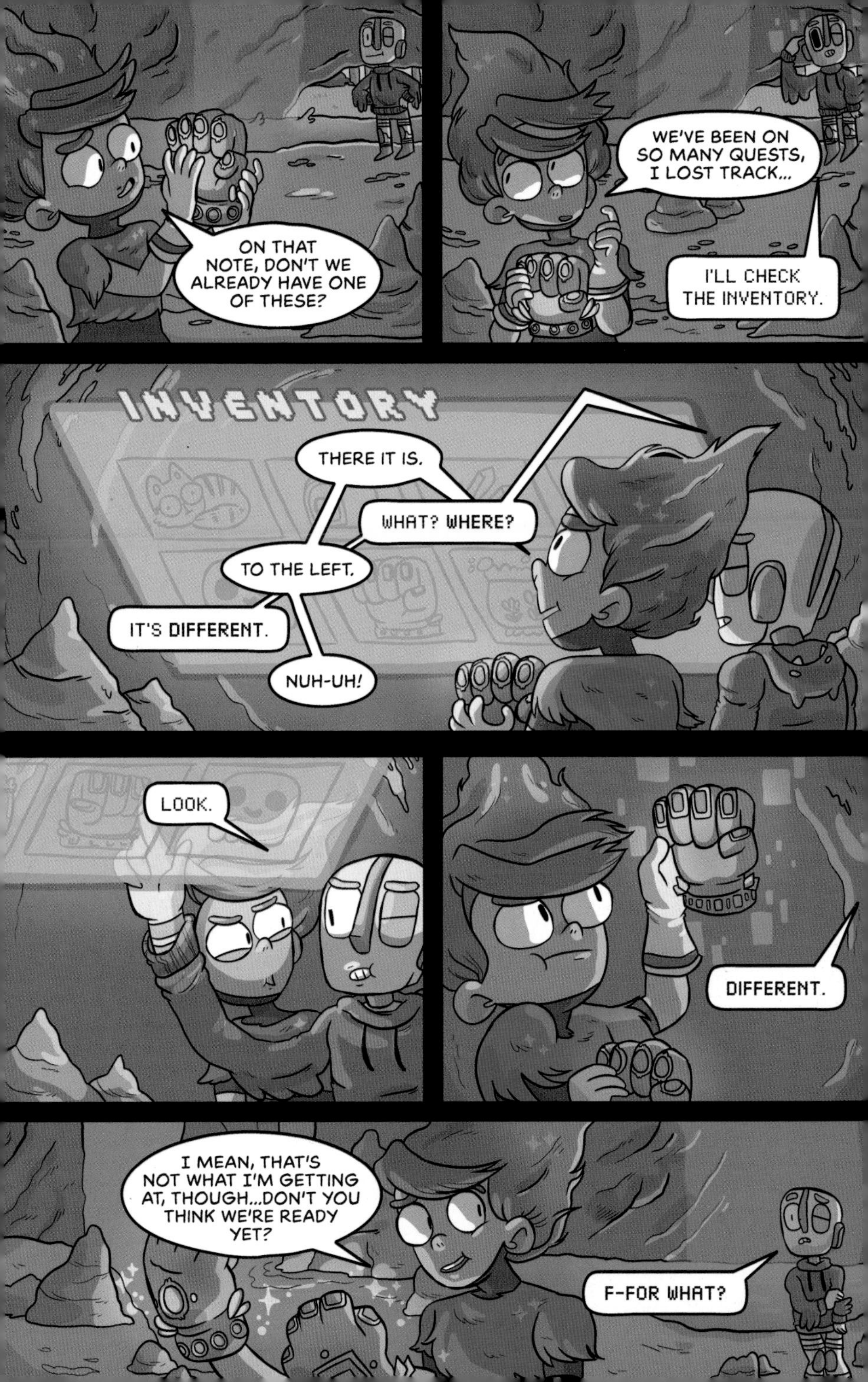

ON THAT NOTE, DON'T WE ALREADY HAVE ONE OF THESE?
WE'VE BEEN ON SO MANY QUESTS, I LOST TRACK...
I'LL CHECK THE INVENTORY.
INVENTORY
THERE IT IS.
WHAT? WHERE?
TO THE LEFT.
IT'S DIFFERENT.
NUH-UH!
LOOK.
DIFFERENT.
I MEAN, THAT'S NOT WHAT I'M GETTING AT, THOUGH...DON'T YOU THINK WE'RE READY YET?
F-FOR WHAT?

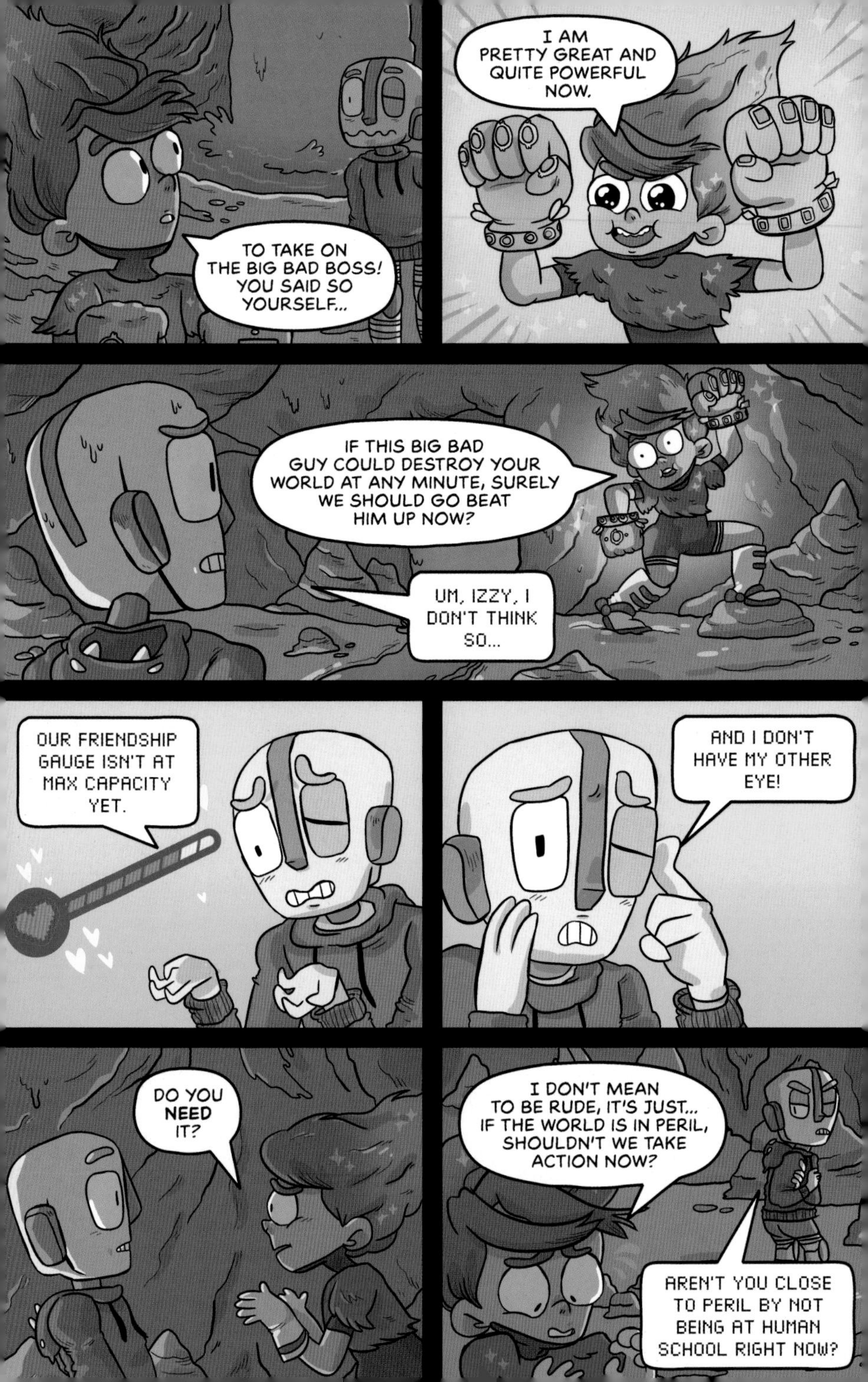
TO TAKE ON THE BIG BAD BOSS! YOU SAID SO YOURSELF...
I AM PRETTY GREAT AND QUITE POWERFUL NOW.
IF THIS BIG BAD GUY COULD DESTROY YOUR WORLD AT ANY MINUTE, SURELY WE SHOULD GO BEAT HIM UP NOW?
UM, IZZY, I DON'T THINK SO...
OUR FRIENDSHIP GAUGE ISN'T AT MAX CAPACITY YET.
AND I DON'T HAVE MY OTHER EYE!
DO YOU **NEED** IT?
I DON'T MEAN TO BE RUDE, IT'S JUST... IF THE WORLD IS IN PERIL, SHOULDN'T WE TAKE ACTION NOW?
AREN'T YOU CLOSE TO PERIL BY NOT BEING AT HUMAN SCHOOL RIGHT NOW?

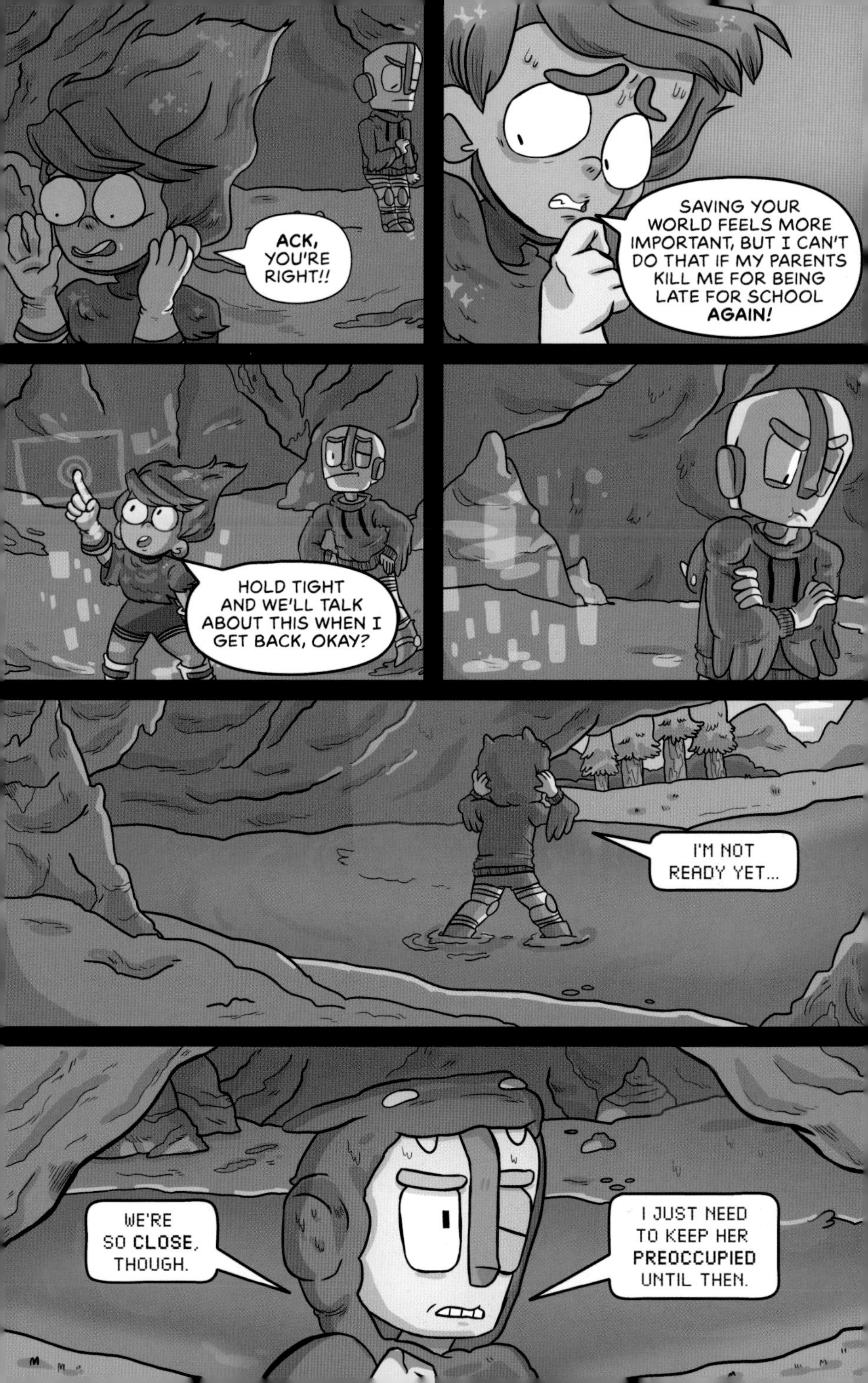

ACK, YOU'RE RIGHT!!
SAVING YOUR WORLD FEELS MORE IMPORTANT, BUT I CAN'T DO THAT IF MY PARENTS KILL ME FOR BEING LATE FOR SCHOOL **AGAIN!**
HOLD TIGHT AND WE'LL TALK ABOUT THIS WHEN I GET BACK, OKAY?
I'M NOT READY YET...
WE'RE SO **CLOSE**, THOUGH.
I JUST NEED TO KEEP HER **PREOCCUPIED** UNTIL THEN.

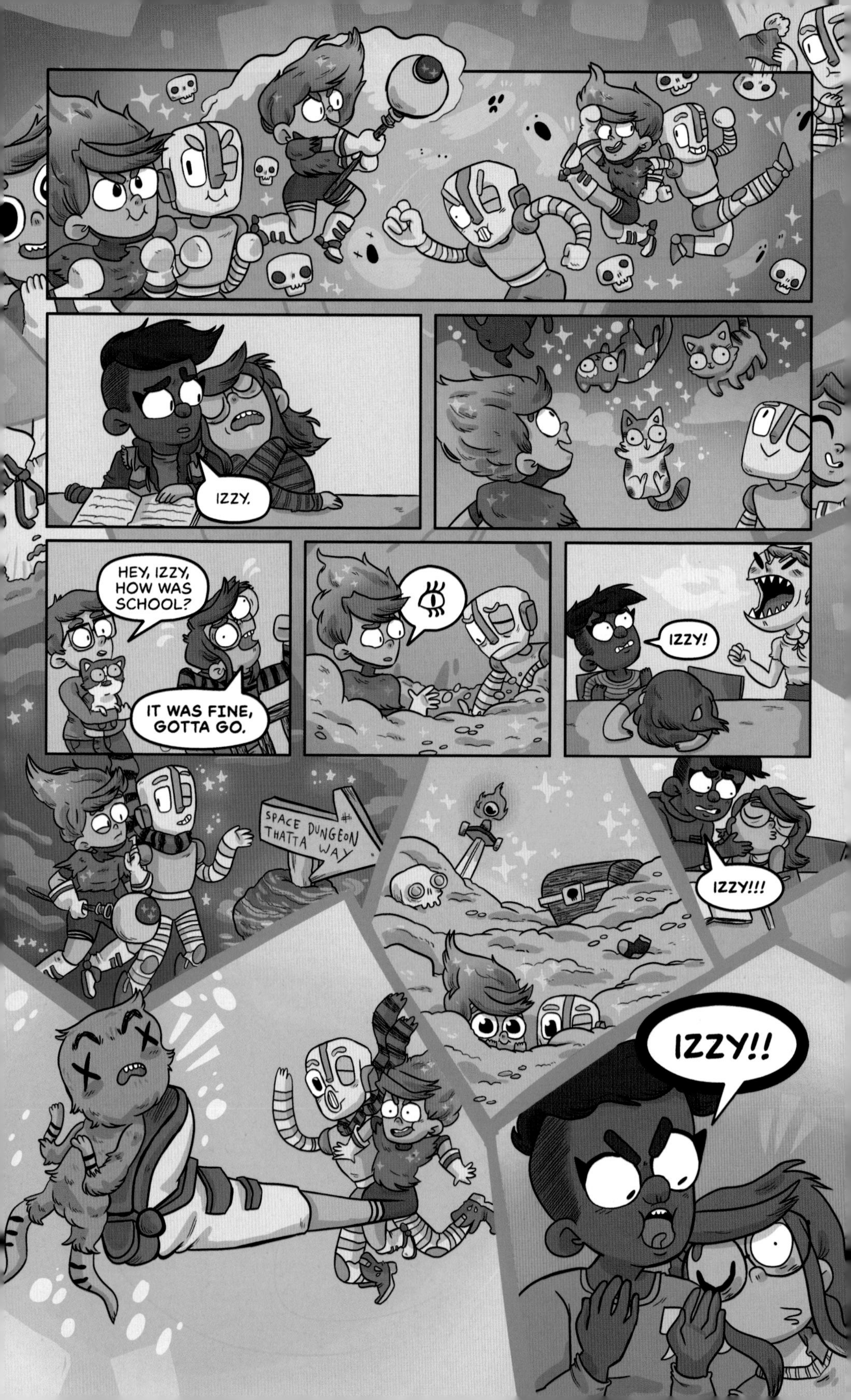
IZZY.
HEY, IZZY, HOW WAS SCHOOL?
IT WAS FINE, GOTTA GO.
IZZY!
SPACE DUNGEON THATTA WAY
IZZY!!!
IZZY!!

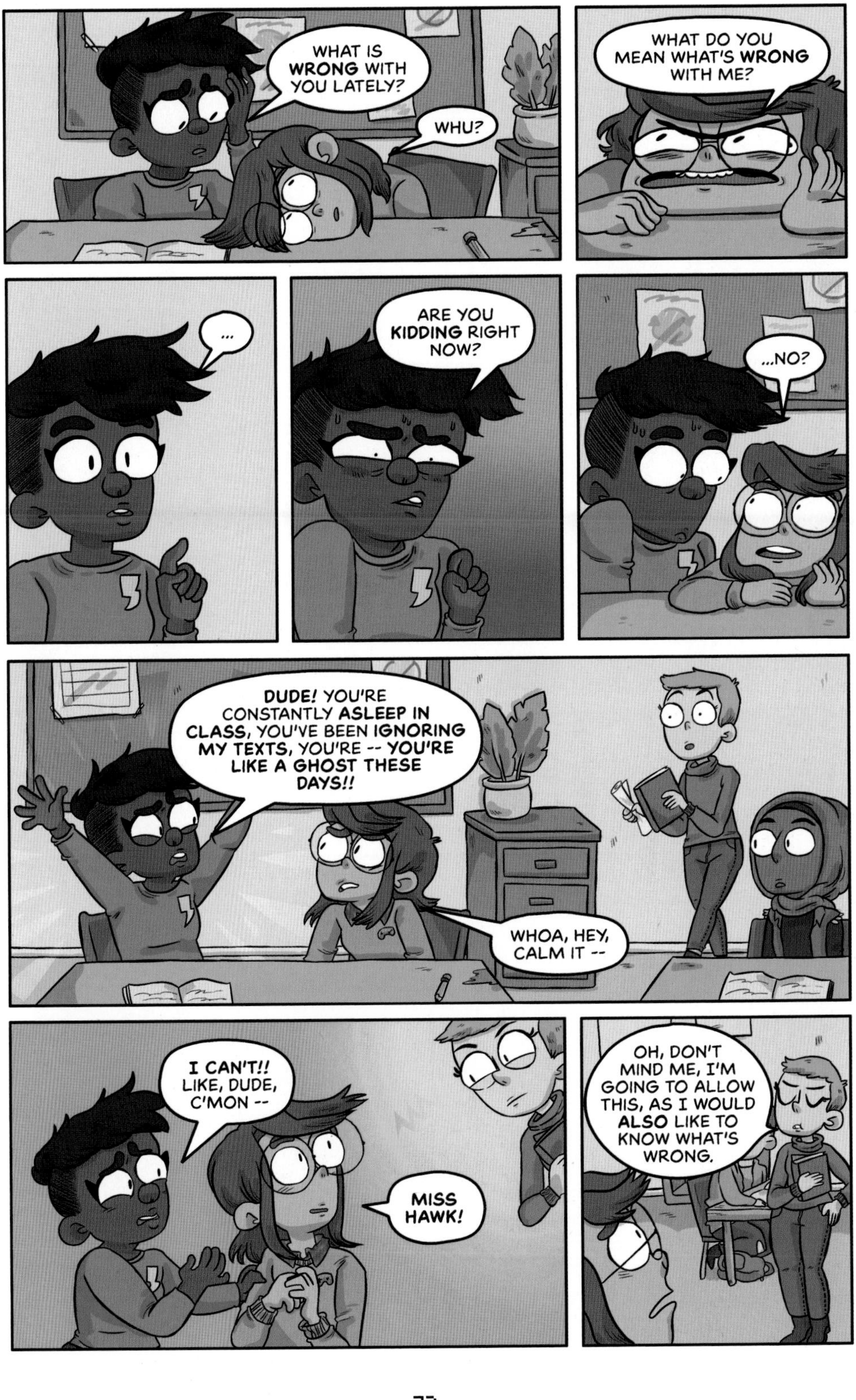
WHAT IS WRONG WITH YOU LATELY?
WHU?
WHAT DO YOU MEAN WHAT'S WRONG WITH ME?
...
ARE YOU KIDDING RIGHT NOW?
...NO?
DUDE! YOU'RE CONSTANTLY ASLEEP IN CLASS, YOU'VE BEEN IGNORING MY TEXTS, YOU'RE -- YOU'RE LIKE A GHOST THESE DAYS!!
WHOA, HEY, CALM IT --
I CAN'T!! LIKE, DUDE, C'MON --
MISS HAWK!
OH, DON'T MIND ME, I'M GOING TO ALLOW THIS, AS I WOULD ALSO LIKE TO KNOW WHAT'S WRONG.

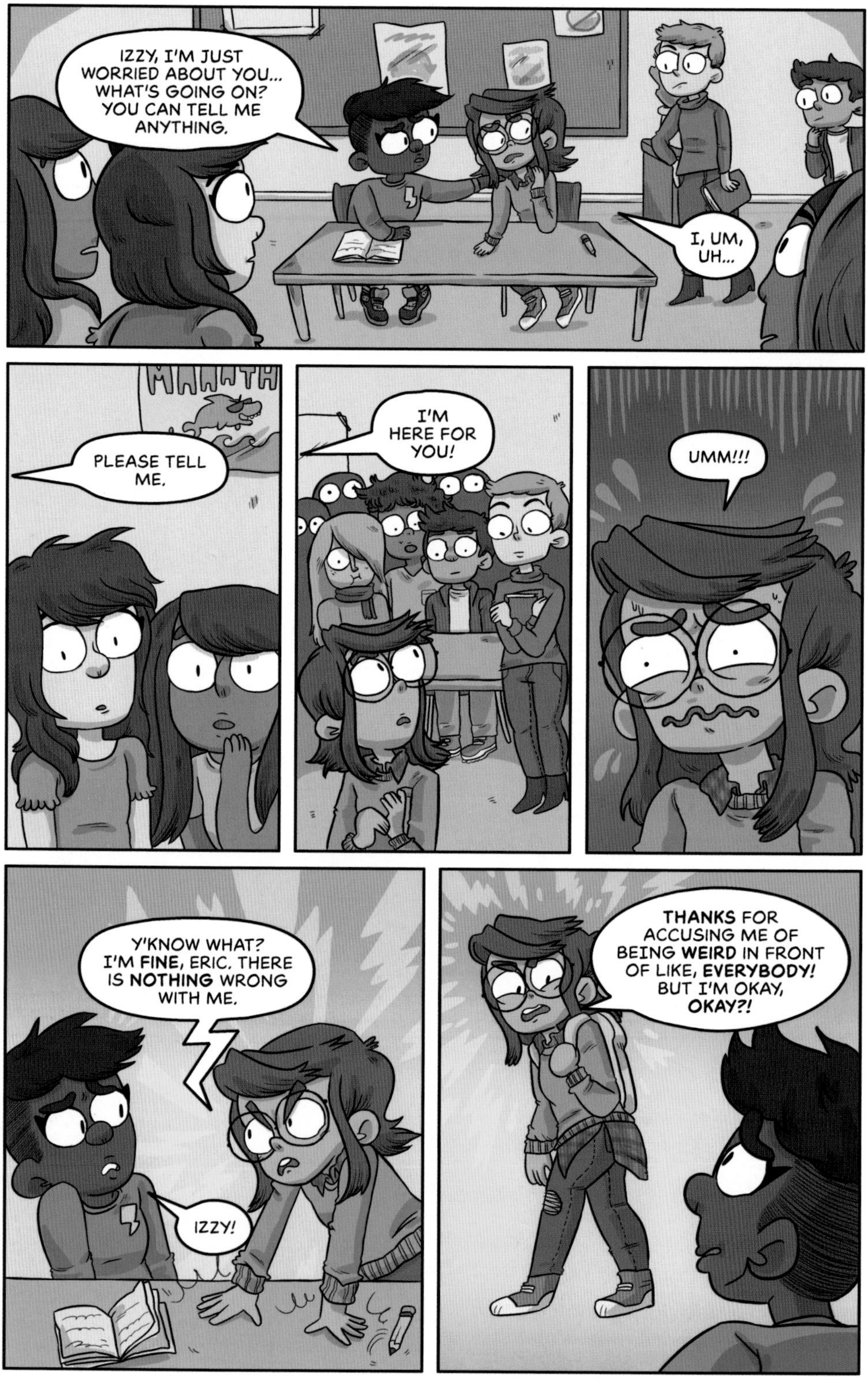

IZZY, I'M JUST WORRIED ABOUT YOU... WHAT'S GOING ON? YOU CAN TELL ME ANYTHING.
I, UM, UH...
MAAATH
PLEASE TELL ME.
I'M HERE FOR YOU!
UMM!!!
Y'KNOW WHAT? I'M **FINE**, ERIC. THERE IS **NOTHING** WRONG WITH ME.
IZZY!
THANKS FOR ACCUSING ME OF BEING **WEIRD** IN FRONT OF LIKE, **EVERYBODY!** BUT I'M OKAY, **OKAY?!**

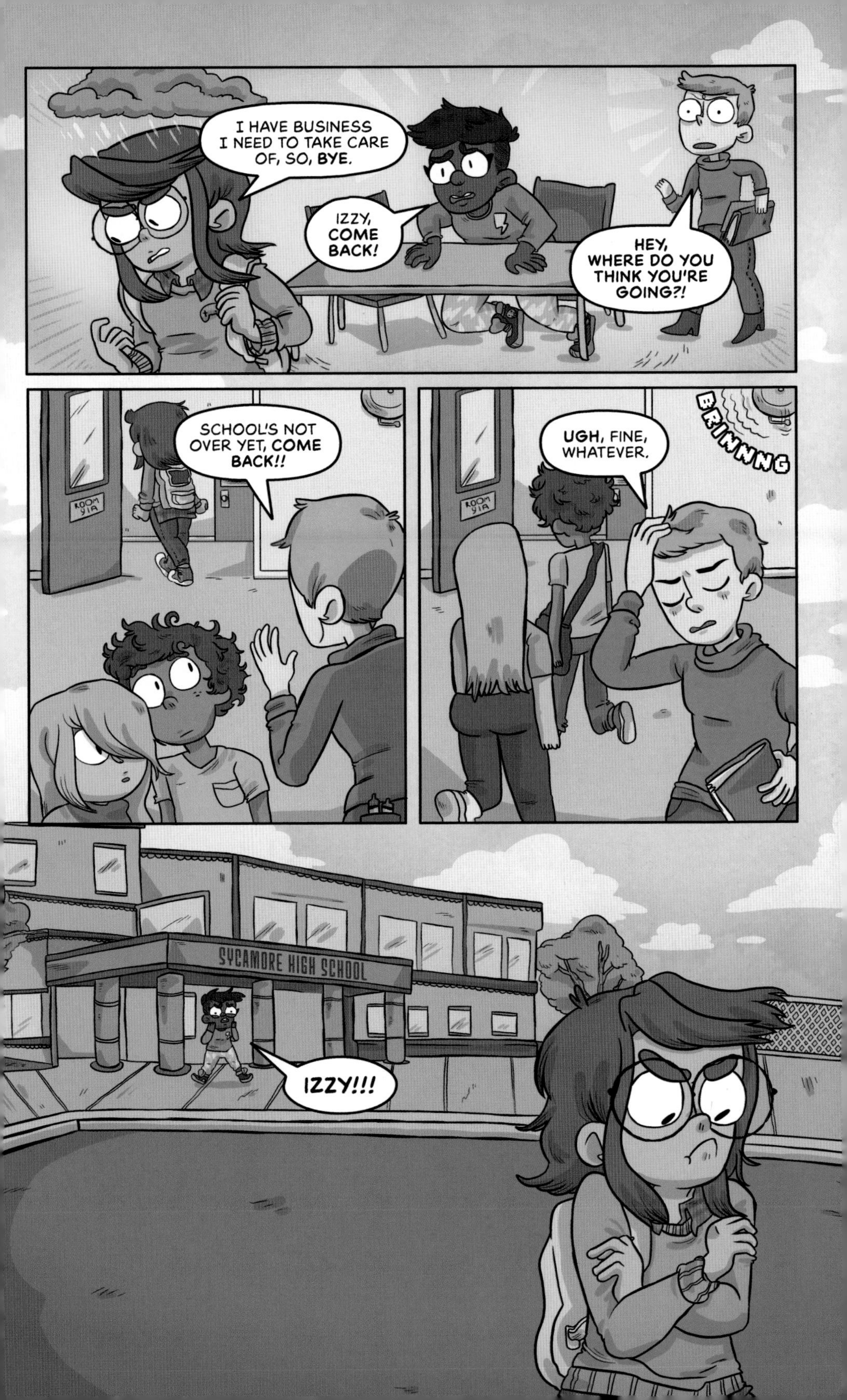
I HAVE BUSINESS I NEED TO TAKE CARE OF, SO, BYE.
IZZY, COME BACK!
HEY, WHERE DO YOU THINK YOU'RE GOING?!
ROOM 91A
SCHOOL'S NOT OVER YET, COME BACK!!
BRINNNG
UGH, FINE, WHATEVER.
SYCAMORE HIGH SCHOOL
IZZY!!!

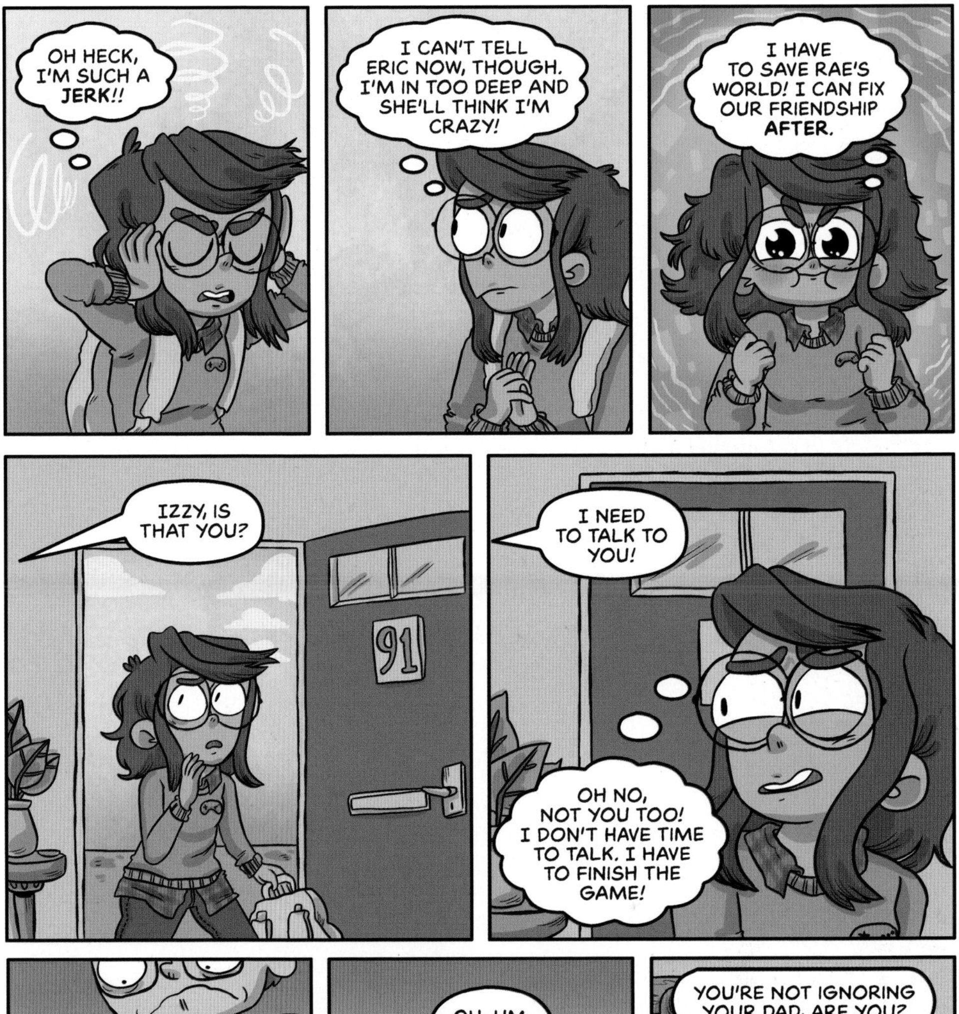
OH HECK, I'M SUCH A JERK!!
I CAN'T TELL ERIC NOW, THOUGH. I'M IN TOO DEEP AND SHE'LL THINK I'M CRAZY!
I HAVE TO SAVE RAE'S WORLD! I CAN FIX OUR FRIENDSHIP AFTER.
IZZY, IS THAT YOU?
91
I NEED TO TALK TO YOU!
OH NO, NOT YOU TOO! I DON'T HAVE TIME TO TALK. I HAVE TO FINISH THE GAME!
BOOMF!
OH, UM, HEY.
YOU'RE NOT IGNORING YOUR DAD, ARE YOU?
WHO?? DAD?? NOOOOOOO?

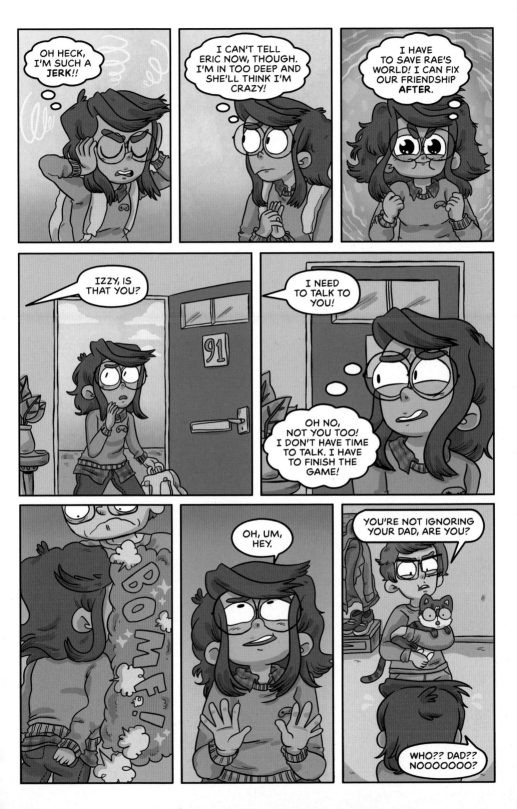

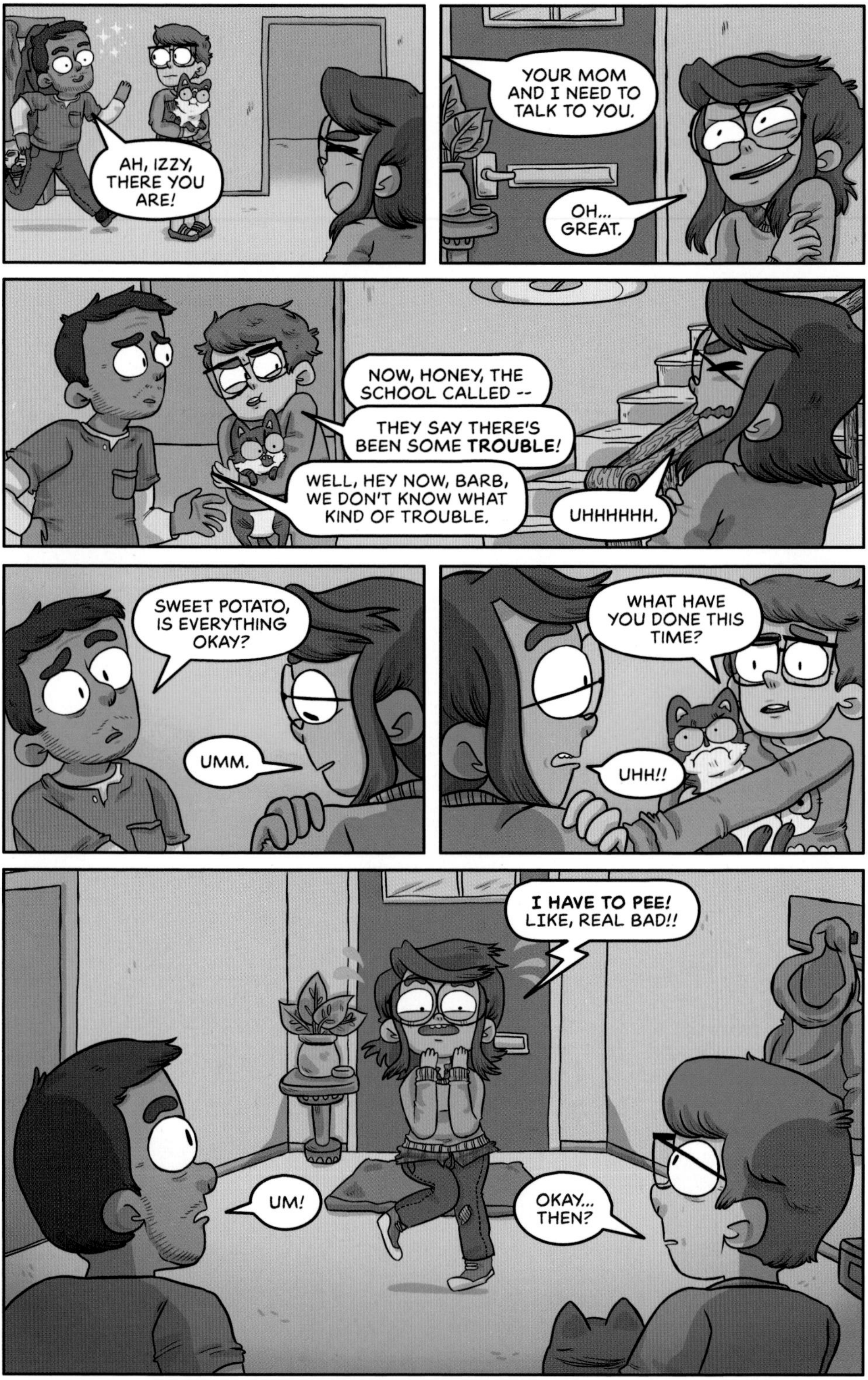
AH, IZZY, THERE YOU ARE!
YOUR MOM AND I NEED TO TALK TO YOU.
OH... GREAT.
NOW, HONEY, THE SCHOOL CALLED --
THEY SAY THERE'S BEEN SOME **TROUBLE**!
WELL, HEY NOW, BARB, WE DON'T KNOW WHAT KIND OF TROUBLE.
UHHHHHH.
SWEET POTATO, IS EVERYTHING OKAY?
UMM.
WHAT HAVE YOU DONE THIS TIME?
UHH!!
I HAVE TO PEE! LIKE, REAL BAD!!
UM!
OKAY... THEN?

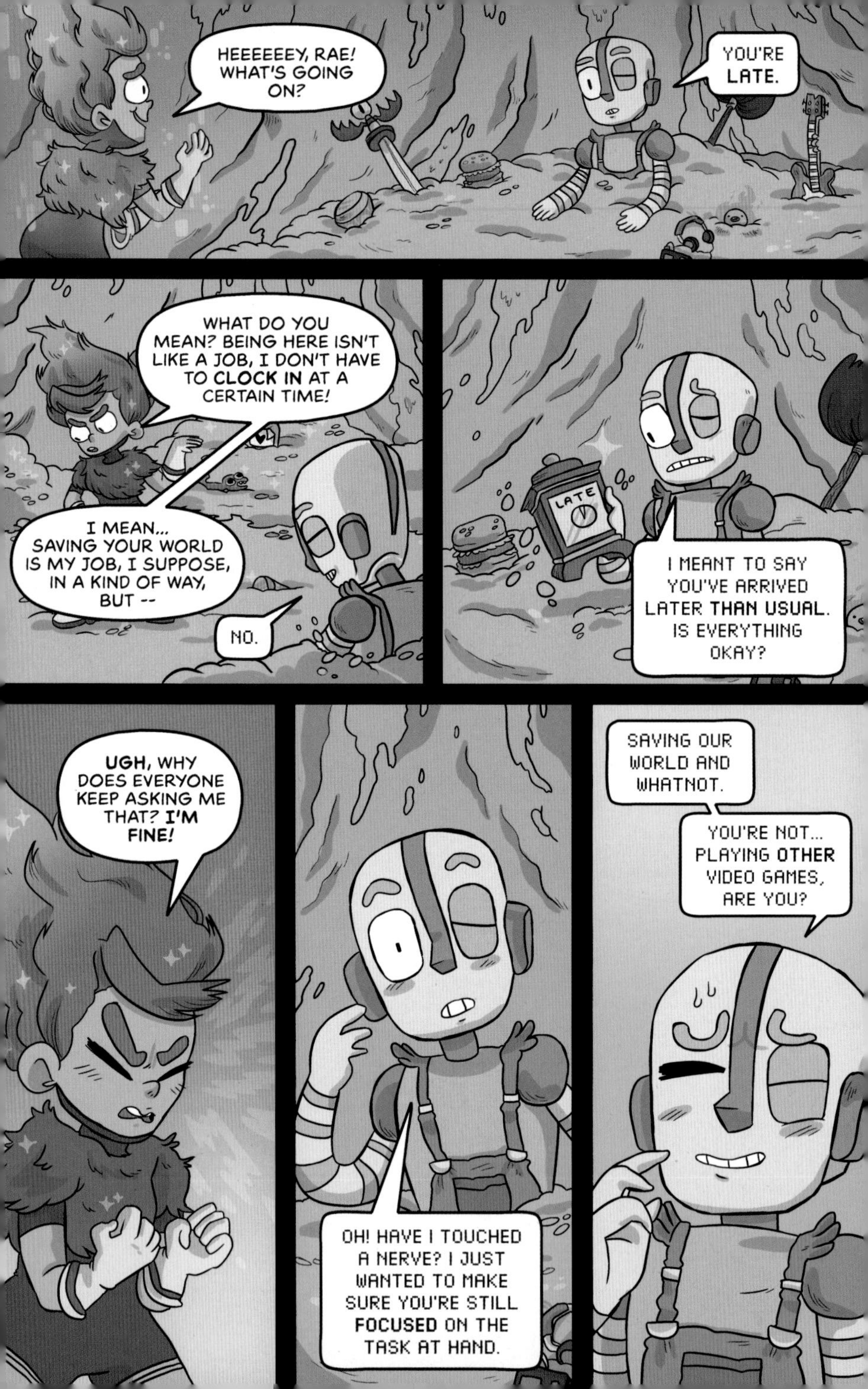
HEEEEEEY, RAE! WHAT'S GOING ON?
YOU'RE LATE.
WHAT DO YOU MEAN? BEING HERE ISN'T LIKE A JOB, I DON'T HAVE TO CLOCK IN AT A CERTAIN TIME!
I MEAN... SAVING YOUR WORLD IS MY JOB, I SUPPOSE, IN A KIND OF WAY, BUT --
NO.
LATE
I MEANT TO SAY YOU'VE ARRIVED LATER THAN USUAL. IS EVERYTHING OKAY?
UGH, WHY DOES EVERYONE KEEP ASKING ME THAT? I'M FINE!
OH! HAVE I TOUCHED A NERVE? I JUST WANTED TO MAKE SURE YOU'RE STILL FOCUSED ON THE TASK AT HAND.
SAVING OUR WORLD AND WHATNOT.
YOU'RE NOT... PLAYING OTHER VIDEO GAMES, ARE YOU?

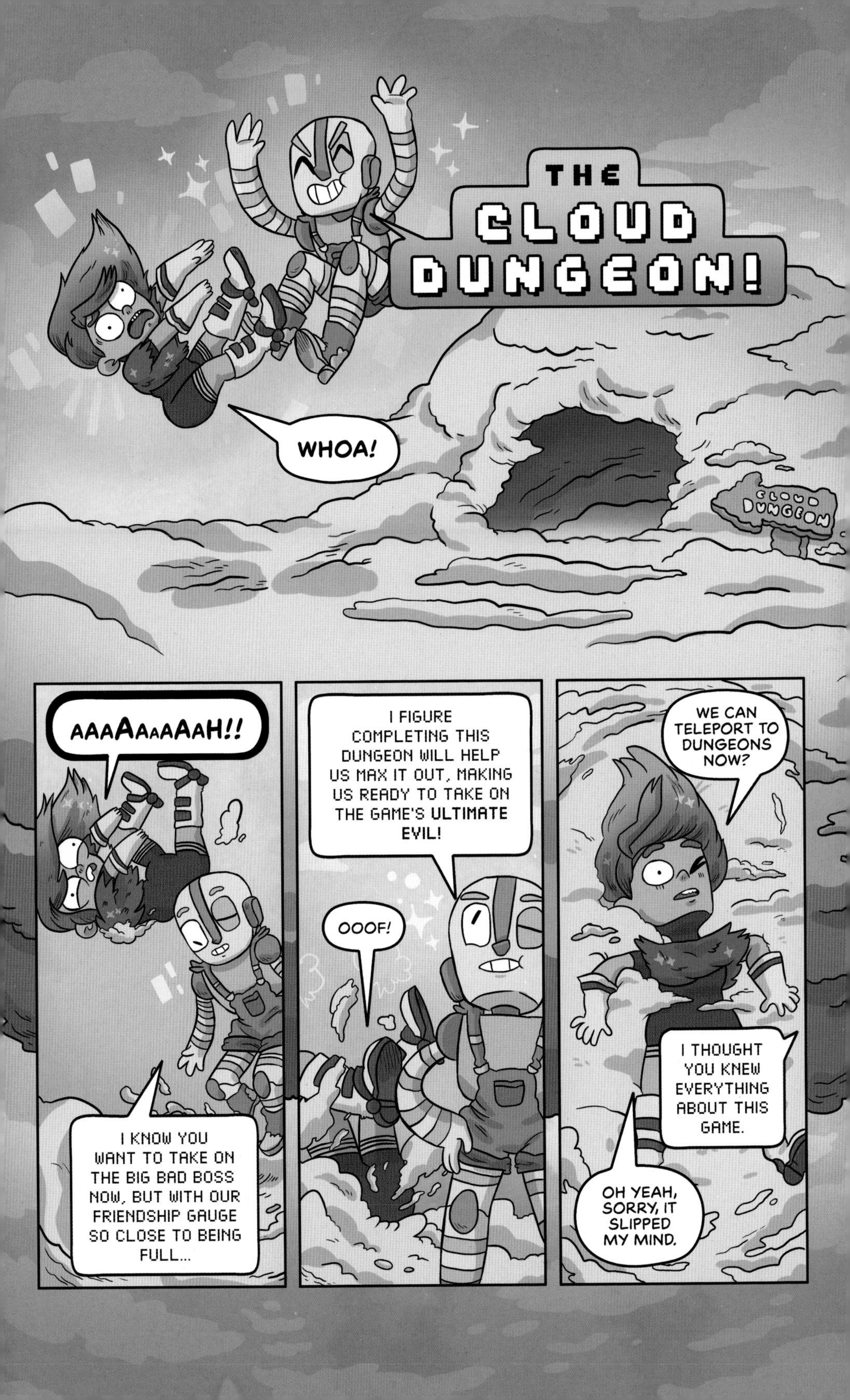
THE CLOUD DUNGEON!
WHOA!
CLOUD DUNGEON
AAAAAAAAAH!!
I KNOW YOU WANT TO TAKE ON THE BIG BAD BOSS NOW, BUT WITH OUR FRIENDSHIP GAUGE SO CLOSE TO BEING FULL...
I FIGURE COMPLETING THIS DUNGEON WILL HELP US MAX IT OUT, MAKING US READY TO TAKE ON THE GAME'S ULTIMATE EVIL!
OOOF!
WE CAN TELEPORT TO DUNGEONS NOW?
I THOUGHT YOU KNEW EVERYTHING ABOUT THIS GAME.
OH YEAH, SORRY, IT SLIPPED MY MIND.

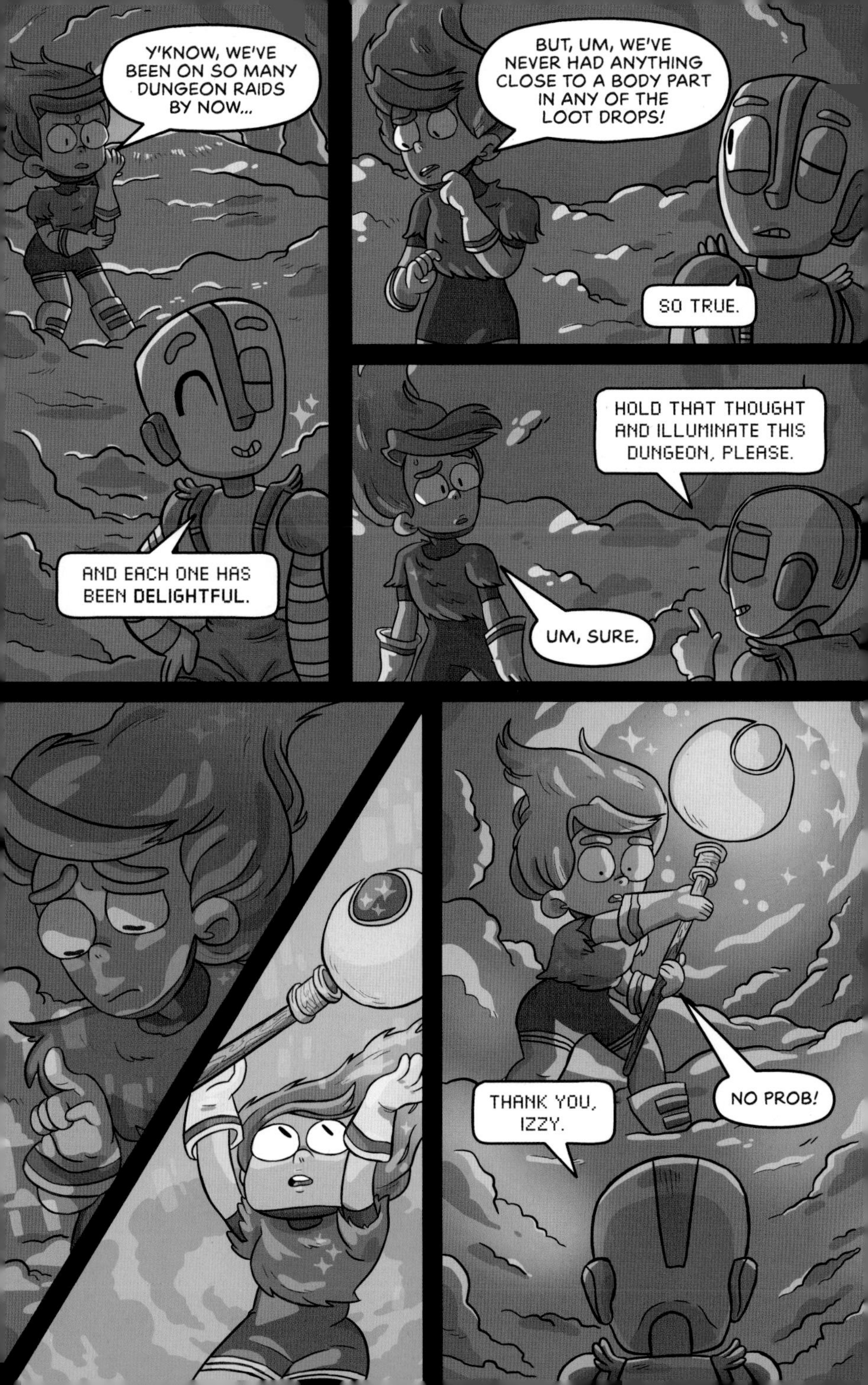

Y'KNOW, WE'VE BEEN ON SO MANY DUNGEON RAIDS BY NOW...
AND EACH ONE HAS BEEN **DELIGHTFUL.**
BUT, UM, WE'VE NEVER HAD ANYTHING CLOSE TO A BODY PART IN ANY OF THE LOOT DROPS!
SO TRUE.
HOLD THAT THOUGHT AND ILLUMINATE THIS DUNGEON, PLEASE.
UM, SURE.
THANK YOU, IZZY.
NO PROB!

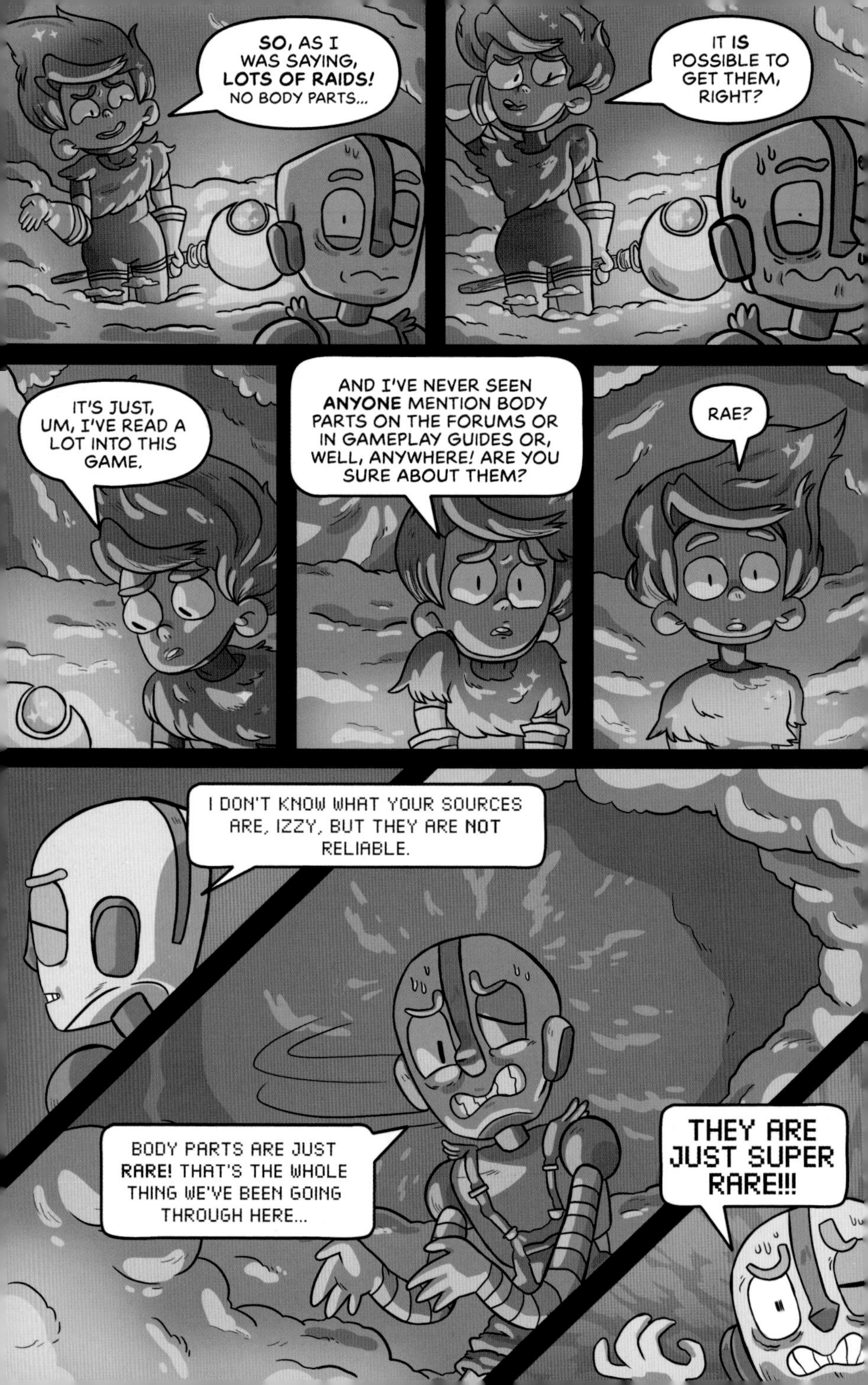
SO, AS I WAS SAYING, LOTS OF RAIDS! NO BODY PARTS...
IT IS POSSIBLE TO GET THEM, RIGHT?
IT'S JUST, UM, I'VE READ A LOT INTO THIS GAME.
AND I'VE NEVER SEEN ANYONE MENTION BODY PARTS ON THE FORUMS OR IN GAMEPLAY GUIDES OR, WELL, ANYWHERE! ARE YOU SURE ABOUT THEM?
RAE?
I DON'T KNOW WHAT YOUR SOURCES ARE, IZZY, BUT THEY ARE NOT RELIABLE.
BODY PARTS ARE JUST RARE! THAT'S THE WHOLE THING WE'VE BEEN GOING THROUGH HERE...
THEY ARE JUST SUPER RARE!!!

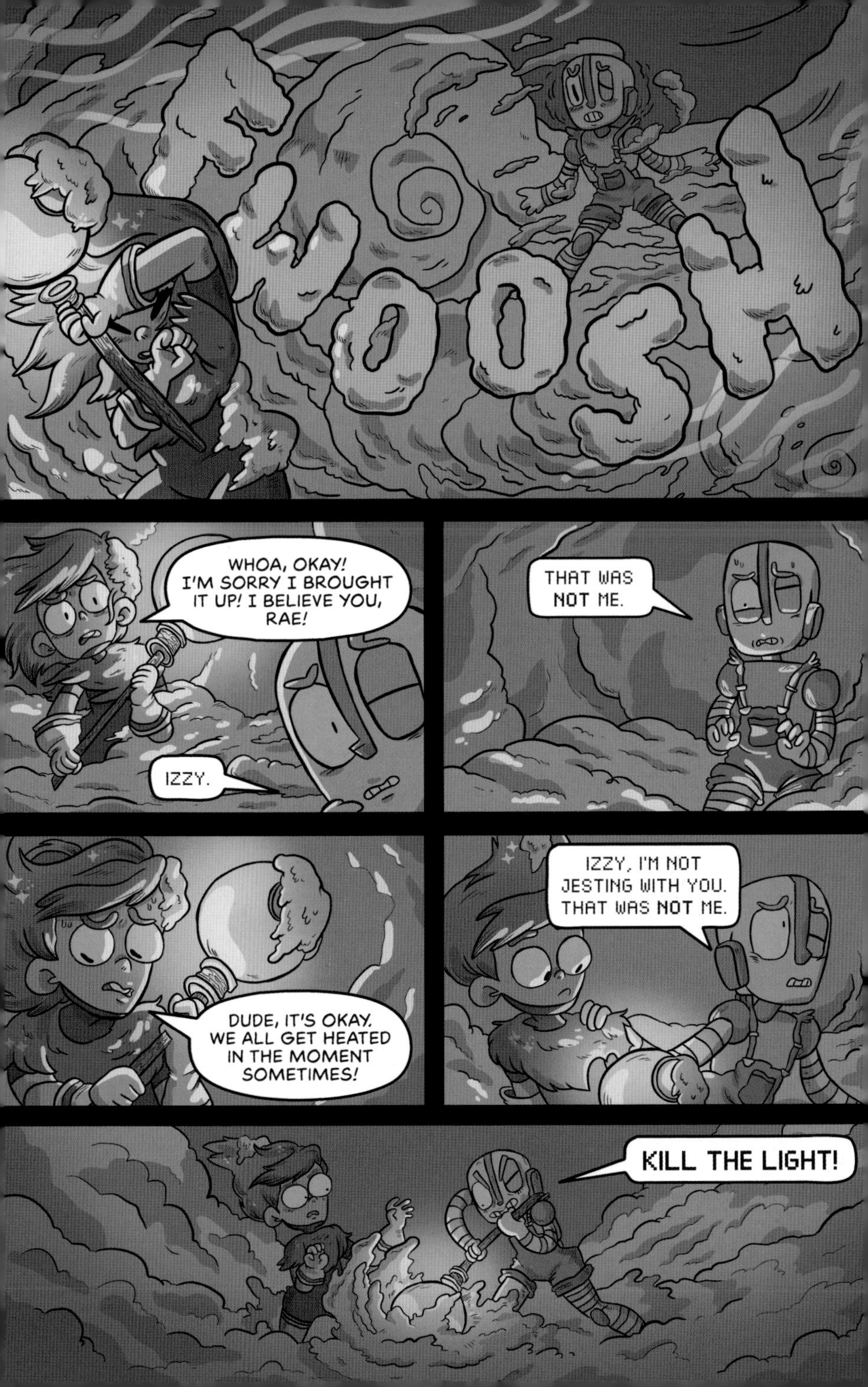
WHOOSH
WHOA, OKAY! I'M SORRY I BROUGHT IT UP! I BELIEVE YOU, RAE!
IZZY.
THAT WAS NOT ME.
DUDE, IT'S OKAY. WE ALL GET HEATED IN THE MOMENT SOMETIMES!
IZZY, I'M NOT JESTING WITH YOU. THAT WAS NOT ME.
KILL THE LIGHT!

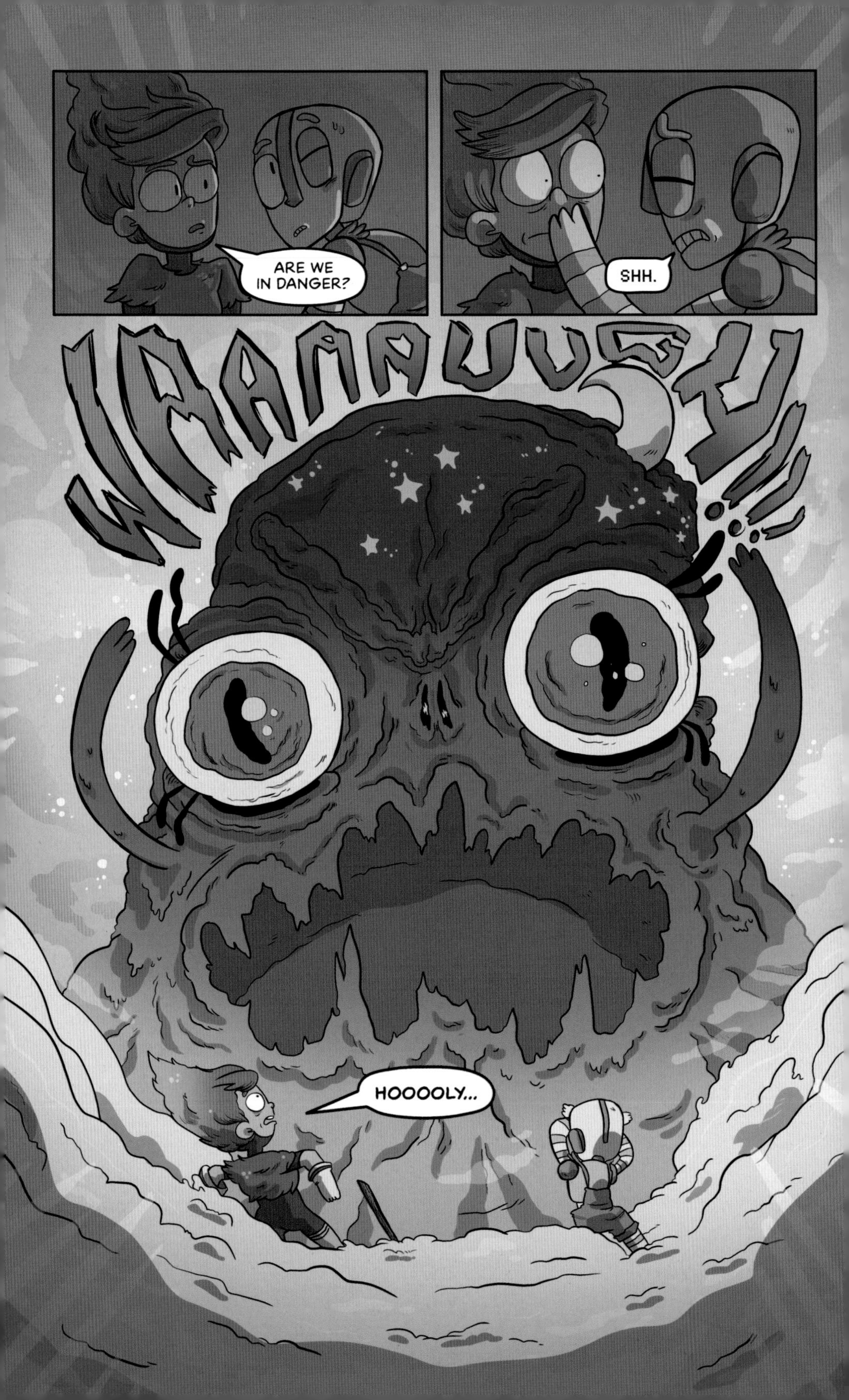
ARE WE IN DANGER?
SHH.
WAAAAUUGH
HOOOOLY...

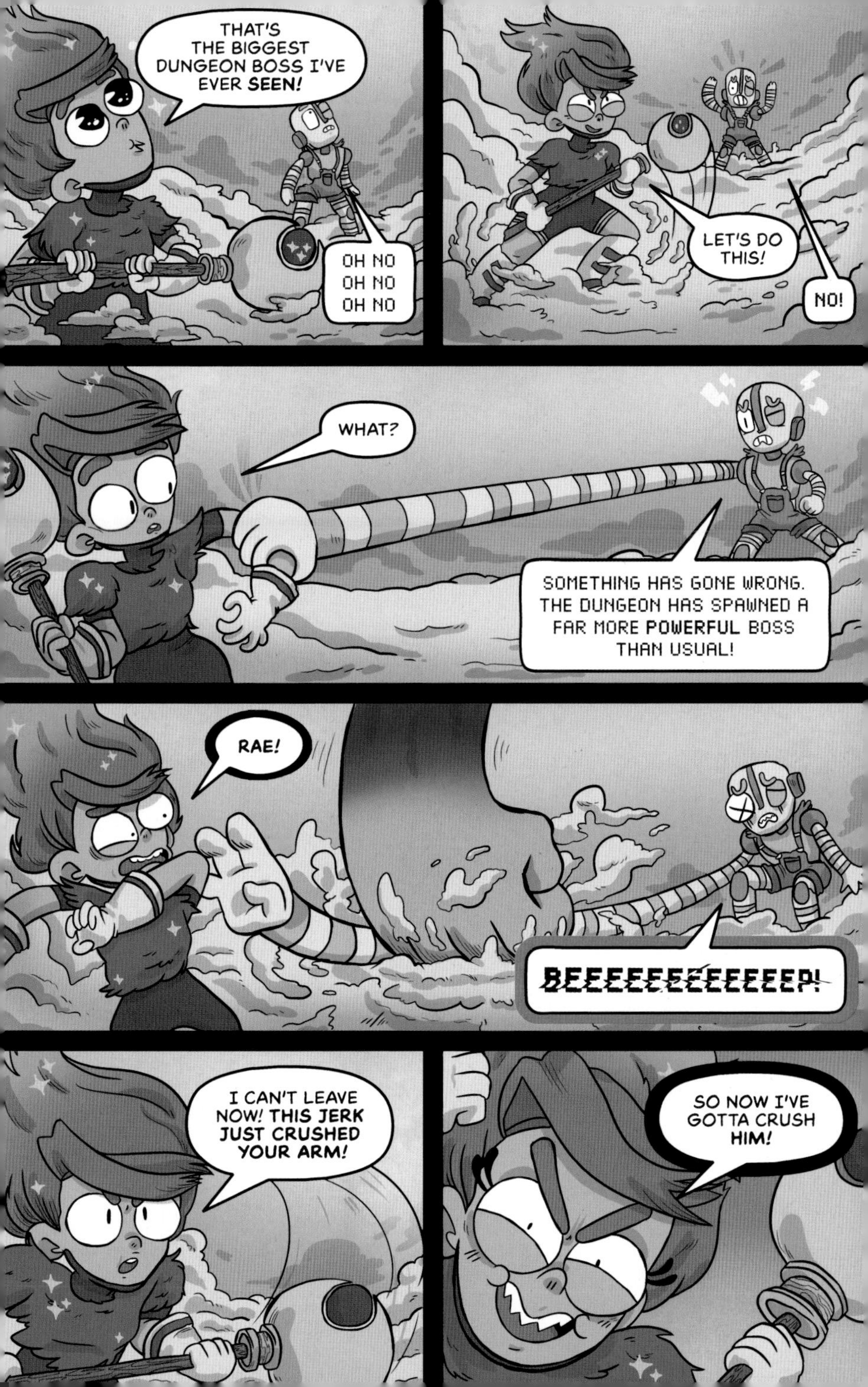

THAT'S THE BIGGEST DUNGEON BOSS I'VE EVER **SEEN!**
OH NO OH NO OH NO
LET'S DO THIS!
NO!
WHAT?
SOMETHING HAS GONE WRONG. THE DUNGEON HAS SPAWNED A FAR MORE **POWERFUL** BOSS THAN USUAL!
RAE!
BEEEEEEEEEEEEEP!
I CAN'T LEAVE NOW! **THIS JERK JUST CRUSHED YOUR ARM!**
SO NOW I'VE GOTTA CRUSH **HIM!**

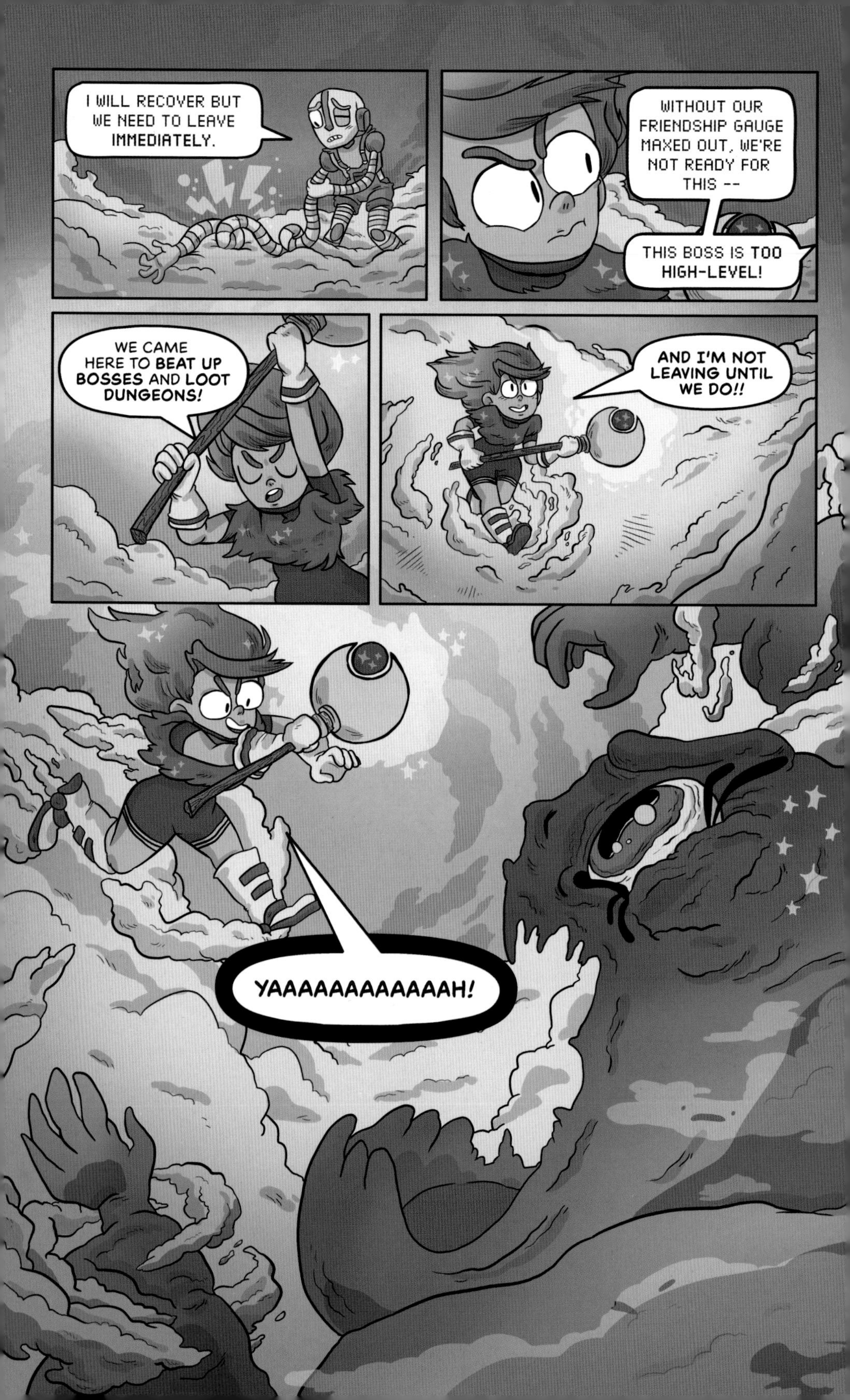
I WILL RECOVER BUT WE NEED TO LEAVE IMMEDIATELY.
WITHOUT OUR FRIENDSHIP GAUGE MAXED OUT, WE'RE NOT READY FOR THIS --
THIS BOSS IS TOO HIGH-LEVEL!
WE CAME HERE TO BEAT UP BOSSES AND LOOT DUNGEONS!
AND I'M NOT LEAVING UNTIL WE DO!!
YAAAAAAAAAAAAH!

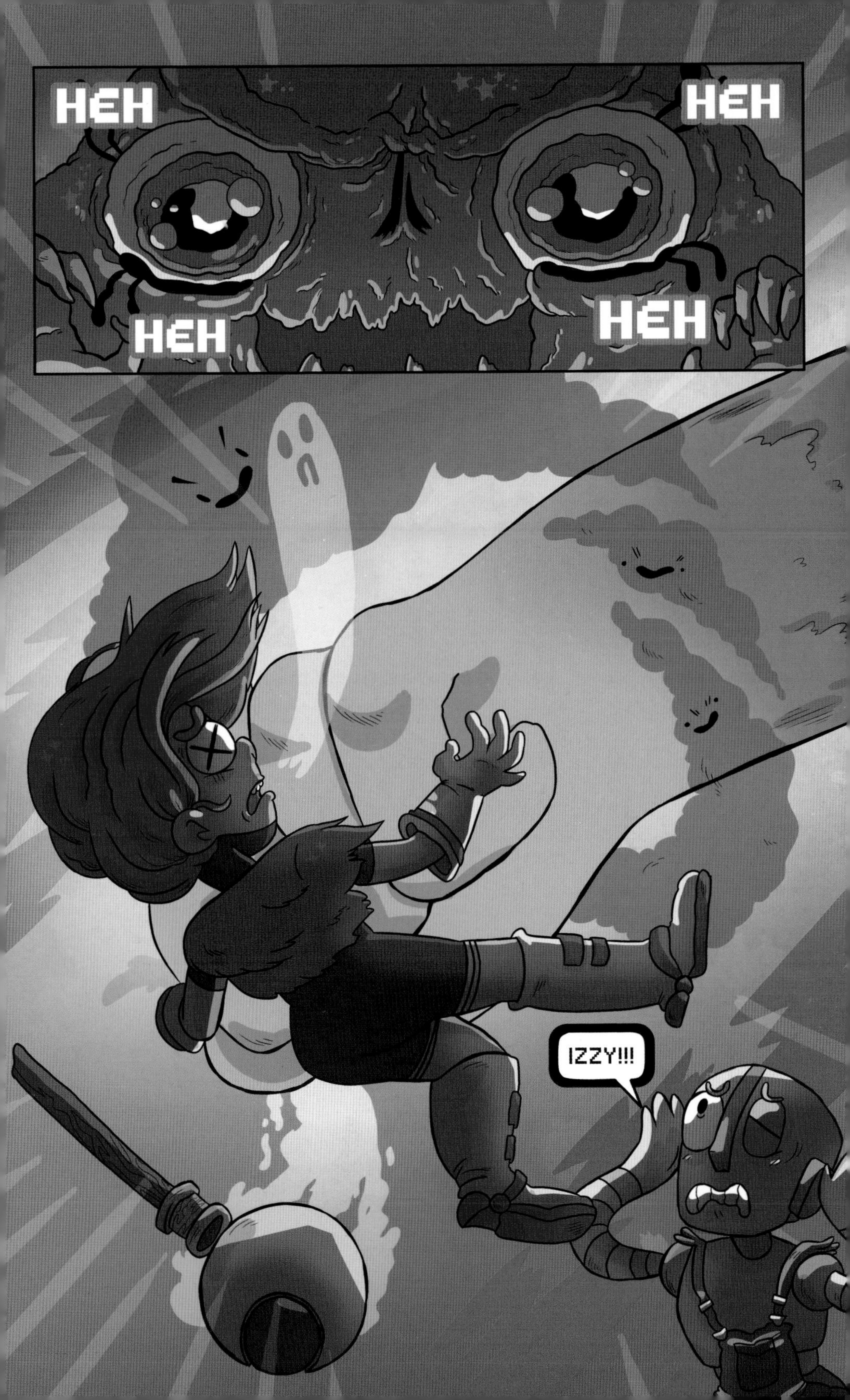
HEH
HEH
HEH
HEH
IZZY!!!

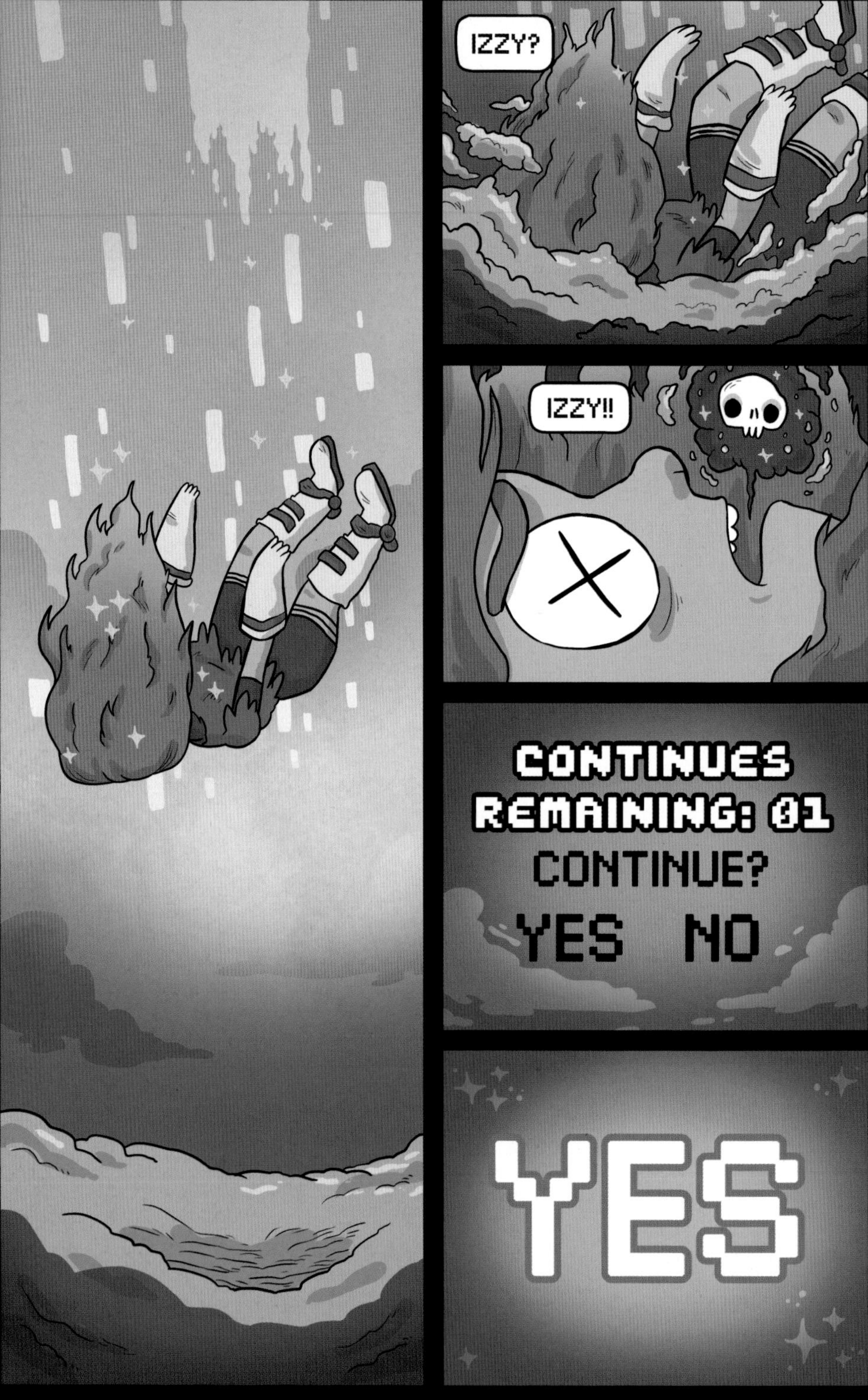
IZZY?
IZZY!!
CONTINUES REMAINING: 01
CONTINUE?
YES NO
YES

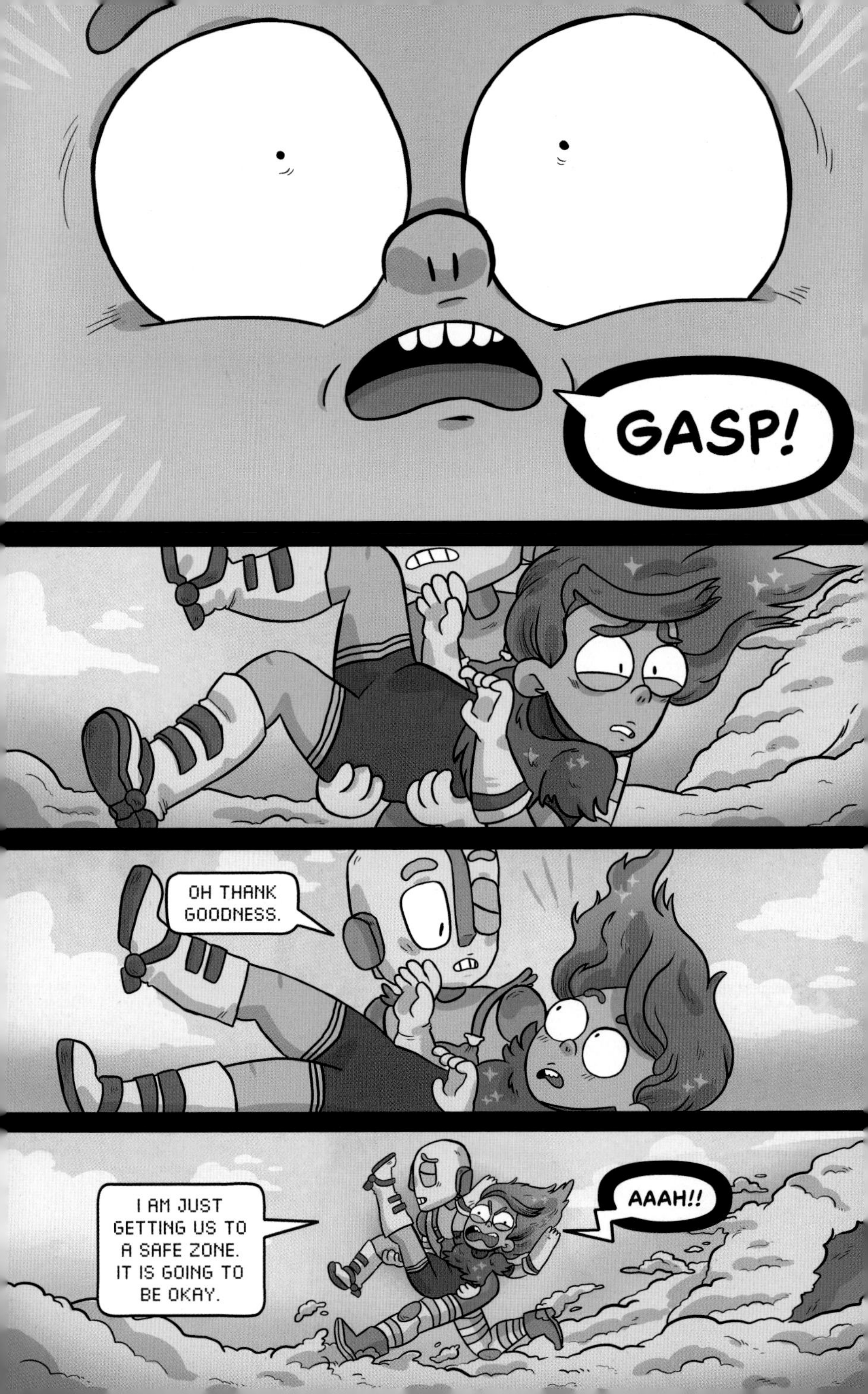
GASP!
OH THANK GOODNESS.
I AM JUST GETTING US TO A SAFE ZONE. IT IS GOING TO BE OKAY.
AAAH!!

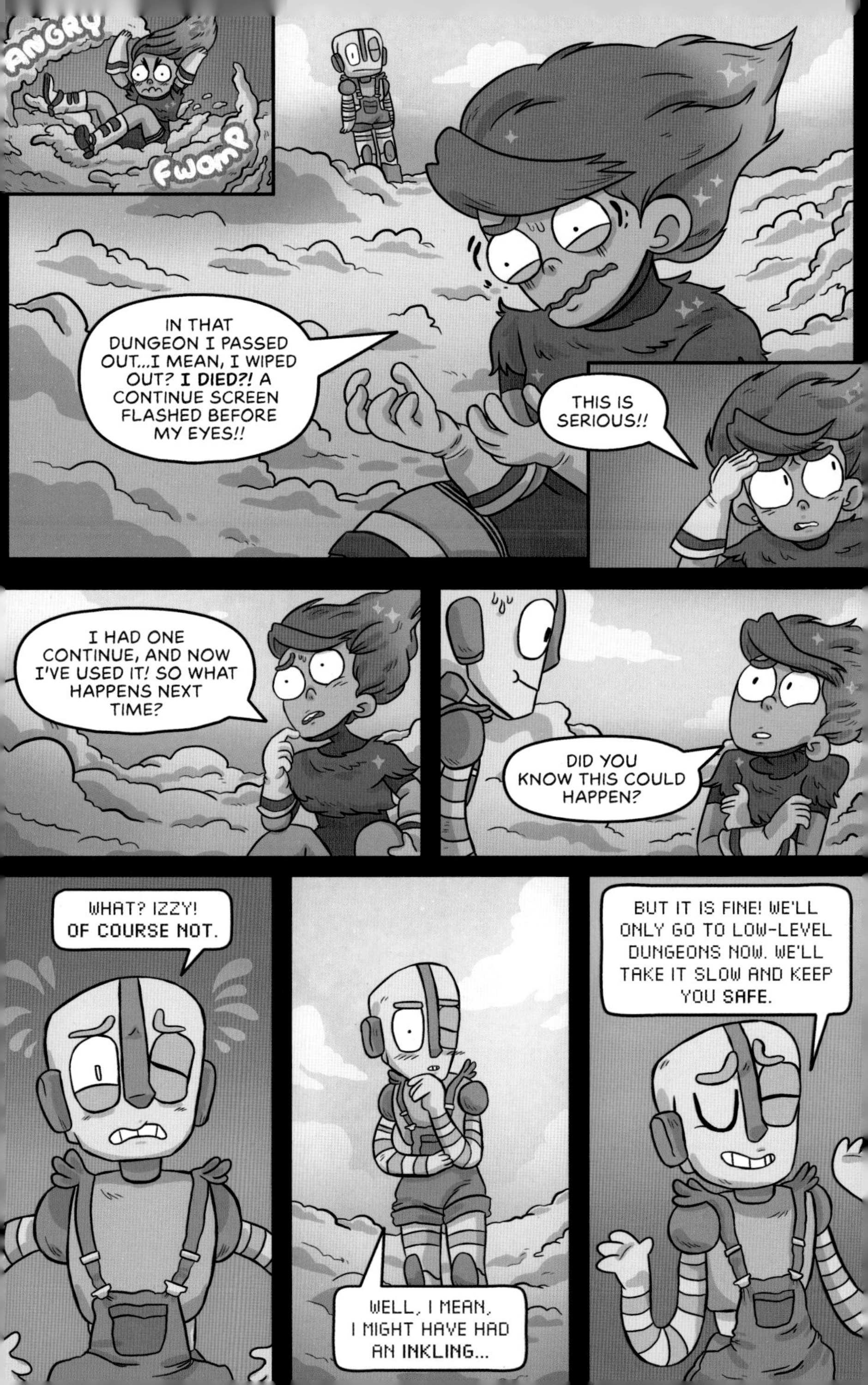
ANGRY
FWOMP
IN THAT DUNGEON I PASSED OUT...I MEAN, I WIPED OUT? I DIED?! A CONTINUE SCREEN FLASHED BEFORE MY EYES!!
THIS IS SERIOUS!!
I HAD ONE CONTINUE, AND NOW I'VE USED IT! SO WHAT HAPPENS NEXT TIME?
DID YOU KNOW THIS COULD HAPPEN?
WHAT? IZZY! OF COURSE NOT.
WELL, I MEAN, I MIGHT HAVE HAD AN INKLING...
BUT IT IS FINE! WE'LL ONLY GO TO LOW-LEVEL DUNGEONS NOW. WE'LL TAKE IT SLOW AND KEEP YOU SAFE.

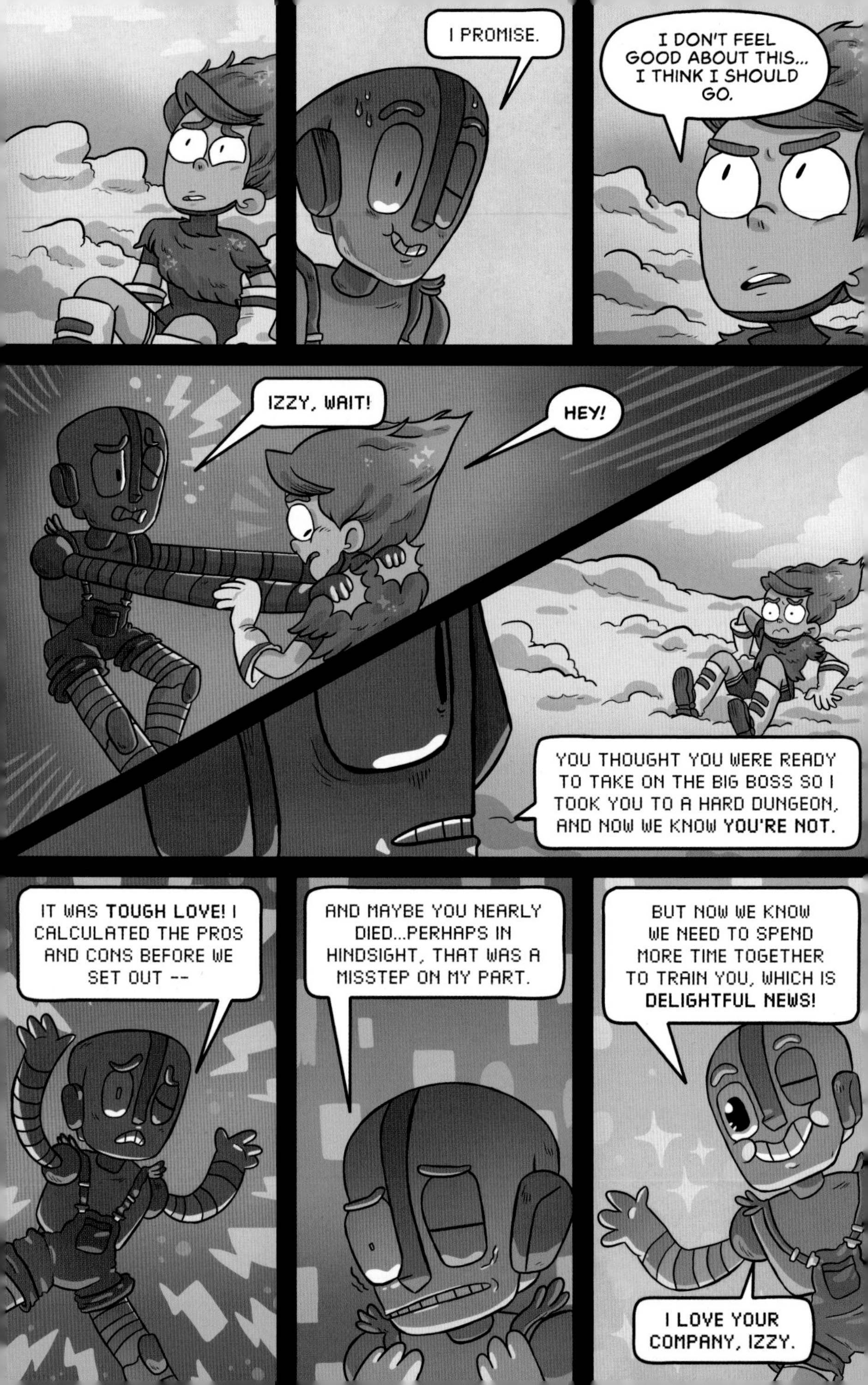
I PROMISE.
I DON'T FEEL GOOD ABOUT THIS... I THINK I SHOULD GO.
IZZY, WAIT!
HEY!
YOU THOUGHT YOU WERE READY TO TAKE ON THE BIG BOSS SO I TOOK YOU TO A HARD DUNGEON, AND NOW WE KNOW YOU'RE NOT.
IT WAS TOUGH LOVE! I CALCULATED THE PROS AND CONS BEFORE WE SET OUT --
AND MAYBE YOU NEARLY DIED...PERHAPS IN HINDSIGHT, THAT WAS A MISSTEP ON MY PART.
BUT NOW WE KNOW WE NEED TO SPEND MORE TIME TOGETHER TO TRAIN YOU, WHICH IS DELIGHTFUL NEWS!
I LOVE YOUR COMPANY, IZZY.

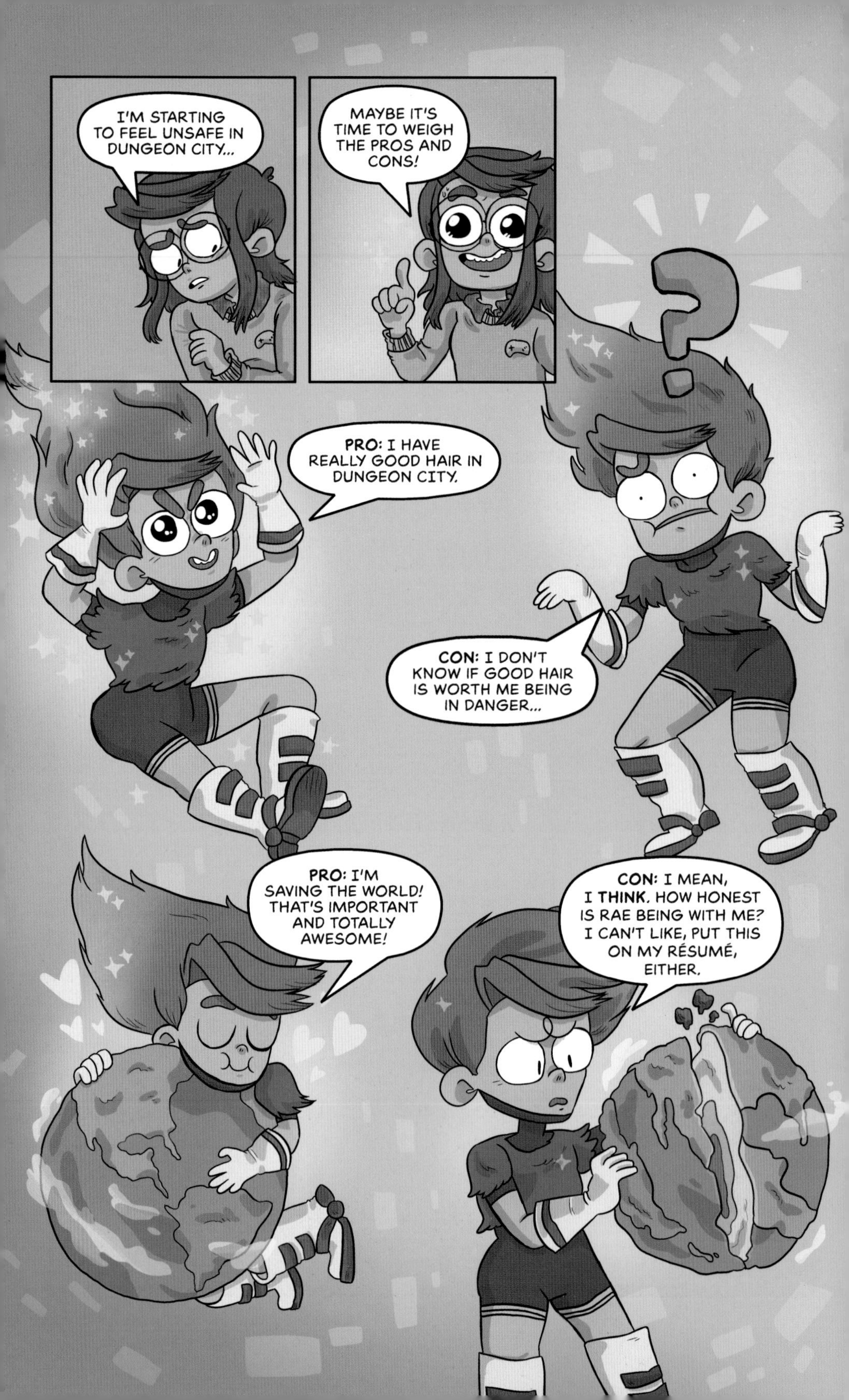
I'M STARTING TO FEEL UNSAFE IN DUNGEON CITY...
MAYBE IT'S TIME TO WEIGH THE PROS AND CONS!
?
PRO: I HAVE REALLY GOOD HAIR IN DUNGEON CITY.
CON: I DON'T KNOW IF GOOD HAIR IS WORTH ME BEING IN DANGER...
PRO: I'M SAVING THE WORLD! THAT'S IMPORTANT AND TOTALLY AWESOME!
CON: I MEAN, I THINK. HOW HONEST IS RAE BEING WITH ME? I CAN'T LIKE, PUT THIS ON MY RÉSUMÉ, EITHER.

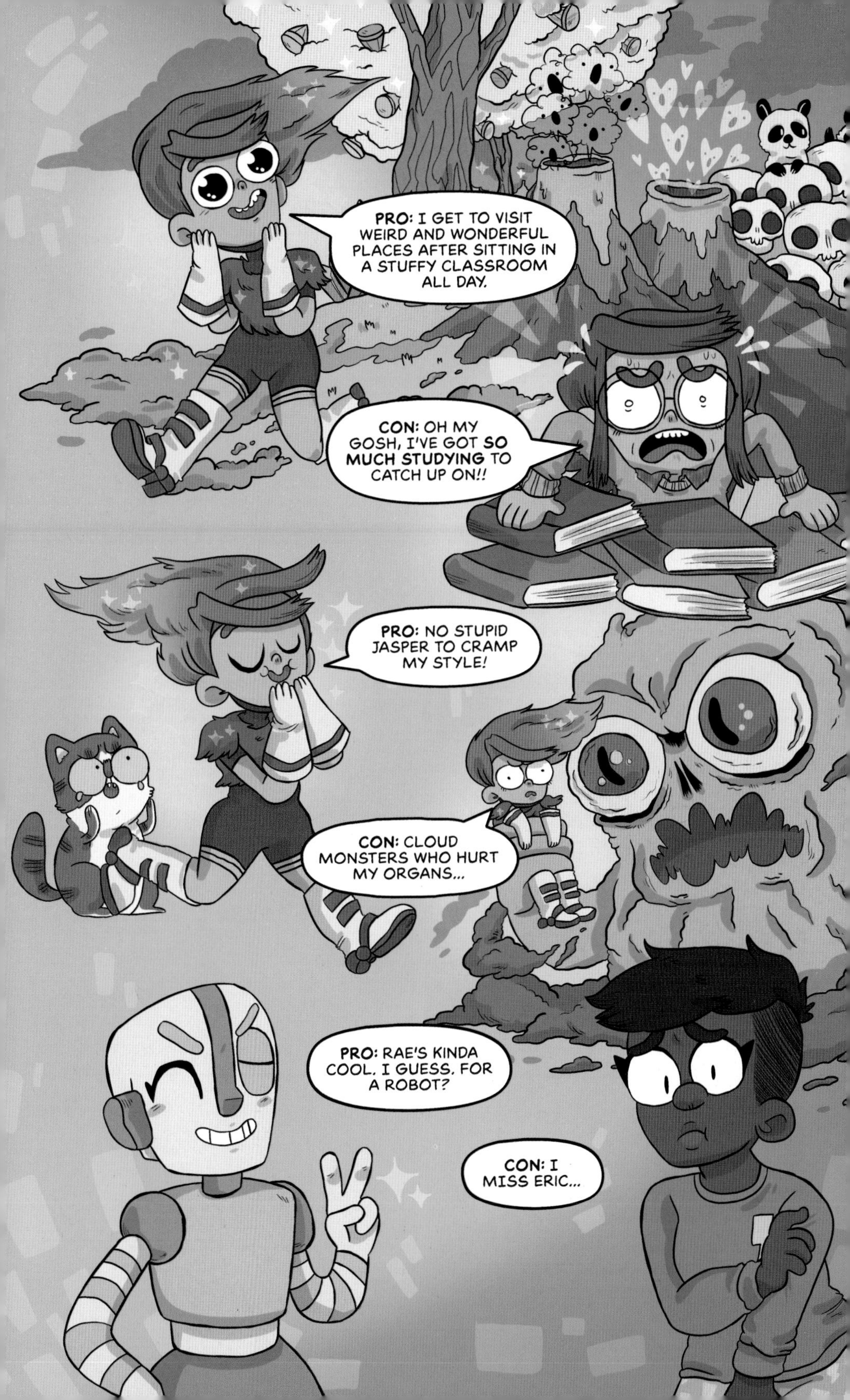
PRO: I GET TO VISIT WEIRD AND WONDERFUL PLACES AFTER SITTING IN A STUFFY CLASSROOM ALL DAY.
CON: OH MY GOSH, I'VE GOT SO MUCH STUDYING TO CATCH UP ON!!
PRO: NO STUPID JASPER TO CRAMP MY STYLE!
CON: CLOUD MONSTERS WHO HURT MY ORGANS...
PRO: RAE'S KINDA COOL. I GUESS. FOR A ROBOT?
CON: I MISS ERIC...

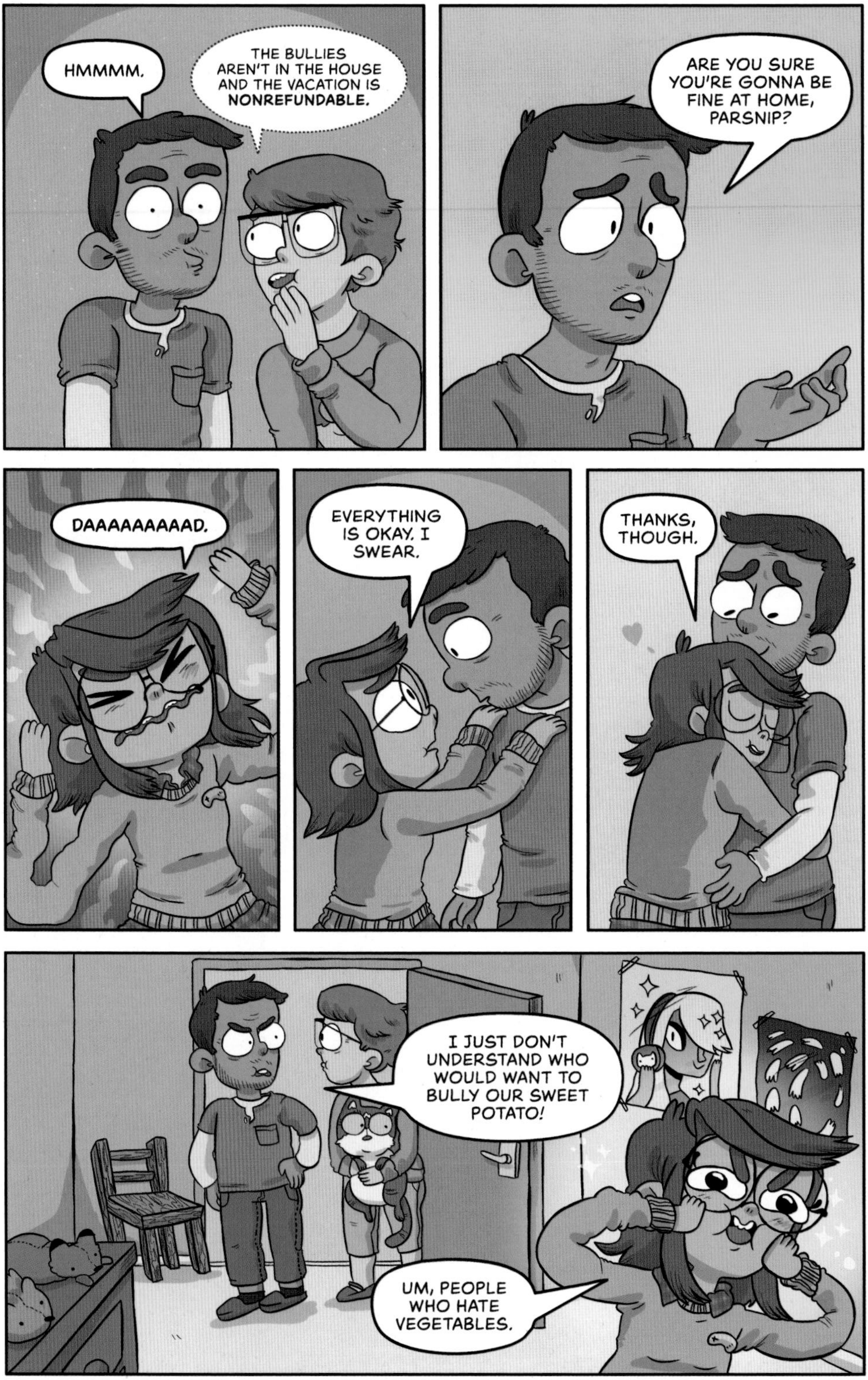
HMMMM.
THE BULLIES AREN'T IN THE HOUSE AND THE VACATION IS NONREFUNDABLE.
ARE YOU SURE YOU'RE GONNA BE FINE AT HOME, PARSNIP?
DAAAAAAAAAD.
EVERYTHING IS OKAY. I SWEAR.
THANKS, THOUGH.
I JUST DON'T UNDERSTAND WHO WOULD WANT TO BULLY OUR SWEET POTATO!
UM, PEOPLE WHO HATE VEGETABLES.

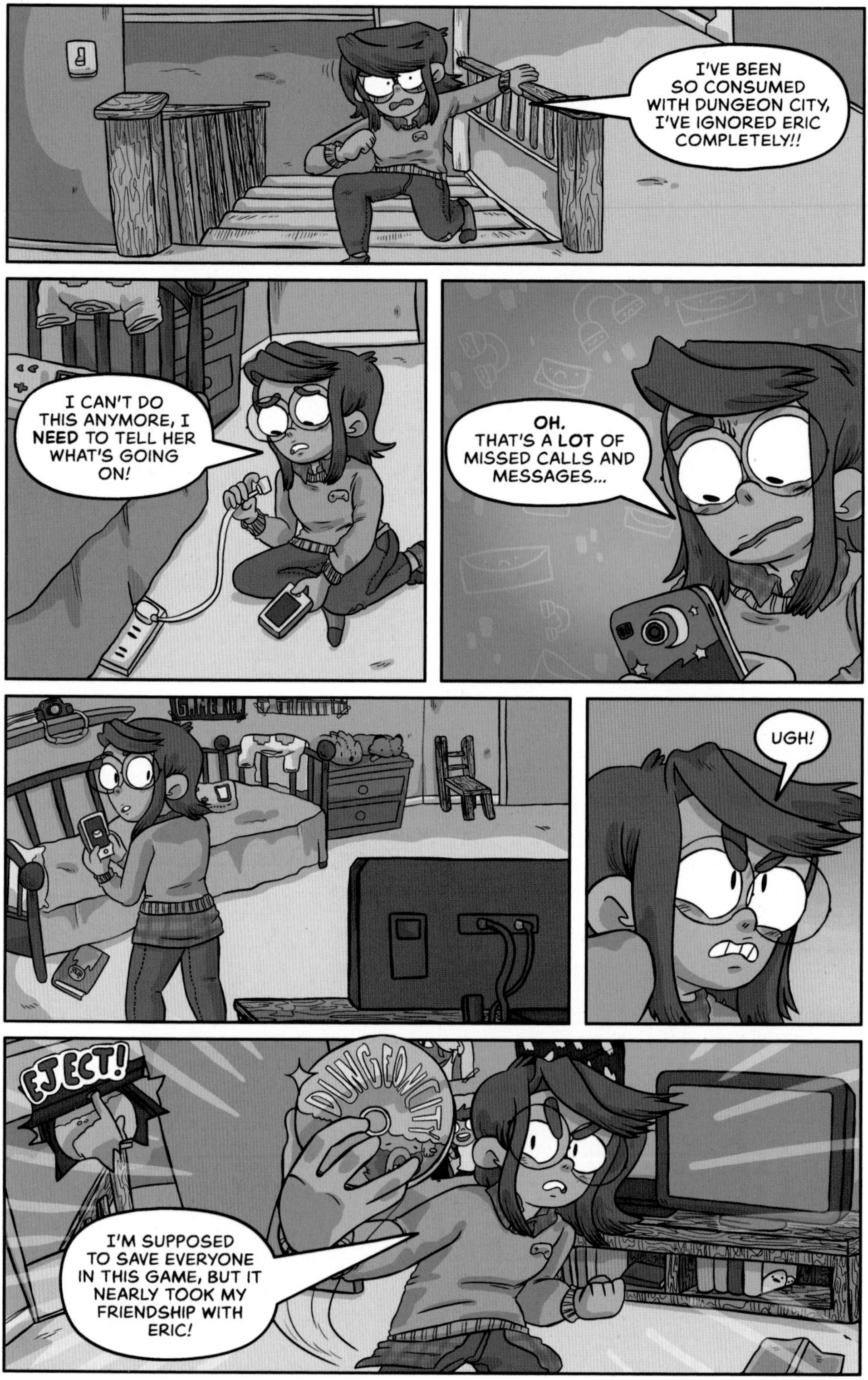
I'VE BEEN SO CONSUMED WITH DUNGEON CITY, I'VE IGNORED ERIC COMPLETELY!!
I CAN'T DO THIS ANYMORE, I **NEED** TO TELL HER WHAT'S GOING ON!
OH. THAT'S A **LOT** OF MISSED CALLS AND MESSAGES...
UGH!
EJECT!
DUNGEON CITY
I'M SUPPOSED TO SAVE EVERYONE IN THIS GAME, BUT IT NEARLY TOOK MY FRIENDSHIP WITH ERIC!

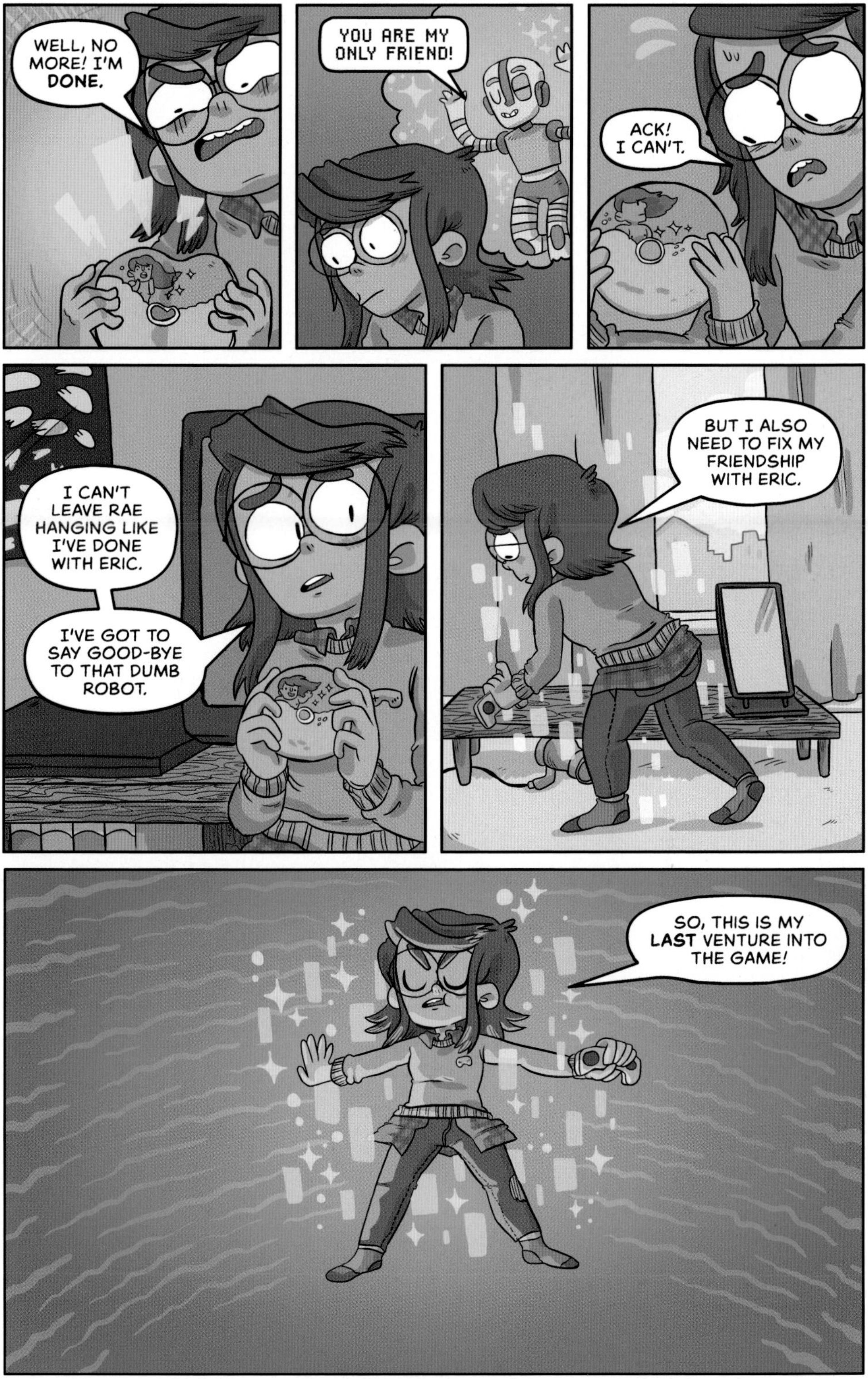
WELL, NO MORE! I'M DONE.
YOU ARE MY ONLY FRIEND!
ACK! I CAN'T.
I CAN'T LEAVE RAE HANGING LIKE I'VE DONE WITH ERIC.
I'VE GOT TO SAY GOOD-BYE TO THAT DUMB ROBOT.
BUT I ALSO NEED TO FIX MY FRIENDSHIP WITH ERIC.
SO, THIS IS MY LAST VENTURE INTO THE GAME!

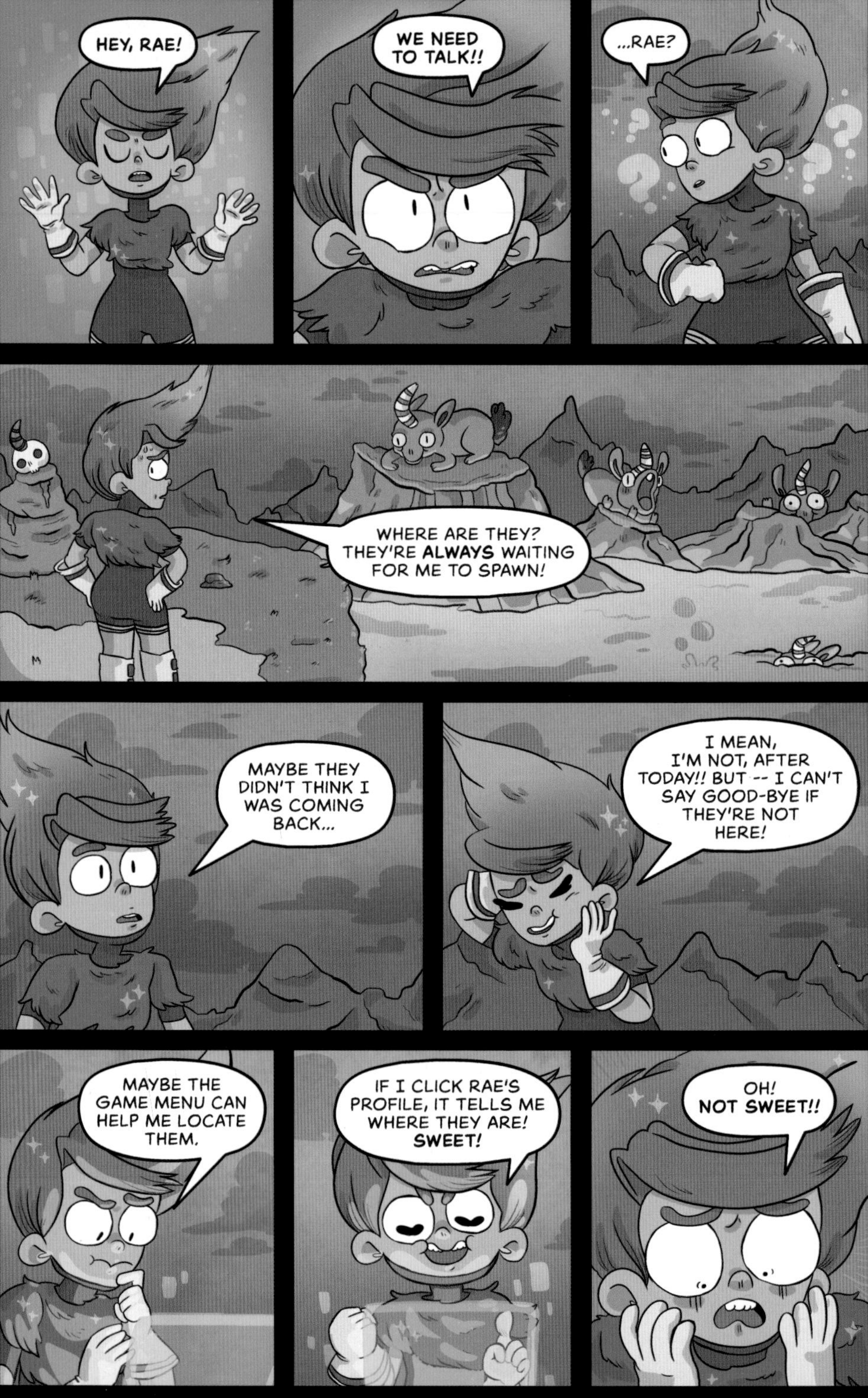
HEY, RAE!
WE NEED TO TALK!!
...RAE?
WHERE ARE THEY? THEY'RE **ALWAYS** WAITING FOR ME TO SPAWN!
MAYBE THEY DIDN'T THINK I WAS COMING BACK...
I MEAN, I'M NOT, AFTER TODAY!! BUT -- I CAN'T SAY GOOD-BYE IF THEY'RE NOT HERE!
MAYBE THE GAME MENU CAN HELP ME LOCATE THEM.
IF I CLICK RAE'S PROFILE, IT TELLS ME WHERE THEY ARE! **SWEET!**
OH! **NOT SWEET!!**

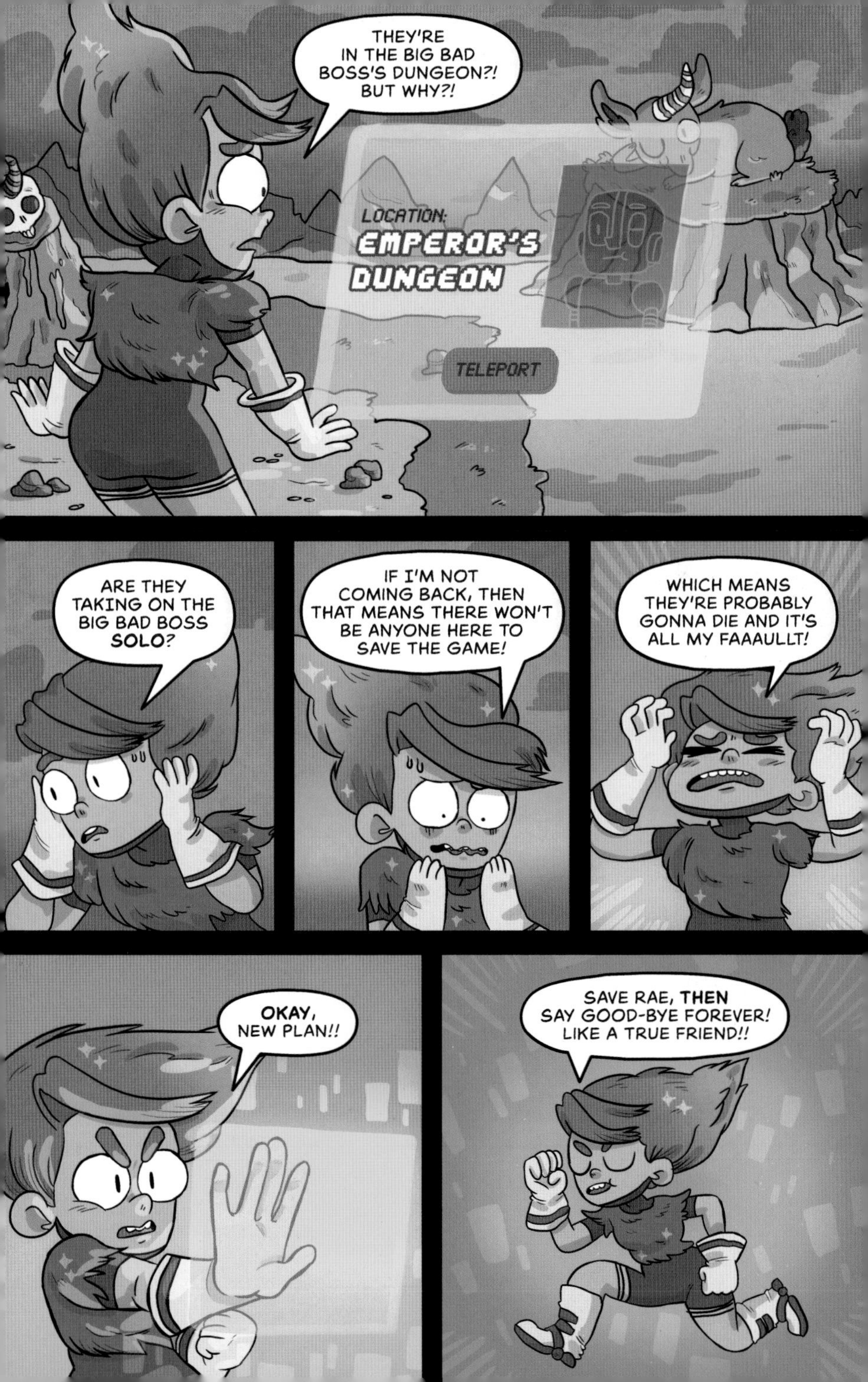
THEY'RE IN THE BIG BAD BOSS'S DUNGEON?! BUT WHY?!
LOCATION:
EMPEROR'S DUNGEON
TELEPORT
ARE THEY TAKING ON THE BIG BAD BOSS **SOLO**?
IF I'M NOT COMING BACK, THEN THAT MEANS THERE WON'T BE ANYONE HERE TO SAVE THE GAME!
WHICH MEANS THEY'RE PROBABLY GONNA DIE AND IT'S ALL MY FAAAULLT!
OKAY, NEW PLAN!!
SAVE RAE, **THEN** SAY GOOD-BYE FOREVER! LIKE A TRUE FRIEND!!

EEEEEEEEEEEEEEEEEEEEEEEEEEEEEEP!

IT'S SO BIG! AND HAUNTING! AND...

STILL? IS THAT THING MOVING?! IS IT EVEN ALIVE?! WHAT THE HECK.

IF IT'S NOT, THEN...WHO'S MAKING THAT NOISE?

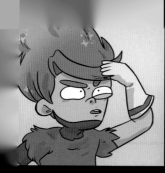

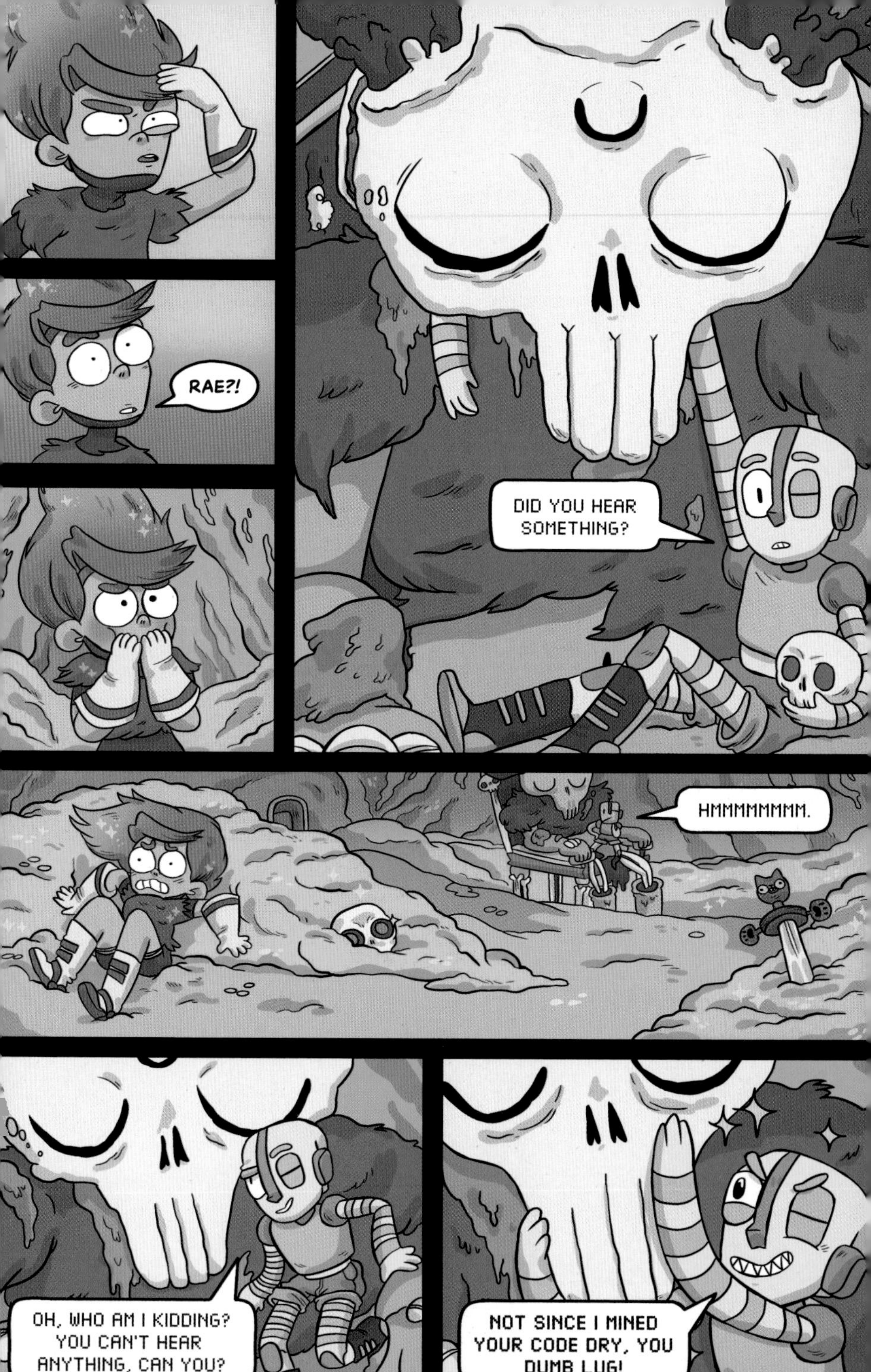
RAE?!
DID YOU HEAR SOMETHING?
HMMMMMMMM.
OH, WHO AM I KIDDING? YOU CAN'T HEAR ANYTHING, CAN YOU?
NOT SINCE I MINED YOUR CODE DRY, YOU DUMB LUG!

113

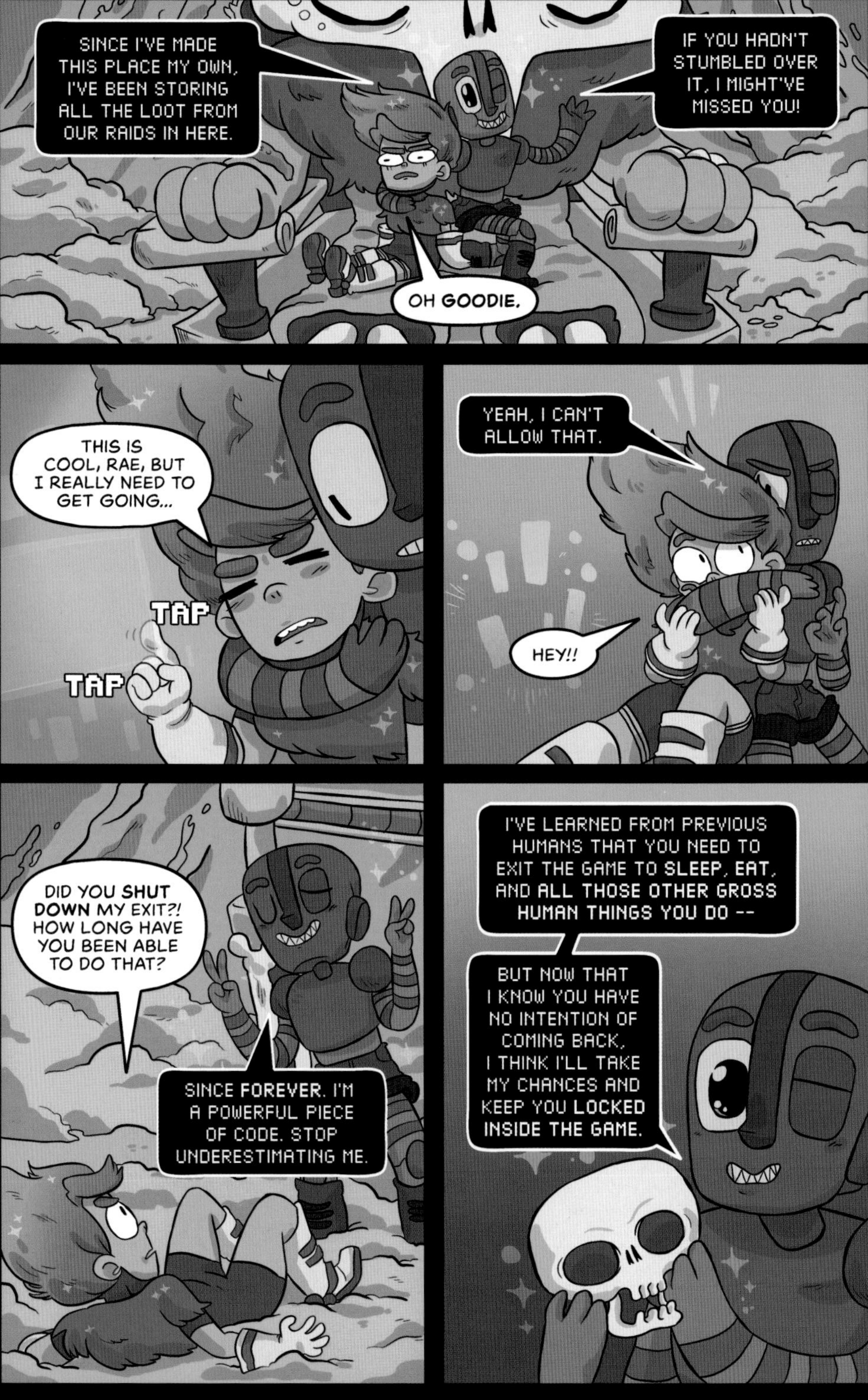

SINCE I'VE MADE THIS PLACE MY OWN, I'VE BEEN STORING ALL THE LOOT FROM OUR RAIDS IN HERE.
IF YOU HADN'T STUMBLED OVER IT, I MIGHT'VE MISSED YOU!
OH **GOODIE.**
THIS IS COOL, RAE, BUT I REALLY NEED TO GET GOING...
TAP
TAP
YEAH, I CAN'T ALLOW THAT.
HEY!!
DID YOU **SHUT DOWN** MY EXIT?! HOW LONG HAVE YOU BEEN ABLE TO DO THAT?
SINCE **FOREVER.** I'M A POWERFUL PIECE OF CODE. STOP UNDERESTIMATING ME.
I'VE LEARNED FROM PREVIOUS HUMANS THAT YOU NEED TO EXIT THE GAME TO **SLEEP, EAT,** AND **ALL THOSE OTHER GROSS HUMAN THINGS YOU DO --**
BUT NOW THAT I KNOW YOU HAVE NO INTENTION OF COMING BACK, I THINK I'LL TAKE MY CHANCES AND KEEP YOU **LOCKED INSIDE THE GAME.**

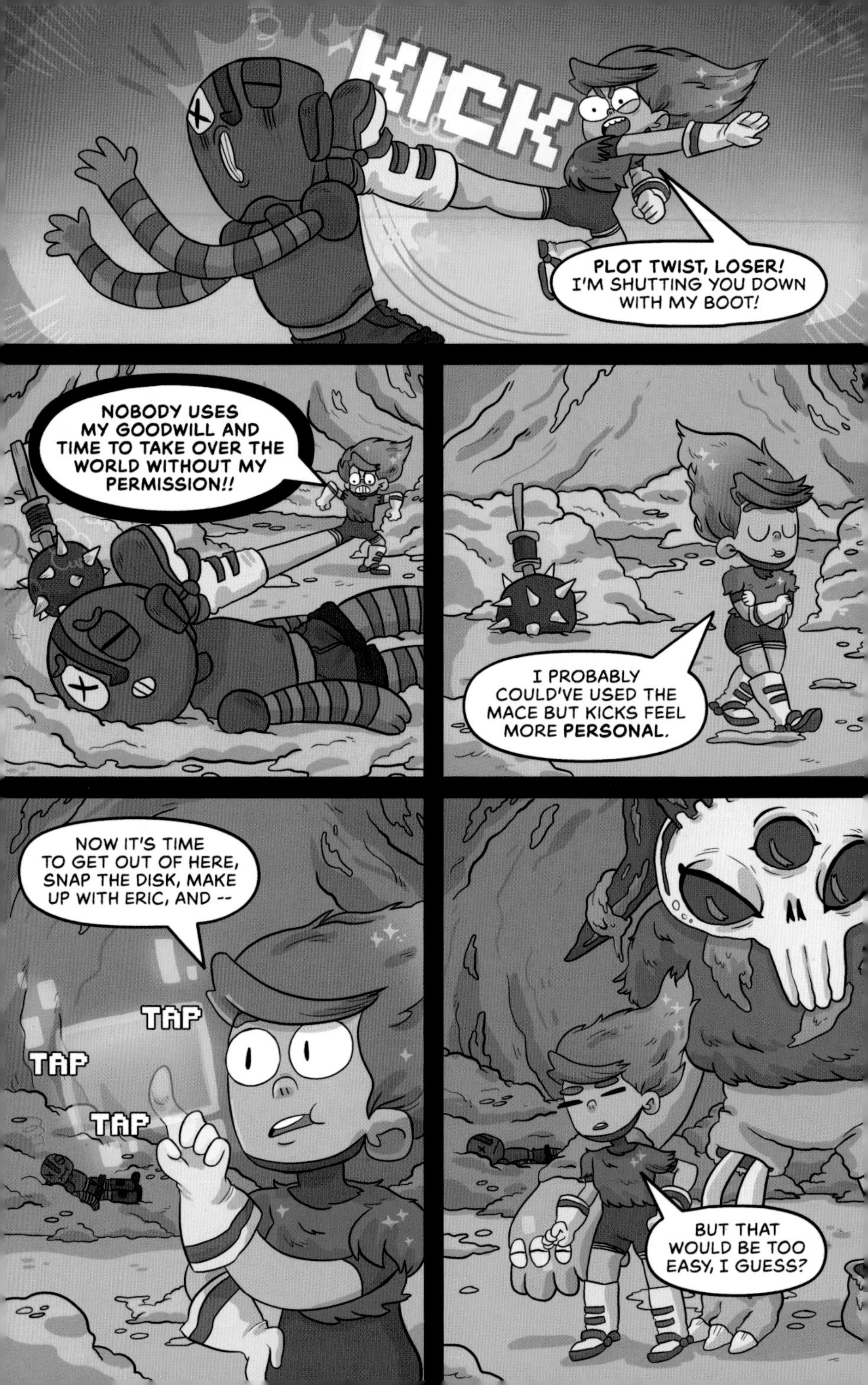
KICK
PLOT TWIST, LOSER! I'M SHUTTING YOU DOWN WITH MY BOOT!
NOBODY USES MY GOODWILL AND TIME TO TAKE OVER THE WORLD WITHOUT MY PERMISSION!!
I PROBABLY COULD'VE USED THE MACE BUT KICKS FEEL MORE **PERSONAL**.
NOW IT'S TIME TO GET OUT OF HERE, SNAP THE DISK, MAKE UP WITH ERIC, AND --
TAP
TAP
TAP
BUT THAT WOULD BE TOO EASY, I GUESS?

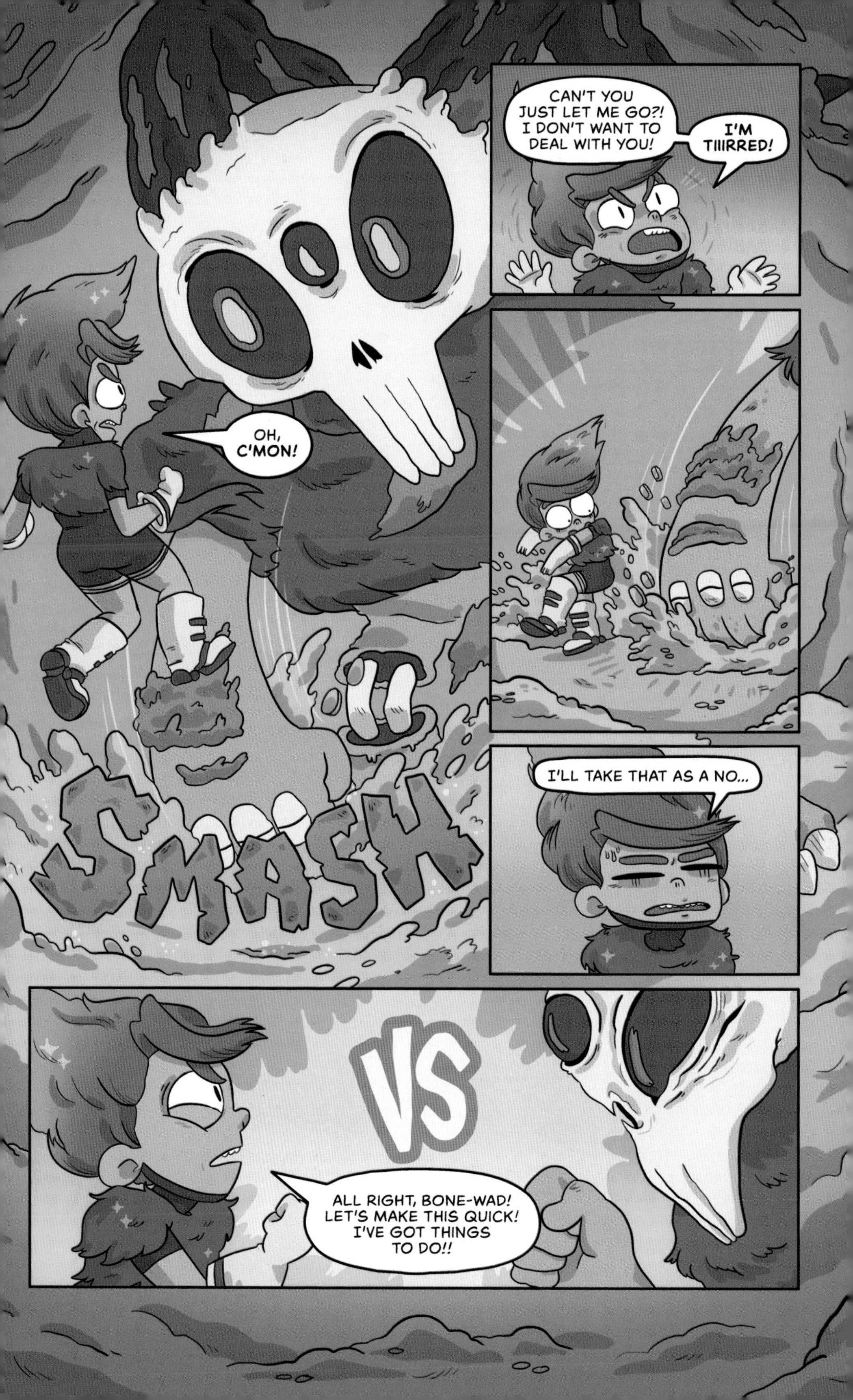
OH, C'MON!
SMASH
CAN'T YOU JUST LET ME GO?! I DON'T WANT TO DEAL WITH YOU!
I'M TIIIRRED!
I'LL TAKE THAT AS A NO...
VS
ALL RIGHT, BONE-WAD! LET'S MAKE THIS QUICK! I'VE GOT THINGS TO DO!!

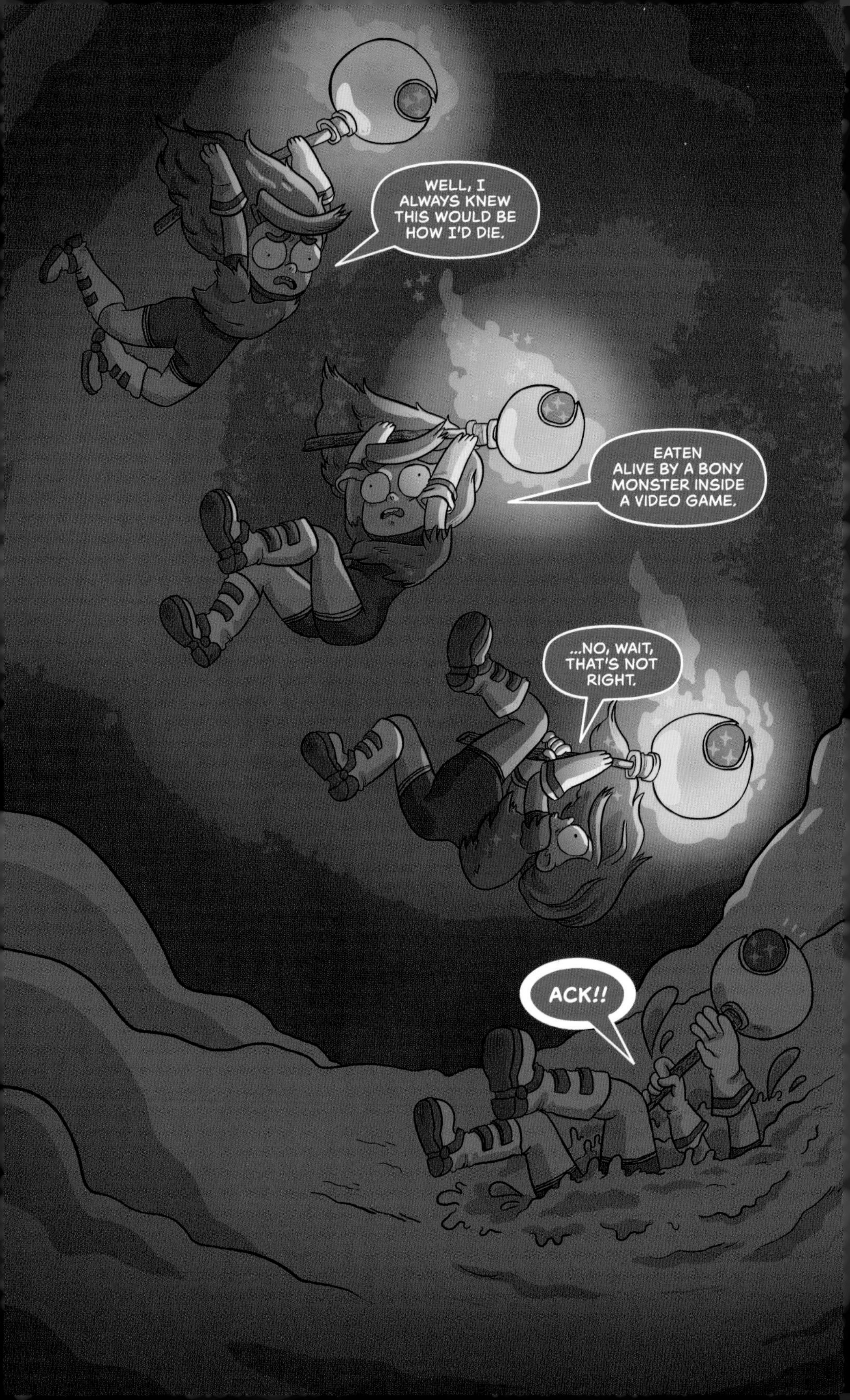
WELL, I ALWAYS KNEW THIS WOULD BE HOW I'D DIE.
EATEN ALIVE BY A BONY MONSTER INSIDE A VIDEO GAME.
...NO, WAIT, THAT'S NOT RIGHT.
ACK!!

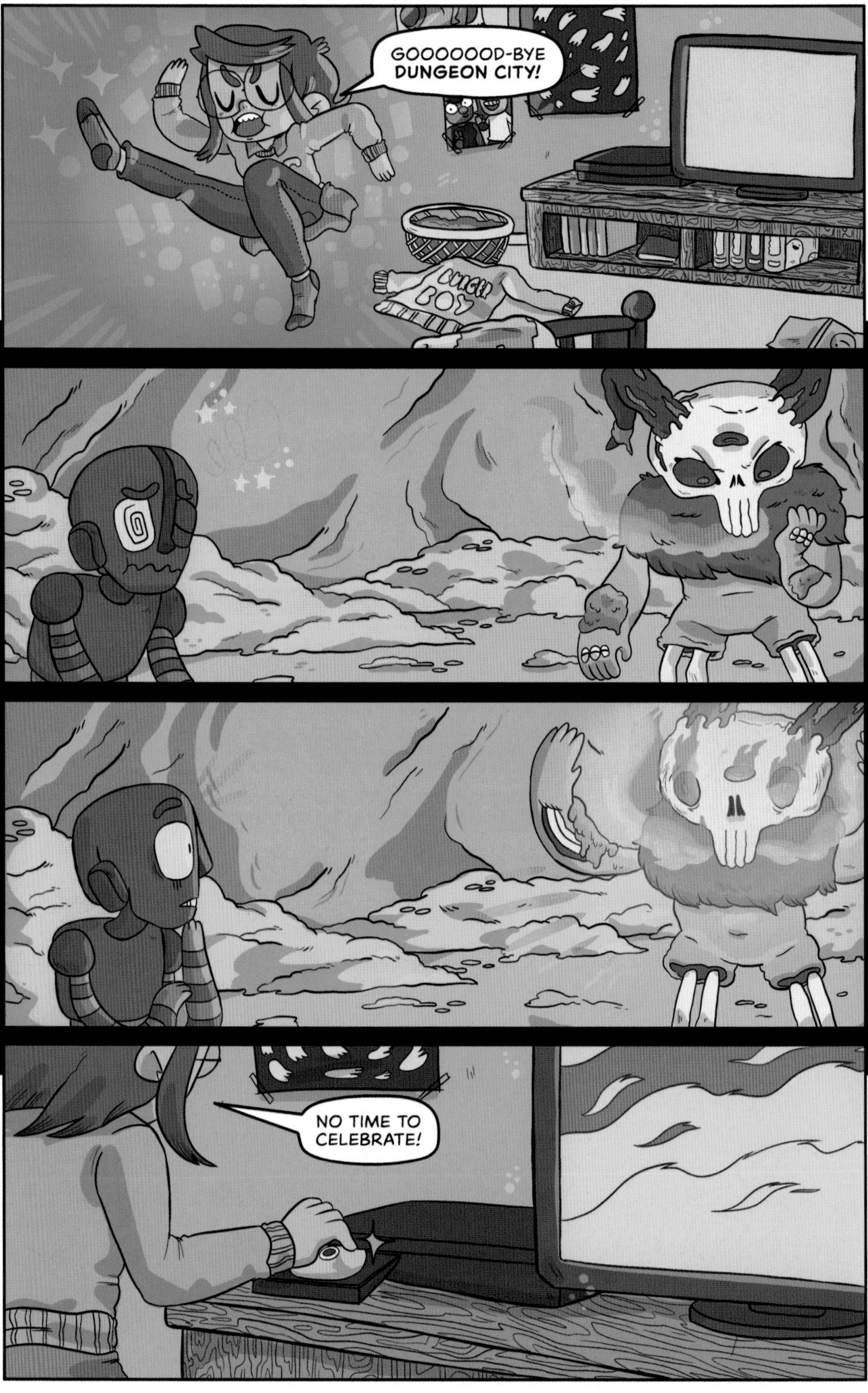
GOOOOOOD-BYE DUNGEON CITY!
NO TIME TO CELEBRATE!

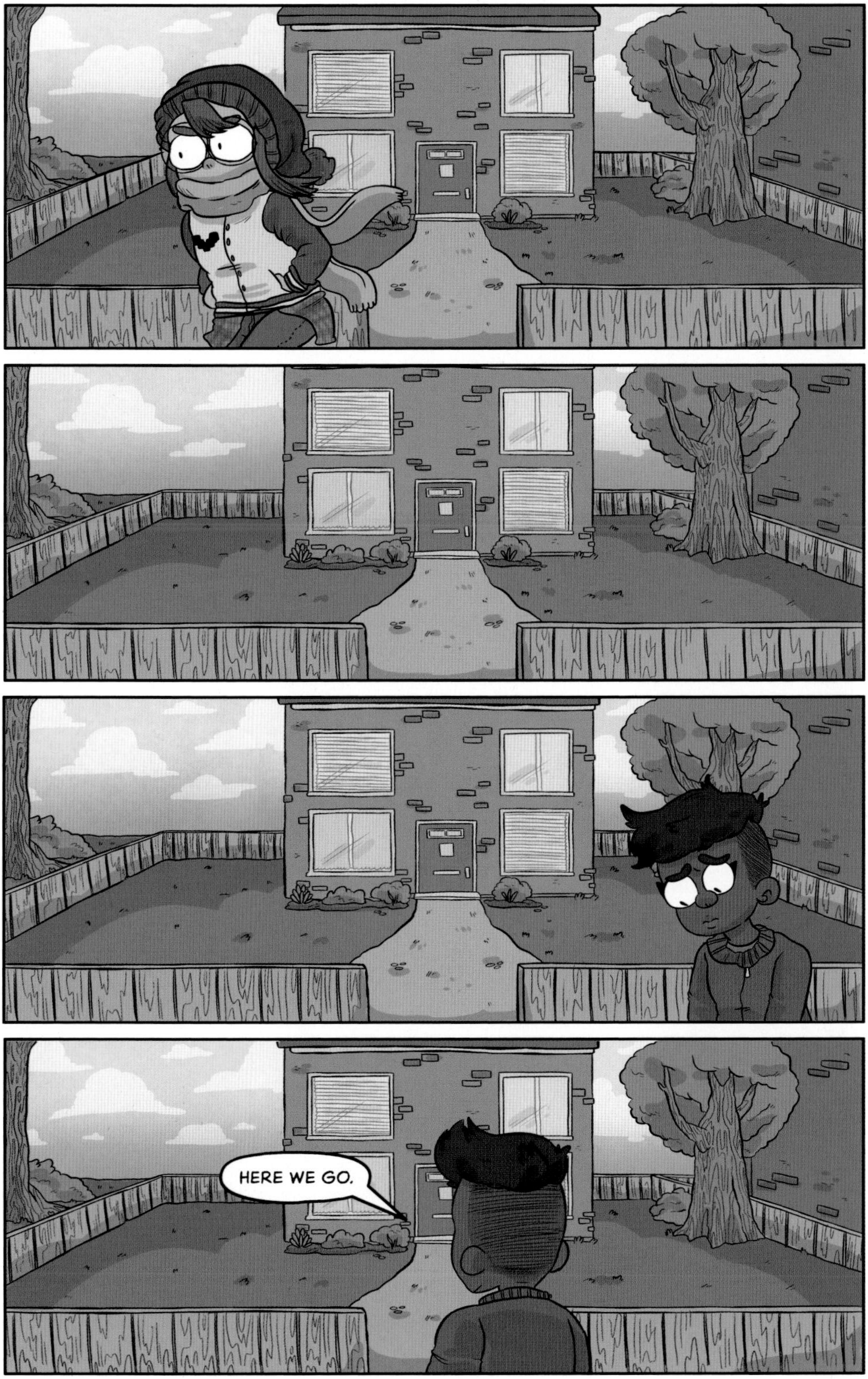
HERE WE GO.

138

139

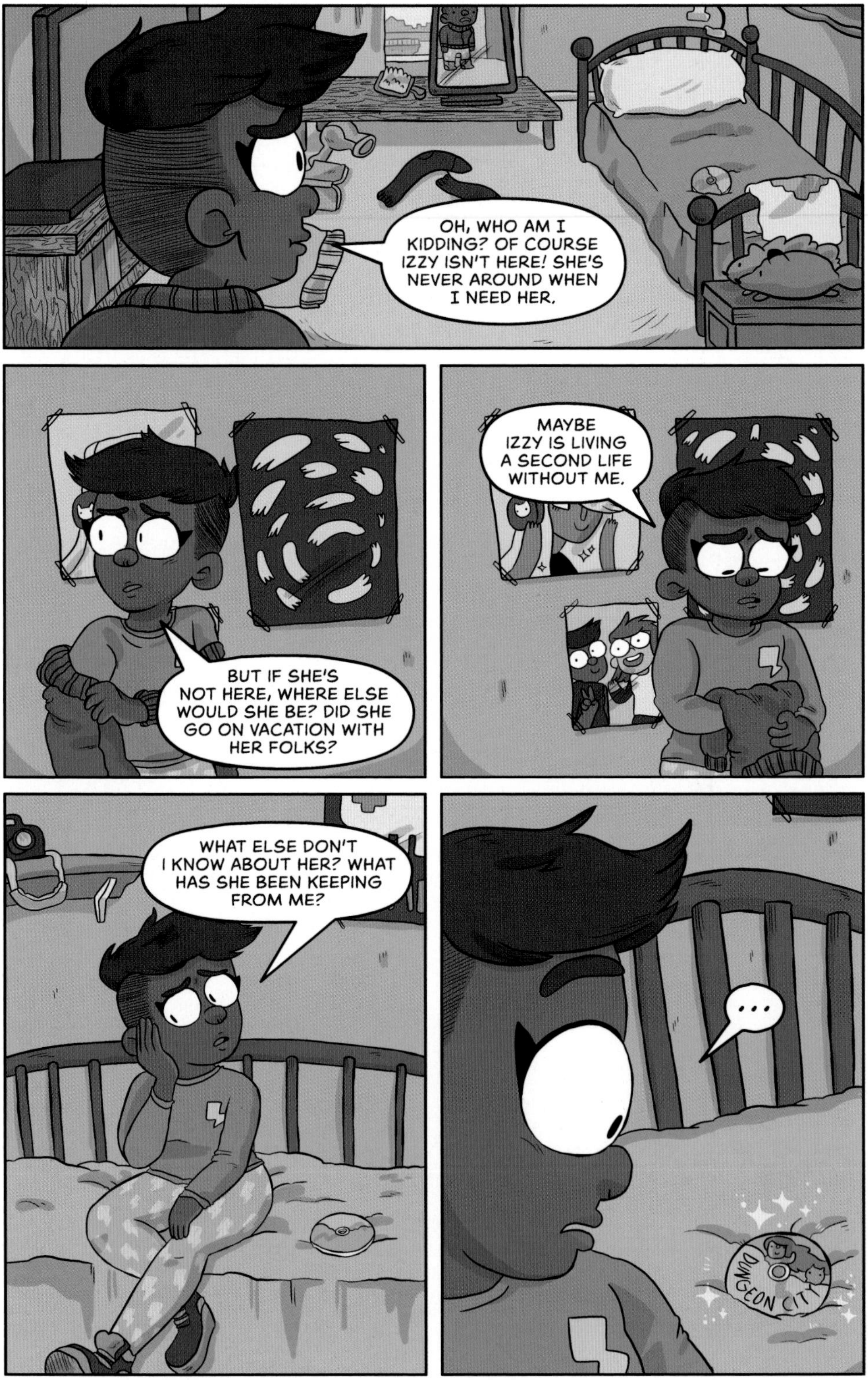
OH, WHO AM I KIDDING? OF COURSE IZZY ISN'T HERE! SHE'S NEVER AROUND WHEN I NEED HER.
BUT IF SHE'S NOT HERE, WHERE ELSE WOULD SHE BE? DID SHE GO ON VACATION WITH HER FOLKS?
MAYBE IZZY IS LIVING A SECOND LIFE WITHOUT ME.
WHAT ELSE DON'T I KNOW ABOUT HER? WHAT HAS SHE BEEN KEEPING FROM ME?
...
DUNGEON CITY

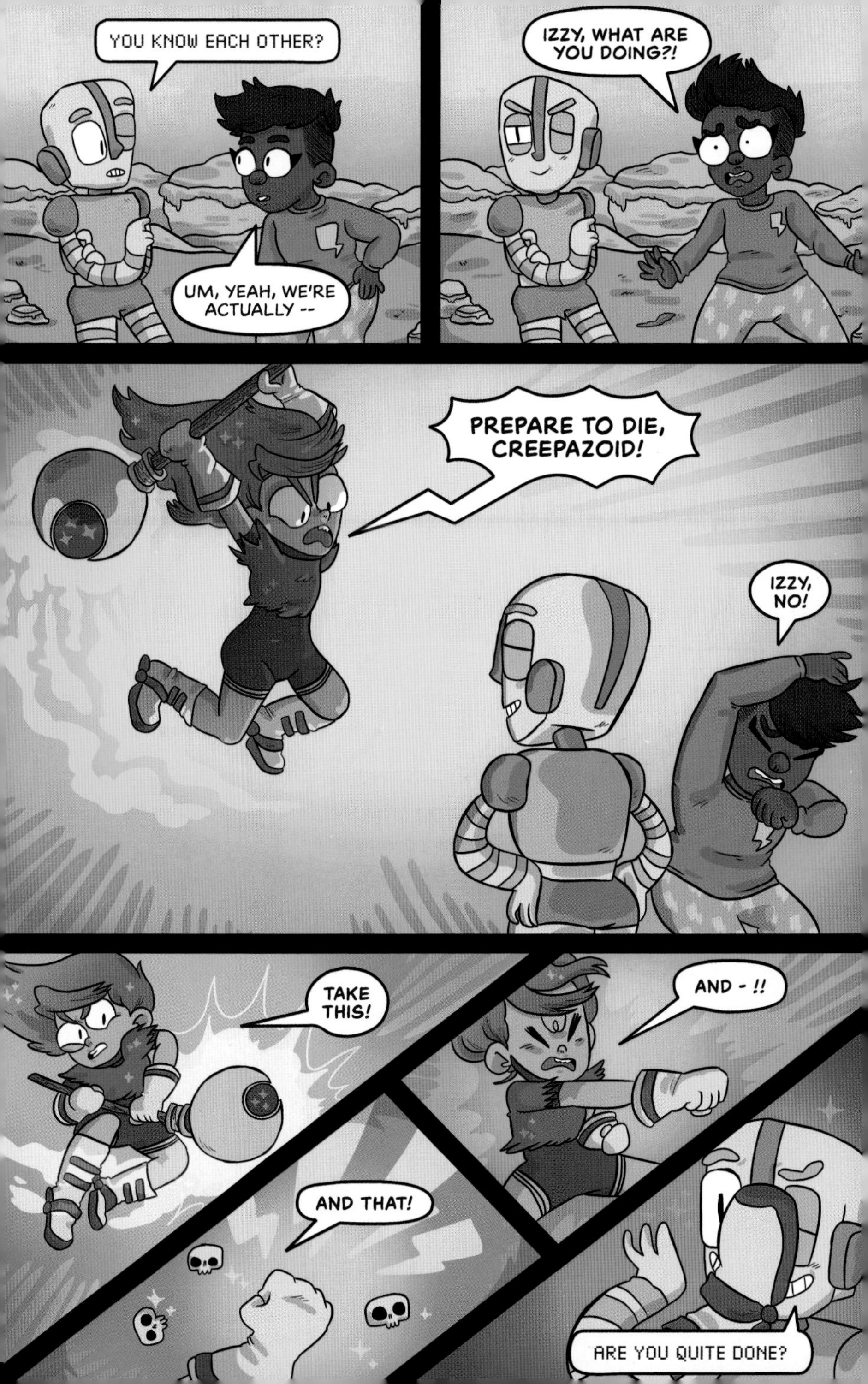
YOU KNOW EACH OTHER?
UM, YEAH, WE'RE ACTUALLY --
IZZY, WHAT ARE YOU DOING?!
PREPARE TO DIE, CREEPAZOID!
IZZY, NO!
TAKE THIS!
AND THAT!
AND - !!
ARE YOU QUITE DONE?

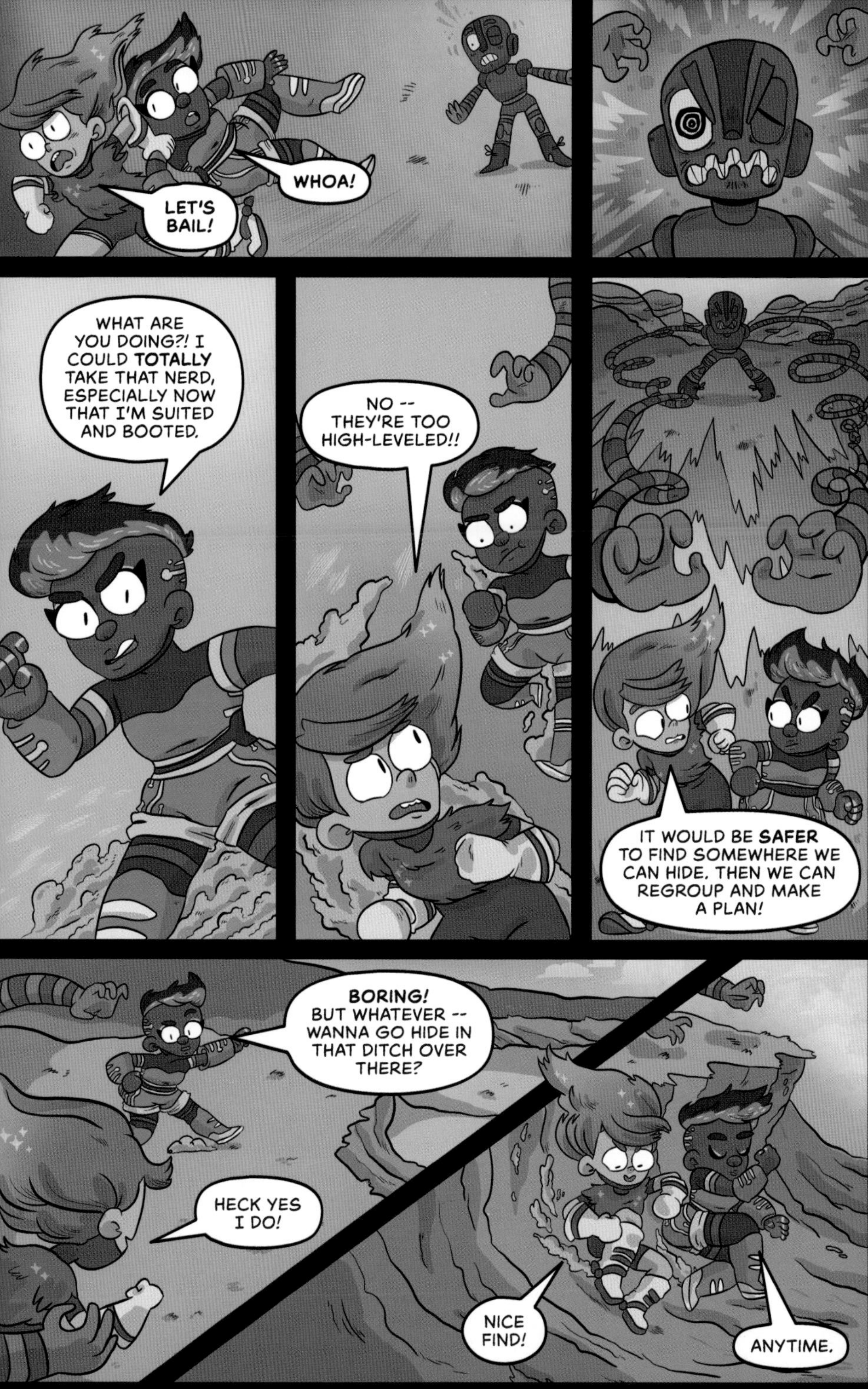
LET'S BAIL!
WHOA!
WHAT ARE YOU DOING?! I COULD **TOTALLY** TAKE THAT NERD, ESPECIALLY NOW THAT I'M SUITED AND BOOTED.
NO -- THEY'RE TOO HIGH-LEVELED!!
IT WOULD BE **SAFER** TO FIND SOMEWHERE WE CAN HIDE. THEN WE CAN REGROUP AND MAKE A PLAN!
BORING! BUT WHATEVER -- WANNA GO HIDE IN THAT DITCH OVER THERE?
HECK YES I DO!
NICE FIND!
ANYTIME.

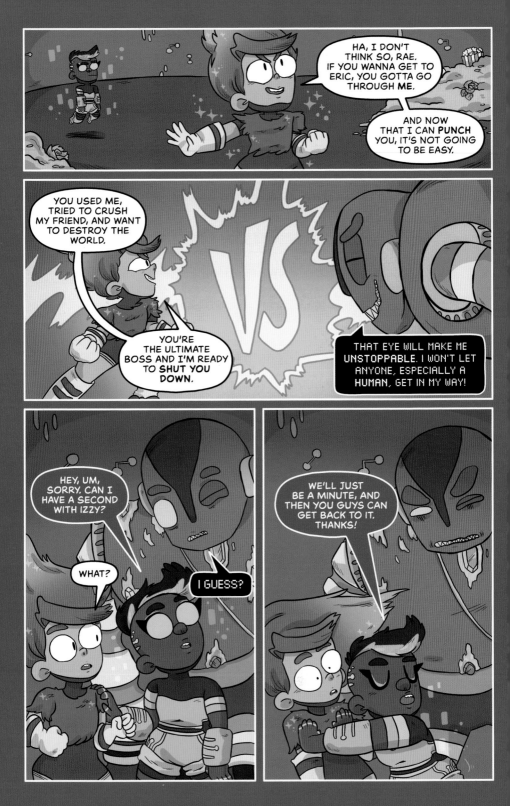

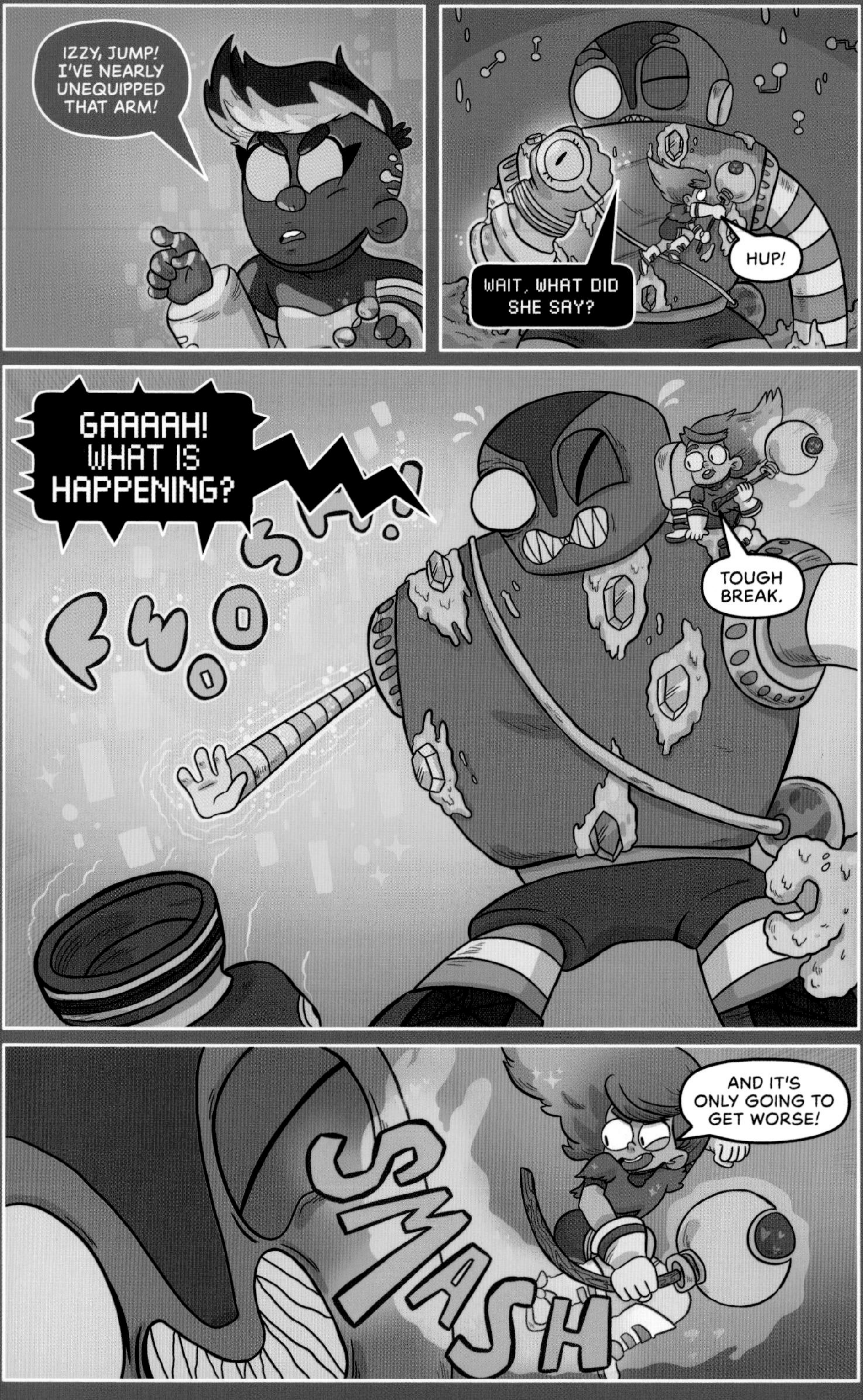
IZZY, JUMP! I'VE NEARLY UNEQUIPPED THAT ARM!
WAIT, WHAT DID SHE SAY?
HUP!
GAAAAH! WHAT IS HAPPENING?
TOUGH BREAK.
FWOOSH
AND IT'S ONLY GOING TO GET WORSE!
SMASH

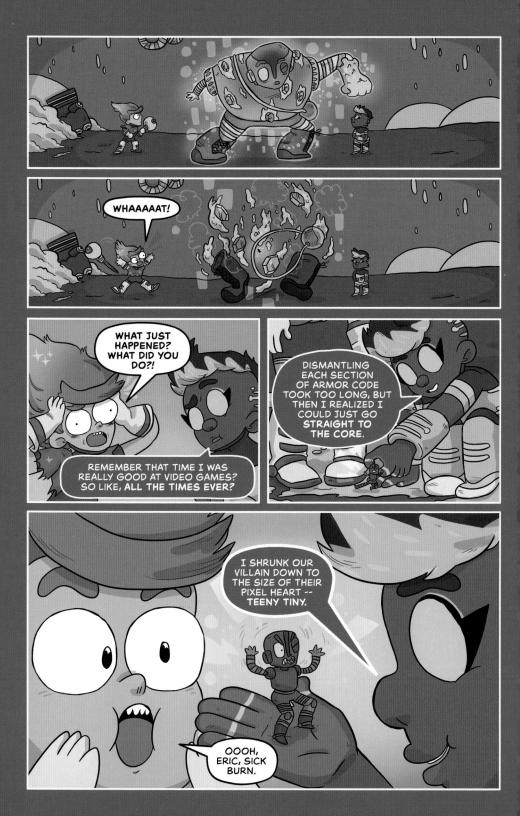

185

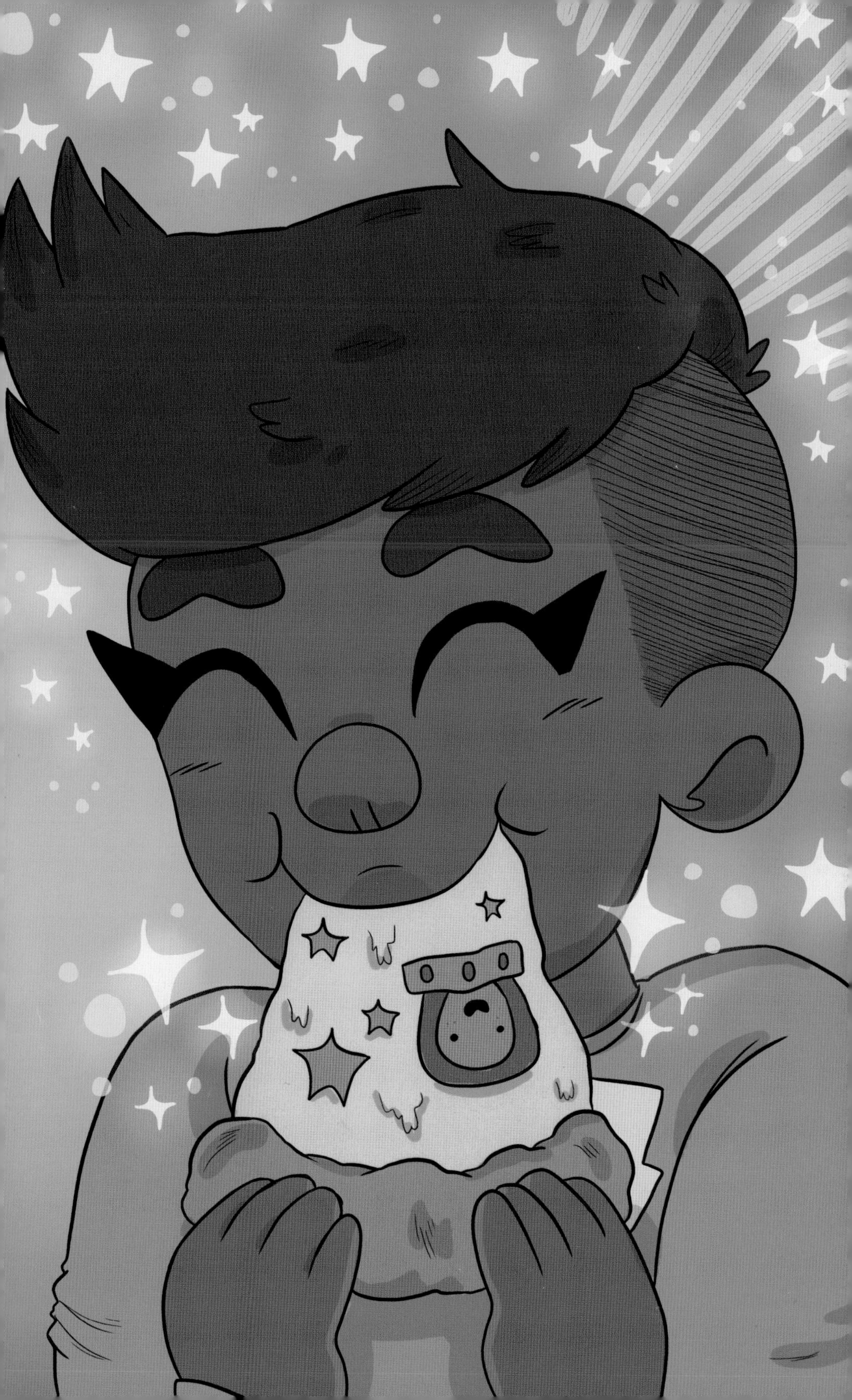

ACKNOWLEDGMENTS

I'd like to thank my parents and family for supporting me and listening to me ramble on about the video games that captured my imagination at a young age.

I'd like to thank my partner, Stef, for helping me figure out the twists and turns in the story early on and for doing a wonderful job in lettering the book, too.

Thanks to my incredible agent, Steven Salpeter, who was instrumental in getting my story out into the world, and the team at Curtis Brown who work their magic behind the scenes.

A huge thanks to Cassandra Pelham Fulton, David Saylor, Phil Falco, and everyone else at Scholastic for helping make this story into an actual real book that exists in the world. Their guidance has been indispensable.

Finally, thanks to my cats for always keeping my lap warm while making this book, and a special thanks to you, for reading this adventure!

ABOUT THE AUTHOR

Sarah Graley is a cartoonist who lives with four cats and a catlike boy in Birmingham, UK. She is the creator of *Kim Reaper*, and the writer and artist for the Rick and Morty comics miniseries *Lil' Poopy Superstar*. She was nominated for the Emerging Talent category at the 2015 British Comic Awards for her long-running diary comic *Our Super Adventure* and original titles *Pizza Witch* and *RentQuest*. Visit Sarah online at sarahgraley.com.